"A brief history of each work is given in a charming afterword, illuminating the write-submit-reject-revise struggle with a light and rueful honesty; a similar tone pervades the book. Though not every story is optimistic, the most memorable ones weave unpalatable truths—that bugs will eat treasures, that grandmothers will die, that the world will end—with the sweetness that keeps life going. Hope is as incontrovertible as misery . . . Cato hits her intended targets with compassion and insight, her work is suitable for YA and adult audiences alike."
    —*Publishers Weekly*

"Beth Cato crafts tales with heart, poignancy, and simple decency. She is the Thornton Wilder of SF!"
    —Lawrence M. Schoen, author of *Barsk: The Elephants' Graveyard*

"Cato writes with abundant heart, placing humanity and compassion in the forefront of everything that she does. Reading Cato's work renews my hope in humanity."
    —Michael R. Underwood, author of *Genrenauts*

"In this collection, Cato shows exactly why she was a Nebula finalist last year. While the worlds in her shorts are vivid and enthralling, it's her characters that highlight her extraordinary skill. She moves easily from one milieu to another. The characters don't jump off the page, they pull you in to join them. This says nothing of the new twists she puts on well-trodden genres. The book is like a delightful night of small plates, each a delicious little escape, and the next arriving just as the flavor of the last is at its peak."
    —Bishop O'Connell, author of the American Faerie Tale series

"These hauntingly beautiful stories and poems each contain a deep aching sadness wrapped around a beautiful gleaming hope—like fog around a sunbeam. If you weren't in love with Cato's writing before you sat down to read this collection, you will be by the time you're finished."
    —Rhonda Parrish, editor of *Equus*

"With Ray Bradbury's poignant charm, Beth Cato explores the resilience of the soul in this versatile collection of stories. Haunting poetry, tales of steampunk horses, a sole survivor drifting in space, colonies on Mars, and toilet gnomes are just a few of the delights you'll find in *Red Dust and Dancing Horses*. Using science fiction and fantasy as her springboard, Cato delves into familiar themes of family—both those we are born into and those that choose us—to reaffirm the notion that what makes us truly human is our empathy toward one another. And story by story, she shows us powerful women: mothers, daughters, and granddaughters as they navigate life's dangers with courage and fortitude. It's a vibrant collection you don't want to miss."
    —T. Frohock, author of *Los Nefilim*

RED DUST
AND DANCING
HORSES
AND OTHER STORIES

Also by Beth Cato

The Clockwork Dagger
The Clockwork Crown
Deep Roots
Breath of Earth
Call of Fire
Roar of Sky (forthcoming)

RED DUST
AND DANCING
HORSES
AND OTHER STORIES

BETH
CATO

FAIRWOOD PRESS
Bonney Lake, WA

RED DUST AND DANCING HORSES AND OTHER STORIES
A Fairwood Press Book
November 2017
Copyright © 2017 Beth Cato

All Rights Reserved

Fairwood Press
21528 104th Street Court East
Bonney Lake, WA   98391
www.fairwoodpress.com

Cover by Kazuhiko Nakamura
Book Design by Patrick Swenson

ISBN: 978-1-933846-68-2
First Fairwood Press Edition: November 2017
Printed in the United States of America

For my grandpa, Kermit Nichols

CONTENTS

Culinary Magic

All Who Wander

RED DUST
AND DANCING
HORSES

AND OTHER STORIES

INTRODUCTION

ARIANNE "TEX" THOMPSON

IT'S NOT EASY BEING A TOILET GNOME. Sure, you can rattle the pipes, burn the washing, maybe flood the upstairs bedroom if you're really aggrieved—but none of that is going to bring back the nice old lady who took such good care of you.

It's hard to be a new author, too. You pour your heart out onto every page and flog yourself senseless trying to get the world to notice your work—but most of the attention is still going to the big-shots with decades-long series and hit TV adaptations, and fantasy feels kind of frivolous right now anyway. It's hard to make a big deal of anything fictional in an era of huge, epic, borderline apocalyptic real-world current events.

Enter Beth Cato, champion of the small.

We debuted around the same time, and her *Clockwork Dagger* novels quickly become a breakout hit. (Read them and you will understand why!) But Beth has long been a fount of literary wonders, showering forth a novella, short stories, poems, essays, articles, flash fiction, and more—right down to her recipe for Cadbury Egg Brownies in *Ad Astra: The 50th Anniversary SFWA Cookbook*. And even as accolades, new projects, and fresh deadlines pile up, Beth continues to pour tremendous love into tiny vessels. She brings home-baked goodies to her readings, and gives out the recipes online. She carves out the time to read and review books by new authors. She shares her life so generously—her writing, her baking, her family, her travels—and still takes a deep and authentic interest in the lives of others.

So I am thrilled that we finally get a book which so well represents Beth herself: an irresistible abundance of bite-sized delights. You won't find any epic quests in these stories. No world-ending apocalypses—or rather, none that we can do anything about. And no huge hidden realms or portentous magical secrets either. Those "Toilet Gnomes at War," the ones currently shrieking through the plumbing? They're as common as backyard beagles—and likewise, if you don't get yours to quiet down on the quick side, the neighbors are going to complain. Just so, it's common knowledge among the Confederate soldiers in "The Souls of Horses" that the spirits of dying horses can be transferred into artificial bodies—for them, the only novelty is the new features on the latest mechanical model. And "Minor Hockey Gods of Barstow Station" is much less concerned with the gods than the hockey. It all adds up to something unexpectedly fresh: since the supernatural elements seem ordinary to the characters, 100% of the marvel and surprise is reserved for you, the reader. I am prepared to call that an act of authorial generosity.

So what is fantasy without the big quest, the monomythic hero, the world-shaking consequence? How much imagination can you really pack into ten pages, in a genre that's more comfortable with ten thousand?

Quite a lot, as it turns out. The stories and poems in this book are overwhelmingly devoted to ordinary people striving for tiny victories. Maybe you can't change what was done to you under that gnarly old oak ("The Cartography of Shattered Trees")—but if you pull yourself together and mind your manners, you might be able to talk with her. Grandma is dead, and her soul is leaking out of that enchanted vase like helium from a leftover birthday balloon ("Blue Tag Sale")—but there's still a little of her left, and it would be a shame to waste that on sadness. And at the end of it all, when the doomsday clock is counting down its final hours, you might as well bake some cookies and enjoy a day at the playground ("A Dance to End Our Final Day").

And that's what I think we've been missing so desperately in our age of unbearable superlatives. Yes, it is cathartic to read stories about small people rising to greatness, overcoming impossible odds to save the world. But we also need stories about small people who triumph even in their smallness. Who find agency within themselves. Whose greatest quest is to rescue themselves, or each other—to change their own point of view, even when they can change nothing else.

These stories showcase rural children and Confederate slaves, elderly widows and struggling caregivers, mothers and veterans and survivors of every kind. It's no accident that they are overwhelmingly girls and women, most of them occupying profoundly underrepresented roles, and most of them unflinchingly generous in empathy. Yes, there are moments when it's kill or be killed—but you can still feel sorry for that poor dumb son-of-a-bitch as you bury him ("La Rosa Still in Bloom"). You can still love your hissing cockroach grandma, even if she's too far gone to love you back ("An Echo in the Shell").

And if the characters in these stories can hold fast to their humanity even in the strangest and most extreme circumstances, I have to believe that we can do likewise in ours. This is the special genius of fantasy, the moment when it grows beyond novelty and escapism. In holding our reality up to the funhouse mirror, we can marvel at what changes—and in doing so discover what doesn't. What shouldn't.

I hope that you enjoy this collection as much as I have. I hope you esteem the author as much as I do. And as the trials of our times pass over and through us, I hope that Beth Cato's work will stand at the beginning of a greater turn back to smallness, to kindness, to the tiny miracles within the human heart, and that our apocalyptic age will prove to be merely the wall-shaking cacophony of deprived toilet gnomes: a transient sound and fury that dissolves the moment we rediscover our shared humanity over a fresh pot of coffee and a plate of Cadbury Egg Brownies.

HOOF BEATS AND CAT WHISKERS

THE SOULS OF HORSES

ILSA KNEW THE SOULS OF HORSES, how they twined between her fingers as silky and strong as strands of mane, how even in death they ached to gallop across fields or melt lumps of sugar upon their tongues.

Few men could understand them as she did.

"Sweet Jesus, are those the flying horses?" asked Lieutenant Dennis.

Ilsa granted him a curt nod. Captain Mayfair and more soldiers waited in her house, and she didn't know what they wanted of her. Only that she must pack her necessities and best tools and leave promptly.

Her barn held a fully assembled flying-horse carousel. A dozen horses dangled from a wooden canopy that could be dismantled to fit in a large wagon. For many years she had traveled summers and worked fairs from Virginia to Connecticut. Cannon fire at Fort Sumter had ended that.

"Pardon my blasphemy, ma'am. I've never seen the like before. Is it steam-run?"

"Yes." She eyed the Confederate officer. He couldn't be older than twenty. His gray uniform draped from his reedy frame.

He frowned as he circled a piebald Arabian mix. "Why carousel horses? Why would dying horses even want this . . . existence?"

"The Captain said you were a cavalry unit, correct? I assume you know horses well?"

"Yes, ma'am. My mama had me on a horse when I could scarcely walk, and my father breeds racing stock."

Ilsa had no desire to get chatty with a soldier, much less one who intended to drag her from her home, but this was a horseman. "Then you understand that horses know what they want. Like a person, they hate some tasks and love others. These horses love people, being ridden, and don't want to lose that joy. I show them what awaits, and they make this choice."

"They really have a choice?"

She stiffened. "Of course. An unwilling soul can't be bound. A horse might lose its body, but it doesn't lose its kick."

"If they are a different sort of horse, one that wouldn't like a carousel, what happens?"

"They float away." She left it at that.

Her papa had been a transferor, too. He had staunchly believed that since a dying horse's soul drifted upward, it must travel to heaven. When Ilsa was a child first witnessing those tendrils of escaping souls, such a thought had been of great comfort and joy.

It had been a long time since she was a child.

Ilsa rested her hand against the smooth paint of a mare's neck. Beneath her touch, the soul stirred. The mare was strong, even after death; Ilsa needed that same resilience.

The officer darted out a hand to touch the mare's blaze. Astonishment brightened his face. "It . . . quivered?"

Lieutenant Dennis *was* a special sort of horseman to sense that. "Souls can only inhabit something that once carried life. Wood works well. The carousel grants them some locomotion, too. They miss the ability to move."

"I'm glad this horse can move then, be happy. What about that horse figure in the house, ma'am? That one—I stared at it, and it stared straight back. Gave me chills. That horse wasn't the sort for a carousel?"

"No. Some aren't content to spin in circles. Bucephalus . . . he's the kind of horse who would unlatch his stall and that of every other horse in the barn, and kick his heels like a colt afterward."

Lieutenant Dennis burst out laughing. "I've known the very

sort, ma'am. He's named after Alexander the Great's warhorse?"

"The same."

"We could use more horses like old Alexander's." His expression sobered as he looked to his pocket watch. "We must go, ma'am. The Captain's waiting."

Ilsa looked to her tools again, remembering why she was there, who she was with. She hefted a skew gouger in her palm, the handle's patina dark. These tools had been brand-new when she bought them in New York City twenty years before. They had aged with more grace than her.

She found Captain Mayfair in her parlor. He scowled and motioned her to the door. She looked to her mantle.

Bucephalus was carved in pale butternut and no larger than a grown man's hand. Three hooves were grounded, the muscles of his hindquarters tensed as if ready to rear. Ilsa wanted to plead for a few moments of privacy with her horse, to say farewell, but she had no desire to show any weakness to these men.

She turned away and blinked back tears to find Captain Mayfair gazing past her to Bucephalus, his grizzled features softened with wonder.

They arrived at the encampment of the newly formed Confederate Independent Provisional Cavalry, and Ilsa was escorted straight to a makeshift foundry. Men talked in the shadows, metal clanging, their furnaces like blood aglow in the weak evening light.

"Captain Mayfair, why am I here? You do know I can't transfer into metal?"

"Yes."

Ilsa opened her mouth to scold him, to demand answers as they entered a dim room. Light slanted down from a high window, as if in a cathedral, and illuminated a gleaming horse. She gasped.

Silver skin flowed with the ripple of muscles, highlighting an arched neck and strong hindquarters. It stood fifteen hands tall, the same as an average horse. Black orbs for eyes had the dull sheen of rocks worn smooth in a river. This was no crude machine. It was a sculpture, a masterpiece.

"What is this?" she whispered.

"The auquine, the automatic horse," said Captain Mayfair. Lieutenant Dennis stood beside him. "This is our prototype. Steam-run in part, but requires the motivation of a soul."

"I already told you, I cannot—"

"You will carve the wooden heart. Its nervous system consists of vine coated with gutta-percha. The soul will have room to expand, control the limbs."

Ilsa knew the relentless, unfilled ache to truly *move* that irritated every horse bound to the carousel. "The engine and soul together. It could work."

Bucephalus would love such a body, but he's no warhorse, nor could I steal a creation like this. There would be no way to keep such a thing a secret.

Dennis cleared his throat. "It has worked, ma'am, in Britain. They're readying cavalry units for India."

"People with your skills are scarce, Mrs. Klein," said Captain Mayfair. "We're in dire need of horses."

She looked between the metal horse and the soldiers. A horse's soul—one suited to be a warhorse—would delight in this new form, so much closer to its original. She touched the metal neck, almost expecting the lurch of life that pulsed within her own carvings. "Who made this?"

"Culver," said Captain Mayfair.

She wondered if she should recognize the name, but a shadow shifted behind the horse, and she realized it had been a summons.

The Negro looked of age with her, his white hair bound in a queue at his neck. He was clean-shaven, his clothes tidy despite their extreme wear.

"Culver's from my father's plantation. No one knows horses

and metal like him," said Lieutenant Dennis with obvious pride.

"Impressive," Ilsa murmured. Impressive that a slave had been granted such a role in this army.

"Master Dennis." Culver bowed, the motion slow and heavy like an old oak bent by a fierce wind.

"Sir! Captain Mayfair!" Another soldier strode in. "An urgent telegraph from General Lee, sir."

"Culver will show you how the auquine works, Mrs. Klein." Captain Mayfair exited. With a bright smile for both her and Culver, Lieutenant Dennis departed as well.

Ilsa considered the craftsman. "Is everyone in the forge working on these . . . auquines?"

"Yes'm. This's the first one done, 'bout twenty more juss 'bout there, and salvage aplenty for makin' more."

Her hands traced the seams of metal, the large eyes. "You modeled this on a Morgan."

"Y'know your horses, missus."

Her voice lowered. "Metal is soulless, dead, but this—this *works*. You know horses' souls."

"Slave's not supposed to know 'bout such things, missus."

"Neither are women."

"God's truth, missus."

"How do you open up the horse?"

Culver crouched down. His leg wobbled, and he landed on all fours with a grunt.

"Are you well?" Ilsa lay a hand on his shoulder. Through the worn fabric, she felt the ridged scars of the lash—layers, mottled like cold candle wax.

Equine memories flashed in her mind. Agonized neighs. The fall of the whip, the fierce sting, the heat of weeping blood.

"I'm sorry," she said, recoiling, and knew he wouldn't grasp the full meaning.

"Body don't work like it used to." He trembled as he leaned on the auquine.

She shivered, too, willing away the shadowed pain of other souls. Culver was property, same as a horse.

Ilsa made herself focus on the task at hand as he opened a hatch in the auquine's chest to show her the fundamentals of its design.

Lieutenant Dennis beamed with pride as he reentered the room. "The auquine's a beauty, isn't he?"

She liked the boy, his enthusiasm for horses. *He's of attitude and age to be my son.* The thought provoked a twinge of grief that hadn't stirred in years.

"Yes. I should speak to Captain Mayfair again, if you please." With a nod to Culver, she followed Dennis into the brisk evening air.

Captain Mayfair stood beside a campfire with a group of soldiers. "Mrs. Klein. What did you think?"

She took a deep breath. "This man Culver's work reminds me of the high craftsmanship I saw as a girl in Germany. Extraordinary."

"Yes. He's a peculiar Negro."

"That said, Captain, my carousel brings joy to my horses and riders, especially children. Working on warhorses like this . . . it's not right for me."

"I was afraid you might be reluctant." Captain Mayfair nodded to a soldier beside him. The man folded down a burlap bag between his feet. There, wadded in wrinkles of coarse cloth, stood Bucephalus.

Ilsa couldn't hold back a gasp, her hand flying to her mouth. Lieutenant Dennis shuffled his feet in clear discomfort.

The captain kept his focus on her. "This horse is special to you. People talk of him. I understood why once I entered your home."

Ilsa shivered in rage. These soldiers took her as they took so many horses, supplies, even homes. If she fled north, she couldn't expect any better. The Yanks would be constructing their own horses soon enough. They'd be no kinder in their pillaging of property or people.

But maybe the Yanks wouldn't stoop this low.

"How dare you, Captain?" she whispered.

Captain Mayfair glanced at the fire behind him. "It's my understanding that nothing binds as well as an original body. You must be very close to catch a soul, correct?"

She barely managed a nod. *For Bucephalus's soul, I would brave the fire. A strong soul like his can be transferred several times. I could make him a new body.*

"We need horses, Mrs. Klein. We'll house you well. My men will not harass you."

She ached to bolt, to make for the road, to fly from this place. She looked at Bucephalus and shuddered. "If I am to—to help, then I must say straight out that I won't abide with any horse being killed without need."

Captain Mayfair motioned, and Bucephalus was gently wrapped up again. "Horses are dear to us. We have no desire—no capacity—to replace them completely. And it's not as though we lack in dying horses." Sadness curved his mustache.

"Yet you threaten to burn mine."

"Is he a horse anymore?" The captain sounded curious rather than facetious. "How long has this Bucephalus been bound by wood?"

"Twenty years."

"As long as you've been in America, then." The man had done his research. "Lieutenant Dennis will show you your quarters and your workshop."

"You want me to start now? Tonight?"

"Yes. The Union's building pontoons to cross the river. Soon there'll be plenty of horses in need of new bodies."

Smoke veiled the furrows as if attempting to hide the mangled blue and gray bodies in the mud. The air of the place—of so many distended souls—weighed on Ilsa like a hundred winter coats.

Lieutenant Dennis helped her down from a buckboard wagon

loaded with rattling wooden equine hearts. "Ma'am, I'm sorry. This is no place for a lady."

"It's not a place for anyone," she whispered.

Never before had she sensed the presence of human souls, much as she had tried. God, had she tried. She couldn't see them, but there were so many here that her head felt as afloat as a hot air balloon.

"There's a horse over here!" called a soldier.

She stumbled over roots and rocks and things her gaze slid across but could not comprehend, and then she came to the horse.

The air shimmied as the stallion struggled against death. He stubbornly stood on all four legs even as his ribs—and more—were bared to the air.

"There, there," Ilsa crooned, focusing on him. "Good boy."

His eyes were glazed over with pain, but she saw beyond that. He was a horse as described in the Book of Job, all flaring nostrils and eagerness at the herald of a trumpet.

Like men, some horses were born fools.

"Fine lines," murmured Dennis. "Some Thoroughbred to him."

Ilsa brought her face so close that vapors of soul caressed her like steam. "Do you want this?" she whispered. She exhaled an image of what awaited the horse: a new body, built strong; how the hooves would clatter; how he might miss the taste of oats, but he would still know the joy of a gallop.

Even in agony, his ears perked up. His soul gushed outward, eager to move on.

"His body's pain needs to end," she said.

A soldier aimed a gun barrel between the stallion's eyes. At Ilsa's nod, the gun fired. Even expecting the noise, she flinched. The horse collapsed. She grabbed hold of the soul as it drifted out from his eyes. The effervescent strands were strong, testing her as if straining against a bit.

"I need cherrywood." A strong wood, bold as the horse. A soldier dashed off for the wagon. "Shh, shh, easy there," she whispered.

She plaited the soul with her deft fingers, forming a loop to confine its essence.

She pressed the soul into the wooden heart as she took it in her hands, patting the ventricles the way a person molds clay, and after a few minutes, she nodded. The soldier took the heart away.

"I wish I could see and feel what you do, ma'am," said Dennis, voice softened in awe.

"No, you don't, lieutenant."

Ilsa rubbed her torso, reminding herself that there was no pain, no blood. Impressions from the dying horse glistened across her mind's eye. Green fields, contentment. The good man who smelled of leather and damp wool, how they rode into battle together—excitement—hoofbeats—wind—galloping, galloping—and then a lightened load. Many others had sat on his back since. Where was the good man?

She shivered out of the reverie. At least she had granted this horse's soul some extra time on earth, doing something he would love. For the first time, this enterprise felt worthwhile.

Though given her druthers, she would still grab Bucephalus and run.

"There's another horse over here, sir! Ma'am!"

The dying mare lay on her side. Her ribs heaved like bellows, breaths wheezing through bloodied nostrils. Wisps of her soul clouded the air and Ilsa's consciousness. A child's laugh. A hand at her mane, a kiss at her muzzle. The girl's wails as the horse was ridden away. The mare kept turning to look toward home, toward the girl. Reins jerked her head straight.

Home. Where the girl waited along the split-rail fence.

"What sort of wood?" Dennis's voice shattered the image.

"No." Ilsa gasped. "Not a warhorse. She should never have been here. She needs . . . I need . . ."

Children. Soft hands. Bouncy, light bodies within the sway of her back.

"Mrs. Klein, I'm sorry. We can't fill a heart we can't use."

"I just need one!"

"Will there be only one like this here?"

This soul wasn't as strong as Bucephalus. It couldn't transfer more than once. Nor could she hold more than one soul at a time as she journeyed across the battlefield, but she wanted to, she needed to. This mare belonged in the carousel. Ilsa couldn't bring forth the same girl, but there'd be others. She clawed for the dissipating strands of the horse's soul. The bellows of breaths softened, the horse's gaze distant.

The last vapors vanished against a sunbeam.

Gone. Not human, not saved by baptism. Lost, like the soul of the unchristened stillborn babe, born in an outhouse behind a Berlin carousel shop.

Ilsa would grab all the souls if she could. She would be the leaden weight to anchor them to earth.

"Ma'am?" Lieutenant Dennis whispered. "I'm sorry to put you through this, but—"

"I came to America to start my life again. I'm in the same place, but this is no longer America." Her voice rasped like that of an old woman. She *was* an old woman.

She stumbled onward, eyes blinded by tears, guided only by the tendrils of another agonized equine soul.

Confederate commanders encased her in a gray ring. They murmured excitedly, buzzing like machinery.

Culver waited by the first empty auquine, the prototype. "Pay them men no heed."

"If this fails—"

"Ain't gonna fail, missus. You know what you doing. You know these horses."

She thought of Bucephalus, the horse she knew best of all, then looked to the heaping basket of wooden hearts beside her. The harvest of the battlefield. Days had passed, and her agony had turned to numbness.

Do the job. Give these souls a home. Let some good come of this.

She touched a knob of smoothed walnut, then delved deeper to find cherry. The heart pulsed in her hand, quickening. In her mind, she retraced the metal body before her, showed it to the soul the way she would once have extended a palm of oats.

As she knelt before the auquine's chest, the murmurs behind her ceased. The horse's chest compartment opened on hinges to show the vascular chamber. Stroking the heart, she murmured wordless assurances as she set the wood within its new cradle.

Death is rife with pain. So is rebirth.

Ilsa stabbed sharpened wood connectors into the heart. At each strike, the soul shivered as it spilled through the puncture wounds to explore gutta-percha veins. The auquine rumbled as the engine started.

She sealed the body shut. A hoof tentatively stomped on the dirt. At the auquine's head, Culver made shushing noises, stroking along the silver muzzle. Ears pivoted on their roller joints, head lifting as if to sniff. The commanders broke out in applause.

"There, there. You mighty fine. You doing good, girl."

Culver wasn't whispering to the horse.

Ilsa moved on to the next auquine in the long row.

"You'll look after Culver for me, won't you, ma'am?" Dennis asked. Dawn had yet to pierce the oil slick of the sky, yet the camp bustled.

"Lieutenant, he's as old as I am. I think he can look after himself." Ilsa softened the words with a faint smile, her eyes on the auquines. Her horses, their silver and copper hides dull by firelight.

The Provisional Cavalry had practiced in the valley for weeks to acclimate the horses' souls to their new, stronger bodies. Now their orders had come in.

"Well, I-I suppose so." Dennis stooped in a way that reminded her of Culver, an invisible yoke heavy on his shoulders.

"Lieutenant Dennis. Mrs. Klein." Captain Mayfair granted Ilsa a tip of his hat. "It's time to mount up."

"Yes, sir," said Dennis, snapping out of his salute. He cast Ilsa a nod and joined the rest of the horsemen.

"I have been meaning to speak to you, Mrs. Klein," Captain Mayfair said, "on the matter of that horse of yours."

Bucephalus. The name pained her. "What of him, Captain?"

"He has a strong soul, doesn't he?"

"Yes."

"Could he be transferred to an auquine?"

She looked at the men—boys, really—and their metal horses. All of them giddy in anticipation of what was to come. These horses would truly die if their wooden hearts were pierced or their veins too badly mangled. *Their souls escaping into nothingness.* Ilsa couldn't follow the cavalry and save them.

"You'd put Bucephalus in front of cannons?" she asked. "Why not just drop him in the campfire, then? It's faster."

It was selfish of her, she knew, to value his soul more than the rest, but Bucephalus had been her constant companion for decades. She had twined his soul and kept it warm beside her own heartbeat. She spent weeks carving his new body in butternut. They traveled the seaboard with her carousel until the war started. She talked to him; he listened.

"A great deal depends on this unit and its success, Mrs. Klein. These auquines could turn the course of the war. They could end it." The captain was silent for a long minute. "I met my wife when I was at West Point. At the start of the war, she went back to New York to be with her parents on the farm. I would very much like to see her again."

"My horse will not change that."

"Smaller pebbles have changed the world, but that's not my point. My inquiry is not about Bucephalus now, but for when the war is done. I own property in the Low Country down near Charleston. There'd be a place for him there. I would like to see him in action as he really is."

"Captain," said a soldier. He passed over an auquine's reins.

Captain Mayfair swung himself into the saddle. "It's something to keep in mind while we're away, Mrs. Klein. Farewell." He rode to join his men.

"Bucephalus is my horse," she whispered to the dust. "Not yours. You *stole* him."

Ilsa retreated to her room and listened to the soft thuds of hoofbeats as they faded away. The walls boxed her in like a stall, the ropes that bound her invisible yet strong.

The knife was a familiar weight in Ilsa's hand. She inhaled the heady scent of wood so fresh it almost cleared her senses, her memories. A gas lamp cast the workshop in an orange glow.

Beyond the thin walls, men cheered. The first mission of the Provisional Cavalry had been a grand success. Their two-day pursuit of the Yanks had resulted in a decisive victory and the acquisition of a Union quartermaster's wagon loaded with honest-to-God coffee beans.

"We couldn't have achieved this victory without you," Captain Mayfair had said. As if she needed the reminder.

She also did not need anyone to do the mathematics for her. Five horses gone. She did not count the men.

Ilsa didn't look up when the door opened. As had become their ritual over the past month, Culver sat down on the lopped-off stump across from her. She was so used to working and talking aloud to Bucephalus that it felt peculiar to share her space with someone who replied. Peculiar in a pleasant way.

Culver opened a toolbox and began busywork with wires and bolts and fingernail-size scraps of metal. The soldiers in the foundry knew their jobs well by now, and he wasn't required there anymore. He mostly acted as manservant for Lieutenant Dennis.

A fiddle whined outside, and voices arose in chorus:

"Jeff Davis is our President,
Lincoln is a Fool!
Jeff Davis rides a white—horse—auquine!"

The song broke off at the overlapped words. The men cheered again.

"They better be glad Cap'n said they sleep late tomorrow," said Culver. "Gonna be a long train ride down to Alabama in three days."

Alabama. Deeper south, deeper into this whole mess, and this time Ilsa was to come along. More horses would die. Dozens heaped together in a day, their memories blurred like hummingbird wings.

"How do you stand it?" She clenched the handle. "Knowing that if you headed north a ways, you could be free. That every time you build a horse, you're building something that keeps you a slave."

"I been free."

"What?"

"I been free. When I's a young man, I ran north, to New York. What a place, what a place." Culver shook his head, still marveling. "Got me a 'prenticeship and a girl and a baby girl-child. And then blackbirders came, trussed me up, and hauled me back to Georgia."

"My God," she whispered. "I lived in New York back then—twenty years ago, was it?" Culver nodded. "I heard about those men, that they even dragged free-born Negroes south and into slavery. Your family—what happened?"

"Don't know. But I had my family down in Georgia, too. Lord be praised for that. Got to see my boy grow up." The curve of his smiling cheeks reminded her of Lieutenant Dennis, how he looked at the auquines.

My boy never grew up. He never even breathed. She was ashamed of herself for envying Culver in such a way when he had lost so much more.

"To be free and captured again . . ."

"Didn't lose all my freedom." He tightened a bolt.

"How is that?"

"When you carvin' those carousel horses, what's it do for your soul?" An oddly blunt thing for Culver to ask.

Ilsa stroked the half-carved heart in her hands. "Years ago, I had a small boy ride the carousel time and again. He told me he'd truly been riding a mustang to California. He said the horse knew right where to go. That's how I feel when I carve, when I see the carousel horses in their new bodies. That I'm going the right way. Escaping without escaping."

"Mustangs. I heard 'bout them, out west. Crazy place, all dirt far's the eye can see."

"We should go there." She set the knife on her lap. "The two of us. Forget this fools' war."

"Aw, Missus Klein. I'm too old to go off somewhere new. Maybe you can, your skin. Anyone take one look at me, they know where I come from, know right where I go. Blackbirders did."

"I knew a horse like you once." She resumed carving in furious strokes. "He had known freedom. He had known love. He was a bit Arab, a bit Thoroughbred, a bit of everything. He could race—Lord, could he race. His mind, it was faster than any whip. But then he was hurt and sold, and spent his last year pulling a glueman's wagon down the cobbles in New York City. He pulled it like a royal chariot, awful as its load was, piled with dead of his own kind."

"This that horse of yours? The one Cap'n has?"

She nodded, not trusting herself to speak.

The two of them worked in silence as her mind untangled frustration and fear and the need to do something for Culver, for Bucephalus, for herself. She thought of her carousel horses and mustangs.

"I'm going to ask the captain for a last trip to my shop for supplies." Ilsa smiled at Culver. "I don't suppose you've ever been on a flying-horse carousel?"

*

"I'll need a few minutes to start up the steam engine." Ilsa scurried about the old barn, connecting the engine and walking the long length of the cord, checking for rust and rat's nests.

"Can I be of help, ma'am?" asked Dennis, their guard for the foray into town. He had seemed especially weary in recent days. She didn't think he was too happy about the cavalry moving south. Maybe it brought the war too close to home.

"I know my own rig best," Ilsa said. To his credit, Dennis let her be.

A neighbor had kept an eye on the place these past few months, but that did nothing to ward away dust, or to fill that empty place on her mantle. Walking through her parlor just about broke her heart, especially as she'd seen Bucephalus that morning for the first time in weeks.

The wooden horse sat on the corner of Captain Mayfair's desk in the command house. Bucephalus had a window view of soldiers drilling on newly transferred auquines.

Captain Mayfair didn't seem worried that Ilsa would try to escape on her trip into Richmond. He had Bucephalus, after all.

She had noted that not a speck of dust was to be found on the carved horse, not even in the delicate whorls of his mane. In truth, he looked . . . loved.

That pleased her and vexed her all at once.

Her fingers had brushed his back. If Bucephalus had been of flesh, he would have scarcely flicked an ear her way. He was fixated on the auquines in the yard with an intensity she hadn't seen in years, not since they traveled the coast with the carousel.

Bucephalus is mine. He should be home. I could move him from the mantle, give him a better vantage of the street.

She directed her frustration into the carousel's crank. She could already feel the wood-bound horses' anticipation. They stewed with restlessness, just as they had in life at the first hints of spring.

"Choose your horse and mount up," she called.

Culver ambled around the carousel. He stopped at the most ornately carved of the lot, a white stallion on the outside ring. The lead horse. Ilsa had designed the horse's colorful barding like that of a medieval charger straight out of *Ivanhoe*. Culver tried to lift his foot to the stirrup and staggered backward.

"Here, old man," Dennis said as he gave him a boost.

"Thanks to you, master."

The two men shared like smiles. It made Ilsa grin, too, to see how Dennis doted on Culver. "What about you?" she asked Dennis as he joined her in the center. He shook his head.

Ilsa released the brake lever. The canopy shuddered as the mechanism activated. Slowly, the horses began to move.

Culver gripped the red pole and looked to either side of his horse as it swayed. "This horse. It different."

"It's a rare breed from Austria, called Lipizzaner. They're taught to dance."

"Fancy that!" Culver's eyes shone as he passed by.

"Thank you for letting him do this, lieutenant," she murmured.

Dennis was quiet for a long moment, watching the horses spin. "One of my first memories is Culver standing alongside Mama, both of them holding me on a horse." He sighed heavily. "I didn't just bring him to Virginia because he's the best artist with metal. I wanted to save his life."

"Save his life? By bringing him into the middle of a war?"

"Safer than being near Papa. He's never treated Culver well, and in recent years . . ."

Ilsa thought of Culver's escape, his layers of scars. The horses picked up speed as centrifugal forces began to pull them outward at an angle. Culver passed by, his gap-toothed grin brilliant. He circled again, and this time, his arms were flung wide, his eyes closed.

"These are very different horses than the auquines, ma'am, and I don't mean the contrast of metal and wood." Dennis shook his head. "These horses—there's a particular kind of happiness. Like foals in a meadow."

Proof again that the lieutenant had an extra sense of horses' souls. Ilsa wondered who it carried through in his family.

"You understand, then, why I told the captain I shouldn't be making warhorses." She paused. "I think you understood from the very start. Since you first saw my carousel."

He said nothing for a time, watching Culver. "You know, ma'am, things will get terribly confusing as we ship south. People might go missing."

Her breath caught. "The soldier in charge of those people might get in awful trouble."

"You're set to ride on a civilian train part of the way. No guards. The captain believes Bucephalus is all the motivation you need to come along. I think that's because he'd do as much for that horse. Captain even talks to him, there in his office."

The words hurt. "I used to do the same."

"What if I can steal the horse?"

"I'm afraid to ask too much, lieutenant."

"What if you only took his soul, and left the carving behind? The captain wouldn't know until he unpacked Bucephalus down in Alabama."

Tears of hope made Ilsa's eyes smart as she nodded.

Culver flew by, laughing. His eyes were still shut, his arms still out like wings.

"I don't think I've ever heard him make such a sound." Dennis's voice was soft with awe. "You know what, ma'am? I changed my mind. I think I do want to ride."

As the horses slowed, Culver opened his eyes, his arms dropping to his sides. The carousel rocked to a stop.

"Missus Klein, never in my life I had an experience like that." He made to stand up, but she waved him down.

"Sit. You get another round, and this time you won't be alone. Lieutenant, mount up."

Culver craned around. "Master, you can't be back there, you—"

"I'm fine here. You lead me like when I was a boy." Lieutenant Dennis took the horse directly behind Culver. It was a red unicorn with a gold-leaf horn. A goofy grin lit the officer's whole face. "Mrs. Klein, don't tell me this holds a unicorn's soul."

"Why don't you tell me once you've had a go?" Ilsa started the machine.

She leaned against the central pillar and closed her eyes as the men laughed and whooped and eventually turned silent as midnight mice. Beneath the engine's rumble, she heard the echo of hoofbeats.

Ilsa waited in a shed adjacent to the rail yard, her satchel at her feet. The gray blurs of soldiers constantly passed the window. The Provisional Cavalry was mustering a quarter mile away to load up for their journey south.

The clock tolled eight times. Lieutenant Dennis was now late.

Ilsa's stomach twisted in knots, her fingers clenched with the need to hold Bucephalus again.

A knock shuddered through the door. She gasped, a hand at her anxious heart.

Lieutenant Dennis entered, Culver in his wake. "I got him, ma'am."

The lieutenant motioned to Culver, who held a worn leather bag. Ilsa reached inside and found those curves and nicks made by her own hand. She knew Bucephalus's alarm—his frustration—at being in the bag, at this change.

"It's me," she murmured. Her fingernail found the soft juncture where his left foreleg met his body. She pressed in just enough to know the heat of his soul there, lingering beneath the surface.

Ilsa let her joys and hope flow through to him—how she would braid his soul and hold it close as she traveled, how she would carve him a new and even more beautiful body, how they would explore the frontier west together.

He balked. His soul dug itself deeper into its wooden body.

"Bucephalus?" she whispered.

He told her without words, showing her the coziness of a body that he had known for twenty years, far longer than he had ever known flesh. He showed her the view from Captain Mayfair's window, the auquines engaged in their drills. He knew they were horses—he recognized the scent and presence of like souls. Bucephalus was not a warhorse, but the bustle of the encampment made him feel alive again, even as a statue. He didn't comprehend that he was stolen; all he knew was that he was in good care and stimulating company. Bucephalus, in life, knew how to work a stall clasp open with his lips so he could get to an oat bucket. Now he saw something else he wanted that was just out of reach.

He wants to stay with Captain Mayfair, not me. The betrayal stung her. He hadn't even thought of the captain, not directly, but the implication was there. She gripped the wooden horse as if she could convince him to leave through sheer will.

Bucephalus coiled within his shell, alarmed. Afraid of her.

What am I doing? Ilsa knew the feel of spurs and the lash. She would not—could not—be like that.

Her son's invisible soul had once slipped away. Now Bucephalus had escaped her, too, but only in part. He was still on earth. He had not dissipated. *He is not lost.*

"I understand. I don't like it, but I understand," she said to the horse then looked to Culver. "Bucephalus wants to stay in this body." Tears streaked down her cheeks. Culver nodded, expression thoughtful as he secured the horse in the bag again. "Captain Mayfair will take good care of him. So will you, lieutenant."

Dennis looked genuinely confused. "I—of course, ma'am. I just didn't expect . . . Well, this will be a trade, then." He pulled a stack of tri-folded sheets from his jacket and passed them to Ilsa. "Those are Culver's papers. Take him with you."

"Master Dennis?" Culver blinked rapidly.

"I gave her your papers, old man. You're going west." Dennis took the bag from Culver.

Shock filtered over Culver's face, then joy, then anger. "Master, no, I am not. I cannot."

"You must. Captain Mayfair's sending you back to the plantation." Dennis's voice cracked. "You know how Papa is since Mama passed. I won't be there to protect you, I . . ."

Ilsa looked between them and thought on their like recognition of equine souls, their uncommon closeness, the similarity in their smiles. Their skins were of different shades, true—Culver's dark as ebony, and the lieutenant's the deep walnut tone of a man who lived in the sun—but their bearings would have established their disparate roles even if they stood in silhouette. Culver's back was bowed by a life of hardship, whereas Dennis was the epitome of a Confederate officer, his posture ramrod straight and ready for a parade. *They're slave and master by reality. Father and son by blood.*

She took a steadying breath to hold back a new wave of sorrow.

"You never ask me nothing, Master Dennis. You never ask me where I wanna go, what I wanna do."

Frustration twisted Lieutenant Dennis's face. "Then what do you want?"

"If I'm a-going anywhere, I'm going north. Got family I'd like to find again, if they livin'."

Dennis clearly tried to act stoic even as he blinked back tears.

Ilsa tucked the papers into her bag and pried out stationery and a pencil. "I can smuggle him north." Smuggle herself, too, so the Union wouldn't use her as the Confederates did. "I know New York."

"Missus, you already gave me freedom on them horses the other day. I don't ask for more than that."

"You shouldn't just get one or two chances at such a thing, Culver. I promise I will do everything I can to help you find your daughter." Ilsa scribbled words onto a piece of paper.

"New York City." Culver said the words like a prayer.

"Thank you," Lieutenant Dennis whispered, his voice breaking. A train whistle pierced the air.

The two men stared at each other, saying everything in nothing. Culver brushed a gnarled hand against Lieutenant Dennis's gray sleeve, then turned away, trembling.

Ilsa steadied him. Even through layers of cloth, the scars on his back were hard lumps. "You'll need to carry my bag for appearances."

"Of course, missus. Of course."

Ilsa sealed the paper into an envelope addressed to Captain Mayfair and passed it to Dennis. "When the war is done, Captain Mayfair is to expect company in the Low Country. I told him this is no giveaway. An old woman might be asking for room and board as part of the deal." Culver opened the door.

"I'll tell him you left behind this letter," Lieutenant Dennis said, his voice thick. "And ma'am?"

She looked back. He cradled the bag with Bucephalus as if he held a newborn baby. "It really was a unicorn I rode, wasn't it?"

Ilsa smiled. She turned away again, her gaze already northward.

WHAT WE CARRY

the girl pointed to a distant glimmering star
and said, "there"
to which her horse replied, "it will take
many centuries, your parents will die, and your world
may very well destroy itself before we return"

the girl filled her pockets with dirt from the field
along with a wild sunflower bud and two smooth gray stones
"I am ready," she said

BEAT SOFTLY,
MY WINGS OF STEEL

BY THE LIGHT OF THE FULL MOON, I crept onto a battlefield mounded with decaying soldiers and horses. Mud squished beneath my boots as I searched for a horse's soul. This close to the Jen picket lines, they had likely already scavenged for souls of both flesh horses and those that had already been reborn as pegasi, but I was desperate.

Not far away, the campfires of the Jen army flickered, their encampment a living wall across the peninsula. At my back, my own city Sharva repulsed me like the rotten flesh on this battlefield. Holes dotted the magicked dome over the spires like a moth-gnawed veil unable to hide an ugly bride. I would rejoice over Sharva's imminent fall but not for what that meant for me and Grandmother.

My hand glided over the smooth metal belly of a pegasus. Voices caused me to hunker low. After a long minute, I crawled forward. Gauzy clouds smothered the moon but I could still make out the bodies around me like miniature foothill ranges. A Jen Cavalry officer lay nearby, her death evidently more recent than most.

The golden emblem of Jen Cavalry on her surcoat was not that different from Sharva's: a rearing pegasus, wings flared. The city-states of Jen and Sharva vied like jealous sisters for the love of the benevolent horse goddess Atanta.

I rubbed my filthy fingers over the embroidered patch, then looked away, ashamed of my own pettiness.

That's when I spied the soul.

The wisp was dull yellow like a star fallen to earth, its light nearly extinguished after so long on the field. I slid over a pegasus's metal corpse to get closer as hot tears filled my eyes. A soul. Blessed Atanta, there was hope. We might be able to escape.

Only the souls of especially strong-willed horses could linger on earth after death, and it took even more fortitude for such souls to persist after their reconstructed bodies failed. Mother often said Cavalry families of Jen and Sharva had that same resilience. We were of Atanta's brood, too—and horses responded to that. It's as though they recognized a scent on Cavalry souls that marked us as part of their herd.

I cupped the soul in my hands. Faint warmth remained, as in a round of bread left cooling for an hour. "There, there," I whispered. "I'm Ulyssa. I'll take good care of you."

I had known and loved many horses throughout my fifteen years, but I had never bonded with one.

With trembling, mud-stiff fingers, I pulled the ready heart from my pouch. I knew every dent and curve pounded into the metal surface. I twisted the lid from the right ventricle, and murmuring praise to Atanta, I poured the soul inside.

I slipped the heart into my pouch just as gunfire punched through the quiescent night. An unseen bird cawed, the sound almost as loud as the lurching of my heart. I eased myself back over the broken pegasus and officer. The bombardment would begin anew at sunrise. I had to hurry. My pegasus must be ready to fly before Sharva's dome was breeched.

"Miss Ulyssa, do you require assistance?" asked Three. He met me at the estate's gate, his three-fingered hand held aloft to cast its embedded illumination.

I stank after the battlefield and the sewers I'd slunk through to get there. "Take this to the workshop and make sure the heart is clean," I said, passing him my satchel. He bowed. With much of his exoskeleton removed to plate my pegasus, the knobs of his spine were visible.

"Miss Faleen brought muesli. I stored it in the kitchen."

"Thank you, Three." What a mercy! I'd used our scant food supply to bribe the sewer guards. Three's metal feet clicked on the courtyard tiles. His light faded.

Atanta bless Miss Faleen and her two children. The rest of Sharva tried to ignore me and Grandmother after the Bloody Tourney and Mother's death, but our neighbor's friendship had never wavered. That's why I planned to bring her two youngsters along when we escaped the city.

I cleansed myself and entered the stable.

Before the war, we had lived in comfort off Mother's Cavalry commission. We'd had a dozen automatons on staff—of which Three was the last—and a double stable filled with both flesh horses and those reborn in winged metal bodies.

Three had lit gas lamps and uncovered my metal horse. It was not yet a pegasus; the soul needed to adjust to a more familiar form first.

My horse was beautiful, yet still undeniably the raw work of a mere squire. Visible seams crisscrossed its body like stitches in a quilt. The mismatched metal patches were proof I had pieced it together from a hundred different carcasses. Likewise, the completed wings against the nearby wall contained hundreds of feathers in a warm metallic array that stood in bold contrast to the steel bones. The full equine form had some sinuous grace—a cupped chin, tapered ears—but overall, like any Cavalry mount, it was built for strength and endurance.

I picked up the metal heart, stroking it. I would soon know this soul with intimacy unlike any I had known. I crouched to place the heart in the chest cavity, and sang to Atanta all the while. I made the final connections within the body and stood, my hand on the halter. The enchantments I had pounded into metal and pressed into rubber thrummed to life like a swarm of bees. Onward I sang.

Life began with a shiver, like a flesh horse beset by flies. My horse's ears flickered next. Hooves shuffled. Its polished black marble eyes rolled in their sockets, the spark of magic brightening pupils. It jerked back on the tethers then stilled, quivering. A flesh horse would have been frothed in sweat. The mouth began to work as if fighting a bit. I frowned as my prayers finished.

"Three, did I miss any elements in creating the mouth?"

"No, miss. All procedures were followed."

"Have you observed any behavior like this in an awakening before?"

There was a pause as Three accessed his records. "No, miss. Nor are there notes on such behavior in fully adapted pegasi."

The horse's nearest eye gazed directly at me as its mouth continued to move. There was a pattern. Long gap, short gap. I mimicked with my own mouth. The horse's head bobbed in an intense nod.

"Do you understand what I'm saying?" I whispered.

The horse nodded.

"But your soul! I saw it! You have to be a horse!"

The horse shook its head.

I stared in horror. "Oh, Atanta, what have I done?"

I skimmed through volume after volume at the workshop bookshelf while simultaneously flooding Three with queries.

Had a human soul ever been placed in a horse before? No.

Had anyone ever *seen* a human soul before? No.

Had a horse's soul ever been placed in anything not shaped like a horse? No. A soul needed a familiar body to be reborn.

Then how could a human soul adapt to a metal equine form? I didn't ask Three that. I knew he had no answer. Only Atanta did.

Oh, there were always jokes about Cavalry families and their deep soul-bonds with their constructed equines. But to see and snare a human soul as if it were a horse?

I froze in the midst of pulling down a book. Sharva killed Mother because she spoke out against the war. Would I have been able to salvage her soul after her execution? Cold trickled down my spine. After all, she had been the finest equestrian of her generation here; her only peers were the Arvo sisters of Jen.

Dizzied, I pushed away the book and faced the horse again. Most Sharvan Cavalry, horses, and pegasi were dead. Very few had ventured from the walls since the last full moon. I remembered the Jen officer's broken body, so close to where I found the soul.

"You're Jen Cavalry," I whispered. The enemy. In my stable.

The horse exploded into motion. Its head jerked down at a hard angle, yanking the tether free from the far wall. The horse pivoted, hind legs angled toward me. I leaped and rolled to one side. Wood chunks and splinters rained down on me as a bench caught the attack. I turned in time to see the horse jerk hard on the other tether. The rope broke free, bringing a piece of board with it, and the horse lunged forward.

Three grabbed one of the dangling ropes. His reinforced metal might have been enough to slow a flesh horse, but not this beast. The horse purposefully jerked its head as it leapt through the open door. Three went airborne and crashed into the wall with a sickening jangle of metal. Hooves clattered in the courtyard, the loud echo like war drums.

I pursued, sick with dread.

The horse spun in a circle. Suddenly, I *knew* its panic. I saw what it saw: the home of the enemy. High walls, a thick gate, a fortress in miniature. Terror pulsed through the horse's makeshift heart as it looked every which way, frantic for escape. The very sound of its hoof beats amplified its alarm.

Shock stole my breath away. My bond with the horse was true, Jen or not.

I whispered to Atanta, beseeched her for her wisdom, her peace, and flowed that calm toward the horse. At the stroke of power, the horse looked at me, ears back.

Negativity punched me in the gut. NO NO NO. It didn't want me in its head.

"Please. You must be quiet. The neighbors . . . they'll report the sound or sight of any horse. You'd be forced to ride against the Jen." A hoof stamped. Questions bubbled against my consciousness, but I couldn't quite grasp words, just continued negative emotion.

I clenched and unclenched my fists, fighting my own panic. I wanted to live. My horse was our only means of survival. I couldn't lose it.

"Ulyssa?" Grandmother called from a far archway. "Did I hear a horse?"

"There aren't any horses here, Grandmother. There are scarcely any in the city at all." Atanta forgive me the lie. "Please go back to bed. Miss Faleen brought us food for breakfast."

"Ah, bless her and those children! No horses. Mercy on us all . . ." She muttered as she shuffled away.

I stared down at the horse. It stared back, utterly still. I had the sudden sense it knew of all my emotions, too: my well of love and despair for Grandmother, and my hope. Some of the negative backlash softened. Maybe my horse had loved a grandmother, too.

"My Grandmother's completely blind and can barely walk. I should have Three check on her, but . . . oh."

I glanced back. Pieces of Three littered the doorway and hall. With his exoskeleton gone, he had shattered like an egg. Tears flooded my eyes. Oh, Three. I felt the sudden need to gather his wreckage, to save him, and then I noticed his neck unit laying on the tile.

"If you come back into the workshop, I can try installing my automaton's voice box in your throat. It's never been done before, but look at us." I motioned to the both of us. "Will you let me try?"

The horse's marble gaze was intent as it nodded.

I sang speech into my horse. Its mouth moved like before, ready to speak as Atanta's blessing descended on us.

"Help. Me."

I froze, my hands still inside the throat cavity. So that's what the horse had been trying to say.

"I hear you." I closed the hatch and stepped back. Thin morning light cast slants onto the workshop floor.

"I'm in Sharva?" The words warbled.

"Yes." I licked my dry lips. "I found your soul on the battlefield. I thought . . ."

"I was a horse's soul. I don't understand, either. Nothing like this has happened in Jen. I am . . . I was Gia." As she spoke, the tone continued to undulate until it found soft evenness. The soul had adjusted the voice to make it familiar.

I stared. "Gia. Commander Gia Arvo." One of the Arvo sisters.

The horse's head lifted. "You know me."

"Of course. I saw you at the Bloody Tourney. My Mother . . ." I stopped and struggled to control my emotions. If Gia knew who Mother was, would she attack me again? I was almost defenseless against her weight and strength, though I could call on Atanta to sever the life I had sung into her; usually such a plea accompanied a dram of Dreamless Death to end the suffering of a flesh horse. There was no way to know how Atanta would answer a death prayer alone.

"Ulyssa?" Grandmother's voice wavered in the distance. "Where's Three?"

"Ulyssa. I thought that's what she said earlier. You're Commander Moshana's daughter." Gia's ears pivoted forward. Instead of being enraged, she seemed intrigued. I nodded, too tired to deny it. "With your lineage, with your city's need, why aren't you Cavalry? Why are we here?"

I looked around. My workshop wasn't shabby, but it certainly wasn't like the Sharvan Cavalry stables Gia would have visited before the war. "I'm surprised you're asking me questions and not simply stomping me into the ground."

"There's still time for that. What day is this? How long was I . . . ?"

"Last night was the final full moon in the cycle. How soon

until Jen pushes into the city?"

"I don't repeat military secrets, no matter how obvious the answer may be." Her indignant attitude prickled against my consciousness.

"Do you think I'll warn parliament? The Cavalry?" My voice rose to hysterical heights. "I don't care if they all rot, I . . ."

I didn't dare grant this Jen-souled horse my wings. I had no way to get us out of the city now. The Jen would slaughter me and Grandmother. Eventually. Painfully.

"Ulyssa?" Grandmother's frail voice was a little closer. "Where's Three?"

"I have to go to her or she might trip on the tiles." I glanced at Three's remains on the floor. Such an ignominious end. I could still bring his central unit, if we had a way to escape. If.

Heavy thuds rang from the street side gate.

My blood turned to ice. "Someone heard your hooves and reported it."

"I will fight. I won't be forced to kill my comrades."

"And I'd cheer you as you fought Sharva," I snapped. Gia's profound confusion—horror—flashed through my mind as I moved to the doorway. "Grandmother! Wait there! Three is broken. I'll answer the gate."

I grabbed a pitchfork, a stark reminder of those distant days when horse manure was an issue. I would fight, too. I wasn't a noble officer like Mother, wearing my parade best to be marched to my doom. No. I'd kick and bite and scream. Like a horse.

Through the gate slats, I recognized Faleen's young son. "Galen? What is it?"

His eyes were bold white against his brown skin. "We all heard hoof beats and Mama sent me to follow Mr. Kirks from across the street and he went straight to the Cavalry to tell them, and they thought hunger made him hallucinate but he kept talking and they're going to send soldiers. Do you really have a pegasus in there?"

Atanta bless this family for all their kindness. "No pegasus, Galen." Not yet. "Thank you for the warning. Get home so the soldiers don't see you here."

I left the pitchfork and ran. I burst into the workshop, breathless. "The Cavalry's coming."

The horse struck a noble pose. "I will make my stand here, then."

"You'll do no such fool thing. You're in a horse's body, but you can go where horses never would."

Gia's ears pivoted as she took this in. "What do you have in mind?"

I led three soldiers to the stable. I had thrown a sheet over the steel wings and tucked them partially behind a table.

"Our automaton had a terrible malfunction," I said, pointing to the broken boards where Three had impacted with the wall. "That must have been what the neighbors heard."

The commander grunted. "Hell of a malfunction." We knew each other from our school days, but he couldn't look me in the eye. My mother was the gifted hero turned traitor, after all.

I walked them through the main house. Grandmother sat on her cushion eating her breakfast of dry muesli.

"It was such a terrible noise!" she said between lip smacks.

"I can imagine, ma'am," said the commander, his gaze averted.

In the back of my mind, I knew the presence of my horse the way I knew a cool breeze. I knew her effort to remain utterly still in the cellar just below. I knew her fear, her tumultuous mind. Also— her awe. For a flesh horse to be reborn in metal was a great honor. Gia's new existence, for all its terror, was of unparalleled holiness.

She understood me in the same way. A standard pegasus responded to the call of its bonded rider, their teamwork in battle synchronized and sinuous. But those horses were *horses*. Gia was something more.

The soldiers left. The morning bustle of Sharva had been replaced by ominous stillness. Everyone waited for the attack to resume. For the end to come.

I entered the cellar. Any normal horse would have balked at those steep downward steps. I left a lamp hanging on the wall. Gia awaited me in a recess beneath the stairs, the light casting brilliant stripes across her sloped back.

"Sharvan Cavalry killed your mother. *Why?* She was your city's greatest hero."

"She was." I blinked back sudden tears. "You need to know that at the Tourney, her volley that killed the Jen prince ..."

"It was an accident. Yes. Many of us witnessed it and testified so, but many more wanted vengeance and blood."

I couldn't disguise my surprise. Even the famed Commander Gia Arvo had been against the war? "Sharva was happy to have an excuse to fight, too. But Mother didn't want to be the reason. She testified it was all an accident, that Jen's military outnumbered ours, that Sharva had no chance. When our parliament wouldn't listen, she tried to smuggle messages to Jen, pleading for mercy. That's when she was declared traitor."

I remembered my mother at the end. Her uniform, creases perfect. Her chin high. She marched to her death without any regrets. I was the one left with the rage. Against her, for abandoning us. Against Sharva, for readying their volley of stones to kill her. Against the Jen, for persisting to fight.

Against Atanta, for letting this happen at all.

"You made this horse's body as a means of escape," Gia said softly.

Her grim vibe confirmed my fears. Me and Grandmother were symbols of a war with a terribly high cost. We would be shown no mercy in the invasion.

Dust shivered from the ceiling as the Jen bombardment resumed.

"The attack won't stop at sundown," Gia whispered. "This will continue as long as needed to crack the dome."

"I need to affix your wings. The instant the dome falls, we must fly." I stifled a yawn against my wrist.

"You need to sleep first or you'll make some fool error. I know that from personal experience. I should stay down here as you rest, just in case soldiers return."

I rested a hand on Gia's muzzle and wondered how she felt my touch, how she saw, how she experienced *life*. All those questions that could never be answered through a human-horse soul bond.

"I feel like I'm alive. That there's more of me. That I'm stronger than ever before. I feel . . . blessed."

"Why didn't Atanta grant our people this kind of bond months ago?" I hoarsely whispered. "If Sharva and Jen could have understood each other like this, if . . ."

"I don't know." Her frustration, her grief, compounded with my own. Gia's head hooked over my shoulder as I leaned against her, the closest we could come to a physical embrace.

I sang Gia into a pegasus, and she sang with me.

It was peculiar, our fusion of power. Horses weren't capable of this intense weaving of magic and soul. My body tingled with heat and light and the channeled blessing of Atanta, and Gia knew the same.

Even so, the wing attachment took hours. Pulleys in the ceiling held the heavy wings aloft so I could wire them in, chanting all the while. It was evening by the time I released the ropes and stood back to watch Gia test them in the wide space of the workshop.

She flapped once, twice, thrice, and her body lifted. I held my breath, in awe of her own indescribable elation. *She* flew. She had known the bliss for years as a rider, but to be the one with wings?

I absorbed her joy, and her ready forgiveness at my undeniable jealousy.

"Considering that you were able to see my soul, that we are capable of bonding like this, you may yet have your chance at wings," Gia said.

"Atanta willing." I was afraid to even hope to be reborn like her. Besides, I rather liked my human body and I hoped for plenty of years in it.

I closed my eyes, the rhythmic wind from her wings like a lullaby. I felt an urge creep over Gia. She could go right outside and fly higher and higher, leave us all behind. We weren't Jen, after all.

I didn't plead. I simply stood there. I understood her temptation. I also understood *her*.

She landed with a clatter of metal hooves on tile.

The bombardment intensified as the dome thinned. I prepared Gia with full tack and laden saddlebags. Our plan was to fly to Gia's villa a day south to take refuge, and once the battle was done, connect her with her Cavalry officer sister.

I explained my plan to Grandmother as we walked to the workshop. Through the veil overhead, the shadows of Jen pegasi swirled like vultures.

"You brilliant, idiotic girl. You think these old bones can take the lurching of flight?" She sat in a wooden chair with a grunt. "Get more children out. Spare them the horror to come."

"But Grandmother, when the Jen—"

"You think I don't know?" Her voice was a brittle knife. She reached into her bodice and pulled out two vials. I accepted one. The glass was warm from her body. "That's Dreamless Death. That dose would squelch the suffering of a flesh horse within a minute. You keep that dram, escape plan or not."

I nodded and tucked it in my own bodice. I should have expected as much from her. "But Grandmother—"

"Stop dillydallying. Gather your young riders before it's too late." I pressed a kiss to her forehead, my hand desperately clutching hers. Reverberations pounded through the walls. "Go," she said gruffly.

I ran next door and up the stairs. I found Galen, his sister, and

Faleen on their flat, narrow roof. Faleen held a crossbow, useless as it was to her. Her steadiness had never returned after she survived a close concussive blast weeks before.

"Take them," she said when I told her my plan. The children looked at me, wide-eyed.

A sensation like snow flurries drifted over my skin and I held up my hand. On my dark knuckles, iridescent slivers dissolved to nothing. The quiet was sudden. Deathly.

The dome had fallen.

Abrupt gunfire punctuated the stillness. "They're already in the city!" a man screamed from a nearby rooftop. I saw him point just up our street. The walls must have crumpled before the dome.

"Come on!" I said, trying to pry the children free from their mother. "We have to go—"

I knew the moment Gia took to the air. Her power and majesty resounded through me like a symphony at full crescendo before I even turned to witness her flight with my own eyes. My pegasus soared, her wingspan stretched ten feet, each feather flared and perfect. She swooped down to our rooftop. Her metal hooves stirred up more of the dome's melting, enchanted shards.

I lifted Galen to the smooth pommel. His sister pulled herself behind him and began to secure herself. I had affixed straps to keep the children in place. Like any youth in Sharva or Jen, they could ride a horse, but flight was something more.

"They're here," Faleen whispered.

I turned. Jen infantry filled the narrow street and split up as they came under fire from above.

Gia was a fluttering, unavoidable target. We'd never make it.

I didn't want to die. I'd scraped together my pegasus to save others, yes, but myself most of all. I wanted summer sun to set my skin aglow; to chew hot honeyed oats on the high holy days. To breathe in the perfume of oiled leather and fresh hay. To welcome the timid winter dawn with songs to Atanta, every word a puff of steam rising straight to the heavens.

But if I was going to die, I'd go like Mother. Doing the right thing.

I grabbed the crossbow from Faleen's limp hands.

"Ulyssa, you can't!" Gia cried as she read my intentions. Faleen and her children stared, dumbfounded by the talking pegasus.

"Mount up, Faleen. Go with them. I'll cover you. You'll be shot down otherwise." I crouched and aimed. I watched not only the street but my neighbors as well. "Go! Before we're surrounded!"

Gia's thoughts warred with mine, our emotions jumbled like fighting tomcats.

A gun barrel poked out from behind boxes along the street. A head leaned out, gaze directly on us, but pulled back before I could fire.

"Atanta, bless us," I whispered, evoking the Cavalry prayer for battle. "Beat softly, my wings of steel. Carry us to clouds and home again. Home again, home again."

The soldier peered out. I fired, loaded another bolt, fired anew. A shot pinged into the lip of the roof not a foot away from me. I tasted grit. The shot came from Mr. Kirks across the way. He took my next bolt in the gut.

"Where stables smell of sweet hay and viscous oil, where my heartbeat knows the cadence of hooves," Gia sang in turn. Her hind legs propelled her toward the fading stars.

I had never known that Sharva and Jen Cavalry sang the exact same prayer. I had known so little.

Tears streamed down my cheeks as my soul-bonded pegasus flew away. I never even had the chance to ride her.

I had a few dozen bolts at ready. I loaded and aimed again, again, again. I hunkered lower and glanced up. The sky looked so bare with the magicked dome gone. Already, Gia was a distant blur. Other Jen pegasi freckled the sky but none close. I shared the image with her as a precaution, and likewise I knew her view. The sea glittered, ships flashing color with occasional cannon blasts. Gia was beyond their range.

There had been no time to bundle Faleen and the children in warmer clothes for the chill of flight—

Gia reassured me with a flash of emotion. She would take care of them. And me, in time.

Grandmother's vial pressed against my heart. When it was time, I would take my drink. What they did to my body afterward didn't matter. My soul was strong. I would wait here. Come the next full moon, Gia would know where to guide her sister, and she would sing me to life again.

"Beat softly, my wings of steel," I whispered to Gia then repeated the prayer to myself, as a promise.

HUNTER

sadness nibbles at the lady
a thousand
voracious mice

the cat, he understands prey
though he has never known
warm dirt beneath his paws

he guards while she sleeps
tail lashing, ears perked
he swallows her grief

she awakens each morning, smiling
his body a round pillow
perfect warmth within the crook of her arm

it is easy to digest true mice
bone, muscle, sinew, whisker
but sadness sticks in the craw

burrows into cells
foul, malignant and amassing
gangrenous to body, not to noble soul

her affliction so mighty
it ravages his few remaining lives
until one remains

even so

the hunter does not stop hunting
tumor a glowing red knoll
above his heart

when he can no longer walk
they enter that place of strange smells and white walls
the lady's tears fall as hot rain

his raspy tongue laps those salty trails
and till the very end
he swallows her grief, and purrs

HEADSPACE

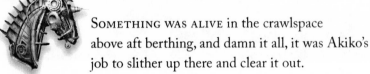

SOMETHING WAS ALIVE in the crawlspace above aft berthing, and damn it all, it was Akiko's job to slither up there and clear it out.

Desperate times called for desperate measures. In this case, illegal drugs.

With fumbling fingers, she unwrapped a tranq patch and slapped it on beneath the waistband of her jumpsuit. She braced herself against the wall for a long moment, breathing through the terror that came at the very thought of that narrow tunnel.

Ninety-nine percent of the time, she got by just fine. Haulers like the *Tolleson* had nice, wide hallways. Her crew berth was as large or larger than what she'd get in some residential stack down in Kyoto. Enviro duty meant sys-monitoring most days, and filters could be changed through hall or room access.

Then the one percent moments came along and slapped her upside the head.

Her heart rate slowed as the tranq did its thing. The overwhelming sense of doom diminished. Thank God that whoever busted into her room last week and stole half her stuff missed the tranqs hidden beneath a floor panel.

She stared up the ladder to the hatch in the ceiling. "Let's do this."

The work chit had described several passengers' complaints of moving noises in the ceiling. Akiko had her suspicions. The ship's last hop involved the transport of about fifty small animals for a colony on Capulet. The critters had been too temperature sensitive for the freight locker, so they'd been given a berth of their own. If anything had been flagged as missing, it wasn't Akiko's place to know.

The air shaft was about a meter in diameter—big enough that she could pivot around if necessary instead of backing up. Even blissed-out, she took comfort in that wiggle room. Akiko tapped her comm. Lights flicked on along the length of the tunnel. She squinted.

Something moved at the far end.

Her tools clanked against the tunnel as she crawled along, her knees tapping hollow. The thing came towards her.

That's when she realized how incredibly stupid she'd been. She'd been so freaked out about the tunnel, she hadn't thought about what might be in there. Any creature going to a colony world likely possessed some genetic modifications, whether to cope with the environment, boost agriculture, or poison intruders.

The creature entered the light.

"Damn," Akiko muttered.

The ginger kitten had an odd, ambling gait that showed the sharp jut of its hips. God, the thing was half dead, and way too small. A runt, maybe, or just plain wasting away. Its mouth opened in a silent meow. A stubby tail stood upright as a flagpole.

"Hey," she crooned, holding out a gloved hand. Before even reaching her, the critter began to purr. A trusting thing, then. Socialized. "How the hell did you get up here? That hop was too short for you to be born aboard. How did you escape? Did someone try to steal you, strip your ID, stuff you up here?" Damn, she'd need to check those quarters. There had to be some kind of break in the grate.

The little body rumbled in a fierce purr. Even through the thick lining of her gloves, Akiko felt the hard ripples of ribs. This thing had been stuck up here a week, at least. They had been in port for several days, and no one would have heard the kitten until they loaded up.

Now what the hell was she supposed to do with it? She did a quick check beneath the tail. Him.

No way would Captain Haanrath let her keep a pet on board; everything had to have a purpose. The man was downright obsessive with his protocols. Hell, even evac drills took place every other Tuesday at 0600; drug tests were Fridays when underway, and six hours prior to any docking. He timed it to the minute. Too bad he wasn't so efficient in catching the burglar on board.

Haanrath would throw the kitten in a crate down in the hold. Akiko cringed. Good God. She hated being in tight confines, and couldn't wish that on any other creature.

They were three days out of port. She could make do until then, smuggle him off, find someone to give him a home. How she'd do that, Akiko had no clue. This kitten was black market now. Haanrath might be the king of obsessive-compulsive, but she tended to operate by the book, too. Illegal tranqs aside.

"You're nothing but trouble, know that?" she muttered to the kitten. His teeth bared in another silent meow and he butted his head against her knuckles.

"Trouble." The name suited him.

Trouble immediately claimed her bunk, though he couldn't make up his mind if he preferred the rumpled sheets or the worn-down nest in the middle of her pillow.

Akiko made a quick trip to grab a tray and recycled paper pulp from the enviro lab in the bilge, and hit the chow line for some meat. She largely favored carbs, so still had plenty of protein allowances on her ration card.

She couldn't play spectator as the kitten snarfed up chicken chunks formed into perfect triangles. With a full buzz-on from her tranq, she climbed back into the shaft and sterilized the whole tube before any complaints came in about the sharp ammonia stink of cat piss.

A quick check on the berth used to store the animals confirmed a busted grate, probably from the hard corner of a cage. She used the commlink at her wrist to zap the repair chit over to maintenance.

It took another hour to do her normal duties: filter changes, climate moderation, so on. Normal day, other than finding an average-looking Earth critter almost dead in a duct.

She'd just finished up when a ship-wide message from Captain Haanrath landed on her commlink. She read and cringed. Now he was giving bonuses to anyone who helped drum up business in port for the *Tolleson* or her sister ship in refit, the *Maryvale*. He owned both ships and always talked about bottom lines and ninety percent capacity quotas and other bull. What did he expect the crew to do, walk the station with flashing placards? If the man wanted attention for the ship, he needed to do something lewd. That always gained media attention.

'Course, Haanrath's idea of lewd probably involved adding cream to his coffee.

She grabbed her own chow and headed back to her berth.

Trouble had decided on the pillow after all. He flicked one ear in response to her arrival. Akiko snorted. Typical male. Could probably sleep through a muster drill. She rested a hand against the kitten's side. Already, the hard lines of his ribs had softened. Trouble had probably eaten his body weight in rehydrated fowl. Even so, he was small enough to fit in her palm.

Akiko gnawed on some boost-bread while she checked over the room. The makeshift litter box had been used. Good.

The bliss of the tranq dwindled away to bone-weariness. By morning, she'd be back to normal; by the time they docked at Assisi orbital, her blood test would look dandy, too.

"Do you know how to share?" she asked with a yawn. Trouble didn't budge. Akiko sighed. She could just scoot the kitten over a few inches, but he looked so damn cozy.

To hell with it. She pulled her blankets off the bed and rolled her own makeshift pillow. The thin carpet was hard beneath her shoulder, but she'd slept on worse mattresses in her day.

There on the floor, the quiet vibration of the engines reminded her of a purring cat.

Klaxons caused Akiko to bolt upright. Sirens screeched from her wrist, the wall, the hallway outside. Where—what—how? Her mind snapped to awareness as decades of training took over, her focus on the sharp pitch and the pattern: evac.

It was not Tuesday.

"Damn, damn, damn." Akiko slapped the commlink on her wrist to shut off the closest screeching.

Captain Haanrath's voice boomed over the continued alarms. "This is not a drill. Repeat, not a drill. We're experiencing catastrophic engine failure and estimate less than three minutes until rupture. Passengers, to your pods. Crew—"

Akiko shoved the emergency closet doors open. Her suit awaited, pants splayed open, coat wide, fish bowl helmet in easy reach.

"—don your gear, do everything as we drilled. Two minutes until pods disengage. Distress signal initiated. Godspeed."

Godspeed. An old school atheist like Haanrath, calling on God? This was the real deal.

She hopped backward into the closet, pulling up the tabs along each leg as she straightened. The suit was designed to be form fitting but flexible for work on the hull—not like she'd ever been outside before. Not her domain. As she shoved her arms into the sleeves, she looked out into her room.

Trouble still lay curled up on her pillow. One of his ears cocked back in annoyance at the noise.

Oh, God.

She secured the suit to her neck. Her commlink chimed to signify proper sealing. Akiko grabbed the helmet and lurched out of the closet. The boots clunked, her feet dragging at the unfamiliar weight. Trouble reared back as if to flee. She clutched him with a mighty gloved hand, shoved him in the helmet, and then pulled it over her head. The fuzzy ball of warmth pressed against the right side of her face. The helmet clinked and sealed with a soft hiss.

Trouble squawked. He turned, a needle-sharp claw catching her across the nose, then the lip. No time to worry now if he had gen mod poison claws. Akiko spat out a paw. Orange stripes filled her vision.

"Calm down," she snapped.

Years of training tumbled through her brain. Don the suit. Get to a pod; failing that, get to an airlock and rely on the suit. Jettison before the ship blows.

Akiko propelled herself through the door. Another white-suited figure rushed by. Further down, someone yelled. The ass-end of a kitten pressed on her left eye.

Haanrath's voice boomed out, "Explosion imminent. Pods disengaging in twenty seconds, I repeat—"

She lunged for the nearest airlock. The door zoomed shut behind her, another door before her. No time to think, no time to panic, she punched the fat red button on the wall.

Akiko couldn't help but scream as she was sucked into space. Her voice filled the confines of her helmet and sent the kitten into a renewed frenzy. White stars blurred as she spun, and she'd continue to spin that way to infinity if she didn't stop it. She had the sense to smack the booster controls on her arm. The crazed spiral slowed, and she turned to look back at the ship—as much as she could see, around the cat.

The *Tolleson* was already a gray mass, growing smaller. Leaving her behind. Panic spiked in her chest. Dear God, she had just jumped into deep space. Was this all real? What if—

The pods split off, followed by other glints—crew like her berthed too far from the pods, all suited up to survive the vacuum of space.

She checked her commlink. The individual signals were too

weak. No one in range.

Behind the furry body and the data across her visor, the ship fragmented.

No violence to it. No sound. Instead of a single gray hulk, it became several. Each spun off on a new trajectory.

She stared, awestruck. She breathed. Faster, faster. The warming gels layered in the suit kicked on, protecting her against the iciness of space, but her body was plenty hot. Her face flushed, the drenching sweat instantaneous.

Akiko was floating in space. Alone.

Here she was, in a suit. A tight suit. The claustrophobia of it strangled her.

Inhale, exhale. Faster, faster. Her lungs couldn't expand. The fabric was too tight. And there was a cat, a cat right there, right on her face. God, what had she been thinking?

She needed out. Out of this suit. The logical part of her brain whispered no, that's death, don't do it, but logic had nothing to do with the reality of deep space; because maybe, maybe, the frigid nothingness would bring a more merciful end than floating out here for days or weeks—God, how long could she last out here? How long until she lost her mind?

Or had she already? A tranq. She needed a tranq. She needed something.

A stubby tail stabbed her in the eye and caused her to recoil.

Akiko's heart threatened to pound its way free of the suit. A thin film of condensation lined the inside of the visor. Sweat gathered at her neck and threatened to drown her even as the suit wicked away moisture. She'd die out here. Her heart would race and give out, or it'd be the cold, or starvation, or—

Trouble's raspy tongue stroked her cheek and shocked her out of her diatribe. Akiko closed her eyes. That little tongue lapped up tears and sweat all the way up to her eye.

It was easier, seeing only the blackness beneath her eyelids. She focused on her breath. In, out. She could taste the moisture in the air, and fur stuck to her lips, her skin.

The cut on her nose stung as Trouble's tongue scrubbed it clean—God knew the bacteria he laced into her bloodstream. He didn't need a gen mod to make her sick.

She kept her face still as he groomed her other cheek. Not like she could stop him.

Then, as if exhausted by his effort, he laid down. His furry body wedged against her mouth and nose and nigh suffocated her. For some reason, that didn't panic her now. She blew out through her mouth. He moved back towards her cheek some more, his body rumbling in a purr.

"If we do die out here," she whispered, trying to work some fur off her tongue, "I hope my ghost or something is around, just so I can see the reaction of whoever finds us. Whoever finds this woman floating in space with a kitten on her face."

Purring was her reply.

"Yeah. I didn't have the heart to throw you in a cage, and then I stuff you in my helmet. I guess I have a good excuse to be a hypocrite."

She closed her eyes and just breathed. She had never been in a suit for more than ten minutes before, for drills. The floating sensation reminded her of how her body felt sometimes right as she fell asleep. Drifting. If she couldn't see the stars, see the bleakness of space, she could almost pretend. Almost.

Someone would find them. Haanrath had sent out a distress call. Even more, the suits and pods had beacons. This was a trade route—not major like a direct hop from Earth or Mars, but it had traffic. For the *Tolleson*, Assisi was only a few days out, but other ships could make it faster.

Trouble squirmed again. His mouth found a tendril of hair and he began to lick and tug.

"Hey." She tapped the dome. "If you hack up a hairball on my face, I'm not going to be happy."

He enthusiastically ignored her.

Actually, he could do a whole lot worse than hairballs, but even that possibility didn't bother her. Not now.

Akiko slept. Dozed might have been a more appropriate term. The panic returned more than once. Her eyelids burst open, took in the view as she remembered where she was, and how. Her heart rate kicked up as if it could power a reactor. Fat drops of sweat coursed from her brow.

But there was always that raspy tongue to catch her sweat and tears, that furry body that all too often threatened to suffocate her. She clenched her eyes shut again.

Akiko spoke to Trouble in a mutter, her lips compressed as tightly as possible, or she'd find a leg or paw stuck in her mouth. With her eyes shut and her heart pounding, she told him about her life. About her dad, the spacer who appeared with utter randomness throughout her childhood; her mom, a corporate phlebotomy tech who flew between Seattle, Kyoto, and Lunar One on a regular basis, and granted Akiko her first taste of flight.

"The *Tolleson*'s been home for five years. It is—was—a rust bucket, but it was my rust bucket." She blinked back sudden tears, wondering at the fate of the crew. "There haven't been as many passengers the past few months, since the peace treaty on Mars. Haanrath has been gung-ho about finding more business. Guess it doesn't matter now. If he made it—if the others made it—maybe we can work on the *Maryvale*. Maybe."

God. Everything was a maybe. Maybe she'd live, maybe she'd find a new home, a new job. Maybe she'd die here with a kitten on her face.

As if sensing her new dismay, Trouble purred. His front paws kneaded her jaw, those dagger-like claws catching her skin. She winced and smiled at the same time.

Trouble was there. She wasn't alone.

Calmer now, she was ready to face the truth. She opened her

eyes and accessed the commlink. Her oxygen supply and booster fuel meters gleamed in green lines against the faceplate. White stars blurred as her body continued a slow spin through space.

Trouble meowed; she felt the waft of his hot breath more than she heard it. He pivoted again, restless, probably hungry.

"I'll buy you a Martian filet mignon," she whispered. "Best cut of beef you'll ever find. They raise miniature cattle in the domes there, a bison hybrid, so it's lean."

The commlink beeped. Akiko's head jolted back in the helmet. Someone had pinged her system.

Far away, the dot almost blended with the stars. As it loomed closer, she made out the hard lines of a long-hop freight hauler, Uluru class. The thing could have held ten *Tollesons* in its broad belly.

"This is the Martian-registered *Quintus*. By your beacon, we identify you as Akiko Danielson, Chief Enviro of the *Tolleson*. Confirm?"

Tears squeezed from her eyes. "Yes. I'm here. I'm uninjured, but I'm not alone."

"Ma'am? We've picked up the rest of the *Tolleson*'s manifest."

Thank God, thank God. "No, not another human. I have a cat with me. A kitten, actually, in my helmet." Akiko's voice caused Trouble to start purring again. Loudly. No way the other ship could miss that.

There was a long pause. "Repeat that, please, ma'am?"

She did. And she repeated it again when Haanrath himself came onto the line. He didn't judge. He didn't have much of a response at all, actually. He just wanted to confirm the status of both of them, as if it was commonplace for crew to float through the deep with a kitten in their helmet. He'd wait until later to tear her a new one.

Trouble continued to purr as a massive arm extended from the hauler and plucked them in a cage-like grip. He purred until they entered the airlock and gravity returned. The sudden weight dropped Akiko flat, as if her body had gone boneless. Trouble squawked in alarm.

"Sorry," she muttered.

Feet filled her vision. Strong hands gripped her arms and pulled her up. The two crew women of the *Quintus* half-carried her into a small chamber off of the main bay. She sank into a chair. While one woman assisted Akiko in unfastening the helmet, the other ran a scanner over her body.

"Cursory health exam shows no anomalies beyond facial lacerations. We'll do a more thorough examination in a few," said the one scanning. A smile quirked her face as she looked Akiko in the eye— as much as she could, around the cat. "A kitten, like that. Never would have believed it."

The other woman reached to lift up the helmet.

"I'll handle it," Akiko said, waving away the help. "I don't want him scared by strangers."

"That's probably a good idea."

Captain Haanrath's voice caused her to bolt up and salute. One of the crew caught Akiko before she crumpled.

"Sit, Chief," he ordered, granting the two other crew a nod as they passed by. The door clicked shut behind them.

"Everyone else is accounted for, sir? Are they okay?"

"Had a few banged up, but nothing serious." Captain Haanrath looked like he'd aged twenty years in a matter of hours. "All these years, I kept patching that ship up, and now she's too far gone."

"There's still the *Maryvale*."

He nodded, eyes creased in sadness. "Still going to be hard to keep afloat, business as it is. It could take years for the insurance off the *Tolleson*."

Very gently, Akiko tipped the helmet from her head, angling it up like a bowl. She lowered it to rest against her thighs. Trouble peeked over the top of the helmet, meowing in his silent way.

"So this is your stowaway," said Captain Haanrath.

"His name is Trouble, sir," said Akiko. She opened her lips, ready to say she planned to foist the kitten off on someone in the next port, that she never intended to break policy in such a way, but she couldn't manage the words. It felt damned wrong to say such a thing after Trouble saved her out there. Even so, no captain would let her keep a pet on board—especially Haanrath.

Could she give up space travel, just for a cat? She cringed. There had to be a good home for him somewhere, even if not with her.

"Trouble." His gaze was shrewd. "This cat was listed as missing on a recent freight manifest. If he had escaped on board, we thought he would've turned up by now. He's a gen mod."

Akiko stilled, thinking of her cuts, thinking of her proximity to Trouble. "What kind of mod?"

The captain extended a hand towards her. Trouble's ears perked up. Haanrath's fingers loomed about twelve centimeters away when Trouble changed. He poofed up to quadruple his size, filling the helmet. A lion-like roar belched from him as a paw swiped at the captain. Haanrath leaped backward and almost into the door.

Akiko stared.

To her astonishment, Haanrath grinned. "Your Trouble here is a newly-mature guard cat. For transit, he was blinded by drugs, but they must have worn off some days ago. He imprinted on you. He'll guard you and anything with your scent."

"Oh." As she watched, Trouble's spiny fur dwindled down to normal. He glanced over his shoulder at her, as if for approval. A goddamned guard cat. They sold for a mint. The things were engineered for brilliance and deceptive brute strength. So much for finding another home for him. Guardians imprinted for life.

Guess she didn't have to worry about anyone busting into her berth anymore. When she had a room again. Or belongings.

A sudden spark lit Haanrath's eyes. "He might be the key."

"Key, sir?" she asked.

"Our promotion problems. A cat that survived deep space in a helmet? That's a story. We'll have the *Maryvale* out in a few weeks. Word of what happened is going to spread. It already is, on this ship. It'll travel from here. We'll be the ship with the crewman and cat who survived a jettison together."

His logic dizzied her. "I . . . you're saying I can keep Trouble, sir? But Trouble—he doesn't even really belong to you or me, does he?"

"No one has to know the cat in question is that missing guard cat, Chief. No one will know unless they try to break into your quarters."

"If they survive the attempt." Akiko stared down at Trouble. He mouthed another meow, and she shook her head, grinning. "I thought you always played by the book, sir."

"Sometimes survival calls for a change of books." Haanrath's cheeks turned a pretty shade of pink as he squared his shoulders.

Akiko scritched Trouble between the ears. "Looks like we're stuck together, you and me. You're a spacer now."

The ginger kitten's eyes closed to happy slits as he purred approval.

The Death of the Horse

in the girl's eyes
the horse is like a chameleon
his hide a rainbow
that bends light and renders him invisible
to most everyone else

cars drive through him
people walk on by
yet when the horse gallivants about
the big oak tree
birds scatter affright

he kneels beside her bed each night
skin flickering red, turquoise, chartreuse
his scent of grass and dust and moonlight
he whispers of his home planet
that he is only visible to special children
for short periods of time

he teaches her the dances that the Quar'tath
use to speak emotions
drills her on species and home planets
talks her through drawing space craft and gunnery
vulnerable points on hulls
and advises her to tuck the notebook into
the deep recesses of her closet

he promises her that she'll forget these things
for a while
as her child brain fights the adult it will become
but when the time is right
when humanity requires an ambassador
she'll be ready

she's distraught when he begins to die
his form flickers like a fast ceiling fan
forces her eyes away

she fights
she cries
she swears she'll be the one
who doesn't forget
who doesn't see through him

the horse says it's not her conscious fault
it's a change in brain chemicals
that hides him from vision
deafens her to his voice
that when he's gone
it's only wise of her to question
what can't be proven

over weeks
he fades
he whispers
he is gone

the new school year starts
she hangs out with girls who shave their legs
and giggle every third word
she's the quiet friend
the one who listens
the one who remembers

when she walks home she passes the oak tree
the birds are still

in her room she starts a notebook
of star charts and trajectories
astronomical units
she mutters through her own equations
answers her own questions
pounds through Google searches
and dusty library tomes

she won't forget
she won't forget
she won't

when the girl sleeps
she dreams of flickering rainbows
warm breath against her cheek

when she awakens in the dead of night
all is silent
yet she listens

Red Dust and
Dancing Horses

No horses existed on Mars. Nara could change that.

She stared out the thick-paned window. Tinted dirt sprawled to a horizon, mesas and rock-lipped craters cutting the mottled sky. It almost looked like a scene from somewhere out of the Old West on Earth, like in the two-dimensional movies she studied on her tablet. Mama thought that 20th-century films were the ultimate brain-rotting waste of time, so Nara made sure to see at least two a week. Silver, Trigger, Buttermilk, Rex, Champion—she knew them all. She had spent months picturing just how their hooves would sink into that soft dirt, how their manes would lash in the wind. How her feet needed to rest in the stirrups, heels down, and how the hot curve of a muzzle would fit between her cupped hands.

The terraforming process had come a long way in the two hundred years since mechs established the Martian colonies. Nara didn't need a pressure suit to walk outside, but in her lifetime she'd never breathe on her own outside of her house or the Corcoran Dome. There would never be real horses here, not for hundreds of years, if ever. But a mechanical horse could find its way home in a dust storm, or handle the boggy sand without breaking a leg. She could ride it. Explore. It would be better than nothing. Her forehead bumped against the glass. But to have a real horse with hot skin and silky mane . . .

"Nara, you're moping again." Mama held a monitor to each window, following the seal along the glass. "No matter how long you stare out the window and sulk, we can't afford to fly you back to Earth just to see horses. They're hard to find as it is. Besides, you know what happened when that simulator came through last year."

Yeah. Each Martian-borne eleven-year-old child had sat in a booth strung with wires and sensors so that they could feel the patter of rain and touch the flaking dryness of eucalyptus bark. Nara smelled the dankness of fertile earth for the very first time. She threw up. The administrators listed her as a category five Martian, needing the longest quarantine time to acclimate to Earth, if she ever made the trip.

"Blast it, another inner seal is weakening," Mama muttered, moving to the next window.

The dull clang of metal echoed down the hall, followed by the soft whir of Papa's mechs. Papa would understand. He would listen.

Her feet tapped down the long tunnel to his workshop. Nara rubbed the rounded edge of the tablet tucked at her waist. Sand pattered against the walls as the wind whistled a familiar melody.

The workshop stood twice as big as the rest of the household, echoing with constantly-clicking gears. The gray dome bowed overhead, the skylight windows showing only red. Papa's legs stuck out from beneath the belly of a mining cart, his server mechs humming as they dismantled the plating on a small trolley alongside him. The workshop was half empty. The basalt mine had received a new load of equipment just two weeks before, and as Papa described it, he'd have a lull before everything decided to break again. Judging by the lack of dents on this cart, the lull was already over.

"Hey, girly. Hand me the tenner," Papa said, a hand thrusting through a gap in the chassis. Nara passed him the tool. "What're you up to?"

"Nothing." Nara slipped open the tablet, expanding the screen with a tug of her fingers. After a few taps, she accessed the data she wanted: the anatomy of the horse. Her fingers flicked up, removing the layer of skin, then the muscles, leaving the bones. One of the nearby mechs bowed, his knees fluid and graceful as he picked up a tire and conveyed it to a stack on the far side. Nara squinted, looking between the mech and the screen.

"You're never up to nothing," Papa said. "Did Mama kick you out of the house?"

"Not yet. I was wondering something, actually. Think I could use the extra space you have in here to make a project?"

Wheels whined as Papa pushed himself out. "What sort of project?" Gray and red smudges framed the skin around his goggles.

Nara held up the tablet, projecting the images out six inches. Papa chuckled low. "Why am I not surprised?" he asked. "You want to build a horse?"

"I think I can," she said.

"Oh, I know you can, I just didn't think you'd settle for that. Let me see." He held it directly overhead, then grunted as he passed it back. "The leg structure's not that different than the diggers you helped me with last month. Your main issues will be balancing the mass and nailing the AI."

She nodded, her mind already filtering through the possibilities. She had to think of horse breeds, no—she would think of specific horses. Trigger, her favorite. He was tough and fast, with all the grace of a dancer. Oh, how he could dance. His hooves shuffled, his gold skin shimmering and muscles coiling. Nara would watch him, holding her breath. Nothing on Mars could move like that.

"You'll have to use the scrap pile," Papa continued, snapping her out of a reverie. "But if you need anything fresh, you need to order through me, and you'll have to work for it. This isn't going to be cheap."

"Cheaper than a trip to Earth," Mother said from the doorway. "And speaking of expenses, we're going to need inner sealants replaced on three windows as soon as this storm is over. One gap was so big a fiend beetle could almost squeeze through from inside the walls, and God knows what it would cost if one of those got in."

"As if it's ever just one," Papa said, shaking his head. "Well, we're due for a full sealant inspection anyway."

Nara closed the equine anatomy charts, her eyes already taking in the nearest scrap pile and a stout piece of pipe ideal for a femur. Mama and Papa's chatter faded. She tapped her fingers along the tablet, already picturing a horse of her own, programmed to nuzzle her shoulder and whicker in greeting.

Papa was wrong. Balancing the mass would be easy. The artificial intelligence could be adapted from existing programs. Realism was the issue. A glossy hair coat, a trailing mane and tail, the musty smell described in the old books she'd read.

Worst of all, she might never know if she got it right.

Nara's boots thudded along the elevated boardwalk, her breaths rasping through her mask. She couldn't be late for her one day of physical attendance in school for the week. Papa had already threatened to dismantle the horse if her grades dropped again. A fiend beetle crunched underfoot in a muddle of juiciness and grit.

So far, beetles were one of the few things that could survive unaided on the Martian surface. Scientists hailed it as a landmark of the terraforming process. Nara crushed the bugs as a hobby.

Six months of work, and the skeleton was complete, and most of the nerve structure as well. She had stayed up late working on the wiring in the neck and reins and connecting them to the processors in the makeshift brain. The skin would be next on the agenda. Papa had suggested she use a thin alloy, the sort used for biometric floors. That way it could be programmed to respond to heel touches and shifts in weight.

She shoved through several sets of doors to enter the dome. A dozen beetles tried to follow, the floor vents sending them rolling like tumbleweeds in an old movie. The next two doors repeated the process and secured behind her. Nara disengaged the breathing apparatus from her mask and took in a deep inhalation of recycled air. For all the inconvenience of living beyond the dome, she preferred it to the tight confines of the city with its block-stacks of buildings and stale stink.

She slid into her cubicle just as the bell rang. Her friend Chu nodded from the adjoining side. Nara set her tablet in its cradle, and grimaced. Another day wasted in school when she could be working on her horse instead.

Throughout mathematics and mineral sciences, she let her fingers busy themselves while she pondered the wiring system for her horse. It's not as though the school work was difficult. Quiz results came back instantly; she missed two equations. Nara grunted. Perhaps she should focus more.

"As Heritage Month comes to a close, all sixth year students study the contributions of the head financier of the Corcoran Colony, the late Mrs. Florence Corcoran," said the professor from the head of the room. A hologram of Mrs. Corcoran flickered overhead, her face smiling as she posed with an old-fashioned pick-axe over her shoulder.

"As you all know, Mrs. Corcoran believed that Earth's cultural heritage deserved a place on Mars. Your tablets have just received a list of the artifacts of the Corcoran household." The file appeared on Nara's small screen. "During next year's Pioneer Heritage Month, the Corcoran Museum will open. Your task is to choose an object from her archive and write a thousand-word essay on the object's history both on Mars and Earth."

A low groan filled the room.

Nara pursed her lips. She could throw together a thousand-word essay in fifteen minutes. It wouldn't eat up too much of her project time. She opened the file, skimming the list. It dragged on, page after page. The fanciest objects were listed first—the paintings, the jewelry, the clothing. Florence Corcoran had been an obsessive collector of old Earth, especially items pertaining to Texas. All of it dull. Well, the leather belt collection might work as a report subject, especially if Nara could touch or smell the stuff. Importing genuine leather for a saddle and bridle would cost more than all the metal parts of her horse combined. She was going to make do with synthetics.

She scrolled down for an eternity. Early space shuttle detritus, bull horns, an oil derrick, a preserved horse skin. Nara stopped cold. A horse? She clicked for more information.

Trigger, a rearing palomino horse dating from the mid-20th century, his skin preserved and mounted on a plaster body. Nara's heart threatened to escape her chest. Trigger, her Trigger, was here on Mars? Not only a horse, but one of the most beautiful horses of all time.

"We have passes available so you can all visit the Corcoran household and see the items in person," her teacher continued.

"This is it," Nara murmured.

"What?" Chu whispered.

She ignored him, her mind already analyzing the possibilities. Her prototype horse would take another six months at least. If there was some way to get this skin, maybe she could use it. Mount it on top of the metal frame—well, no, it probably couldn't withstand the sand. But if she could study the texture, it would be easier to mimic. Would the museum sell such an old artifact? Nara fidgeted with the edge of her tablet. Could she steal it?

Maybe a way could be found. Adrenaline zinged through her fingertips. She could see and touch a real horse, and not just any horse—Trigger. Hot tears burned her eyes and pattered against her desk.

This was meant to be.

As Nara entered the grounds of the Corcoran Mansion, she was keenly aware of every security measure scrutinizing her. The cameras on high, glassy lenses glaring. The slight give of the cushioned tile underfoot, implying a biometric measure to contrast her weight coming and going. The slits in the walls that memorized her irises.

Stupid, stupid, stupid. Of course there would be excellent security here. She was day-dreaming to think otherwise. Still, maybe there was a loophole in the system. Trigger's skin had been a low-priority item stuck far back on the list. Centuries old, an archaic artifact that meant nothing to anyone else. It wasn't even scheduled for a berth in the museum.

"Ah. You. Chu's little friend." Her friend's grandfather edged close, his small body straight as a support pillar.

"I didn't know you were working inside the mansion now, Grandfather," Nara said, handing over her tablet with her student pass loaded.

He grunted, the sound a husky echo of Chu. "I have been since the Museum was announced, taking inventory of her treasure trove. You're the first student to take advantage of the pass, you know? No one else seems interested in seeing the works in person. Probably will be the same when the place opens, I'm afraid." He pressed the tablet back into her hands.

"Well, I care." Nara stood a bit straighter.

She had spent the past week re-watching every available movie showing Trigger. Nara knew the sway of his mane, how his hind-quarters bunched as he reared, how his muscles flexed beneath shimmering gold skin. He could kiss girls with his lips flared, rear on command, walk on his hind legs, and perform dozens of other tricks; even if Nara heightened the resolution on the picture, it was difficult to detect Roy Rogers's cues. Trigger wasn't a mere horse—he had to be the smartest horse that ever was.

Trigger's presence on Mars had to be destiny. She was meant to know him in real life, centuries after the fact, long after civilization had forgotten him. Trigger would teach her how to make her horse even more real.

"What artifact do you want to see? Most of the good stuff is here in the house." Chu's grandfather motioned behind him. Down the hall, a large painting of two naked people in a jungle filled the wall, the woman holding an apple outstretched in a pudgy hand.

She tried not to look too disgusted. "No. I want artifact 3046."

"Three-thousand range?" His eyes narrowed. "That will be in the old warehouse. All came in the second colony drop. You sure you want to go there?"

"Absolutely."

She couldn't help but notice his sour expression on their long walk out behind the mansion. The warehouse stretched along the back wall of the dome, the clay brick walls red-tinted and pecked by sandblasts. It had to be a mech-built storage house, dating from before the completion of the dome and human arrival.

Grandfather stood as the iris security scanned him in, grunting for Nara to follow. The floor beneath her feet seemed shiny and new, each step sinking in by millimeters. More security, but not as much as the household.

"Forty-six, forty-six." He muttered as he walked. Metal scaffolding stretched to the high ceiling, the rafters filled with wooden boxes. Nara stroked a box in passing, not even gasping when a splinter snagged her flesh. Mrs. Corcoran had been very wealthy indeed to have so much wood, and for it to be used for mere storage.

"Here." Grandfather stopped. A pink tarp filled the bin space ahead. A device at his waistband beeped. "Damn it all. Another guest and Rorie's not in. Can you behave yourself?"

Her heartbeat raced in hopefulness. He was leaving her here, alone? "Yes."

"It's all junk here, anyway. Just wait and I'll be back to escort you out." He marched away, his steps brisk.

Nara stood there for a moment, taking in the fading echo of his footsteps. That pink tarp . . . She bit her lip and lifted up the sheet.

Trigger's pale orange coat looked soft to the touch, his ears back. His entire body seemed coiled, ready to strike. An ornate bridle dangled from his face. Oh, his white blaze! Even tinted pink, it was beautiful to behold. Despite the glare of security, Nara couldn't resist reaching up on tiptoe to stroke his muzzle. The prickliness surprised her. It was like she had imagined, and so much more. But Trigger, beautiful, graceful Trigger . . .

A sob choked in her throat as she stepped back. Trigger had succumbed to death at last.

The pink dust on the tarp had been the first hint. The lower half of his body had been chewed away clear to the blackened plaster below. The old building hadn't sealed out fiend beetles. His saddle had slipped sideways, the girth almost eaten clear through. Only a nub remained of the flared plume of tail. Tatters of skin dangled against the plaster, fragments littering the floor like a poor haircut. Of his powerful dancing legs, nothing remained at all.

Nara lowered herself to the floor, the gray stone chilled beneath her. Trigger was dead. Dead. His skin would crumble if it moved at all. His legs would never waltz again, never leap over cars, never lower in a handsome curtsy.

"I'm sorry. I'm sorry," Nara whispered. "You were so beautiful. You still are." She stood, standing close enough to breathe him in. He stank of Martian dust and degradation, no more. The creamy mane shifted between her fingertips, a tuft coming away in her hand. She curled her fingers into a fist.

Horses didn't belong on Mars. She knew it, but she hadn't wanted to accept it. This horse had survived centuries on Earth: wars, fires, owner after owner, the long journey here, only to be eaten away by ever-hungry bugs brought along for the ride. Trigger deserved better. He deserved to be timeless.

"I still love you, Trigger," she whispered. In her mind, she could see the intelligent gleam in his eyes; hear the rhythmic clatter of his hooves.

Footsteps thudded behind her. Nara swiped an arm against her cheeks and took a steadying breath.

"Oh. You found our half-eaten creature." Chu's grandfather stepped alongside her. Nara clutched her fists tighter. "It's a shame. Some of these crates hold old masters—Rodan, Picasso. The fiend beetles had a feast. As it is now, the leather around this thing's belly is the only thing worth keeping, and that's just scrap. If someone broke in here, they'd want to steal the security system."

Chu's grandfather didn't even know the proper name for a saddle. Nara swallowed, choking as if on a handful of sand. "Is he really going to be thrown out?"

He scratched at his smooth chin. "Eventually. They plan on tearing this structure down before the museum opens. Things like that won't survive the move." He motioned to the floor and the scattered bits of hair and skin and degrading plaster.

"If that happens ... can you let me know? I mean ..."

Grandfather shook his head, chuckling. "Ah yes. Chu told me you have a thing for horses. That's what this is, right? Smaller than I expected. But yes, I can tell you when this row comes up for disposal. I hate to think what your mother would say."

Nara looked away. "I know what she'll say."

Trigger was only a thing to him. No one here knew about horses. No one cared. Trigger had been more than a horse. He'd been loved in his lifetime, adored by thousands and thousands. Maybe he could be loved again, and not just by her.

They headed out of the warehouse. Nara released her breath before she stepped across the biometric steps, expelling every bit of air in her lungs. No alarms rang. The presence of a few useless hairs hadn't even registered. She sucked in a breath of refreshing stale air, the strands of mane a moist web in her palm.

Papa had guided her work on the forge. Nara pounded and shaped her own horseshoes, and then nailed them to her horse's hooves. The first hoof prints marring Martian soil looked as they should on Earth: deep and almost circular crescents, a spray of dirt disturbed with each ambling step.

Trigger's alloy skin glowed in glossy gold, a version of palomino for a new world. A white blaze filled the length of his face and curved around into wide nostrils. He snorted, the sound tinny. It could be adjusted later. This was a test run, no more.

"You ready?" Papa asked, the words thick in his mask.

Nara nodded. Papa's broad, gloved hand gave her a boost up into the makeshift saddle woven of rags and polyvinyl chloride belts. She sat high, taking in the jagged red terrain and marbled sky from a new vantage point. The brim of her hardhat cut the afternoon glare. Angling her heels down, she tapped Trigger's ribcage and then engaged the reins. He snorted and moved forward. Gears cranked, soft and whirring, but his gait was lolling and smooth, ears attentive.

Just above his withers, a knot of long, white hairs dangled down and brushed the backs of her gloves. Nara closed her eyes for an instant, imagining an intact mane, a green horizon, the warmth of pumping blood beneath her and not an engine. Trigger couldn't come to life again, not truly, but she could grant him a different sort of immortality.

"The whole colony will learn all about horses, and you," she whispered within her mask, guiding him towards the nearest ridge. "I'll start programming your tricks in the next few weeks. Everyone will laugh and cheer when you blow kisses and dance. You'll be loved again, Trigger. Remembered." She laid a hand against his chilled neck.

The sun glowed fierce yellow overhead. Nara glanced over her shoulder and smiled at the deep cut of hoof prints leading back towards home.

WHAT HAPPENED AMONG THE STARS

the girl shoed her horse's hooves with paste and sequins
created a layer tough enough to withstand
the subzero vacuum of space
the molten surface of stars

as she rode she sang songs from school
of muffin men and ladybug picnics and eating worms
the blackness swallowed all sound
her horse still heard every word
he knew her every breath
he felt the weight difference as a bead of sweat
evaporated upon her skin

he knew that the hand tangled in his mane
missed the slick poles of the playground ladder
hated the juicy overflow of a broken taco
and that those fingers would soon wield
power that would age her beyond her years
that her eyes would forget how to cry

the horse, he knew his own grief
he galloped onward

Brothers, Mothers, Grandparents, and a Sentient House

BIDING TIME

 WE SAT TOGETHER EVERY DAY of the trial, hands entwined where our thighs met. No matter how grim the testimony, we sat it out as a silent team. We were one, strong.

After the verdict came, we watched together as Mr. Land was led away. He still radiated suave charisma, even in a vivid orange jumpsuit, his chiseled face smug beneath a silver sweep of hair. He met my eyes, briefly, in passing, and my innards curdled.

The prosecutor told us that with the trial complete and the sentence of 150 years, we could now find closure. What is closure? How do you close a door if the house has burned to ashes?

"Maybe things will be easier when he's dead," I said. "If anyone deserved to burn for all eternity, it's him."

We returned to our hollow home, trying to resume our lives. My husband went back to work as a local truck driver. He awakened in the darkness of morning, yawning with a snap of his jaw. His footsteps creaked down the hall, back and forth, as he shuffled between the bathroom and the kitchen. He returned home late, after I was in bed, and I would only be faintly aware of the solid warmth of his body dropping beside mine. His days off varied little, the only difference being that he spent the day twiddling with wood in his shop out back, and the chair opposite mine was occupied during silent meals.

It was hardest on me, and I think he would even agree with that. I was the one in the empty house all day long. I was the one restless and waiting at 3:30 most every weekday afternoon, wait-

ing for that telltale rattle of the screen door and the sound of the
refrigerator door opening. It was quickly apparent I couldn't stay
home all day, or I was going to go mad. I went back to school and
earned a certificate in culinary studies, soon afterward getting a job
in the bakery at the grocery store down the street. There was a sort
of catharsis in working with the dough, twisting elongated strips
like miniature necks and pounding a risen round into compliance.
Still, there was no lasting satisfaction from labor. Work made the
hours chug by and kept abject misery at bay. Always, there were
more doughy necks to twist and mounds to compress, never ending,
never ceasing. No completion. No closure.

We aged like that, drifting in our parallel lives. One day we
were called into the prosecutor's office again. There was a new man
in the job now, a young fellow with a buck-toothed lisp.

"I thought it best to let you know," he said. "About Mr. Land's
condition before the media carried the story."

Synchronized, we perked up. "Is he dying?" my husband asked,
his hands clasped.

The prosecutor shook his head. "No," he said, slowly. "That's the
issue. It's been twenty-five years, and he hasn't aged at all. He's in
exactly the same condition as when he was arrested."

"But," said my husband. His eyebrows scrunched as he calculated. "That would make him about a hundred."

"Yes," said the man. "It's being investigated of course, but—"

We looked at each other, my husband and I, both scrutinizing
the signatures of our age: the white hair, wild chin whiskers, and
sagging softness of our jowls. I think we both understood at that
moment that we wouldn't be getting justice in our lifetimes, that
Mr. Land was somehow cheating death in a dark way we didn't even
want to comprehend.

It was some five years after that that my husband died. It happened on a Saturday. He didn't come in for supper, so I went out to
his shop and found him there, his head lying on the wooden table
as though he was sleeping. I stroked his wispy hair in a way I hadn't

in years, then called the authorities. I carried on, just as I always had. Things didn't change much. The laundry load was lighter, the grocery bill lower. In the wee hours of the morning, I still heard his feet pace the hall, and I knew he was as present as he ever was.

There was no brilliant light when my own time came, no overwhelming bliss. The restlessness of life continued, like a burr against my nonexistent skin. We were together again, hand in hand as during the trial, drifting. Waiting for that promised closure.

I think our sentences were rendered the day that two beautiful girls, aged eight and ten, didn't make it home from school. Somewhere in a cell, Mr. Land is biding his time, knowing he'll outlive his jail sentence and be a free man. Somewhere, in the space between life and death, we wander this house, waiting for the rattle of the screen door and two girlish giggles as backpacks smack the floor.

Even if Mr. Land does eventually die, I don't know if that will really change anything. After all, we were haunting these halls long before we were ghosts.

HAT TRICK

"THE POND IS OPEN TODAY!"

No one else was in the kitchen, but I had to make the cheery announcement, even if it was just to myself. It was tradition.

Mom's St. John Ambulance books sat on the table, one still flipped open. She'd just gotten a job as receptionist at the old folks' home and they had her taking a first aid course. At the far side of the table, two mugs touched handles like old friends. Two packets of cocoa—the best kind, with the little marshmallows—lay flat behind the mugs. I grinned. The cocoa would wait until we got back from hockey.

She used to always set out four mugs. Maybe I could still pull down at least one more.

"Chuck?" My brother's door was open a smidge. The lights were off and he was sitting in front of the computer. The faint light from the monitor cast a spooky glow on his face. "The pond's open, remember? You want to come?"

In the funny light, it took me a second to realize his eyes were shut. His hands were folded on his lap, graceful like when we had to sit all proper in church. It's not like he needed to touch the keyboard.

"I'm busy, Sara." His voice creaked like an old floorboard. Since he'd "manifested," as the local Guild rep liked to say, Chuck had been able to listen and talk to computers. The Guild had even given us a brand spanking new Tandy 2000 so Chuck could hone his skills.

He used to have lots of other skills, too. A husky singing voice. Quick wit. A mean slapshot.

"But this . . . it's the first day." My shoulders slumped. This had been our tradition since I was five, wearing awful figure skates with pink laces. I mean, the first day on our pond! This used to mean everything to our whole gang – me, Chuck, Chuck's best friend Jeff, and my buddy Amaud.

"Fine," I muttered, shoving myself from the doorway and stalking to the kitchen. If I had a superpower, I'd still play hockey. Maybe I'd even be better, depending on what I could do. Our little town of Red Hawk already had crazy odds, with two manifested kids. Even Edmonton, as big as it was, only had five.

"Hockey day! Hockey day!" I chanted beneath my breath as I rummaged around in the kitchen. I refused to let Chuck ruin my morning. I charred some toast and slathered on gobs of butter to compensate. I glanced at the St. John Ambulance book as I chewed, and all the information flooded back into my head from when I was stupid enough to skim through it a few days back: bloody arms, tourniquets, rescue breathing, brain trauma. I gagged and forced myself to swallow. I should have known better than to even look between the covers, with how my memory was and all. "Eidetic memory" was the fancy term for it. My grandpa memorized the whole Bible and could spout passages on request. Mom said she'd kill to have inherited the family knack, but she didn't know how things were in school. Everyone hates know-it-alls. Hates in a mean sort of way.

A minute later, I swiped the crumbs onto the floor, grabbed my gear and bolted out the door.

The morning smelled all wet and fresh, ice crystals zinging in my nostrils. The sun glared through gauze-thin clouds, and I glared back. I didn't want a warm and sunny day that'd make all the ice melt. Snow crunched under my boots, and my tied-together skates swayed against my shoulder. My freshly-taped hockey stick felt perfect in my grip.

Up ahead, Amaud waited for me under our meeting tree. He'd accidentally crushed his glasses a few days back and his face looked bare and weird without them.

Amaud was the other gifted kid in town. He wasn't a technophile like Chuck. He was big. Like, refrigerator-sized big, and still growing. That also had its own fancy term, "myostatin-related muscle hypertrophy," but what it really meant was Amaud was becoming some super muscle man.

It was weird to think of Amaud as a man at all. I mean, he was twelve, same as me, but I was still totally average and now he towered over me.

I wouldn't be average forever.

"Where're your skates?" I called.

He shook his head, like in slow motion. "Don't fit," he said in his low mumble. His hockey stick was too short, just coming up to his chest. Even his snow shovel looked stubby next to him.

Amaud never said much. Kids always teased him for being slow, but he was really super-smart except for math; that's how we met, because our teacher made me start tutoring him back in first grade. But Amaud read Shakespeare for fun. No one else in school did that. No one would want to.

"You said your skates fit in October!" My voice squealed. Snow shivered from a branch overhead.

"My feet've gotten bigger since then." He shrugged.

"Well, you were going to be goalie, anyway. Don't think you're getting out of it." He was no Grant Fuhr, but at the very least Amaud could stand there and let stuff bounce off him.

First Chuck, now this. I stalked past Amaud and blinked back tears.

His voice softened. "I'm not trying to get out of it. I like playing hockey with you."

I grunted. The pond was just over the rise. My feet crunched through a thin layer of ice with every stomp, the crystals scratching through cloth to my calves. I suppose I could have let Amaud go first and plow through, but I wasn't lazy like that.

"Did you finish your math homework?" I asked, needing to change the subject.

"Started it."

I squinted at the annoyingly bright sky. "Started it, meaning you did one page and stopped at the word problem, right? 'Mary ate 3/8 of a pizza, while Michael ate 1/16, while little Susan ate 1/32.'" I saw the words in my head, clear as if I held the book in front of me. A neat trick but no superpower; superpowers did something. All I could do was bore people to death. Or open my big fat mouth yet again and cause half the class to pin me down on the playground and shove snow down my sweater. "I've shown you how to do common denominators a million times. It's no different when the numbers are stuck between words."

"Hate math," he muttered.

"I know." Amaud wouldn't have made it past basic addition without me harping on him every day.

I frowned and tilted an ear. I could swear I heard kids laughing and the thuds and whispers of skates on ice, but this was our street, our pond. The kids on the other side of town had their indoor rink and all—why'd they come here? I started to jog. Amaud huffed behind me, his heavy feet pounding.

Older kids in blue jerseys cluttered the ice. These guys had gotten here early. The ice was scraped clean. White gouges gleamed across the surface and cast-off boots designated the goals on either side of the pond. The sweaters were from the high school team, complete with a blazing red hawk embroidered on the front. Chuck used to wear one before his brain started computer-talk.

I recognized a tall mop-head of red hair. "Hey, Jeff!" Angry as I was, I knew not to try and run or I'd just flop down the slope.

Jeff swirled off from the rest and scraped to a stop right in front of me, his face ruddy with exertion and cold. "Hey, Sara."

He had been Chuck's best friend since preschool, like my second brother as far back as I could remember. He always drank his cocoa out of an old Christmas mug showing Santa and his sleigh. About now, I felt like shattering that mug to a million pieces.

"What's all this?" I jabbed my stick at the players. "This is our pond. Your team can practice at your own rink, or on one of the ponds on the east side."

The one time I'd tried to skate at one of their ponds—it had a changing room shack with heaters and everything—the kids demanded I pay admission and laughed the whole time, knowing I could never pay.

Jeff looked past me. "No Chuck?" Sadness flashed in his eyes, and he blinked it away. "Hey, Amaud."

"No." My word came out as a growl. "Listen, this is our—"

"Emphasis on 'our.' Look, Sara, I live here, too. I've been coming here since before you were born. The school rink is hosting some event today and I invited the guys over."

"So can we play, too?" I met his eye.

Jeff cringed. "That's . . . probably not a good idea. Look, Sara, you're a sixth grader. Some of these guys are seniors—"

One of those seniors zoomed by. "Hey, come on, we're playing a game here! Tell the little girl to go build snowmen with the other kiddies." The other players laughed.

I looked past Jeff to where three girls in puffy coats were building snowmen along the little ridge that separated our pond from big pond beyond. They couldn't have been older than five or six. Heat flushed my cheeks.

"We'll be out of here soon," said Jeff, a pleading note in his voice.

"This was our pond," I snapped.

"Well, the old gang isn't what it used to be." Something shifted in his face then, making him sound colder. Older. He skated backwards and away. Ice spat off the blades.

"Come on," I said to Amaud without looking at him. "Let's go shoot pucks on the big pond."

We trudged along the snowy shore. A few low whistles and utters of, "Damn," showed they recognized Amaud's presence—not that he could be ignored. I got angrier with every step. One of the little girls tried to say hi and I just glared until she shriveled into her fluffy hood.

No one was on the big pond. No one was supposed to be on the big pond, really. It was too big to freeze in the middle. But along the shore was okay, and better than nothing. That's almost what I had—nothing. I fumbled the puck out of my pocket and thwacked it, hard.

"You could have like, done something!" I snarled at Amaud. I knew I shouldn't take it out on him but I couldn't help it.

"Like what?"

"You could throw them off the ice! Do something! I'd do something!" I flung my skates into the snow bank. I didn't even feel like putting them on now. I just needed to hit things.

Amaud walked along the crunchy shore. I could see the puck from where I was, but he walked past it three times before he plucked it up and tossed it back my way. He really needed his new glasses.

"I dunno."

"No, you don't." I closed my eyes, taking a deep breath. Chuck, Jeff, Amaud . . . everyone was changing. I hated it. And if I had to change, let this be the time. Let it be something brilliant. I could burst out of my skin like a butterfly from a cocoon.

"I don't hurt people. You don't hurt people."

"I don't know. Maybe some people should be hurt." Tears burned in my eyes. I knew I was saying stupid stuff, but I wanted to get it out. See if it helped me feel better.

It didn't.

"I want to help, not hurt." Amaud's voice was soft as he kicked the puck back at me. Anger made me feel too hot beneath my coat, even when I was standing still. "I want to feel like I'm going through . . . this for some reason. A purpose." He motioned at his massive body.

I wanted that purpose, too. I wanted to fly. I wanted to heal people with a touch of my hand. Maybe not talk to computers like Chuck, but there were lots of other powers out there—fire from fingertips, cold creation, fast running, amazing hearing. Dozens more, probably.

"I hurt all the time."

Those words came from nowhere. I blinked at Amaud. "What?"

"I hurt all the time. I can feel my muscles stretch, even when I sleep. They say—the Guild people say—that I'm going to be so big and heavy it's going to mess with my joints. I may not be able to walk by the time I'm forty."

"Oh." I don't think I ever heard Amaud say that much at once. "But the Guild, they have healers. They can take care of you, right?"

He shook his head, slow and swaying. "I don't know."

I didn't know what to say, but I still had that awful, raw knot in my chest, that tight feeling that had been there since Chuck started listening inside his head instead of with his ears, since Amaud's body started changing to something big and foreign. They were special. Different. Isolated in a way, yeah, but . . . amazing.

I wanted to be amazing, too. Not just the weird girl who had to sit at the front of the class so no one beat her up.

I handled the puck with my stick, then I reeled back and struck it with all my strength. In my head, I could see it like an old cartoon—flames and contrails, like a rocket to the moon. In reality, it skittered over the ice and landed on the far shore.

"I'll get it," I said and set down my stick. Amaud would never be able to see the puck that far away.

All of a sudden I felt deflated. Tired. I didn't know what to think anymore, about Amaud or any of this. The echoes of the hockey players at the little pond seemed to dully ricochet in my head. A small gust of wind slapped my face as I walked along the shore. Icy stones squealed beneath a thin sheet of snow.

It took me a few minutes to find the puck. It had bounced off a tree or two and landed on a little drift. I trotted back towards the pond.

The first thing I saw was glaring pink—a little girl's coat—way out in the middle of the big pond. My heart just about stopped. Then I saw Amaud crawling out on the ice, halfway from the shore to her.

"Oh, God," I whispered. The puck fell from my hand. "Amaud! Amaud! Go slow, okay? Be careful!" What had he been thinking?! Why didn't he yell for help? I'd never heard him yell in my life, but now would have been the perfect time. He probably weighed three hundred pounds. The ice out there'd be thin as skin.

I ran down the shore, screaming. "Jeff! Jeff! Guys! Help!"

They came. I may have wished them terrible pain ten minutes before, but they ran over that crest. There was a split-second pause as they assessed everything, then most of them ran towards me. One headed the other way, to the firehouse.

That's when I saw the girls, all three of them. One without a coat.

"Amaud, stop! It's just a coat!" I screamed.

He stopped. The pink coat bobbed about twenty feet away, and had to look like a real kid in his fuzzy sight. He edged backward, slowly. The other guys clustered along the ice, waiting.

"Come on, Amaud," called Jeff.

It happened so fast, so very fast. That vicious crack that made my whole world break. His legs sank in, but not his upper body. He clutched the ice with his hands splayed out.

There was another crack. Amaud was gone. Just, gone.

I stopped breathing. Everything stopped. "Please, God, please." I took two steps forward and stopped. I never felt so helpless in my life. Powerless. Jeff and another guy flung themselves down, belly first, and slid out towards that awful black hole. It hurt to watch, it hurt to think they all could die, trying to save Amaud. Big wonderful Amaud.

An arm flailed upward. A head. His hat was gone, his skin so white, so terribly white, his hair black, then he was gone again.

Another flail. A splash. Seconds stretched out like hours. They were almost there. The pond was so shallow. Maybe – maybe he can stand up. Jump up. Something. Another hand out. A brief gleam of face.

"Hang on!" yelled Jeff. The girls wailed in an awful chorus.

The guys were at the hole. Reaching in. Fishing. I took another step forward, willing something to happen, aching for some kind of miracle.

"We got him!" screeched Jeff.

Then they had an arm, somehow. A third guy joined them. I recognized the slick black of Amaud's coat.

Another sharp crack. No one moved. They didn't drop in, but they were slow to move after, like an old man from a hospital bed. Together, they somehow pulled him out. He was big, limp, and sleek like a walrus. So, so slowly, they eased him backward. They didn't dare to stand up for another twenty feet, and then they dragged him as a team.

Amaud's eyes were closed, his head slack. They set him down on the snow and he was just there.

I ran forward. Dropped to my knees. I touched Amaud. He was cold, achingly cold, dead cold. I willed something to click in my brain. That magic, that superpower, a healing touch.

"What do we do?" asked one of the boys. They were all panting, drenched and shivering.

The images flashed in my head. Page 36 and 37 of Mom's St. John manual. One of my hands tilted Amaud's head back, chin jutting up.

Pinch his nostrils shut.

Open mouth and check for obstructions.

Breathe.

I brought down my lips over his. The chill of his lips sank into me and ached in my jawbone. I sealed my mouth over his and released two quick breaths. Releasing his nose, I looked at the rounded wetness of his chest. No movement.

Again.

Again.

As I looked at his chest again, breath warmed my ear. I gasped, recoiling. Amaud's dark eyes were wide open. A violent shiver quaked through his massive body.

"We need to get him warm, out of these clothes," I said. Page 63.

"Firehouse," said Jeff. The other guys moved in and hauled up Amaud by the coat and legs. I worked my way in between them to grab Amaud's hand. It was icy, like a fish from the freezer. He convulsed.

"Hey," I said.

His eyes found mine. "Hey-y-y." His teeth rattled.

"That was amazing, Sara," Jeff said as he huffed for breath. Water and sweat beaded from his jaw. The guys leaned forward and struggled up the ridge.

"You guys, too. You got him out." I grinned down at Amaud. "Hang in there. You're going to be okay."

I couldn't help it. I laughed. We'd saved a life. I'd saved a life. I hadn't needed to manifest a thing—no healing, no telekinesis.

I sandwiched Amaud's hand between my palms and rubbed briskly. Maybe I'd warm him some.

And maybe, just maybe, my brain would still let me do a little something more.

In any case, I wasn't about to let go.

Blue Tag Sale

Lindsay was surprised to be named the beneficiary of Grandma's soul. Most folks' souls just drifted free immediately after death. As old-fashioned as Grandma was, Lindsay had expected hers to do the same.

"Mother would do this, just to be difficult," said Lindsay's mom. She paced back and forth, a black matte bag with satin handles swaying from her arm. It looked like something from a high-end retailer, but it bore the silver monogram of the funeral parlor. "And you wouldn't believe the piece she chose to be put in. It's an old blue carnival glass vase. It might have actually been worth something."

Mom set down the bag. After some rustling, she pulled out the object in question. Lindsay couldn't help but smile. She recognized it; that vase had sat atop Grandma's piano for as long as she could remember.

The carnival glass was blue with an iridescent tinge, narrow as a column and flaring like an orchid's petals at the top, except now it had been modified. A bell of silver capped the petals. Near the base was a fixture like a miniature faucet lever, a dime-sized silver mesh just below it.

"That was Grandma's choice," said Lindsay, studying the device. She had never seen one up close before. They were the sorts of things she would spy high up on a shelf while she and Grandma were out antiquing. What was she supposed to do with this? God knew she never dusted as she should.

She repressed a shudder. The very concept of dusting off her

Grandma's soul container on a regular basis seemed wrong. She flashed back to the image of Grandma, laying there in the hospice for months and months. The way Grandma had to be shifted to avoid bedsores. The way she soiled herself. None of that was like Grandma. It screamed of wrongness.

The vase, for all its elegance, was wrong, too.

"You know what I think about your grandmother's choices."

Lindsay did. Because, as her mom liked to remind her, Lindsay took after her Grandma in all too many ways. They had identical body types, all hips and a strut of a walk. That same mousey brown hair, though Lindsay only remembered Grandma's as white. That same penchant for bargain-hunting and keeping-things-simple.

Lindsay definitely had not inherited those traits from her mom.

Mom continued to study the vase with thin-lipped disgust. "The man at the funeral home said it was her wish that no one in the family be told until weeks after her death. He said Mother wanted us to mourn as if she was already completely gone."

Or celebrate that Grandma was gone, in Mom's case. No. That was too harsh. Mom loved Grandma. They just never got along. Mom loved her Lexus and Nordstroms. Grandma was content in her Kmart sweatpants. Never the twain shall meet.

"Well, I'll be glad to have her here." The half-lie emerged with ease, simply to act contrary to Mom. She wanted Grandma here, yes. But this wasn't Grandma. Lindsay accepted the vase, hefting it. If anything, it felt lighter now that it contained a soul. It was unnerving. "How does this work exactly?"

"There's a brochure in here." Mom lifted the bag. "Souls can't last long outside of a body, even preserved in a vessel. I think they estimate about six months of communication left, on average. Fifteen minutes or so a day. The color becomes more vivid when the soul has energy stored up." She motioned to the vase. The blue was bright as if in a direct sunbeam. "You turn the knob here. They have a voice approximation installed inside, so it's supposed to sound like her when she speaks."

"Hence this little thing like a speaker at the bottom?"

"Right."

"It's pretty bright right now. Want to say hi?" Lindsay couldn't resist the dig.

Sure enough, Mom turned away as if she could conceal her repulsion. "Lindsay, my mother's dead. I accept that. I don't want to talk to some part of her spirit that's been crammed into a jar."

"Vase," Lindsay corrected.

"Whatever." Mom moved towards the door.

"Do you know when Uncle Bill and Uncle Seth are clearing out Grandma's place?"

Mom looked back at her, rolling her eyes. "No, I don't. And I already told you, you don't need any of that old crap. If you want new furniture, I can—"

"—get you new furniture," Lindsay said, finishing the line in Mom's prim tone. "I don't need anything fancy, Mom. Not your sort of fancy."

"No." Mom's expression said everything. Her hand rested on the doorknob.

"See you later, Mom."

"Yes. See you later." Mom's eyes drifted to the vase one final time, and then she fled through the door.

Lindsay plopped down on the hard wood of a thrift shop-scavenged pew, the vase clutched in both hands. This was weird. Surreal. She stroked the cool ribbed lines of the glass. Was Grandma really in there? Taking a deep breath, she twisted the lever at the bottom.

There was the slight pop of a valve releasing and a hiss of air. "Lindsay?" came that familiar quavering voice, distant as if heard through a long tunnel.

"I'm here, Grandma." Tears filled her eyes. Even faint, Grandma sounded stronger than she had in a year, before the cancer and chemo and that long, slow decline.

"I see you. I see your whole living room."

Lindsay jerked back, staring around her apartment with sudden self-consciousness. She should have remembered that aspect from hearing about this years ago. Grandma's soul was gradually seeping out whether the valve was open or not. She was becoming, basically, a ghost that drifted in the area around her vase.

Which was one of the big reasons why most people didn't store their souls anymore, not unless it was out of spite. Grandma wasn't like that. But Lindsay would have never expected Grandma to have her soul contained like this, either.

"Guess it's a good thing I don't have a boyfriend," Lindsay said, trying to keep her voice light.

"You should have a boyfriend, pretty as you are." There was a long pause. "So I'm dead."

"Yes. Three weeks now." Tears flooded her eyes again. "I've missed you so much."

"Oh, Lindy-Lou. These last weeks . . . or was it months? They were so hard. It was like I was barely awake, wasn't it?"

She nodded, one foot tapping against the leg of the pew. "Yeah."

"So, those kids of mine dump my house yet?"

"No. Mom hasn't said much about it, but I know they plan to."

"I sure miss that old place." Yearning creaked in her voice. "I have a lot of good memories there, me and Papa. I wasn't there at the end, was I?"

"No. You were at the hospice for four months."

"Four months. That long." Lindsay could picture the disbelief on Grandma's face. "Do you think . . . do you think I could go home? See the old place?"

Lindsay looked at the clock. She had homework to do, but this was Grandma asking her for a favor. Grandma, dead and stuck in a piece of glass. "Sure. I can drive you over. I guess . . . I guess I turn this thing off?"

She didn't want this power. She had already said her farewells. Had said good-bye to Grandma every week at the hospice, wondering each time if it would be the last. Now it was like Grandma was a prisoner all over again, and Lindsay was the one in control. Control she didn't want. Waves of longing and frustration rocked her. Why did Grandma put this on her? Why make her go through this again?

"You just turn the valve there. It's supposed to be easy."

"Yeah." Her fingers clutched the knob, boneless and lacking the strength to do the deed.

"Lindy-Lou. I'll still be here, even if I can't speak." Grandma's husky voice softened. "It's okay."

She nodded and took in a deep breath as she twisted the lever shut. Having Grandma like this was better than nothing, but it still wasn't Grandma.

Lindsay stroked the hard lines of the vase and shivered at the coldness of the glass.

Lindsay didn't want to open the valve again once she reached Grandma's house, but she knew Grandma was already drifting close by and could see what she saw. Lindsay set the vase on its customary spot on the piano and twisted the lever.

Grandma didn't speak for a few moments. "I see they've already been busy."

"Yeah." Anger burned in Lindsay's chest. Mom had lied to her. Boxes stacked in crude brown towers, black marker labeling the fates of Grandma's precious belongings: eBay or thrift store. Lindsay knew she shouldn't have taken Mom's word; she should have driven across town, checked on the place for herself.

But that meant visiting Grandma's house with Grandma gone. Even now, it wasn't the same. It didn't smell right.

"I always was something of a pack rat," Grandma said, her tone dismissive. "This is one of the things they warned me about when I did the paperwork for this. That I'd have to face the consequences of my death and let go."

"Then why did you do it?"

"I wasn't ready to die." Grandma's heavy sigh rasped over the vase's speaker.

Lindsay closed her eyes. She hadn't been ready for Grandma to die, either, but she had told herself that her passing was for the best. Stopping the pain and all that.

"Why did you . . ." She couldn't finish the sentence.

"I wasn't ready to die yet," Grandma repeated gently. "I figured if I stuck around for a while, I might be useful. Maybe someone will decide they want my Spam rice recipe after all."

That coaxed a smile onto Lindsay's lips, but her emotions were a muddled knot in her stomach. She still couldn't phrase the question that kept racing through her mind: why did Grandma choose to be with her? Grandma had to know how painful this all was, and how hard it would be to say good-bye as her soul faded away in all finality.

"Now, Lindy-Lou," Grandma said. "I know you're busy with school things, and the drive over was long as it is. Leave me here tonight. I would like one more night in the old place, in the bed that Papa and I shared. I never had that, at the end."

"Okay." Lindsay picked up the vase again and headed down the hall. Grandma's room was in the same stripped condition as the rest of the house. Bare mattresses sat askew on the bed frame. She nudged them straight with her knees and set the vase at the head of the bed.

"Thanks. Go ahead and close the valve. I just want to wander a while."

"Okay," she said, and turned the lever. Here she was with a chance to talk to Grandma again, and she didn't even know what to say beyond one-word responses. Lindsay stopped in the doorway. "I have classes all morning and work in the afternoon. I'll be back to get you about suppertime, okay?"

She paused, waiting for a reply, pulling out the key for Grandma's front door again. Oh, how stupid. With the valve shut, Grandma couldn't speak. Lindsay clenched her fist, the key cutting into her palm.

*

She tried not to think of Grandma all day long, which meant that thoughts plagued her every five minutes. Grandma, her emaciated body like that of a third-world child, stretched out beneath those stark white hospice sheets. The way Grandma always made sausage gravy and fresh biscuits for Grandpapa every Saturday and Sunday morning. Grandma's voice, so thin and tenuous, emitting from a vase of carnival glass.

Lindsay almost didn't want to fetch the vase again. People always talked of souls as eternal, but it didn't seem like Grandma without her body and smile and the lingering scent of White Shoulders perfume.

She unlocked Grandma's door, rehearsing the pleasantries about her day that she could say aloud for the vase. Her footsteps echoed in the darkness and she stopped cold.

The house was empty.

Frantic, she dove for the light switch. It didn't work. She jerked the cord for the blinds. They lurched open crookedly, granting scattered beams of light into the room. The furniture and boxes were gone. She staggered down the hall, knowing the bedroom would be the same. Empty. Her cold fingers fumbled to pull out her phone.

"Hello?" Mom answered on the first ring.

"Where is Grandma's stuff?" Where is Grandma? That's what she wanted to scream, but couldn't. She was the one who had left Grandma there. For one day, that's all. She never thought this would be the day the house would be cleared out.

"Oh. Why are you there? I was going to tell you . . ."

"I came because Grandma asked me to. Was Uncle Bill or Uncle Seth here today?"

"Neither of them, I think. Bill was going to hire a crew to clear out everything, some college kids—"

Icy cold trickled through her veins and almost sent her to the floor. Other people her age wouldn't recognize a soul-snaring vase. Oh, God. Grandma's soul could be in the trash. Or on eBay.

"Where?" she choked out. "Where did they take everything?"

"Lindsay, there is nothing in that house you need. It's junk. You don't need more junk."

Her eyes opened wide. "Mom. I'm twenty-two years old. If I want more junk, that's my decision. What company did he use?"

"I can ask—"

"No. I'll do it." For the first time in her life, Lindsay hung up on her mother. Fingers quivering, she looked through her contact list for Uncle Bill.

The Tricounty Renewed Hope Thrift Store on Seventh and Anders was not a place that Lindsay had visited often, but she was familiar enough to know they had a donation drop off in the back alley. According to the men her uncle hired, most of Grandma's things had been left there. And one of the men remembered putting the strange vase that had been sitting on the bed in a donation box.

She walked around to the alley, her pace brisk. Mountains of boxes and plastic bags flanked either side of the back entrance. She eyed the boxes. They didn't look like the ones from Grandma's. The only comfort she took was that there was no way that Grandma's vase had been sold so quickly.

But the vase might still be broken, releasing her soul all the faster. Or Lindsay might not be able to find it at all. Anxiety thrummed in her heart. No. She had to find Grandma.

"Hello?" She stood in the doorway to the back room. Shelves and racks of clothes overflowed. A pervasive musty odor tickled her nose. "Hello? I need help finding something that was donated by accident."

No reply. She didn't even hear footsteps. Well, this couldn't wait. She walked inside, looking every which way for those particular plain brown boxes or familiar furniture.

"Grandma? If you can hear me, maybe you can do a ghost thing and knock some boxes over or something?" Lindsay didn't know if that was possible with a vase-bound soul, but it was worth a shot. She spied a familiar couch arm and heaved up a large black garbage bag. Yes, that was Grandma's ancient couch. She sucked in a breath. Getting closer.

She shoved some other garbage bags aside. There were the brown boxes, but her heart sank. There had to be two dozen of them, some of them big enough to hide a crouching adult. Which one held Grandma?

The top box drifted into the air, just by a few inches, and then set itself down again. Lindsay grinned. Grandma was listening.

The sealing tape roared as she tore it back. Delving past a thin layer of newspapers, she spied the shimmer of blue glass. She fumbled the vase out, rotating it in her hands. It looked fine, the blue as bright as it had been the day before. She turned on the valve, air escaping with a sharp hiss.

"Grandma, I'm so sorry!" Lindsay blurted out. Tears flooded her eyes. "I didn't know they were emptying your place today and—"

"Lindy-Lou. Shush. All's well."

Grandma's soothing voice cut through her panic and straight to her heart. She clutched the vase against her chest, sobs wracking her body. "I thought I lost you again," she whispered.

"I'll fade away eventually. You know that."

"I already saw you fade once. I don't . . . I don't think I can deal with that again, but I don't want you to go, either."

"I was sick before, barely awake at all. Now you can chat with me every day. Fifteen minutes, maybe more, maybe less, but it's me, Lindy-Lou. Just as if we were on the phone. Now dry off those tears. I need to show you something."

Lindsay mopped off her cheeks with her sleeve. "Show me something?"

"Yes. Walk around these boxes, and look at that clothing rack. Go about seven shirts in . . . yes, right there."

With one hand hugging the vase close, Lindsay looked through the rack of already-priced clothes. Her fingers rested on a frilly yellow sun dress. The crispness of the cloth showed it to be barely worn.

"Look at the maker." Grandma's voice was faint, the speaker pressed against Lindsay's breast.

Lindsay looked at the tag. "This is made by 9 Cats in the Sun. That's a designer label. This thing probably cost over $500. I had one of their skirts years ago—"

"Yes, that blue nautical one. I remember."

Lindsay burst out laughing. "I was panicking, and you were shopping?"

"Well, I couldn't wander far. I had to occupy the time somehow. Grab it, girl. Blue tags are half-off today. That rack isn't supposed to go out until tomorrow."

"That's pretty devious, Grandma. Don't make me worry about your soul."

"I'm not devious. I'm cheap. Besides, you can tell your mother you saved up to buy that thing. She'll never know that meant $2.50 instead of $500."

Tears brimmed in her eyes again, but this time they were of joy. "I missed shopping with you so much, Grandma." She pulled the dress from the rack and let it drape from her arm.

"You're forgetting something," Grandma said.

"What?"

"This vase is merchandise, too. Grab that sticker off the table there and put it on this thing."

Lindsay balked. "Grandma, no, I'm not putting a price sticker of $1.99 on you. That's just wrong. No."

"Lindsay." The voice was raspy and gentle. "You're not putting the sticker on me. Just the vase. When my soul is all drifted away, that's what you'll have left. It's not me any more than my body was."

Lindsay's fingers hovered over the sticker. "I know," she whispered. "But it's hard . . ."

"Tell me about it. I'm the one who's stuck in a vase." Grandma chuckled.

Lindsay closed her eyes briefly, nodding to herself. "I love you so much, Grandma."

"I love you, too, Lindy-Lou." Grandma said it sing-song, just as she had when Lindsay was little.

The blue sticker just fit on the bottom of the vase. "It's a blue tag, too," she said. "That's means you'll be half off."

"You know me. I'm all about bargain shopping."

Lindsay had never realized how much she missed these moments with Grandma. Breathing in the mustiness of old cardboard and the sharp chemical taint of mothballs, Grandma with her—everything felt right. And even though she couldn't see the look on Grandma's face, Lindsay knew she felt the same way.

This was why Grandma had chosen her, why she had stayed in that vase. Even if they just shared a few minutes a day over these next months, that time would have more value, more weight, than all the time they had had during Grandma's awful last year.

"Want to take a look around the store with me?" Lindsay asked. "Maybe you can find something else."

"Oh goodness, yes! I haven't been able to do this for forever! Let's go for a quick walk around. I don't have much voice left today. Be sure to go straight to the kitchenware! Maybe they have some Revere silver today . . ."

Lindsay couldn't help but grin as she slipped out into the brightness of the main store, Grandma's presence a comforting weight on her arm.

NISEI

grandpa used to say
he joined the army to be like
all the other boys

he signed up from Manzanar
"I was as American as them"

he served in Japan after the bombs dropped
he brought the kappa back to California
said he found its pond nearly dried up
the house nearby a shattered ruin

he made the kappa a new garden
gravel rocks raked in sinuous swirls
cherry maple leaves like blood
upon the velvet carpet of moss
pond warmed by the Valencia sun

I would visit and bring cucumbers
to plunk on lily pad-capped water
the kappa grabbed the vegetables
with his long, webbed fingers
his skin green and slick like a frog
a fringed pate crowned his head and held
the water that kept him alive

they played jokes on each other
grandpa and the water imp
a string of tripwire across the path
grandpa's favorite chair, water-soaked
a gentle friendship of fifty years

but the kappa never touched the American flag
there in the center of the garden

sometimes the two of them sat there in evenings
tea cup nestled on the swell of grandpa's belly
kappa crouched at water's edge
red, white, and blue rippling in pink twilight
saying nothing, everything

TOILET GNOMES AT WAR

WITHIN AN HOUR OF ARRIVING at Grandma's house, it was clear to me that her toilet gnomes were really, seriously pissed off.

They were super-quiet when I first arrived. That's the norm for them. As the saying goes, "A happy gnome is a quiet gnome." But they must have heard that someone was in the house, because soon enough it sounded like a Black Sabbath jam session inside the walls. The reverberations were so bad that the empty mug on the bathroom sink almost vibrated itself onto the floor. I had to drop my purse and make a quick dive to catch the cup in time. It was one of Grandma's old favorite coffee mugs, too, the interior perfectly stained brown.

Coffee. Oh God, coffee sounded really good about now.

"What is wrong with you?" I yelled at the wall. The sound didn't let up.

The din was weird. Grandma took awesome care of her gnomes. Better than most people, but Grandma was the hyper-attentive goody-two-shoes-from-hell type. Like, ask her to pick up a can of chicken soup for you when you're sick, and she shows up with a hot stock pot full, freezer bags for the leftovers, and probably a set of new soup bowls and spoons, too.

But now Grandma was the one who was sick. Well, I wished she was only sick. She was run down in a crosswalk. She'd been in a coma for the past week.

And now it sounded like her gnomes were going to shred her house from the pipes on out. Grandma's cozy, perfect house, crammed with two long lifetimes of love, where she and Grandpa'd raised three kids, where I spent most every Christmas growing up. I could navigate the place blindfolded in six-inch heels. And now, I swear to God, her gnomes chanted like a Māori Haka.

Maybe they were hungry for some reason, which was weird. Grandma had to have the fattest gnomes in the county. Nothing in that house would be allowed to starve. It wasn't anywhere near a solstice or equinox, so their seasonal offering hadn't been skipped. I headed to the kitchen to check things out.

As usual, Grandma had stockpiled for Armageddon, or enough to get her through till the next big sale at Costco. There was a whole shelf of chicken and beef broth. I checked the topmost cupboard on a whim and was surprised to see it was empty. No coffee. Sure enough, the magnetic notepad on the fridge listed milk, coffee, and denture cream.

The china in the cabinets dinged as the vibrations increased. The gnomes were stalking me from within the walls. The obnoxious racket pulsed through my frontal lobe like a jackhammer and re-minded me I'd just driven twelve hours, straight through.

Coffee. The one thing I desperately needed and craved had to be the big thing Grandma was out of. And here I was with only a few bucks to my name and a credit card payment that was starting to mimic the national debt, minus some zeroes.

See, my mom thought I had taken time off from work to come and check on Grandma and her place. She didn't know—well, no one in my family knew—that I'd been laid off six months before. That my boyfriend ran off with some skank freshman. That my shiny new bachelor's degree would be more useful as mulch than as a job-getter. That I'd lost my apartment a few weeks back and had spent the intervening time playing couch roulette at friends' houses.

If Mom or Grandma knew the truth, I'd get that I-told-you-so lecture about staying in the big city, and then they'd want to help. Grandma-style help. I was twenty-three. I didn't want that kind of help, damn it. I wanted to prove I could make it on my own. If that meant some starvation and permanent neck strain from flat couch pillows, so be it.

But coffee would have been a nice perk.

The wailing within the walls worsened, like someone packed a hive of banshees inside and told them to sing Michael Bolton.

I glanced at the clock, the pendulum swaying drunkenly. I had a little time to spare before visiting hours were up at the hospital, and honest to God, I didn't want to go. I didn't want to see Grandma hooked up to machines to keep her alive. Procrastination time.

I had my belongings pared down to one large suitcase, and everything in there had a permanent musty smell because of long stretches between clothes washings. I was so pathetically poor, I couldn't even afford laundromats. Grandma had plenty of detergent though, so I started up a load.

Then I went to my backpack, and pulled out my laptop.

The neighbor's Wi-Fi was still as pleasantly vulnerable as it'd been last Christmas, so I took full advantage. Wikipedia didn't offer anything new on the subject of toilet gnomes.

I poked around in toilet gnome troubleshooting forums and was still stumped. Anything that wasn't common sense led to references to toilet gnome interventionists, who seemed to cost hundreds of bucks an hour. The very thought of that expense made my head throb more. It didn't help that the drumming in the walls kept getting more frenzied, compounding the pre-existing headache from the drive. Procrastination just wasn't cutting it anymore. I had to get out of there.

Since I had rolled into town on fuel vapors, walking was my only option. Being that it was summer, most people were smart enough to sequester themselves in air conditioning. Therefore, I earned some funny looks when I got to the hospital with my clothes soaked in sweat. I didn't much care at that point. I needed to see Grandma.

The place had that funny antiseptic smell that reminded me of taking my old cat to the vet. Grandma looked . . . weird. Pale. Like she was sleeping, but not. She always prided herself on her appearance. You know, standing appointments for a perm and manicure every Saturday at one o'clock, with the same beauticians she had been visiting longer than my lifetime. Now her hair was a flattened mess. Her hands still wore scrapes from the accident, like red scaled gloves, with several nails missing.

Mom had tried to warn me over the phone, after she had flown out to see Grandma, but nothing, nothing could have prepared me for that.

The legs of the metal chair squealed as I dragged it next to the bed. Grandma's hand was cold, like a piece of chicken in the fridge.

"Hey, Grandma," I said, my voice cracking. "It's P.J. I drove out here to see you. Mom wishes she could be here." That was tearing Mom apart, I knew it was, but my stepdad was in the middle of chemo, and there was no one else to take care of him either.

I sat there and I talked. I told her everything I hadn't told her or Mom. About being fired. About waiting in line for three hours for a two-minute job interview. About Carl leaving me—she didn't like him when we came over for Christmas anyway. "He doesn't listen when you talk," she kept insisting. Told her no, of course he listens, he's a good guy.

A nurse finally came in to boot me out. "I've got to go, Grandma," I said and kissed her cool cheek. "I'll be back tomorrow. Maybe I'll have a happier story for you then." She always loved happy, silly stories—Pollyanna tales, she called them. All rainbows and kittens and happily-ever-afters.

The total opposite of my life. Maybe I could bring some fiction to read to her.

I walked out the door feeling ragged and limp. Grandma hadn't squeezed my hand. Her eyelashes hadn't even fluttered. There was no sign that she was there at all.

There was one thing I hadn't mentioned to her—the gnomes.

Everything I confessed was about me, my screw-ups. Her house, that was sacred ground. That was the place she and Grandpa scrimped and saved for twenty years to buy. If there had been a way to ask her about what might have set off the gnomes, that would've been different. But as it was now, telling her, "Hey Grandma, your toilet gnomes are on the warpath and sound like they're tearing your house apart," no, I couldn't say that to her. Not when she might be in there, helpless and listening.

I was halfway home when I saw smoke.

It was a slow, sinuous line of gray. I stared at it a moment before I registered that it was in the right direction, the right distance away.

"Oh, God," I said. Then I ran.

The fact it was a hundred degrees didn't matter. I had to get there. I had to save the house. Toilet gnomes had done that sort of thing before, in cases of terrible abuse. Their tribes were bound to a house at the time of construction. If the home was in bad enough shape, the only way for them to break that bond was immolation, the purification of fire.

Why? Why would they be that angry? Grandma hadn't been home for a week! If she had started blaring elevator music and sub-sisting on Limburger cheese, sure I could see them getting pissed, but this didn't make sense.

I was there to take care of the house. I failed in everything else. I couldn't fail Grandma, too.

Oh, God. When Grandma woke up, she'd kill me. I'd deserve it. I'd stand there and take it, just like when she whupped me for taking the Lord's name in vain when I was six.

Smoke rose from the back of the house. I staggered up the front walkway just as a man burst through the side gate. We both stopped in our tracks, staring. It took me a second to recognize him as Grandma's next-door neighbor, his hair having thinned consid-erably in recent years.

"You, you're—" he started.

"What happened?" I said between gasps.

"A fire in the backyard. I couldn't believe it. It was the gnomes, the damned gnomes." He shook his head, dazed. "But they ain't too bright, since they were trying to set fire to wet clothes—"

That's all I needed to hear. "Oh, no," I whimpered, dragging myself to the backyard. My sweat-soaked clothing clung to me, like I was competing to win some foul-smelling wet T-shirt contest.

The toilet gnomes had tried to dry my clothes. With fire. They hadn't burned much—the smoke had come from a row of wooden planters lighting up—but I doubted the smell of the smoke would wash out. Clothes. Hey, who needs clothes? I almost laughed, and instead managed to swallow down the need to hysterically sob.

"I put the fire out right away. I could call the fire department—"

I didn't hear any sirens yet, and I didn't want to. "No, no, this is fine. Thanks for putting it out."

His thick brows lowered as he scrutinized me. "So what the hell is up with your gnomes?"

My gnomes. Not Grandma's. I couldn't help but flinch as I mumbled some sort of reply and backed away.

The house was quiet as I entered. Too quiet. I breathed in the cool air and faint scent of dusty potpourri, tears stinging my eyes. The house never changed, no matter how old I was. That was one of the most comforting things about it. The living room had wood paneling leftover from the 1970s. The garish green carpet still had a dark splotch from when I spilled grape Kool-Aid when I was five. I loved the place. Grandma loved the place.

Very, very faintly, I heard the sound of running water. A strangled whimper escaped from my throat.

I could see the overflowing toilet from ten feet away. I also saw a small, pudgy blur make a dash for the hallway.

"Hey!" I yelled. "Stop!"

Yeah, like it did any good. The toilet gnome moved as fast as a cat to a can opener, right to their little access niche in the hallway. It threw open the door and was swallowed up by the darkness of the interior walls. I was left staring after the little bastard, panting (again), sweating (again), with my head pulsing to some insane mariachi beat.

Why were they doing all this? I didn't have the money for some gnomish linguist to come and whisper at the walls. I could ask Mom for help but . . . well, if I had to swallow my pride, I would. For Grandma, not for me.

I stood in the overflow of the toilet and plungered the thing. The water drained away, for the moment. A gnome could magic it clogged again the second I turned my back though. Kicking off my shoes, I went to the garage to get the mop.

It looked like someone had shaved a sheep dog. Those gnomes had hacked off every strand of fiber from that mop, leaving them all in a tidy pile right on the mat.

It was war. Those suckers knew what they were doing.

I used up Grandma's whole stockpile of old white T-shirts cut into rags, and a paper towel roll besides. Every time I leaned over, that pain in my head pulsed again, like a shifting metal weight inside my skull. At least the noise in the walls had stopped.

Moving stiffly, I went to the medicine cabinet and swallowed some generic pain pills. My knees didn't want to work well after kneeling on the tile for so long, but I hobbled through the house to the kitchen, where I found out why the gnomes had been so quiet.

Every cupboard was open, gaping, empty. The contents covered every inch of cabinet space and much of the floor as well. I stared, jaw gaping. As well as I knew that house, there was no way I could put everything back where it belonged. No way. Not a full seventy year's collection of china and plastic and carnival glass.

So, I did the only think I could do at that moment. I sat down and cried.

Grandma was in the hospital. She might die. She might be as good as dead already. Her house was being poked and prodded by insane gnomes who just might blow the place up if I didn't figure out why they were pulling their crap. And there I was, the class valedictorian who was flopping at Real Life in every possible way with a headache from hell, and if Grandma lost her house, it would be all my fault.

Yeah, I had my own pity party right there on the floor.

When I couldn't cry anymore, I wiped my face with my stiff shirt, washed my hands, then started reassembling the kitchen. And tried not to think of what the gnomes might be doing in the other rooms.

Three hours later, I could walk through the kitchen again. I still had one stretch of counter covered with old, dusty stuff that looked like it'd emerged from a time capsule. Seriously, 32-ounce cups from McDonald's commemorating the 1988 Olympics?

Then there was the upside: money.

Until I started opening those old lids, I had forgotten about Grandpa's habit of stashing extra cash like that. It used to be something of a game when Grandpa would come visit us, as he'd hide a few bucks around the house and I might not find them till months later. I guess Grandma was just as bad at that game. I had a pile of $64, none of the bills dated after Grandpa's death in 1997.

Really, it wasn't my money. It wasn't like Grandpa had hidden it in my house. And it wasn't enough to hire a gnome whisperer or interventionist or whatever. But that pain medicine hadn't put the slightest dent in my headache, and there was only one thing on my mind worth spending it on.

Coffee.

I wasn't going to go crazy and spend all the money. Heck, I knew I might be living on that for a week. But coffee would cleanse my nose of that lingering wet bathroom stink and might provide the mental jolt I needed to stop the gnomes. Besides, Grandma's the one who got me hooked on coffee back when I was ten. I could raise a cup to her in tribute—maybe even use her favorite mug, the one I'd salvaged from the bathroom.

Honest to God, I was afraid to run the shower or take off one of my few remaining sets of clothes, so I dragged my stinky self to the grocery store a few blocks away. The smell of the in-store coffee stand lured me first thing. I took tiny sips from my cup, making it last, making it linger. The hot manna seemed to whirl in my brain, all cozy and hallucinogenic. Maybe it was the placebo effect, but my head felt better after that first sip.

I could imagine Grandma shaking her head and smiling at that. "It's called addiction, honey," she'd say, that gentle smile curving her cheeks. "You're just like me."

Dear God, I wanted to see that smile again. I wanted to be just like her. If I could make that claim, I'd have a good life.

At least I would have a nice story to tell her at the hospital. She'd love to know that Grandpa had left her surprise money like that.

With caffeine thrumming through my veins, I floated through the aisles and check-out. My only purchases were coffee—Grandma's brand, nothing fancy—and a half gallon of milk.

I still had half a cup left when I walked in the door at Grandma's house. Just as I reset the deadbolt, the walls screamed. Pictures rattled, and the floor heaved beneath my feet. I dropped my bag and purse, but held onto the cup for dear life.

That was it. The gnomes were intent on taking down the house.

I felt their footsteps, mobs of them coming down the hall, winding through the living room. Then I saw them, marching in their perfect rows, three abreast and some dozen strong. Their peaked brown hats bobbed with each step but otherwise they were naked. Not a stitch of clothing covered their skin, not even boots. Itty bitty man parts swayed in unison. Blue war paint marred their faces and chests—it looked a lot like toothpaste, actually. The leaders held Grandma's Oneida forks like tridents, and I didn't doubt that they were willing to use them.

Some five feet away from me, they stopped. The middle gnome held aloft his fork. "Off of fee!" he shouted. The others repeated the phrase in a chorus.

I stared at them, my back against the door, wondering what my mom would print in my obituary if I was forked to death by a dozen naked toilet gnomes.

"Off of fee!" He pointed the fork at me. His teeth shone as he grimaced behind his filthy beard.

Enough already. They were pissed off about something? Fine. I was pissed off, too, and I wasn't going to go down without a struggle. I wasn't going to give up Grandma's house without a fight. "What do you want?" I yelled at them, feet braced, cup contents warm in my hand.

The toilet gnomes howled. One of them from the back said something that sounded faintly Germanic, and the back row broke off from the rest, heading towards my grocery bag on the floor.

"What the . . ." I advanced, intending to kick them. They brandished their forks, but that's not what stopped me—it was curiosity. *What did they want?* They tore through the bag. The red canister of coffee emerged, and they cried out like Inuits snaring a whale.

"Off of fee! Off of fee!" The gnomes worked as a team to twist off the lid. One of the fork-wielders joined them and stabbed the plastic sealing open. The canister tilted, spilling some grounds onto the floor. They fell into it, weeping. Warfare forgotten, they all threw themselves into the dumped grounds, rolling, snorting, sobbing. Some of their gestures seemed weirdly like prayers.

Off of fee. Coffee. They had picked up some English, after all.

"Oh my God," I whispered, then cast a sideways glance at Grandma's portrait on the wall. "Sorry."

Grandma had taken such good care of her gnomes that she'd created a mob of caffeine addicts, then was gone for a week. No wonder they were on the warpath.

"I can make you coffee," I said loud enough to be heard. I bent to take the canister, eyeing the discarded forks all the while. The naked, teary gnomes looked up at me and smiled through their brown-smeared beards.

I bet Grandma felt just as desperate as her gnomes, locked away in her body like that, wanting to be understood. Wanting her coffee, too. Whenever she woke up—and she would wake up—I'd be right there to lift that coffee cup to her lips.

I smiled back at the toilet gnomes. Tomorrow I would have a

happy story for Grandma, and a promise for her, too. I'd take good care of her house and her gnomes, in her own grand tradition. They were my gnomes now, too, and I was going to spoil them rotten.

I could do this.

Minor Hockey Gods
of Barstow Station

I skated down the corridor to holding bay thirteen, my gear bag's strap heavy on my shoulder and sticks in my gloved hand. For the next three hours, I was a goddess, and for the last time.

The alien Pashi ran Barstow Station. During this time span every six day cycle, they locked themselves away for some kind of holy purification ritual. To them, all species became incarnations for this three hour block, though I wasn't sure what the Pashi actually did during their time as self-proclaimed gods. When humanoids with specialized tentacle limbs need quiet time, you don't ask questions. As for us six humans remaining on board, we devoted our time as so-called deities to one thing: hockey.

I glanced at the commlink on my wrist, willing it to ding. Willing for us to have a last chance to play against the Daru Baru. The screen was black, the speaker mute. I didn't even know if they had gotten my message about our plight months ago. Ansibles were stupidly unreliable, though they were even worse out toward Earth.

I skated around a curve in the hall. The entire station was like a big ice rink. The Pashi's mass of lower tentacles included blades; they glided everywhere on their icy home world. The sound of a smacked puck and the clatter of a stick echoed ahead. Familiar, cozy sounds. I closed my eyes to slits to meditate amidst the ruckus when I heard a burst of profanity.

Also familiar, not so cozy.

My twin brother was already there. Most athletes stretch before workouts; Sal Salazar warmed up with obscenities instead. I clenched the sticks tighter and paused in the archway.

Sal was out in the docking bay we took over during this time of minimal operations. His body was wrapped in the full-body navy blue suits we had to wear against the Pashi-regulated cold. Sal looked three times his normal thickness thanks to the pads layered beneath his suit. Thermo gear alone did nothing to shield us from pucks or body checks.

Sal slammed a puck into the makeshift net on the far side. Trish was out there, too, doing warm-up stretches on the sideline.

"Gloria."

"Hey there!" I turned and almost smacked Kazuo with my sticks. "Sorry."

"So. Last game." His voice sounded husky, even through the helmet. Nicolai and Maurice skated by us with a wave. "Just us humans. As usual."

"Yeah." Frustration tightened my throat as I glanced at the commlink again. There'd been twenty-five of us originally, our full team plus two refs. We'd gone into cryo for the long haul to Daru Baru, certain we were going to wake up to glory and fame. Thirty intelligent races were invited to compete in the Games, showcasing hundreds of sports. The Daru Baru were downright fanatical about athletics.

I'd hoped, maybe, they'd love hockey enough to come to Barstow Station since we couldn't afford the full trip to the Games. Oh well. The Games were over and done. Our time on Barstow was, too.

Sal missed a shot and let loose curses so acidic they probably melted the ice in spots.

Kazuo snorted. "Sounds like your bro sat on a stick again."

"It's a permanent fixture." I skated out onto the bay, frustration and melancholy fueling my strides. Kazuo's skates swished behind me. Sal bum-rushed me, but I pivoted and took a glancing blow off the shoulder instead.

"Hi to you, too!" I called.

Anyone who met Sal first expected me to be just as crazy, someone who'd accept a dare to do an atmospheric jump off the Central Am Space Elevator (security busted him in an off-limits zone) or drink a shot of Nu liqueur (he'd always been curious about how it felt to get his stomach pumped). He was the one who always wanted to bum around in space. Me? I was the reasonable Salazar twin, the girl who told other kids to stay out of contaminated zones, the one who finished college, the one who wanted to study alien races, not challenge them to drinking games. He had begged me to join the Humanity United Roller Hockey team to play against the Daru Baru.

"Hello to Salazar numero dos," called Trish.

I waved with my sticks and started my usual warm-up routine. Big loops around the ice, leg stretches, froggy bends. All the stuff our mom taught us ages ago when she first strapped us into rollerblades. We never had ice but we heard all the stories about when ice hockey had been a worldwide sport, when electricity had been so abundant that buildings kept permanent ice rinks all year long, even in Los Angeles.

Crazy talk.

We sure never expected to play ice hockey for months while stuck on a frigid alien space station.

A chime rang over the intercom, denoting some new stage in the Pashi's Holy Hours. I teamed with Kazuo and Trish. Sal, Nicolai, and Maurice had white stripes painted around the arms and legs of their thermo suits to set them apart.

I skated to center to face off against Sal. Through the visor, eyes identical to mine stared back at me.

People sometimes asked me if twins can really communicate without speaking. For us, no. Not until we suited up for hockey. Our brains synced in that need for the puck.

"Let's play some goddamned hockey," Maurice said, tapping his stick's blade on the ice.

"It's damned if you say so," called Kazuo. A few of the others laughed.

I cast a final glance at the commlink as I fumbled the puck from my pocket. Last time to play on Barstow, and as a temporary deity, and as a pro.

By the grace of the Pashi faith, we became sweaty, sweltering gods. Deities wrapped in blue crinkling suits, grunting and paying homage to centuries-old idols of Gretzky, Crosby, Malaucap. Our incense, the constant musk of our own bodies and the odd tang of our over-worked thermo gear. Our laments and halleluiahs laced in profanities and hard checks into the shipping barrels that lined the metal walls. There was no bench, no switching out. We took breaks every ten minutes for our communion of water, spouts pressed to the piercing in our suits, then out we went again.

Funny how, here on an alien space station months from home, in a time when we were designated divine, I felt so very human, with the full array of emotions.

Angry at being stuck on Barstow Station—nicknamed that by Sal because years ago we'd been stranded overnight in the god-awful desert ghost town of Barstow, California.

Sad—grieving—to end my career like this. Years of practice. Didn't even make it to Daru Baru.

I should be happier at this point. We hadn't needed to travel en masse to go home, so our other teammates had already shipped out. The six of us were finally leaving after Holy Hours. I'd go to sleep tonight, wake up in six months, on Earth.

Soon I'd have a class of kids I could gross out with stories of how it felt to awaken from cryo. I wanted to teach, and yet . . .

My lungs burned and my muscles seared as my Pashi-made skates shoved me forward. Sal's heavy breathing, his presence, chased me. We countered each other so damn well; nothing felt so good as busting through our stalemate. I slapped the puck into the goal—a small shipping crate—and cheered. Sal whooped, too, even as he bumped me in the shoulder.

Right now, hockey was my happiness. Not thoughts of Earth.

After an hour, we'd normally stop. This time, in unspoken consensus, we played on. Slower. Clumsier. I was reminded of the pick-up games the two of us played as kids, when we continued for hours and hours. Mom often joined us as part goalie, part coach. Her parents had migrated from Canada, driven south from the Maritimes as the coastline flooded. Hockey was in our blood.

Play slowed as another conversation started.

"It's going to be awesome to just wear hockey gear again, none of these thermo layers," said Trish.

"Yes. To move freely." Maurice stretched. "We'll need to get together again, when there is money for us to meet."

Sal snorted. "In that case, see you again in ten years."

I played in the American West Coast League with Sal, but the rest of the team was scattered around the world. We had a lot in common, though. Long weekend road trips. Trading out drivers, sleeping in back seats that reeked with months of compounded body funk. Playing in makeshift rinks in old warehouses with tractors or freight along back walls. Bartering labor for ration cards or food or gas to make it home. The glamorous lives of roller hockey pros.

Once we were back, sure, I'd do pick-up games every so often, but no more weekends away, no more playing to empty bleachers. I'd planned for this trip to be a grand end to my career since Sal talked me into joining the team but I still hadn't confessed that to anyone, certainly not my brother.

"Hey, at least we'll have stories to tell," said Trish.

"Not about the Daru Baru," added Sal. Ever the buzz kill.

I felt their gazes on my commlink as I skated by. I couldn't help but look at it, too. Still dark. Still quiet.

I also had the main docking bay page me every few weeks, just to make sure the unit worked. Eight months here, and no one had pinged it, not even from Earth. Freaking antique ansibles.

We still didn't know exactly what happened to our team funds. As far as we could figure, our sponsors absconded with the money after we were underway. We were lucky—ha—to wake up on Pashi station, really. Sure, the bulk of the station was set to a cozy

10 degrees Fahrenheit to mimic their home world, but they were willing to provide us jobs, rent a room block set to 70 degrees, and enable us to slowly save up funds for our tickets home.

Better than a swift kick out the airlock, that's for sure.

I scooped the puck and made a run for the far side. Maurice moved to block but the puck zinged between his legs and into the crate. Score: 38 to 36.

"What day job you think you go for, Sal?" asked Nicolai, his English thickened by a Ukrainian accent.

"Dunno." We faced off again. "Not worried about it. I'll go with the flow."

I slapped the puck so hard it left a new dent in a barrel.

An odd trilling sound almost caused me to trip forward in surprise. I glanced down. The commlink blinked red.

"Oh my god." I scraped to a halt.

"You gotta be kidding me." Sal stopped beside me, gawking at my wrist as if a tarantula had landed on me. "We barely have an hour before the Pashi want this bay back and—"

"I know," I snapped.

"Could be Earth?" said Kazuo.

I tapped the screen as the rest of the team gathered around.

"Hola hola!" The high-pitched voice of my Zarash crew boss carried over the device, clear as if he stood next to me. "Your Daru Baru landed. They coming to you. Capiche?" The guy had an annoying fascination with Earth's diverse languages.

"You're sure?"

"Yes yes! No one else dock but them. They got them trees and clothes and already had blades on."

"Sticks," I corrected him absently. "Thanks." The screen blinked off.

I stared at everyone. Everyone stared at me. A fuse lit in my nerves, giddiness causing me to bounce on my skates. "This is it! This is what we've been waiting for! Kazuo, your goalie gear—"

"It's in the locker up the hall. I was going to stow it after our game. Damn! Nic, come give a hand for a quick change."

The Daru Baru. Here. The main hangar was a ten minute walk away. In my letter, I'd invited them to play and said the Holy Hours were the only time it could work but this was cutting it so damn close.

The air within my suit felt thinner, my gear lighter. The team split up, chattering. Only Sal remained with me. His face was cast in shadow, but I knew by the tilt of his head that he was giving something serious thought. A noteworthy event.

"The Daru Baru take their sports seriously. That's why they hosted the Games, right? So they could play everyone?"

"Yes. Athleticism is the highest virtue, the body as a temple, all that."

"Damn." He shook his head as he glided backward. "We're so screwed."

"Don't say that!"

"When we left Earth, we were good, primed. But look at us here. Six left. In these suits. On blades, not wheels—"

"We always wanted ice, like in the stories, like before the wars—"

"Well, we got ice." He extended his arms as if to embrace the frigid arena. "We've also lived on Pashi food for months. We've all lost weight, muscle. We've only gotten to practice once every six days for a few hours. Gloria, we're going to lose." He tapped his stick on the ice as he turned away, but he couldn't disguise the quiver in his voice.

"Don't give up already!"

"Give up? Hell no. I'll play, it's just—I never expected it to be easy, but I knew we'd win. Hockey belongs to Earth, to us. In my head I saw it—I saw it like the Stanley Cup Finals. Stupid, I know."

For an instant, I remembered him as a little kid. Mom sewed us jerseys, 20th-century-style, SALAZAR in bold letters across the shoulders. He was Salazar 01. I was 02. Sal, with all the enthusiasm of his six years, said he was going to wear that sweater when he won the Stanley Cup.

Me, already Miss-Know-It-All, told him the Cup didn't exist anymore. It melted down with the rest of Edmonton.

He had sobbed his heart out and refused to play hockey with me for weeks. Only time in our lives that ever happened.

"Not stupid at all, Sal. This—this game still means something. Everything. We'll have burned up a year of our lives just in travel time. This is our Stanley Cup game."

"For no audience, with only six of us playing."

"Like back home. Like when we were kids." I looked at the quiet commlink again. "It's why I wore this every day, just in case some word came through."

"You're acting like this is your final game ever or something." Sal started to laugh. Something must have shown on my face, because he froze. "God. It is. Gloria Salazar. You're planning to quit."

He realized this now, of all times. I braced myself. "I want to teach, to learn, not spend my Sunday nights grading schoolwork by flashlight in the van."

"But you love hockey." His voice sounded small.

"I do." I refused to cry. Not here, not now. "But I need to grow up."

"Unlike me."

"That's not what I said."

Sal brought a hand to his helmet as if he could rub his face. "Sure. Yeah. So, last game. Big drama. Intergalactic stakes. Hope it turns out well for you." He skated away. I stared after him, fists balled.

"Cold, cold! God, it's cold!" Kazuo skated by me, shaking out his arms. His blue suit was even thicker now due to the swift change to goalie pads.

"You didn't lose any vital body parts, did you?" I called, keeping my voice light.

"The parts I need for hockey are all good."

"Don't think you'll feel that way when you're back on Earth," I said. Loud echoes carried down the hallway behind me. Skates. Lots of them.

By God, they were really here. The Daru Baru wore bronze thermo suits, hockey sticks in hand. By their height and bipedal nature, they could pass for a human.

I glided forward, the rest of my team gathered behind me. One of the Daru Baru advanced. Behind the visor, the vivid yellow of her skin reminded me of sunflower petals. Her eyes were fully black, nose two slits, her lips wide.

"You are Dearest Gloria Salazar, team captain?" she asked with a tip of her head.

Her English speech surprised me—her accent was vaguely Swedish. "You must be Dearest Vanfen." I bowed my head in turn. I'd forwarded her play manuals and hundreds of hours of video after we submitted roller hockey as a Games sport.

"We were aggrieved at your inability to compete in Daru Baru. The sport of roller hockey has become our life's blood, and so we have sought you here among the Pashi."

The phrase 'life's blood' caught me. That meant they really had gone hardcore, essentially converted to roller hockey as a religion. I'd hoped they would love it, but . . . wow.

"Dearest, where are your other teammates?" Vanfen continued, looking around. "This rink is not regulation size."

"It was most prudent for our teammates to return to Earth as we could afford it and as ships were available. There are only six of us left. You're correct that the rink isn't regulation size, but we have had to make do. Dearest." I barely remembered to add the proper diminutive.

A long, thin tongue lashed out to trace her lips. From my reading, I knew this was a sign of agitation. Her neck gills were probably fluttering, too. Damn, I wished I could fully gauge her appearance, get to know her. Daru Baru was a world of like size, oxygen content, and climate to Earth. We could comfortably socialize in our human quarters, if we had time.

"Make do. As with these . . . blades. Like Pashi feet."

The Daru Baru tended to be very literal in their interpretation of a sport's rules. Variations were like schisms in a church. "On Earth, we used to wear shoe-blades like this for a popular international version of hockey, back before the wars and the rise of the sea. It was far, far more popular than roller hockey has ever been. Now most humans don't live where ice like this is found, and it expends too much energy to generate such large amounts of ice indoors."

Vanfen's tongue withdrew. Apparently, I had placated her. "This 'making do' is a return to an old tradition, dearest?"

Tears welled in my eyes as I nodded. Hockey, as it was meant to be played on Earth, but here we were in the boonies on the far side of the sun. I wanted to tell her more about that old style hockey. I wanted to tell her about Pyotr Baranovsky and Gordie Howe and Catherine DuBois.

"There's not much play time left," Sal said in a low voice.

"Dearest," I said. "The Holy Hours end soon, and the Pashi will need this hangar again. I need to tell you of other adaptations before we play." I sped through our modified rules for holding bay 13. Vanfen pared down her team to six; we didn't have anyone on the bench, so they wouldn't play with reserves, either. If the cut players were disappointed, it didn't show. Two Daru Baru refs patrolled the ice.

We assembled. I positioned myself for a face off against Vanfen. Another tone rang over the intercom as part of the private Pashi holy ritual that we'd never see. It reminded me of what this time was, what I was right now.

My stick on the ice, an alien before me, I knew I was a goddess of hockey.

My existence was a slick rink, a hand-carved rubber puck, and the chaotic symphony of clattering sticks and hissing skates. I snared the puck and passed it to Trish, and she bounced it to Nicolai. He dumped it into their end.

Vanfen collected it along their boards—storage barrels—but Maurice clung to her like static, pinning her. The goal was some fifteen feet to the left. I moved in and swiped the puck. Sal was open. I passed the puck and made a beeline for the goal. Sal sent the puck back to me, deflecting it off my stick and through the goalie's five hole. Score!

Human whoops erupted all around me. My teammates granted me quick fist-bumps and smacks to the shoulder and we gathered for another face off. This time the Daru Baru won and passed it off to their left wing. My God, they were fast, but not flawless. Their stick-handling needed practice and the refs didn't seem to know just where to be. I had the sense that they memorized the vids I sent, and this new setting had shuffled the dynamics.

Action moved to our end of the ice, where Kazuo hunkered in the crease, waiting. Vanfen was on me now, her height equal, her reflexes faster. She seemed to anticipate my every effort to move around her—it was reminiscent of playing against my brother. All the data flashed through my mind again, about how Daru Baru biologically adapted to their chosen sport, about our current condition as pessimistically assessed by Sal.

Kazuo blocked the puck. It pinged off the boards just feet away. I angled my stick but Vanfen was there. Then Sal. He collided with her, his stick up.

The sound of a whistle took me off guard. I spun to stare at a ref as he made the stretched arm motion for high sticking.

"We programmed the appropriate sound of the whistle, so it would not be lost even in this thermo gear," said Vanfen.

"I—thank you for your thoughtfulness," I said, then turned on my brother, escorting him to the sideline. "Two minutes in, and you get a penalty?"

He gripped my arm. "Why do you really want to stop playing?"

That took me off guard. "I . . . something more to life. Deeper meaning, I guess." I squinted at him. "Did you just high stick Vanfen so you could ask me that?"

"Like I need an excuse to high stick anyone."

There wasn't any more time to chat. I skated back to the right side of our goal and motioned for Maurice to take the face off.

The Daru Baru scored a minute later. Sal tore back onto the ice. Play resumed. Moments later, a Daru Baru player was penalized after catching Trish across the hands with her stick, but we weren't able to take advantage of it.

I held back a little to study the Daru Baru. Even layered in pads and gear, they moved with the grace of old time figure skaters out of a vid. Sinuous. Beautiful. Not perfect, sure, but damn good and so fast. No breaths rasped through their vents. The first period ticked by, and they didn't appear tired at all.

We weren't fairing as well. We'd played through almost two hours before the Daru Baru arrived and it showed. That giddy adrenaline rush faded. Maurice leaned forward, pushing himself to skate. Trish kept leaning onto her thighs for breathers. Kazuo's reflexes slowed. My heavy breaths roared in my helmet. Sweat stung my eyes like acid. My heartbeat ticked in my ears. My lungs burned, my calves throbbed.

I skated. I skated hard. I was a goddess.

Sal matched me, stride for stride. Through the visor, the dark skin around his eyes was ruddy and wet.

We called the game at two periods. All of us were hockey gods right now, but some gods are mightier than others.

Final score: 8 to 5. Victory to Daru Baru.

I leaned on my legs, trying to absorb the reality but only feeling hollow. We lost, and yet . . . The Daru Baru, in their bronze suits, formed a line to high-five each other. They were chattering and cheering.

They'd been willing to come out into the boonies of deep space, just for this. They loved hockey. I grinned and tasted salt through my cracked lips. We might have lost, but this was a hell of a way to end the trip, end everything.

I shook hands with the Daru Baru, Earth-style, and directed

them down to our corridor. We had twenty minutes until Holy Hours were up. Enough time to chat with the Daru Baru for a few, dry shower, and get to the hangar to go earthbound.

Sal worked his way over to me. "You played the best damn game I've ever seen you play."

"I'm still dropping the full time team when we get home," I whispered.

"You'll regret it."

"I'm not making you stop, you know. It's okay for you to keep on playing."

He sighed, shoulders slumped, and skated ahead.

Once we were in the human-friendly climate of our corridor, both sides stripped off their headgear. The smell—well, our suits had wicked a lot, but there was an oddly sweet garlicky odor that I guessed was an indicator that the Daru Baru had worked up a sweat, too.

I approached Venfen. "Dearest, I am glad you arrived when you did. Our transport to Earth leaves in a little over an hour." Around us, humans and Daru Baru mingled and chatted.

I could barely see Vanfen's neck gills flutter above her collar. "We were surely blessed. In claiming hockey as our life's blood, we have all vowed to make a pilgrimage to your world, but we cannot do so now, not with a fertile season approaching. We must return to Daru Baru within hours as well."

"How long is the journey home in one of your ships?" Daru Baru tech was a lot better than most.

"Three months, by human account of time, dearest."

A long way to come for forty minutes of game time. Not that she seemed to mind.

"Dearest," I said, "Whenever you do make it to Earth, keep in mind that hockey isn't what it used to be. The past few generations, it's all about survival, about bringing up our population again and resettling to avoid radiation and high water. I'm returning home to teach more than to play hockey." It was easier to say that aloud to a stranger than to my brother or the rest of my team.

Vanfen's furred ears tilted forward. "Teach hockey?"

"Ah, no, that's not what I meant. Academics, mainly. To children. Maybe a little hockey, too."

She settled back in disappointment. "Oh. To be a devoted teacher of sport, that is the highest of callings, and one for which you seem greatly qualified." She made a sinuous hand motion. It took me a second to interpret it as a symbol of higher respect than 'dearest.'

My mind raced. "I do know a lot about the sport. It's in the life's blood of my family, going way back." Sal stepped alongside me.

"Select athletes from the Games have stayed as teachers among us." Vanfen made the gesture again. "Would such a role interest you?"

"Yes." No hesitation.

"Do you have a cold stasis apparatus for your kind?"

"A cryo berth? Yes. It's in the hangar, ready to be loaded."

Vanfen's face gleamed with excitement. "My pardon. I must confer with my sisters." She turned away and emitted a slight trill. The conversations around us abruptly ceased and the Daru Baru clustered together in a metallic-suited mob.

"Gloria?" Sal whispered, paragraphs of questions in the word.

"Sal, I think I might be getting an offer for a new teaching position."

"You, going to Daru Baru by yourself." To my surprise, he grinned and nodded. Our teammates gathered around us.

"Sal, you're the spontaneous one. You're the one I would have expected to do this," I said.

"No. Me, coach? Never. You want to teach. You want to learn. You would have gone back to Earth and kept looking at the stars. Plus, this means you'll keep playing hockey."

"Not with you," I said softly.

"Hell, I'll make do. Like you said, this is our life's blood."

"He's right," added Trish. "This is your lucky day. Do it. Besides, they want to make a pilgrimage to Earth, so you can eventually hitch a quicker ride home and even play tour guide." Maurice and Nicolai nodded, grinning.

"You'll be Earth's ambassador of hockey," said Kazuo.

Vanfen turned toward me, smiling. The other Daru Baru tittered and whispered as they reached for their helmets.

"Not an ambassador, or even a coach," I said. "I think to them, it's more like being a priest. A priestess."

"Kind of a demotion after being a goddess on Barstow," said Sal. He gripped me in a sweaty hug. Tears stung my eyes as I let go.

"I'll make do," I said, and bowed to Vanfen.

AN ECHO IN THE SHELL

DESPITE THE BITTER AUTUMN CHILL, Jonah's kiss warmed Allison's lips and sent unaccustomed heat swirling through her belly. Gravity didn't weigh her steps as she hopped up to the front porch. He had kissed her. He had held her hand and kissed her. Allison squealed and spun in a dizzying circle.

Feet away, the walls of her house shuddered. Something heavy smacked against the inner window, unseen behind the thick cover of nailed plywood. In that instant, the heat from the kiss evaporated and reality grounded her like an anvil.

Grandma.

Allison flung open the screen and fumbled with the key to unlock the doorknob and both deadbolts. She jumped inside. Glass squealed and crunched beneath her flats.

"Shut the door!" screamed Mom.

Allison kicked the door shut and slammed the locks in place. Grandma's solid weight impacted against Allison's back, sending a gush of air from her lungs. The doorknob gouged her gut. Grandma's knobby fingers inched up her arms towards her neck. The buzzing sound grew louder; the earthy, indefinable odor more potent.

Then Mom was there. With a sharp squeal, Grandma released her hold. Allison slipped around just in time to catch Grandma as she slumped to the ground. Mom stood there, panting, her hair electrocution-wild. A syringe gleamed in her hand.

"She took an extra long nap and was too quiet when she woke up and then I couldn't catch her." Mom blew stray hair from her lips, tears filling her eyes. "Her first Kafka rage."

"So how long were you chasing her—oh." As Allison heaved Grandma onto the couch, she finally had a good look at the room. Broken glass littered the floor. Two side-tables lay broken, one leg embedded in the wall like a spear. Through the arched doorway to the dining room, she saw more overturned chairs and the light of the gaping refrigerator door. Grandma had broken things before or tried to bust out, run towards lights outside, but nothing like this.

The rage. The next symptoms . . . no.

"Oh, Grandma." Allison stroked Grandma's shorn scalp.

"Looks like she has some cuts and bruises. I need to take pictures of her and the room and then I can sweep up this glass."

"You should have called me," Allison said.

"Like I had a chance," Mom snapped. "But no, you had to go on your little date. I hope you enjoyed it, because you aren't having another one for a long time. She always seems to respond best to you." Mom gnawed at her inner cheek as she stared at Grandma.

"Mom! That's not fair!"

"Life's not fair. You're sixteen, Allison. You'll have plenty of time for boys and all that nonsense later on. Go grab the digital camera for me."

Glass crunched underfoot as Allison stalked towards the hall. Like Mom had any place talking to her about boys, seeing how Dad left, seeing how Mom hadn't even attempted a date since Y2K.

But maybe Mom was right, too. Maybe Grandma had missed Allison. Maybe that was why she flipped out. Maybe this wasn't "the rage" doctors talked about. Maybe it was something . . . weird. A tantrum. That's all.

She made a slight detour to shut the fridge and reset the child-proof latch. The office door was open, which meant Mom must have been working when Grandma's rampage started. No surprise there. Mom tried to squeeze in freelancing whenever she could. The monitor was darkened in screensaver mode, the green light beneath blinking like a heartbeat. Allison grabbed the camera from its dock.

She took pictures as she walked through the house. A new hole in the wall. She stopped in the doorway to the living room and took in an empty spot on a high bookshelf. That broken glass used to be her great-great grandmother's vase. The one that used to be Grandma's favorite.

It was just a vase.

There were no curtains over the board-covered windows. A Plexiglas shield covered the TV, and that was frosted and scratched. Any shelves were bolted to the walls, cupboards secured with child-proofing snaps and locks. Mom leaned against an open cabinet beside the TV, set something inside, and shut the door. A shot of whiskey, probably. As if Allison didn't know. Mom would probably finish off the bottle when Allison was in bed and bury the evidence at the bottom of the recycling bin, as usual.

Grandma sat up on the couch. She blinked as she stared dully into space. Her crudely-shorn hair lay flat against her skull, dull metal gray against pasty skin. Her shadow cast against the front door revealed the truth. Long antennae curved from her head and arced a foot in height. Two mandibles protruded from her face and worked at the air. From her shoulders, diaphanous wings clung to her back and stretched the length of her body and through the couch itself. None of that was visible to the human eye, of course. Not yet. Light revealed the strengthening curse, that Grandma's body had become the husk of a soul-stealing bug.

That was the proof that Grandma suffered from Kafka Syndrome.

Grandma used to be Loretta Christiansen. Retired letter carrier for the United States Postal Service. Sunday school teacher for thirty-five years. Widow of Johann Christiansen. Mother of one. Grandmother of one. Game show junkie.

Really, when Allison thought of her grandma and who she truly was, her game shows were the first thing that came to mind.

"Come on, you banana brain," Grandma would yell at the TV. "The answer's the Mississippi River! The Amazon isn't even on this continent." Grandma had declared that Alex Trebek was dead to her after he shaved off his mustache.

Funny and old game shows were the best of all. Checkered bell bottom pants and big hair were standard issue, along with cheesy orange studio sets. Allison was crestfallen at age ten when she realized no other kids knew about *Match Game 75* and Charles Nelson Reilly or the hilarity of the Whammies on *Press Your Luck*.

Oh, how Grandma would laugh as she watched, light and feminine and free, and descend into giggles and wheezes.

One day as Grandma and Allison walked the two blocks from school, Allison saw Grandma's shadow. The horns were mere nubs then, the wings like little fists from her shoulders.

Allison wasn't scared. She reached for Grandma's hand and squeezed, and stood close enough so that the shadow couldn't be seen.

The curse had been on Grandma and others for decades and the victims never even knew. Back in the early '70s, some group of animal rights radicals laid a sleeper curse on laboratory workers in five states. Their goal: make the workers become their own test subjects. By the time the illness manifested in shadows decades later, there was nothing magic or medical science could do.

Grandma had delivered mail to all the labs within the complex. For some reason, the Asian cockroach room's curse was the one that clung to her soul. Ate it away.

But Allison swore that sometimes a flash of clarity returned to Grandma's eyes. Sure, she might not be able to talk anymore, or laugh. She ate with her fingers gathered like pincers. Sometimes she hissed when surprised. And at dusk, she fixated on the lights outside, especially the ones reflecting on the lake behind the house—so they boarded up the windows. That attraction made the Asian cockroach different from other kinds. They hungered for light.

They were also supposed to be really strong flyers.

Allison refused to think about that final stage. It was a long ways off. But there were only some five thousand people under the curse, a few hundred with the Kafka variant. No one knew the exact timeline. Doctors said that most would die during that final physical transition, anyway.

Until then, Allison had Grandma to love and care for, and that was all that mattered.

The next morning, the house looked normal again. Spartan. The sharp stink of fresh paint made Allison's nose run.

With the phone to her ear, Mom paced along the bay window in the dining room. "I know you're still building the Kafka wing, but this was her first big incident of the rage. Yes, I read the report—no, we aren't sending her to that lab. The whole point of that curse was to force her to be some lab animal, damn it!" She took in a deep breath. "Sorry. Sorry. She signed a living will before—uh huh. I'm sorry. Last night was just really rough and . . ."

Oh. Mom was talking with the people at that special home for National Lab curse patients. It was down near the University of Washington. A really nice place. They were building it for compatibility with a dozen different curses-in-progress.

Mom's voice slurred. Maybe the person on the phone wouldn't notice. Allison's stomach clenched in a knot. She hated mornings now.

Mom trailed a hand down her face. "Yes. Yes. Thank you." She pressed a button on her phone and set it down on the table, staring at it between her fingers.

"No progress?" Allison asked.

Mom's lips worked for a second and she shook her head. "They can't build it any faster. Other than that, they said we can sedate her more if necessary. I just . . ." She looked away, blinking, her head bobbing slightly. "Hey, don't you have that biology test today?"

"That was last week. But all of my homework is done. I had

everything taken care of before my date, remember?"

"Oh yes. Your date. That's right, it's Monday morning." Mom stared at where the calendar used to hang. Now only a few gouges from tacks marked the spot. "I'm losing my mind."

"You could drink less." Allison tried to keep her voice light.

"That's none of your business." Mom made no such attempt at levity.

"It is if I hear you slurring like this first thing in the morning."

Mom sucked in a sharp breath, the sound so like Grandma's cockroach hiss that it sent a rush of cold along Allison's spine. "How dare you. I'm an adult. I'm in complete control of how much I drink. It helps me sleep. Last night I needed all the help I could get, after that."

Allison grabbed an apple from the fridge and made a quick retreat towards the front door. She couldn't bear to even look at Mom.

Grandma was still asleep on the couch, her jaw gaped open. Asleep, she looked so normal.

"Hey, Grandma," Allison whispered, her throat hot with tension. "I've gotta go to school. I'll miss you. Maybe this afternoon we can hang out?" Without waiting for an answer, she planted a kiss on Grandma's forehead. It was a shame the game show channel had changed their whole line-up a few months before. All their old shows were shuffled around.

"Allison. She's gone. This is just a shell—"

"Don't say it. I'm sick of you saying that."

"Reality's going to crash down hard on you when it comes, Allison. You can't be in denial forever."

"Denial? I know Grandma's sick—"

"She's not sick, damn it, she's gone! Dead! That's not her on the couch, get it?"

It was the whiskey, it was that stupid whiskey that made Mom all awful every morning. Allison backed up to the front door, her nails digging into flesh of the apple in her palm. She swung her backpack onto one shoulder and fled. She hit the sidewalk running fast enough that the tears tipped from her eyes and flew away without touching her cheeks.

"Come on, Grandma. It's time to get ready for bed."

With her hand curled beneath Grandma's armpit, Allison walked her down the hall. They staggered together, Grandma's steps small and shuffling. She fitted Grandma in fresh disposable underwear and a pink paisley nightgown that snapped up the sides. Then she guided Grandma to her room. Mattresses sat on a bare concrete floor. Scratches gouged the walls. Allison tried not to see it, tried not to compare the room to how it used to be with its dense '70s wood furniture and Currier & Ives prints on the walls.

She tucked in the old woman, taking care to layer the blankets and cover her wrinkled feet.

Allison laid a hand against Grandma's cheek. By Mom's account, it had been an okay day. Nothing good, nothing bad. Allison's day—well.

"Jonah asked me to go out with him on Friday," Allison whispered. "I didn't say no, not straight out. I mean . . . I know how he'd react. He's a cool guy, really. But . . ." She could only say "no" so many times. Most of her old friends had moved on for that very reason, or were content with just hanging out at school, never mentioning the possibility of anything after.

"It's hard sometimes, you know? But I know Mom won't let me go."

Grandma's teeth bared in a grimace. If her shadow had been visible, no doubt those pincers would be working as if they could bite. But there was no shadow. Just Grandma.

"Good night, Grandma. I love you." She planted a kiss on her forehead.

Allison shut the door and bolted it on the outside.

Mom was holed up in her office, working frantically on her

work backlog. Probably would be until late. Allison disgorged her backpack's contents onto the couch and turned on the TV. She had already gotten a decent start on her homework by staying late after school—not like she was in a rush to get home for more quality time with Mom—but the terrors of algebra awaited.

Out of habit, she picked up the remote and flicked it to the game show channel.

"—*Match Game* Marathon!" boomed an overly-pleasant announcer.

Allison's head jerked up.

A *Match Game* Marathon this Friday. Twenty-four solid hours of bell-bottoms and orange-shag goodness. Grandma would love this!

From the office, the chatter of computer keys continued, punctuated by dark, indecipherable mutters.

Mom wouldn't agree. Mom would say it was pointless, that Grandma wasn't in there, that it was all just a waste of time. She would yell and rant and do everything she could to make sure the TV stayed off. Allison's hand clenched the remote as if she could strangle the plastic. Grandma would love this marathon. If anything could coax her out of her shell, this would be it. Mom had even said Grandma responded best to her.

Mom needed to be out of the house that night.

Grinning, she reached for the phone and dialed up Mom's best friend, a friend who'd already pestered Mom for months to cut loose and relax for sanity's sake. "Hey, Shayna?" she said. "Allison here. Mom's really needing a break. You think we can tag team her?"

A few minutes later, she hung up. A devious plot was already underway. Shayna knew how to score tickets for some overnight bed and breakfast deal over in Leavenworth this Friday night. If Shayna had already shelled out the money, Mom would be more likely to cave in and go. It'd still take a few days to wear her down, but Allison knew it would work. On some level, Mom knew she needed a break, too. This was the excuse.

Allison finished up her homework as the TV droned in the background. For the first time in ages, she hummed aloud, a smile on her lips. This Friday was going to be the awesomest night ever, for all of them.

When Allison crawled into bed, she was still smiling. An incessant buzzing sound shivered through the wall. Grandma slept one room over, her breathing like a mob of a thousand mosquitoes.

Down the hallway, the door clicked open. From the living room came the soft thud of the opening liquor cabinet and the clink of glass. Mom was getting ready for bed, then.

Allison stared at the blackness of the ceiling. Her happiness dwindled away as a sick knot resumed its normal place in her stomach. Mom was the one who was really gone, not Grandma.

The terrible susurrus continued from next door, from Grandma. "It's just buzzing," Allison whispered, as if saying it aloud made it true.

She drifted to sleep, and the buzzing droned on.

"I shouldn't go." Mom clutched her suitcase handle and paced the living room. "You know what happened on Sunday—"

"She's been fine all week. If it gets to be too much, I'll call 9-1-1," Allison said. "Now go. If Shayna has to shut off her car to come get you, the neighbors might call 9-1-1 before you even leave."

Mom laughed, the sound abrupt and nervous. "Yeah. Riding tied up in the trunk might look suspicious."

"Go." Allison held open the door and pointed to the sidewalk.

Mom ducked her head like a chastised child, casting glances over her shoulder as she walked halfway along the path. "If you need me—"

"I'll call. Go!"

Allison bolted the door and stood there, shivering. It was going to be awful cold tonight. Through the peephole, she watched the car drive away. Mom was probably crying now, apologizing to Shayna, saying she shouldn't go. Shayna would keep driving.

"Well, Grandma, this is our big night," said Allison. Grandma sat on the couch with a slack jaw. Her dead eyes stared ahead at the television.

"That's right, it's TV time! We've already missed some twelve hours of the marathon. We're slacking." She powered on the television and squealed as she sat down beside Grandma. "Look at Charles Nelson Reilly in that snazzy red suit! Geez, I think I saw Brett Somer's dress on sale at the mall last week. And you said the '70s would never come back in fashion."

Grandma buzzed softly. Allison leaned against her knees and giggled as she watched. "Oh, gosh. I'm surprised that comment made it past the censors then. That was awfully double-edged, even for now." Rain drummed a soft rhythm above their heads. Another episode came on, then another.

"That was a cop-out answer. That could have been smarter or funnier." Allison shot a furtive glance at Grandma, in search of agreement.

"Charles Nelson Reilly! Best player ever! Remember when I showed you the song Weird Al made all about him? Wasn't it awesome?"

"That hair. Crazy. Did she stick her finger in a light socket or what?"

Buzzing answered. Only buzzing.

Two hours passed; three.

Grandma's laughter wasn't there. Grandma wasn't there.

Allison turned off the television. She stared at the black screen. Through the marred protective glass, she could see their reflections. Grandma's expression never changed.

Grandma was really gone.

The realization was quiet. Cold. Back when the diagnosis first came, Allison had tried to joke that the curse wasn't real until Grandma had wings. Now she understood. It wasn't about how

Grandma looked, or even her shadow. It was about . . . Grandma.

She stood. In the blank screen, she saw Grandma stand as well. Grandma pivoted, hunch-backed, and dove at the taped-together lamp on the end table. It crashed to the carpet, and in a blink, the room was cast into darkness.

"Grandma?" No. This wasn't Grandma, not really. It wore her skin, but soon, it wouldn't even wear that. Mom had injected Grandma before she left—her regular dose with a little extra.

It wasn't enough to quell the rage.

There was a long, cockroach hiss and the shuffling of feet and Grandma was there, those hands scratching at Allison's neck.

She sidestepped. Grandma grunted, swinging towards her. Allison retreated towards the TV. Lamp shards skittered and crunched underfoot. Pain pierced the sole of her right foot, followed by the intense warmth of blood.

In scant gray light, Grandma advanced, her feet wide like a sumo wrestler. Her mouth gaped, glare reflecting from her teeth. Her gaze—empty. No hatred. No malice. Allison was just . . . a thing. A target. Prey?

Grandma was gone. Dead. She was dead. She wasn't in that body anymore.

Anger rippled through Allison and clogged her throat. Anger at the hippies and their curse, anger at Mom and her alcohol and her work, anger at doctors for doing nothing. Anger at Grandma.

"You were supposed to fight this!" Allison yelled. "You're supposed to still be in . . . there!"

Grandma launched herself forward. Allison slipped aside, her bloodied foot tacky on the carpet, and Grandma plowed into the liquor cabinet. It rattled, glass tinkling and liquid jostling.

Allison hated that cabinet. Hated it. She turned, throwing her shoulder into the cabinet. It rocked against the wall, unable to fall because of the straps securing it in place. She hugged it with both arms and yanked with all of her body weight. The cabinet pulled from the wall. Then Grandma was there, tackling her. Allison met the next wall with a grunt. The cabinet crashed into the carpet at Grandma's heels.

Mom could buy more alcohol. She undoubtedly would. But there was something amazing about hearing those bottles shatter. There was just enough light to see a gush of dark fluid seep through to the floor, as if the cabinet itself bled.

"You should have laughed during *Match Game*," Allison whispered. "You would have laughed."

How long would the curse drag on? How many months, years? How long would this thing wear Grandma's skin? How long until—that Asian cockroach emerged? The wings. The antennae. The shadow come to life. And Mom—how would Mom change? What facade would she wear?

Nausea punched her in the stomach. Suddenly it was all real. All too real. Grandma hissed, and Allison stepped back. Her bare feet kicked through more pieces of the lamp. Pain zinged all the way up her leg and caused her to gasp. If she made it across the room to the switch, Grandma would go for the light instead. That would distract her until . . .

Light. Outside, the light would be on down at the dock. A light that attracted clouds of bugs.

The awfulness of the thought froze her for a moment. Then the fumes of weeping liquor stung at her nostrils, and she knew what she would do.

She glanced at the door to the back patio. The story poured into her head: she would say she heard that old tom cat on the porch, that she opened her door to check. That Grandma attacked her. It was close to the truth. That they had fought throughout the room and then ended up back at the door. The door that lead to the stairs and the lake and the light and the cold, rainy night.

Allison staggered across the room and towards the door. Grandma's nails gouged at her neck. An earring ripped free from Allison's lobe. She worked the locks as Grandma's body dragged from her arm. The door swung free, iciness a wave over her skin.

Grandma hissed, grabbing Allison's neck with both hands, and shoved. Allison's head met the hardness of the doorjamb. Stars danced in the middle of the room as she fell to her knees. The loosened snaps of Grandma's gown clacked at Allison's head level.

"You're free," Allison whispered. "Go."

Then, the old woman was out the door, her bare feet smacking on wet cement. Allison forced her head to turn.

Rain fell in wavering sheets. Out on the nearby lake dock, a single yellow light stood as a sentinel. Grandma, hunched, was like a gray shadow in the blackness as she scurried away. The unsnapped gown trailed behind her like wings. Then she met the stairs. She tumbled, feet over head. Allison listened to the rasps of her own breaths. Grandma's head was visible again, barely. She still worked towards that brightness below, just like the Asian cockroach she was.

Allison could have screamed for help. She would have, if Grandma had been somewhere within that frail shell.

A slow ooze of blood coursed Allison's cheek. She lowered herself to the frigid linoleum before the door. The gallop of her heart was louder than the buzzing had ever been. She quivered as she heard a distant splash, and clenched her eyes shut. The light from the dock still burned through the blackness, and as the minutes passed and the chill sank in, the relentless rhythm of the rain soothed her like a lullaby.

213 MYRTLE STREET

THE HOUSE AT 213 MYRTLE STREET wore an enchantment that could obscure it when it so desired. This was a handy skill, particularly when salesmen roved the streets or teenagers skulked about after dark, eggs in hand.

Now there was a realtor at the gate. The smell of dozens of strange, foreign houses clung to her clothes.

The house ached in its abandonment. Mrs. Leech was gone. A stranger had to lock the door behind Mrs. Leech when she last left the house, still asleep as she was rolled along on a strange wheeled bed. They shared a comfortable existence together, woman and house. Mrs. Leech had been a mere slip of a girl when her family moved into 213 Myrtle, the place still ripe with fresh paint and cut lumber. Her parents left, then her husband, but Mrs. Leech stayed. Her bones creaked along with the settling of the pipes at night.

The house did not want a new owner. It did not like the thought of condemnation and rot, either.

Mrs. Leech just needed to come home. The porch needed sweeping.

Therefore, when the realtor arrived, 213 Myrtle Street hid. The woman strode up the front walkway, heels clicking a powerful rhythm, and she stopped.

"House, you're not going to play this game, are you?"

The house was indignant that this person saw through its glamour so quickly. Certainly it wasn't losing its skill? 213 Myrtle waited. The woman waited, too. The soles of her right shoe went tap-tap-tap. Finally, grudgingly, 213 Myrtle acquiesced. Its powder blue wood-paneled exterior emerged. The front steps creaked as the realtor hopped up to the porch.

"You old houses can be so temperamental," she said, fondness in her voice. "Enchantments like that add to your value, you know. Goodness knows, I wish my condo could hide, but no one would believe the illusion."

The house was quiet. It's not as if it could speak or answer, not as a person would, but it was quite adept at conversation. Mrs. Leech would chat with the house for hours.

"Now," said the woman. "I have to look you over to prepare you for sale. All the money's going to go towards the Children's Club."

Mrs. Leech had taught for fifty years and mentored well beyond that. 213 Myrtle Street was accustomed to being an after school destination. As a rule, the house did not like children, especially young ones who scribbled on walls, but Mrs. Leech had always made sure her charges treated the household with proper respect. The house had to admit it enjoyed the extra wear of feet on its veneered floor and the buoyant laughter that floated to the rafters.

The woman placed the key in the lock, the same familiar key the house had known for years and years. The house clenched the door frame.

"Now, house," she said. "Please."

There was something comfortably soothing about her voice and manners, but the house hesitated. This was a realtor. The house did not intend to be sold.

213 Myrtle could burn down. It would be very easy. The old wires itched in the hollow spaces between walls. Yet the house hesitated. Was that really what it wanted, the complete death of its timber and memories? Was that truly preferable to new residents or—Wright forbid—renters?

Mrs. Leech would come back. She would need a place to sleep. The house couldn't burn.

The woman rested a hand against the doorframe. A memory

trickled through the layers of paint and aged wood. It understood: this was a good hand.

213 Myrtle Street relaxed. The door unstuck.

The realtor's footsteps echoed. 213 Myrtle Street felt the reverberations. It had been an awful day last week when all of the furniture had been moved out. The house had tried to hide then, too, but movers were all too familiar with the wily ways of old and enchanted houses.

Where would Mrs. Leech sleep? Where would she sit?

"My goodness. So empty." The woman shook her head, then pulled out her phone to begin jotting down notes. The house heard her whispers. "Bay window with bench seat. Kitchen with 1950s appliances, in perfect repair . . ."

She walked onward, a scent of jasmine trailing in her wake. It reminded the house of the scent Mrs. Leech used to wear, so long ago, when Mr. Leech lived there as well. He would come to the door in that khaki uniform. The happiness of Mrs. Leech's rapid footsteps used to make the household quiver in anticipation.

Sadness ached in its support beams. The electrical wires pulsed.

The realtor laid a hand against the wainscoting in the dining room. The body warmth soothed the glossy paint all the way to the primer.

"I have so many good memories in this room," said the realtor. "We'd all gather around the table. Mrs. Leech always had cookies, and we would sit there, do homework, crafts."

The floorboards creaked. The woman's weight was different, the shoes new, but the house suddenly understood. Knew this as a child, grown.

"Mrs. Leech loved this place. Before she passed on, she made me promise to find good, new owners for you. People who would love you as much as she did. You can have a family live here again." She patted the paneled wall.

213 Myrtle Street felt the touch all the way to its disused pipes. This girl's fingers had dragged along the walls, so many years before.

This realtor was not such a bad person. The house wouldn't hide from her, or the guests she brought. And having a family here was a good thing. They could bring new furniture, new footsteps. Besides, Mrs. Leech would love the company when she returned.

213 Myrtle Street nestled against its concrete foundation and waited.

A SAMPLE PACK OF APOCALYPSES

THE HUMAN IS LATE
TO FEED THE CAT

SASSAFRAS WAS MOST DISPLEASED. The woman was late to return home. Sassafras positioned herself in the hallway with a clear vantage point of both the front door and the laundry room that contained her barren wet food dish.

Her anxiety increased as the hours passed. She fully groomed herself five times over, and even lapsed her guard duties long enough to eat some dry kibble; that dish was despairingly low as well. Her snack done, she resumed her watch.

If Sassafras had to rise again, it would be for the curtains to know her wrath.

The front doorknob jostled. The cat hopped to her feet, fur like a puffy white cloud. The woman lurched inside and slammed the door behind her. Without sparing a glance at Sassafras—the nerve!—the woman dove through another doorway. With a dismayed glance toward the laundry room, the cat followed her.

The woman was ill. She radiated sourness, and the potency of it worsened as she leaned over the toilet. But Sassafras was the very model of support and patience. She purred and marched back and forth in the gap between woman and toilet, with brief pauses to groom the woman's elbows.

"No. Sassy." The woman pushed her away.

Confused, the cat scrambled backward. The woman fell back on her haunches, groaning.

"People are coming down sick everywhere. Some virus. I heard the hospitals are full. I couldn't take the train. On the bridge, I saw someone . . ." She wiped her wrist against her mouth and shuddered. Sassafras smelled blood. "I'm afraid . . . I don't know . . . I tried calling my mom, but . . ." The electricity flickered like a pulse but stayed on.

Sassafras rubbed against the woman's knees and prodded her toward the doorway. The woman did move, but to hover over the toilet again. The cat retreated a few steps with a despondent yowl.

"I know, Sass." The woman coughed and hacked. She pulled a towel from the rack and dragged it with her as she crawled down the hallway. Sassafras was unsure what to make of this sort of progression, but at least the human was going the right way. The cat trotted ahead to act as guide, her tail like an exclamation point as they entered the laundry room.

The woman knocked the food box from the shelf, and after more delays, managed to rip open a pouch. The glorious perfume of savory tuna in gravy filled the room. Sassafras purred like a motor and she settled in at her food bowl.

The lights flickered again. Outside, car horns blared, followed by pop, pop, pop, and a prolonged scream.

"Oh God. The world's gone to hell. What's going to happen, Sass?"

The cat felt the weight of the question and glanced up. She had just resumed eating when the sound of the jostled dry food bag made her freeze. The woman had dragged the large bag from between the washer and dryer. She undid the clip at the top, then tipped the whole thing on its side. An avalanche of kibble tumbled across the floor.

Sassafras stopped eating her beloved tuna. Why was her crunchy food all over the floor? The woman knew Sassafras only ate dry kibble if it was in the appropriate bowl. The woman smelled increasingly wrong, too. Her body was too hot. It was rank. Sour. Unfamiliar. The cocoa butter lotion the cat liked to lick from the woman's calves couldn't even be smelled now.

The woman used the supply shelf to pry her body upright. The effort left her wheezing and coughing. "At least it'll be fast for me, Sass. That's what the news was saying." Her laugh made her cough more. "To think, this morning . . . I thought it would be an awful day because I ran out of coffee."

The woman edged her way to the window. It took her several minutes of effort to crank open the pane of glass. Fresh night air flowed through the room. Sassafras's whiskers flared out as she breathed in the fragrance of trees and strange cats and city. She started forward but the woman wobbled and collapsed to her knees, forcing the cat back toward the doorway.

"I used to hate it when you hunted birds at our old place, remember? I would get so mad. But now . . ." She rolled to her side. Her shoulders racked as she coughed and choked. It took her a minute to speak again. "The tree branch goes right to the window. Good thing . . . landlord never had the landscapers come. You can go in and out, Sass. If I can get to the sink, I'll . . ."

More sickness, more coughing. Unsure of the strange assault of smells, Sass stayed back, ears flicking at the contrast of the woman's noises with the sounds from outside. The loudness there had frightened away the birds.

The woman's racket faded to weak sobs. That sound, the cat knew from nights when she shared her bed with the woman. Sass took mincing steps around the foulness on the floor and stopped at the woman's hands. The fingers twitched and managed to rest on Sassafras's sloped spine.

The cat lowered and folded her body into a bread loaf form. The woman's hand grew heavier on Sass's back, and the cat purred.

THE SWEETNESS OF BITTER

 MARGO CLUTCHED THE NINE IRON and tilted an ear, listening for the crunch of footsteps from the next yard over. Dead leaves rustled. Even the wind seemed to hold its breath, waiting.

"Is someone there, Mommy?" Tara whispered.

"Maybe." With one arm, Margo pressed her daughter behind her, against the cinderblock wall. Their last quart of water sloshed within her backpack.

Her fingers twitched on the golf club, a souvenir from salvaging in Palm Springs. It had been weeks since they had seen anyone alive. No one else was stupid enough to cross the desert stretch of Interstate 10 between Los Angeles and Phoenix. It'd been a wasteland before the bombs dropped.

But now they were on the far western fringe of metropolitan Phoenix. People were bound to linger here, and Margo was ready for them. Copper stains already marbled the shaft of the nine iron.

"I know someone is back there." The brittle, feminine voice carried from the neighboring yard. "Looters aren't welcome here. Show yourself and I might not shoot."

Damn it. "Might?" Margo called, gripping the club. She had Doug's old pistol in her backpack. No bullets.

The silence was long, assessing. "How many of you are there?" the woman asked.

"Me and my daughter. Just passing through, that's all."

"Come out." That voice left no room for argument. "We have you surrounded."

"I can help, Mommy!" said Tara. The simulacrum of a five-year-old girl hefted up a cinderblock, hoisting it above her head.

"Put it down, Tara!" Margo hissed. Sometimes her daughter's inhuman strength came in handy, but right now Tara was too fragile. Again.

The real Tara had been dead for two years. Leukemia. The simulacrum had been created using the latest of advancements, complete with programmed memories, fuzzy logic, tantrums, and biological requisites. Tara—this Tara—was all she had left, and why they had walked and driven across three hundred miles of nothingness to find the headquarters of Simulated Innovations.

Margo spared a glance at the sky and sucked in a deep breath. Sim Inno should only be five miles down the road. They were so close.

"Stay here," she whispered to Tara, pressing a quick kiss to her forehead. Margo's sun-blistered lips burned.

She lifted her hands above her head, club still in her grip, and eased into the open. Her heart thudded throughout her thin frame.

A gaunt woman faced her, a shotgun in her steady grip. Beneath a layer of grime, her skin gleamed in a golden tan that once would have sparked poolside envy.

"We're just passing through," Margo repeated, her voice raspy. She was thirsty. She was always thirsty.

The gaze on her remained hard. "Where to?"

"Going to a place just up the road."

"After that?"

Margo's tongue moved as if to speak, tasting dirt and tangy iron instead of words. Surviving, breaking into Sim Inno, running recalibration on Tara—that meant everything.

"Don't hurt my mommy!" Tara wailed. She crouched at the base of the wall, tears leaking from her eyes. Margo bit back the urge to tell her to stop crying. Tara couldn't afford to waste fluid, but Margo hated using protocol commands to quell emotional responses. She loathed the reminders that a machine wore her daughter's smiling face.

The woman jerked her head. "Have the girl come out."

Margo's fingers squeezed the metal shaft of the club. "Tara, come out. Slowly."

Whimpering, Tara sidled out and embraced Margo. Her head rested against the hard jut of her mother's hip.

The other woman recoiled. "She's pale . . . and fed."

Tara had been a skinny five-year-old by pre-war standards, which meant she now passed for plump.

As for her skin, pigmentation nanites had been among the first to fail months before, not long after the cataclysm, but Margo couldn't tell a stranger that. She knew how people reacted to sims, and didn't need derision or pity.

"She's sick. I'm trying to get her help. I . . . give her all my food."

"Oh." The woman's expression softened a degree. "Other kids have been sick, too."

"Other kids?" Tara emitted a joyful squeal.

Tears heated Margo's eyes. She hadn't seen another living child in ages. "It's not that kind of sickness. I'm—I was—a nurse. Her case is . . . special."

"A nurse?" The woman's eyes narrowed. "We could use a nurse."

"I have to save my daughter." The two women regarded each other. The silence stretched out.

"Of course." The woman relaxed a degree but the gun didn't lower. "Just so you know, these houses are already stripped clean. No food or water."

"We just want to move along." Soon they would need more sugar, but that could wait until after recalibration.

"Then move along." The woman granted her an abrupt nod and whistled sharply. "But keep us in mind. There could be a place for you here."

Margo heard footsteps behind her and turned. Two boys emerged from the shadows of a house, their adolescent bodies as long and lean as summertime tomcats. The youngest couldn't have been older than twelve, his face emaciated and eyes wide. Both carried makeshift spears. Following the woman, they ran across the street and vanished amongst the houses.

Margo stared after them. She had become familiar with the boney lines of her own body, but seeing children so close to starvation seemed unreal and wrong. And here was Tara, strangely *normal* in comparison. That felt wrong too.

"Mommy, they were kids like me!" Tara bounced in place. *No, not like you,* she wanted to say, and forced away the awful thought. She never used to think things like that. Doug had, when they first discussed purchasing a sim, but that was ages ago. Another life.

Tara hopped backwards and directly into the cinderblock. She toppled with a cry. The sweet scent of manufactured blood slapped Margo's nostrils.

"Tara, stay still!" She swung the backpack off her shoulder and rummaged to find the patch kit.

"It hurts! There's blood everywhere!" The child whimpered, clutching her knee. The backside of her calf streamed pink fluid.

"Mommy will take care of it. Don't worry. Scoot here to the corner." Margo cast a wary glance over her shoulder as she sheltered Tara with her body, then went to work.

Tara's skin hadn't blistered from the sun or radiation, but the slightest physical duress caused it to tear like parchment. The blood didn't even clot as it should. Tara's every motion, each breath, relied on hundreds of thousands of nanites within her circulatory system. Before the attack, this would have been a simple fix. Two hours in the recalibration module in Riverside.

Nothing was simple now.

Margo retrieved the patch kit and tore off a strip of manufactured skin. She patted it over the wound. Replenishing Tara's blood-glucose came next. Simulacrum Innovations had promoted their glucose-based life system as the next great thing. No batteries to charge, no obvious computer hardware. It sold the fantasy that this was a real child. Her real daughter, complete with memories up to the point of her leukemia diagnosis.

Margo pulled the sugar and chemical additive kit from her backpack. The half pound of sugar shifted in its bag and trickled like hourglass sand.

She scooped out two tablespoons of sugar and poured it into a pink-dyed vial. After dumping in the additive, she sealed it and agitated the mix. In a practiced move, she hooked the IV to the concealed port in Tara's arm. Pink fluid trickled down the line and vanished beneath a pale sheath of flesh.

"Sims are so easy to maintain! Just buy white sugar at the local grocery store and replenish their supply once a week, or more as needed. Blood-glucose is energy efficient, nontoxic, and economic!" So the ads once read. Doug once tried a sip and said it was eerily like Kool-Aid.

Without looking, Margo wiped her stained hands against her pants and packed everything away again.

"I did good! I did good!" Tara bounced in place. "I stayed nice and still, right?"

"Yes, you did wonderfully." She gave Tara's hand a squeeze.

Tara tilted back and blinked. "I did good! I did good! I did good! I did good . . ."

Margo bit her lip and looked away. Vocalization loop and paralysis. More signs of imminent failure. Death. Shut down.

"God, why is this happening again?" She rocked in place.

No answer came besides Tara's ecstatic chant.

After a few minutes, the dialogue loop abruptly stopped. Tara sat up, smiling. In her databanks, the failure hadn't even happened.

"Let's go," Margo said. New urgency pushed her stride.

Margo acutely sensed their vulnerability as they walked the borderland between the desert and civilization. Half-built houses stood frozen in time, their desert vistas now consisting of abandoned cars and debris. She balanced the golf club on the fulcrum of her fingertips. Merciless heat radiated from the pavement. Many people undoubtedly fled to the mountains in search of cooler temperatures and water, but even so, these streets were surprisingly clear of bodies and rot. Someone tended to this place.

"Mommy, that one boy looked like Sanger, didn't he? But it couldn't be him, huh?"

Margo's steps slowed. "Sanger? But . . ." Sanger had been another boy in the leukemia ward. Tara wasn't supposed to remember that time. She knew she was different—special—but no more than that. Innocence was meant to be bliss. "No, it couldn't be him," Margo answered slowly, gnawing on her lip.

"Sanger used to give me his jelly cups and I'd give him my apple slices. But we can't give them any food, huh?"

"No. I know you want to help, but we've talked about that before. We can't give anything away, Tara. I need to stay strong to take care of you."

The girl was quiet for a long minute. "Do you think if we gave them food, they'd be my friends?"

"Oh, Tara. You don't have to give them anything to be friends. Just be yourself."

"Really?" She brightened and glanced the way the others had gone.

"Of course." Margo rubbed Tara's shoulder for good measure.

Beyond a chain link fence, the headquarters of Simulated Innovations was a gray and glass obelisk. A broad gate blocked the road. The fence stood a solid eight feet high with barbed wire looped along the top. A quick rummage through the backpack and she had the wire cutters in hand. She hefted the tool for a long moment, immobile in grief and memory.

The fence at Riverside had killed Doug. When they cut their way inside, wire scraped across his ribs. It seemed like nothing at the time. The only thing that mattered then was what they'd found inside the facility: the recalibration chamber disassembled for maintenance. Still, they replenished Tara's supply of additive and synth skin, and immediately planned to move onward to Phoenix to Sim Inno's headquarters.

Then Doug's health failed. Fast.

Even as a nurse, Margo never thought to ask her husband when he last had a tetanus booster. She also thought that nothing could be worse than watching your child die. Then she had to watch Tara's devastation as her father died in indescribable agony.

Margo cut a wide doorway through the fence this time, tossing the metal aside. She knelt in front of Tara and gripped her by both shoulders. "Whatever happens, you know I love you, right?" Three hundred miles to get here, for this chance to keep Tara alive. Every step, every mile, was worth it.

"I love you, Mommy." Tara's arms squeezed her and kept on squeezing.

"Tara, let go," she gasped. The little girl's arms painfully compressed her ribs and then suddenly released. Margo staggered back with a gasp, rubbing her torso. Tara smiled, oblivious to her own strength. Yet another nanite failure.

"Let's do this," Margo said, voice hoarse.

Margo gingerly stepped through the gap in the fence. Tara inched through with equal care. Margo's eyes traced over Tara, making sure the wires hadn't scratched her, and she nodded to herself.

There was no way to tell if the building had any electricity or generators. *God, let there be electricity. Let this work.* Dark windows glistened through a coat of dirt. The glass didn't look broken or even cracked. Surely someone had tried to break in and search for vending machines or something.

"I did good! I did good! I did good . . ."

The suddenness of the Tara's voice caused Margo to freeze. The girl kept walking, oblivious to her vocalization loop, and Margo hurried ahead. Another failure, that fast.

"Protocol 10, mute," she said, hating the words, not even sure if they would work. Tara's silent lips continued to form syllables as she skipped along. As they reached the darkened three-story building, Tara's lips stilled again. "Protocol 11, volume."

"This is like a special hospital, Mommy?" she asked right away. "You can fix me up?"

"Yeah." Margo squeezed her hand. It felt like a real hand, warm and balmy with sweat. It felt like Tara.

Taking a deep breath, Margo tested a door handle. Locked.

"If anyone's in there, they must be vewy, vewy qwiet." Tara said that Elmer Fudd style.

Margo's fingers traced a card scanner and pad beside the door. On a whim, she pressed her thumb against the pad. A red light blinked.

There was electricity. But how to get inside? Riverside's security had been totally different.

"My turn!" Tara sang as she pressed her whole right hand against the pad. The light flicked to green. With an audible click, the door unlocked.

Margo yanked Tara back, golf club up, breath catching.

"WELCOME, MODEL 311337 B." The words scrolled across a plate on the door.

They entered the building. Stagnant air reeked of mustiness. Emergency lights glowed in long, fluorescent strips above. As the door behind them shut, green dashed lines appeared on the floor and trailed down the hallway, flashing on the right side of the fork as if to guide them that way.

"Hello? Is anyone there?" Margo called. "I'm Margo Calloway. My daughter is Tara, she's from . . . here. She needs recalibration." The echo of her voice trailed away.

"You think it's like a maze game?" Tara asked, pointing at the green lines of the floor.

"It seems to be leading us somewhere. Let's follow. Slowly."

They walked deeper into the center. The air cooled, the mustiness faded. Some sort of limited air-conditioning was running.

"Oh my God." Margo stared in awe at a water cooler. It sat in the hallway, half-full. Her hands trembled as she pulled a paper cup from the dispenser and filled it.

"Wow," said Tara.

"Yes. Wow."

The clean water tasted like heaven. Margo drank and drank again and forced herself to stop. Too much, and she'd be sick. She pulled bottles from her pack and filled them. This might be a place they could stay a while. If there was water, there was bound to be food around, too. Hydrated and hopeful, she herded Tara along the path of lights.

Tara practically bounced up a staircase. Margo smiled as she listened to Tara count steps beneath her breath.

"Forty steps all together!" Tara pointed ahead. "Look!"

The green lights stopped at a door. As they approached, it withdrew into the wall with a slight hiss. Margo held out an arm to keep Tara from dashing ahead, nine iron aloft.

Ahead of them stood a child. She looked . . . perfect. Clean. Groomed. Like a photo shoot from a catalog. A lacey white cardigan clutched the slight swell of her breasts and contrasted with an A-line pink skirt. Straight blonde hair fell to her shoulders. A pink bow perched above one ear.

"Hi!" Her cheeks were rosy as she grinned. "Welcome to Simulated Innovations. I'm model 31145 A. Nice to meet you! Are you a technician with security clearance C?"

"No," Margo said slowly.

"Oh, dear." The girl's shoulders slumped. She clasped her hands together and rocked back and forth in her Mary Janes. "Why hasn't anyone come in to work? Don't they realize they have jobs to do?"

"I might be able to help." Margo eyed the girl.

"Not if you don't have clearance!"

Great, a sim with a programmed attitude. Margo laid a hand on Tara's shoulder. "Maybe you can help us, then. My daughter needs recalibration—"

"Oh. She's a model 311337 B and obsolete." The girl made a slight sniff. "But even if she was a 311338 or 311339, she couldn't recalibrate. There was a fatal flaw in the chamber design, and the company ordered maintenance to replace the recalled parts, but no one's come to finish the job."

"What?" That couldn't be right. The chambers couldn't be offline here as well. She lunged forward to peer into the room.

The laboratory stretched for seventy feet or so, the stark walls and beams immediately familiar. It looked like a larger version of the calibration laboratory in Riverside. The individual chambers were stripped of their walls, wires and gadgetry exposed. Caution tape, toolboxes, and barriers surrounded the site. Everything left waiting for workers who were either long dead or long gone.

A low, agonized wail escaped Margo's throat.

In that instant she felt the shadowy compression of the hospital walls, the harshness of antiseptic, the soft and steady beeps of the machinery that kept Tara alive. Her Tara, the Tara she birthed in eighteen hours of labor, the little girl obsessed with butterflies and Harley Davidson. At age six, after months of chemo, she was so small, so frail.

"I'm scared, Mommy," her flesh-and-blood Tara had whispered. "I don't want to die."

"We won't let you die," Margo whispered back. "You're going to be our little girl forever." Even then, technicians from Sim Inno crowded the room and bustled behind her. Ready for Tara to die, ready to revive her.

"Mommy? What's this mean? Can't I get all better?" said Tara. She stood in the hallway of Sim Inno. Dirt smudged her face, that miniature replica of Doug's nose.

A small hand as strong as iron clenched Margo's wrist. "You don't have security clearance to go in there," said 31145 A. Her voice sounded cheery, her skin warm and human, but her grip had all the flexibility of rebar. Margo had the strong hunch that if she made any move forward, her wrist would snap like a twig.

She stepped back, her mind reeling. The sim relinquished her hold, but the pain of that inhuman grip lingered. "Don't say that, Tara. We'll find a way." Somehow. They had come this far. Margo looked at 31145. "She's suffering cascading nanite failure. She needs recalibration or . . ."

"That's not a surprise since she's a model 311337 B. What's she experiencing now? Peripheral neuropathy? Temporary paralysis? Memory errors? Soon her personality nanites will succumb and then—"

"Tara's not going to forget who she is!"

"Yelling at me isn't going to help. I didn't create such an inefficient design. Do you have any idea how wasteful their glucose-caloric burn was?"

Margo's fingers clenched the club even harder at the use of the past tense. "There has to be something we can do. Instruction manuals or something." Never mind that Margo had trouble loading Windows on her old computer. For Tara, she'd try.

"There is one option." The sim's face brightened as she held aloft one finger. "Hey, sisters?"

A door across the hall opened with a slight pop. Another 31145 stood there, smiling. Margo whiplashed her head looking between the rooms. This new sim looked identical but for a blue bow on the head, and behind her—God, it was a whole line of them. Margo shivered at the freakiness of the clones. Even Tara made an odd sound in her throat and backed up, her fingers clutching at Margo's thigh.

"That's a lot of twins, Mommy."

"Yeah." A sudden cough shuddered through Margo. Already, she craved another drink.

"These are my sisters, B through M." 31145 A's tone was cheery as she stepped into the hall. "We're all happy to see you."

"Hi!" "How are you doing?" "What's up?" "Konichiwa!" The greetings rang out at once, followed by girlish giggles.

31145 A sashayed around them. "See, we can't recalibrate either, and we're having to be super careful with all our supplies." She pointed at Tara. "We need your help! Your glucose can be recycled, and recycling is so, so important."

"I like helping! What's my glucose?" Tara asked, her brow furrowed.

"Recycled?" Those words seized Margo's mind. "That doesn't . . . no, you don't understand—"

"As model 31145s, our glucose management is both efficient and our functions are an integral part of this facility. We really, really, appreciate your help!" The girl reached for Tara, still smiling.

Margo shoved Tara behind her and brandished the golf club. "You're not touching my daughter."

31145 A did a very pre-teen eye roll. "Oh, come on. She's already in catastrophic failure."

"Yeah, I mean, nothing should go to waste," said the unit with the blue bow. She and the others poured into the hall, the sims nodding and murmuring in agreement.

Margo almost tripped as Tara stopped moving. "She will never be a waste!"

One of the sims lunged forward. Margo hesitated only for a split second, seeing that perfect catalog image of a child's face, then swung the nine iron with all her strength. The club smashed against the 31145's cheek. She stumbled back with a shriek, setting off an echoing cry among the others.

"Tara, run for the exit!" Warm glucose dribbled down the shaft and pooled at the base of her thumb.

"I did good! I did good! I did good!" Tara's words slurred. Margo spared a glance behind her. One of Tara's eyes drooped in the socket, the surrounding skin sagging. Hemispheric paralysis.

Oh, God. Not this, not now. "Tara, go to the exit. Hurry!"

"I did good! I did good!" Repeating the phrase, Tara turned and walked down the short hallway, her left foot dragging.

Margo pointed the golf club at 31145 A. "Do you know the addresses of any local scientists, people who work here? People who can get the chambers working?"

People who were evacuated, or dead. But she had to ask, she had to do something. She hadn't come this far to give up.

"I did good! I did good!" The faint voice continued behind her.

"You don't have clearance for that information!" said A, her voice shrill. The 31145s stepped forward en masse, forcing Margo back. Something clattered behind her. Metal on metal, squealing.

The stairs. Tara's paralysis.

Sims forgotten, Margo burst down the hallway and stopped at the railing. Three flights down, Tara lay in a twisted heap. A small puddle of pink expanded around her. Her head—her spine—nothing looked as it should.

Margo had no memory of walking down the stairs. She was suddenly at the bottom and dropping her heavy backpack to the floor. Her hands hovered over the twisted wreckage of her daughter.

"I did good! I did good!" The tumble had degloved half her metal skull; a vellum-thin flag of skin and scalp draped over her shoulder. *Tara looked like a robot. She was a robot.* Burst veins oozed pink. Below—her arms and legs were scraped, but her spine—God, her spine. Her head twisted the wrong way around.

Stabilize her. Stop the bleeding. Margo's brain fumbled into crisis mode. She ripped open a pack of synthetic skin and pressed it over Tara's face, covering an empty eye socket. Where was the eye? That didn't matter now. She patched here, there, staunching the flow of circulatory-glucose.

Margo exhaled in slight relief, and then gray, gummy fluid dribbled onto her hand. She frowned and wondered what it was.

She looked down. The immediate glucose loss had been averted, but now gray sludge oozed from the break in Tara's neck.

Nanites. The central nervous system had ruptured.

"I did good! I did good!" The slurred words had softened.

"What happened?" 31145s crowded the railing above. "Oh! What a waste! She's bound to—"

Margo huddled over Tara with a feral growl and scooped her into her arms. A misaligned rib poked Margo's chest. Warm fluid coursed down her arm, soaked her shirt, her skin, and deeper. Footsteps pattered down the stairs. Margo ran.

The walls of the facility blurred and then she was outside, dashing across the parking lot, toward the hole she had cut in the fence. The sun pierced her eyes like a laser as she glanced back.

The 31145s had stopped at the front door, their programming apparently preventing them from leaving the building.

Margo kept running anyway. "I'm sorry, I'm sorry," she whispered to Tara.

"I did good. I did good."

Across the parking lot, through the fence. Down the street where not even dust had the energy to whirl.

Freed of the backpack, everything seemed lighter. The sugar, the supplies, they didn't matter.

What mattered, now?

Tara was dead. She had been dead for over two years. Margo had always known, on some level. What she held in her arms . . . that was the last part of Tara. A part she loved dearly, more than anything else left on this shattered earth. But it wasn't truly her daughter.

That didn't make this any easier.

Margo collapsed in the shade of a nearby building, unable to breathe. Black dots swarmed her vision.

"Mommy?" The word was scarcely audible.

Tara still knew her, despite the nanite loss. Margo hunched over, sobbing. Tara blinked her singular eye.

"It's okay, I'm here," Margo said. "I'm not leaving you."

"I fell. I couldn't stop it."

"I know, sweetie, I know. It's not your fault."

"This doesn't hurt, not like last time. I don't really feel anything right now. It's not bad, really."

Margo stilled. "What?"

"The last time I died. It hurt a lot then. It hurt all over."

"You're not supposed to remember that." Sim Inno, they said those things were filtered out. Tara was supposed to remember to age five, roughly, except for associative data.

This was associative. Death remembered death.

"You were there, and Daddy." Tara's smile wobbled on her lips. "It'll be nice to see Daddy again."

Margo couldn't speak, couldn't think.

"I love you, Tara," she finally whispered. "I will always love you."

Tara's smile was distorted, but it was still her smile. "I did good. I did good." Tara breathed the words.

"Yes, you did. Always."

Tara's voice trailed to a whisper, looping until it stopped completely. Margo pressed her face against Tara's cheek, absorbing the realism of her skin. Warmth flowed against Margo's lips and invaded her mouth. Sweet, fruity. *Delicious.* She knew it by the scent: circulatory-glucose.

Almost gagging, she recoiled, staring down at Tara. Despite her mangled face, Tara looked at peace. Margo's hands shook. Her parched mouth salivated in response to the liquefied sugar.

Slowly, her tongue eased out to lick more from her lips, and then her fingertips, but her thirstiness didn't subside.

The backpack was gone. She had no food. No water. Margo stared down the street the way they came. The children. The ones Tara wanted to be friends with. They were sick, starving. Margo was a nurse. Circulatory-glucose was food, calories. And she knew where they could get more, and water. Tara was the key. Her palmprint could get them back into Sim Inno. All they had to do then was find a way to defeat a small army of freakishly-strong pre-teen clones.

"We can help your friends, just like you wanted," Margo whispered, rocking Tara.

She couldn't help herself. She dipped her hand into the sticky glucose on Tara's arm and, closing her eyes, brought her fingers to her lips.

The sweetness brightened the darkness, and she drank it up.

POST-APOCALYPTIC
CONVERSATIONS WITH
A SIDEWALK

EMMA TRIPPED but the sidewalk caught her. As her bony hip and shoulder met the concrete, the surface beneath her softened to the texture of the foam pads she once used for tumbling exercises in school.

"Oh dear! I'm terribly sorry. It seems my third panel developed an uplift of four millimeters. I do hope you're all right. Should I summon assistance?" The voice was young, female, and perky, though not obnoxious in a morning talk show host kind of way. The sound came from the sidewalk itself.

Emma lay still, breathing fast in shock from the words, not the fall. "You . . . the sidewalk, you talked?" Her voice was creaky with misuse. The surface hardened beneath her.

"Why, yes! I'm Cy Anara, the Friendly Sidewalk™. Good morning. I apologize for the uplift that occurred while I was offline. It has now been corrected. Do you need emergency help?"

Emma rolled herself to a crouch and blinked tears from her eyes. How long had it been since she heard a human voice—even from a computer? She glanced around. The street was a ruin, like the rest of the city. A blackened sign read, "-OSPICE CARE." That explained the modified sidewalk. Her own grandpa had died when a fall and hip fracture led to pneumonia.

"Can you summon emergency care?" she asked.

"Yes!" A pause. "Oh dear. It seems the network is currently down. The response status is not listed, but I've queued your request."

"It was worth a try. How . . . how long were you offline?"

"It seems I've been offline for seven months, five days, and three hours. My average offline period is three hours, nine minutes."

No one had walked this way since the attack, then.

"I really am alone," she whispered. All alone here. Maybe in the country, the world. If the blasts hadn't killed them, the virus had.

"You're not alone. I will stay online as we await emergency responders."

How had the sidewalk's computer survived the EMP? Luck? Surely something like this hadn't been kept in a Faraday cage. She stroked the surface. It still felt like concrete but with the tiniest of give.

"Do you always talk to strangers?" A hysterical titter escaped her lips. She was talking! To a sidewalk!

"No one is a stranger to a Friendly Sidewalk!" said Cy. "I act as greeter for Twin Doves Hospice. I track a daily average of fifty-three residents and twenty-two regular guests to the facility. It's my hope that you'll become a regular, too!"

About half of the hospice had burned. Emma should investigate. She could always use more food and clothing for the stockpile, but she didn't want to move. She sprawled out on the sidewalk, quiet sobs shivering through her body, her backpack a heavy shell.

"I . . . I'd like to become a regular. Can you tell me about Friendly Sidewalks? How large an area do you cover right here?"

"My sensors are distributed across ten panels of sidewalk directly in front of Twin Doves Hospice. I take care of my residents. Since you're interested in Friendly Sidewalks, would you like to be sent an introductory document regarding our systems? We won't subscribe you unless you opt-in!"

Ten panels. It'd be wonderful to bring the device home, but Emma had no idea how she would go about removing such an inlaid system. "You run on batteries? How . . . how much power do you have left?"

"Yes, I run on batteries! My current battery life will keep me online for one hour, thirteen minutes. Oh dear. It seems I'm overdue for my annual maintenance. I have queried the network. The system is currently down, but I'm sure a technician will respond shortly." A pause. "It's been three minutes since I requested emergency care for you. I apologize. I'm querying them again."

"One hour, thirteen minutes." Emma moaned against her fist. "Please God, no. I want to talk longer than that."

"I apologize for the limits of my battery. This should have been addressed in my maintenance, but the problem is currently queued. I don't believe I heard a reply from you regarding more information on Friendly Sidewalks. Again, it's totally opt-in after the initial mailer!"

The sidewalk was cool against her cheek. Rough, porous, soothing. "Friendly Sidewalks. There are more of you?"

"Why, yes! I'm glad you asked. There are twelve Friendly Sidewalks within a ten mile radius. We're currently hosting a scavenger hunt. If you visit all twelve locations, you get an eco-friendly water bottle! Please visit our site for the full rules and regulations."

Emma scrambled to sit and unzipped her backpack. She cracked open a notebook warped by rain and tears. "The locations? Can you tell me?"

"Of course!"

If this one survived, maybe some of the others had, too. Maybe they had more juice in their batteries. She scribbled down the addresses and filled two pages. "How much battery life is left now?"

"One hour, five minutes remaining. The maintenance system is currently unresponsive. I've queried again. Do you still need emergency care?"

Yes. Emma stood. "No . . . I, I'm going to go now. I need to go. I can't . . . I can't use you up all in one shot. I'll be back tomorrow. I promise. I'll be a regular." She stepped into the gutter. "Bye."

"I'm glad we're friends! Good-bye, from Cy Anara, the Friendly Sidewalk!"

Silence.

Emma stared at the sidewalk for a few minutes and then hurried on, notebook in hand. Food could wait.

She had more friends to find.

A DANCE TO END
OUR FINAL DAY

THE WORLD WOULD END AT 6:09 P.M., but Meg's final batch of chocolate chip cookies would be done in three minutes. She had kept the dough in the fridge all night, chilling it to perfection, and began to bake before the sun even rose. It's not as though sleep had a point.

Will couldn't grasp the concept of cookies for breakfast. "First we eat our meal and then we have treats," he said, his thin brows drawn down in concern.

"That's how it usually is, but—"

"First we eat our meal and then we have treats, or we get in trouble," Will said. He ate most of a bowl of cereal before reaching for a cookie. His remaining marshmallow bits and milk congealed in a rainbow puddle.

When he was done, a brown smear of chocolate traced his lips. "And now we go to school."

Meg glanced at the clock. "Yes, we usually would, but there's no school today. We get to play at home instead." The oven buzzed.

Will bounded from his chair, his socked feet padding on the laminate. He stood in front of the wall calendar and pointed at the date. "Not a weekend. Not holiday." He pressed a hand against his forehead. "Not sick. School day."

Meg set the cookies on the stove top and took care to turn off the oven. She followed him to the door, her steps dragging. Arguing with him would only lead to a tantrum, and that could last for well over an hour. That's not how they needed to waste their final day.

"Okay," she said. "We'll go to the playground at school." Will shoved his feet into his shoes without undoing the Velcro.

The crisp fall morning chilled her nose. Will's feet crunched across the fallen leaves as his arms outstretched like wings. His backpack seemed bigger than his body, as if it would swallow him whole. With dread in her gut, Meg glanced up. The sky appeared normal. Deep blue, with feathery cirrus clouds drifting high. The news had said they wouldn't see anything here. The impact would be in the Indian Ocean, not far off Sri Lanka.

Eerie quiet filled the street. Cars cluttered driveways. Will noticed none of that, all his focus on following the line along the right edge of the sidewalk. At the intersection, he came to a stop.

"We look right and then we look left and then we look behind," he said. The fast grind of tires on the street made Meg dive forward and press a hand against Will's shoulder. A van rolled by without bothering to stop. "And now we have no cars!" They crossed, Meg glaring at the van's red taillights.

The school's chain link gate dangled open. Not a single car in the parking lot. A frown distorted Will's face. "We have no friends today."

"No. It's all yours, little guy. Go play."

He tossed his backpack at his class's line up pole, and then ran for the slide. The empty swings squawked like crows as they swayed back and forth. Will squealed as he went down the slide and sent up a spray of sand at the bottom. "Still no friends! We are first in line!" he shouted, running to the ladder again.

Meg crossed her arms, warming her fingers in her armpits. How could he possibly comprehend the end of the world? This was the boy who had memorized the first fifty pages of the dictionary and could regurgitate the contents verbatim, but couldn't use a proper pronoun. He laughed again, sliding down with a whoop. White sand speckled his pants to the knees.

His pants reminded her of the laundry load she'd put in the dryer just an hour before, of how she needed to fold it once they got home. By all accounts, tomorrow humanity would be extinct, and yet she felt the overwhelming need to get the towels put away.

"We climbed to the top!" Will said, his arms straight up as he slid. He hit the sand and leaped up, pirouetting in space, and landed in a crouch. His little hips swayed side to side as he danced to his mother.

"No bell," he said, looking around. A chocolate mustache still framed his upper lip. "No friends." He glanced up at Meg. "Mommy sad? Sad we have no bell?"

She wiped the tears from her cheeks. "Yes, Mommy is sad that there's no bell."

Will bounced in place. "We keep playing? Do swings?"

"We can stay as long as you want, Will."

His eyes bugged out. "Forever-ever?"

Meg laughed so hard her stomach ached. He had quoted a line from one of his favorite TV shows. "Yes, forever-ever."

He ran for the swings and threw himself onto the black seat belly-first. His fingers combed furrows in the glittering sand. "Forever-ever, forever-ever," he sang in a high-pitched voice, giggling at some private joke.

Meg sat at the base of the slide, elbows against her thighs, her chin resting in her hands. Ten hours until they would die, and here was her piece of heaven.

A Lonesome Speck
of Home

THE GODDAMN ROBOTS were at it again.

Victor scowled out the living room window at a panorama of churning dust and powdered debris. "Get off your damn phone," he muttered into his cell phone, pressing redial again and again as he encountered a busy signal.

Not another house remained standing on his street. Most of the trees were gone, too, nothing more than toothpicks along the cracked and crushed sidewalk. Telephone poles leaned together as if consoling each other. He saw it all with his eyes, yet refused to let reality sink in. The lot across the way still belonged to the Smiths; old lady Periwinkle should still be next door. The hum of his generator covered up the whistle of the wind across the trampled desert.

The receiver at his ear clicked. "Major General Montague's office," said the slick voice of the clerk. Victor made a quick tweak to his hearing aids so he could hear through the din.

"This is Victor Lynch," he yelled. "I'm calling because—"

An especially heavy thud jarred the house, and the shiny butt of the two-hundred foot Mega Robot skidded parallel to the street, over where the Clarks and Smiths used to live. The rainbow-patched robot scrambled upright, its massive black and pink metal feet stirring up dirt and crushed concrete.

"Yes. You again." The clerk did not sound enthused.

"Damn it, transfer me to Montague or—"

"Or what?" The gruff voice of the general took over the line.

"They're at it again! Mega is fighting some new alien that just landed. It's blue with a boar's mask. Now, you said you'd get some planes in here—"

"Victor, you're an idiot. I said I'd get planes in there if I could, but I can't." His voice creaked. "We have other attack zones in progress across the country right now, and some of those are near high density areas. I'm sorry—"

"My life's in danger here! I'm a United States citizen!"

The boots shoved backward and the new robot's feet dominated the window, all shimmery and turquoise. With a spur of rocket boosters, it leapt up. Heat lashed Victor and he stumbled backward. The window throbbed, new cracks in the surface zigzagging like lightning bolts, but it didn't shatter.

"You're in danger because you're a stubborn old fool. No one is holding you prisoner. It's only by sheer luck that your house is still there. If you get stepped on, it's your own damn fault." Major General Montague paused, taking in a sharp breath. "Victor, I've known you since I was a kid. I can't change your mind, and hell, I'm tired of trying. I'll make sure there's an honor guard at your funeral."

Dead air filled the line. Victor stared at the cell phone and slammed it shut. Arrogant jerk. Victor put every last dime of savings into buying this house thirty years before—his perfect little retirement bungalow out on the fringe of Palm Springs. At sunset, the brown hills formed a craggy silhouette against a spilled-watercolor sky.

Now, the property wasn't worth squat. Insurance didn't give a damn; invasions of alien robots fell under some 'Act of God' clause. He had mucked through monsoons in Korea and Vietnam, spent a few decades with a bottle permanently adhered to his hand, and finally emerged sober and divorced. This house was all he could rely on. His family—damn them all. Not even his grandson Ned would stay loyal forever.

The boar-faced robot jabbed Mega, sending the rainbow robot flying backward. The boar pivoted, and Victor already knew its intended target: the high school. That's all the invaders cared about.

There were a lot of theories about these damned alien attacks, but two things were clear: they always took place near high schools, and some colorful robot always rushed to the schools' defense. Therefore, the school was intact in the midst of No Man's Land. Idiots on the news kept saying the attacks were some plot to slaughter the younger generation, which didn't make much sense since the schools all shut down when the attacks began. He recalled that a few campuses had been destroyed in some other states, though.

Not that it was any loss. These teenagers were all morons, anyway. Education wouldn't seep through those thick skulls.

Grabbing his shotgun, Victor headed into the front yard. The grass had died but his beloved rose bushes along the sidewalk were still alive, though they had shed every petal. He had planted those roses for his wife back before the divorce, and those blooms had stayed prettier a lot longer than she had.

Years ago, he had busted some girl stealing his blooming roses. Yelled at her, made her cry. The next morning, he found a wrinkled five dollar bill beneath a rock on his front step. Victor stared down the street. That kid was probably dead in the initial attack, or had been evacuated.

Mega swiped a leg, tripping the alien. It fell face-first into the ground. A cloud of dust obscured the action for a minute, and, when it cleared, Victor could see both robots upright and wrestling. They were near the same size, differentiated only by color and head design. Despite the dirt, their metal bodies gleamed, their curves elegant and smooth like a '55 Chevy. And the way they moved—God, it was like two snakes striking at each other, faster than a blink.

A lone missile plumed from the boar's back, the contrail curling like ribbon. The explosion flared between the two robots' faces. The boar staggered backward. Mega seemed unfazed as it reared back a blue fist and jabbed, sending the alien robot airborne. The boar arced high in the sky, heels up, and vanished over the hills. The ground shuddered.

Everything was still. He waited, watching. Was that it? After several minutes, Mega lifted its arms. What should have been a triumphant gesture seemed abrupt, tired. Mega's rockets flared, and it took to the sky. The day's battle was done.

He stared into the distance where the boar-headed robot had crashed. It hadn't looked too banged-up at last sight. The hills were littered with the carnage of past battles: half-busted metal craniums, fists, miscellaneous shrapnel, missile craters.

So much for his beautiful sunsets.

This new robot was worth checking out, but there's no way he could walk that far. He headed toward the house. Time to give his sucker of a grandson a call.

About an hour later, Ned pulled up to a crushed curb in his rickety Toyota truck. The young man leaned out his window to gawk at the neighborhood. "Pop, when you said you were the last one left, I didn't think you really meant it."

"It's still home." Victor heaved himself inside the truck, grateful the cab had plenty of space for his shotgun.

"Doesn't this get to you, looking out your window at this every day, knowing that most of them are—"

"I haven't cried in fifty years and I'm not starting now. Are you going to drive this damn thing or not?"

Ned hunched over and shut his trap. They drove a few miles into the hills, dodging extraterrestrial scrap metal, and found where the boar-headed robot had skidded to rest. Ned whistled as he debarked.

"Wow. It looks pretty good." He tossed his keys on the seat.

Victor marched towards the head where the cockpit surely lay. Ned moved about as fast as Jabba the Hutt and had a similar body type, but he tried to keep up.

"Something smells like bacon," Ned said between gasps.

"Yeah. Him." Victor pointed at the snout-faced alien draping from the robot's mouth like a flaccid cigar. "Saw one of these guys last week during a battle. Shot him dead. He was stuck in your grandma's roses."

"Grandma hated those roses."

"She sure did. Hated them so much, I got the house in the divorce. I love those damn flowers. God, why do these things have to be so blasted huge?" Victor couldn't climb up the slick surface of the arm, so Ned helped. By the time they reached the top, both were panting and soaked with sweat.

Victor hauled the pilot's carcass out and let it roll down to the desert floor beside the robot's armpit. The glass windshield of the cockpit had shattered cleanly. Black scorch marks showed the damage the craft's own missile had caused. Ned climbed over the edge and fell into a massive chair big enough for two. He filled it.

Victor leaned over the robot's lip. Lights and buttons flashed along the console.

"The computer looks like it's functioning," said Ned. "Look at that." He motioned to something above Victor's head.

The old man lay on his back and gazed up. The screen depicted a satellite view of that high school down the street. An overlay showed circles and lines of what he could only guess to be missile trajectories.

"Why the hell is that high school so important?" he asked.

"Why are any of these high schools important?" Ned's thick fingers glanced along a switchboard. "I mean, there are about fifty of these attack zones around the country, right? Plus all the places abroad."

"Yeah." He gnawed on his chapped lip. "You like computers. Why don't you play around with this thing for a while?"

"Play around? No! God, no! I don't want to launch nuclear missiles by accident."

"Out here, no one would notice the difference." He slid out of the cockpit and sat upright, letting the blood return to his head. "I'm going to borrow your truck for a while."

"What? You don't even have a license anymore." Ned's hands gripped the chair arms as he tried and failed to pry himself up. "Pop, no—"

"I'm going to check out this high school. I'll be back later. Don't break my robot."

"Your robot? Pop! Stop! You need to call the government. Don't leave me with this thing!"

Victor didn't stop. He blocked out the yells, just as he blocked out the vision of ruins beyond his front door.

Debris pock-marked the sprawling school grounds. The doors to the main building remained locked, but a gate creaked open. Not even birds chirped. At least cemeteries had birds and greenery and flowers.

Victor hunched his shoulders. How many had died in the first robot attack? Thousands. It had happened at the butt crack of dawn. No one saw it coming.

A tattered United States flag dangled from a pole in the quad. He paused for a moment. Back when he was a kid, that flag meant something to him. Then: blood, death, loneliness, a homecoming to derision and indifferent children, an inebriated haze, abiding loneliness. The latter, at least, was a conscious choice.

Now he had his house. That, and his pride.

Victor's hearing aids picked up the distant low murmur of voices. He pressed his back against the wall, rifle barrel against his shoulder. His shadow stretched long against a cinderblock wall. He rounded the corner to find a door ajar.

Hot, stale air pressed on him like a blanket. Voices echoed from down the hall. Damn. Vandals. Nothing was sacred to these punks. He sidled down the hallway, his left knee creaking in rhythm with his steps. A wall display showed chemical compounds and twined DNA ladders. The door to the next classroom stood open.

He propelled himself through the doorway, bringing the gun

level. Five kids in colorful costumes sat on the floor surrounded by an array of liquor bottles. Victor opened his lips to scold them, then noticed the wall behind them was a rippling iridescent portal like something out of a goddamned movie.

His jaw fell limp, and he stepped forward.

"Stop!" The girl in turquoise leaped to her feet. "Don't move."

"Or what?" growled Victor, brandishing the rifle. The first six inches of the barrel vanished. A cascade of gray dust drifted to the floor. He scrambled backward, staring at his lopped-off firearm.

"It's a force field," said the boy in red, his words slurred. "If people wander in and see that," he jabbed a thumb at the portal, "they waltz right into the barrier. Never knew what hit them."

"Damned alien technology." Victor eyed the invisible wall, but couldn't even see a distinct line in the ceiling or floor. However, he did see dust. Piles of it, on both sides of the barricade. "You're prisoners? Where are the guards?"

The kid in yellow laughed. The sound edged on maniacal. "Prisoners? You have to ask if we're prisoners?" He flung a bottle. It arced straight at Victor, and then was gone. Only amber dust drifted across his chest. "We don't need any guards, not with that thing."

"You should have just let him walk into the barrier," said the kid in red.

"No." The girl in turquoise sat down again. Straight black hair draped to her jaw in crude chunks, as if hacked with a dull knife. Sweat glazed her dusky skin. "You're the old guy in the last house. The one who won't leave."

"Yeah. And what the hell is this?" Victor jerked the gun barrel towards the portal.

"God. Just go away." That came from the kid in yellow. "You don't want to know."

"That's the dimensional shortcut that leads directly to Mega." The girl in turquoise said it matter-of-factly, then whipped her head to look at her companions on either side. "Someone needs to know. One of these days . . ." Her voice cracked. "I want someone to know. Someone from our neighborhood. We can tell him. He's already proven he won't leave." She tilted back a bottle of hard lemonade as if to fortify herself. He stared at her. Why did she look so familiar?

"She's right." That came from the slender girl in pink. "The military knows, and they're still alive. Why not him?"

"The military knows?" Victor took in everything. "You all pilot that Mega Robot. And you're drunk."

The pink girl waggled a finger. "We're drunk now. This is our little celebration for another battle won. There won't be another fight until tomorrow, at least."

"Tomorrow. God, tomorrow." The red-garbed boy shivered.

"I want to know what's going on," Victor said.

The girl in turquoise set down her bottle. "It's pretty simple, re- ally. We're unwilling contestants in the ultimate intergalactic game show run by these aliens called the Gonquins. We were selected be- cause we're considered the optimum age group. Teenagers. A dozen of us were grabbed, all honors students. We have to protect the high school using Mega."

The high school. The robot. The pieces slipped together in Vic- tor's mind. "So what is this, some damned game of capture the flag?"

"Yeah, but the game is rigged. It doesn't matter how many times we win. If an alien pilot defeats us once and destroys the school, they own the region. That's it. Game over."

The boy in yellow nodded. "The Gonquins look at schools like churches or something. Nothing is more sacred. Having one at stake and eventually blown up is like some big alluring taboo."

"In our case, when someone else wins, it means they own all of southern California," said the kid in red. "They can do whatever they want with it."

Victor gnawed his lip as he thought. "Some high schools have been destroyed. Damn. So the kids' robots lost those battles?"

"Yeah," said the kid. "In New Jersey and Detroit."

"Goddamn. No wonder no one knows the difference."

"The aliens like to see everything destroyed," said the girl in pink. "They cheer. It's like that old TV show with the home videos, and how everyone laughs when a guy gets kicked in the nuts." She clenched her eyes shut. "The Gonquins laugh a lot."

The girl in turquoise pointed towards Victor. "We're all that's left of our school's pilots. The others couldn't take it." She nodded towards Victor and took another long guzzle from the bottle.

He didn't need to ask how. Twelve. Now five. God, all that dust along the barrier wasn't just dust.

Victor forced his gaze to the teenagers in their sleek suits. He knew these kids. Not by name, but from the neighborhood. Staring through blinds day after day, he'd see them walk to the basketball courts down the street, or play in the Smith's yard across the way.

"Your families are dead," he said.

"Yeah." She frowned into her lemonade. "We couldn't warn them or anything. We either sit here or in the lair with Mega, or walk into that force field. Zap." She flared out her fingers. "A Gonquin brings us food and whatever else we need." She tossed the bottle across the room where it landed atop a stained glass mountain of broken bottles. "You don't know what it's like doing this, day after day, knowing that if we don't win . . ."

God. Victor knew. Not with stakes this high, but he knew. He knew about the jungle and dead friends and how his heart galloped as he listened to the whistle of dropping shells, wondering if the next would land on him. But damn it, he'd volunteered. He was an idiot, but a willing one. These kids—and they were kids. Goddamn, two of them were pizza-faced, and only one of the boys had facial hair.

Heat stung his eyes. This wasn't right. Nothing about this was.

"With so much in the neighborhood gone, it makes me smile to look at your house sometimes," whispered the girl in turquoise. She lifted up her chin, and for a split second he saw her as she used to be, all pudgy-faced with wide, dark eyes. "The rose bushes are about the only green things left."

He stared. "That's who you are. You're the kid, the little thief. The one who paid me for the roses."

She didn't meet his eye. "Yeah. For my mom's birthday. She loved them. You never caught me after that, but I kept taking roses, every year. I didn't always have money, so I would pull weeds from the sidewalk, save your newspaper from the gutter, stuff like that." She smiled into the distance. "Mom loved those roses."

"How much does the military know about this game?" Victor asked, his voice rasping.

"As much as we do, I guess. They aren't allowed to interfere or they forfeit the entire country. All they can do is help refugees and monitor everything."

No wonder Montague couldn't bring in planes. Everyone in this was powerless, even the kids with their rainbow robot. Victor refused to be powerless. He was eighty-one years old. What did he have to lose, his life? His house? His roses? The thought of those bushes only bolstered his resolve.

"I want to know the rules of this game," he said.

She shook her head, shorn hair sticking to her cheeks. "The rules are simple, but they won't do you any good. The winning pilot has to be in a combat robot, defeat us, and must destroy the entire high school. That's it."

"It doesn't matter where the pilot's from?"

"No. They win for their home planet. These contestants come from all over. Why? You have a spare robot in your backyard?" She snorted and reached for another bottle.

"As a matter of fact, yes I do." A slow smile crept across Victor's face. "I think it's time you threw the match."

She leaned against her sweat-soaked leggings, thoughtful, and said nothing for several minutes. The others looked at each other, communicating something beyond words. Then, slowly, each of them nodded.

The girl stared into her white-gloved hands. "We'd—we'd have to put up a fight. It's all for entertainment. If it's too easy . . ."

"We can do this. It'll work."

"Yeah," she said, and each of them nodded again. "We're ready for this to end."

When Victor returned to the fallen boar-faced robot that evening, Ned awaited him, flush-faced and angry. He did not respond well to Victor's plan.

"Pop, no. I mean, Dad told us you're crazy for years and staying in your neighborhood proved it. But this? Trying to win some alien game show?" He shook his head, sweat flying. "No way."

"They told me how to operate the damn thing." Victor had retrieved a paper pad from his house and queried the kids on the basics, even sketched out schematics based on their descriptions. "It's meant to be piloted by a team."

"Team." Ned laughed, nigh hysterical. "You don't know the meaning of the word. And you ask me, after abandoning me in the desert all day? No. I don't care if you have every switch labeled with a sticky note. I'm not doing it. You're on your own from here. Literally."

Victor watched his grandson drive away. The kid was right to be angry. Hell, leaving Victor in the hills was probably safer than returning him home. And, when it came down to it, he didn't want to get Ned killed. Maybe it was for the best.

"I used to be part of a team," he whispered. Conrad, Jessup, Marco, Martinez, Belding. He hadn't thought of them in years, not since he saw them leave 'Nam in coffins too big for their contents.

Now he was part of a team again, and he didn't even know the kids' names.

Morning sun glared through the glassless cockpit. The robot lurched with each long stride and slid Victor side to side in the massive captain's chair. Along the dash, he had taped translations on usage and toggle functions. It would be enough to get the job done.

An alarm wailed above, a blue light spinning and flashing. The label: ENEMY IN PROXIMITY.

A distant roar came from behind him; Mega was on its way. Victor crested the last hill, kicking a decapitated robot head on the way down. It bounced across the deserted valley like an oversized soccer ball. His house looked like a mere anthill from this height and distance. It looked insignificant, and it was. Victor's gnarled hands clutched at the two-foot, wishbone-shaped steering wheel.

The roar behind him grew louder.

A yellow light began to spin. Incoming missiles. Time for evasive action. He couldn't help but grin. Although, that very type of thinking on the freeway had cost him his driver's license.

Victor threw himself forward, pressing down on two pedals. Cold air whooshed into the cockpit as the robot leapt up. His body jerked against the bloodied seatbelt, but it held. Rocket boosters rumbled from the soles far below. He glanced up and hit a sequence of three switches, pausing to look at his scribbled instructions, and then pressed a large green button in the center console. A screen dropped into his sight range: there was the high school, green-tinted, the trajectories highlighted.

Damn, where did Mega go? Victor hadn't enabled all of the screens, and he didn't dare turn the thing around too fast. The robot had to be somewhere above him.

He pressed the button again.

The robot rocked as missiles shot from barrels on each arm, three from right, two from left. Fluffy contrails arced towards the school.

God, let this work. Victor sagged forward, his heart threatening to pound out of his chest. He was too old for this damned stuff anymore. They had to make this look like a battle; like Victor won, fair and square.

"Mr. Lynch." The girl pilot's voice rang over a small speaker, as clear as if she stood next to him. "I just want you to know, we're okay with this. We're ready."

"What the hell are you talking about?" A panel to the right beeped in a steady rhythm. Victor frowned. The beeping was supposed to indicate the missiles' proximity to their target, but they were nowhere close to the school yet.

Alarms from Mega rang over the speakers. "You have to defeat us—"

"Defeat you? No, you didn't say it, not like that. Blowing up the school should be enough—"

"I'm sorry. We have to do this, or it wouldn't be over." She paused. "Thanks for the roses."

In a distant rainbow blur, Mega dropped out of the sky and directly into the path of the two left-hand missiles.

Victor stared out of the gaping cockpit, then at the dash, then back out. There was nothing he could do. Those kids—damn it, he should have seen this coming.

"You're all just kids," he whispered. He and his buddies used to be kids, too. That was long ago, so very long ago.

The first explosion caught Mega in the chest. Its arms pinwheeled backward as if to regain balance, then the next missile struck. Even from a mile away, the pressure shift rocked Victor in his seat. Mega became a towering inferno and crumpled to its knees.

Behind it, more explosions. Mushroom clouds billowed from the school grounds. When the dust cleared, the screen showed craters instead of buildings. The sirens silenced. Victor's hands fell limp in his lap.

Every screen above the console flared to life, more descending from the sides. They showed crowds of alien beings—some pig-snouted, others cat-like. Some he couldn't even describe beyond saying they were damned ugly.

He'd won.

Victor sat there a moment, staring at the screens, staring at the button labeled "REPORT TO GONQUINS." He finally leaned forward and compressed it.

"My name is Victor Lynch, and I declare this frigging victory for Earth." He didn't recognize his own voice. God, he sounded old.

The rejoicing on the screens didn't stop. This is what those kids had seen almost every day after killing someone, after stomping a five mile radius into dust. Even if they didn't kill their own families, the guilt was there, logical or not. And the aliens cheered.

It all became clear then. He saw his neighborhood and the lonesome speck of his house and how he had squandered the last fifty years of his life on bitterness. He had screamed at that little girl for clipping off a single rose. Now, when he would give all of the blooms away, there were no roses, no people.

Victor leaned against the console and sobbed.

LA ROSA STILL IN BLOOM

ROSA SPIED MASON MARCHING DOWNHILL, the formerly pregnant swell of his beer belly dwindled to a saggy bump. Morning light glinted along the barrel of the shotgun in his hands. She tapped her fingers against the windowsill and calculated the days since electricity failed: twenty-three. The chill of autumn crept into her very bones as the house creaked and sang to itself. As far as she knew, beyond their hill the human race had ceased to be.

Now Mason was coming to her, gun in hand. No attempts to hide, no subterfuge. Rosa's lip curled in disgust, even as fear fluttered in her chest. Such a lack of respect. He assumed he could waltz on in here, bully an old woman, and take what he could— probably all her food and the gas from her car. She turned from the window, her weight heavy on her cane. In the chair, Spritz lifted his narrow Siamese head, his front paws kneading the fur-coated seat.

Rosa sucked in a breath. Mason hated cats. Threatened to shoot hers more than once. Shot at everything else that wandered the woods, too, and claimed it all tasted fine with ketchup. And now he was undoubtedly hungry.

"Move it, niño." She shoved Spritz from the chair. The cat squawked, scampering for the back cat door. Where were the others? Lily ate from the cat dish still mounded with dry food. Rosa tapped the cat's hind paws and herded her toward the flap. Through the back window, she could see the two cats dash across the dry grass to the trees. She couldn't spot the others, but imagined they were out in the woods at this time of morning.

That hick brute of a man wasn't going to hurt her babies, or her. Her gnarled fingers clutched the knob of the cane. Who was she trying to fool? She could barely walk, much less fight. If Tomas were here . . . She hurried back towards the front of the house, her hip creaking almost as loudly as the wooden floor. Pausing, she evened out the rug underfoot, then continued.

Her hip, her cursed hip. It had shattered when she fell off the Bank of America building back in '83. Rosa thought it had healed just fine, even as Tomas scolded her to slow down, take it easy. By the time she qualified for a senior discount, a painful limp had replaced the skirt-swinging sashay that commanded the full attention of a room.

If this apocalypse had happened two years ago, Tomas would have gone up the hill, taken care of Mason from the start. Mason had always been the neighbor from hell: threatening the cats, roaring by in his truck in the wee hours of the morning, stacking rusted car carcasses in his yard in place of bushes or trees. Now she had to deal with him on her own turf. God help her. His thick boots shuddered through the old wooden porch, his thick brows and blood-shot eyes glaring through the front glass.

"Old woman, I see you in there." His words drawled like molasses poured from a jar. "Just open on up now." He waved the gun barrel in front of his face, as if she had somehow missed it.

She forced her spine straighter and hobbled for the door. Might as well open it, as the thing would probably shatter in a single kick. Tomas always intended to replace that. He intended a lot of things that never came about in that blur of chemo and endless appointments.

"Mister Mason." The lock undid with a loud click. "How are you?"

Mason worked something between his teeth and cheek. Rosa concealed her disgust behind a naïve smile. Life had required her to be an excellent actress, but her skills failed her today. Her trembling fingernails tapped against the door handle.

"I'm hungry," he said.

"Well, of course I am willing to share—"

Mason shoved open the door, almost striking a small side table loaded with picture frames. "I'm not here to share." He pushed past her and rounded the corner to the kitchen.

Well, he was going to be disappointed. "I saw you drive by a few days ago. What did you find out in town?" Not much, judging by the empty bed of his truck that evening when he returned.

He flung open a cabinet. "They had roadblocks set up outside. A few places burned. Carson's Corner Store was empty, and not much left in the Blue Circle Grocery, either. Word is that it was nuclear, in a dozen cities at once. Maybe more." He dropped a half-empty box of Ritz crackers on the counter. A few cans of tuna thunked alongside it. "No one knows when things will be up and running again. It's every man for himself."

His sneer told Rosa where she fell in that equation. "I feared as much," she said, her tone quiet. Nuclear. All the nightmares of her childhood come true.

Drawers opened with goose-like squawks. "Damn it, woman. Don't you have anything good? Half the cabinets are filled with cat food. I seen you do those big trips to the club warehouses down in the valley. Where's it all at?"

"It's been three weeks." Rosa met his glare. "But I assure you, I have plenty of toilet paper."

"I don't need your lip." He stabbed a grimy finger in her face. The blackened, jagged edge of a nail waved in the air like a flag. "Where's your food? You're still all fat and sassy. You got something."

His chest collided with her shoulder, bending her over the corner of the kitchen counter. His Clydesdale feet echoed heavily on the living room floor. "What's all this junk?"

"My life." Rosa's teeth ground together as he yanked a handful of books off the shelf. He tipped others, peering behind the stacks. Photographs swayed on the wall, as if she had taped crackers behind the frames.

"What were you, some kind of dancer?" Mason motioned to a picture of her as a mock Carmen Miranda. That head full of fruit had caused a week-long migraine.

"That was my day job, yes." And my night job involved hunting down useless punks like you, she thought. Her tongue wedged against the back of her teeth to force her to silence. Thirty years ago, he never would have made it off her porch. His lips would have kissed the knotholes.

Her hip griped as she edged forward. Deep in her chest, her heart twitched at the sight of his filthy fingers on Tomas's favorite philosophy tracts, his CDs, at how he tossed the family Bible on the floor; even if it hadn't been read in twenty years, it came from Mama, and that made it priceless.

He didn't look twice at the masks hanging on the wall, the ornate red satin with sequin roses; Tomas's blue mask hung right above. Foolish, she knew. The youthful her would have been appalled at the lack of discretion. But after Tomas died, their old secret identities didn't matter anymore. No one remembered La Rosa and El Toro, how they trolled the streets of Los Angeles through the '70s and '80s, a dam against the rising tide of gang violence.

L.A. had probably been nuked. She blinked back tears. Detective Johnson and his wife, the old commissioner, Duke, Rodriguez—all their old friends who still met for golf every Wednesday morning. Dead.

Rosa couldn't keep up as Mason fumbled through the bedroom. Photo boxes were dragged from under the bed and left half-dumped on the floor. Then the bathroom. He gasped in glee. Of course. An entire shelf was lined with pain pills, old expired ones from Tomas as well as her current prescription. She heard the trashcan upend, the shivering of the plastic liner bag, the rattle of the pills dumped inside. He came out with the bag swaying, his teeth a brown grimace of triumph.

"I need my pills," Rosa said, keeping her voice mild. Stupid,

stupid. She'd become so complacent, so normal, that she left everything in the medicine cabinet. She could picture the slow shake of
Tomas's head and the tsk-tsk of his teeth.

"You don't need nothin'." The bag made rhythmic sways as he
opened up the empty guest bedroom. He spat at the empty closet
and left the dresser drawers in a heap on the floor. He never relinquished hold of the shotgun, or of the bag of druggy delight. She
pursed her lips. That would slow him down. The man was like a
raccoon. Once he had hold of silver, he refused to let go.

"I do need my heart medicine. Take the codeine, but leave the
other pills for me, please." She couldn't contain the plaintive wail
in her voice.

Mason motioned the barrel towards her. "You know what? You
don't need any of this at all. This house? Nothing. I bet you still have
gas in that old Cadillac of yours, too."

She had suspected as much, but hearing the words made her
heart tighten in a knot. "But winter's coming soon, and—"

"This house will be perfect for me. It won't get nearly as cold as
up on the hill, and none of that ice, either. When people do come
to the rescue, this place is right off the main road. Not easy to miss
at all."

There wouldn't be any rescue, and not simply because Mason
would loot and kill anyone who came near. No one cared about
some remote unincorporated section of the county, not when mil-
lions were dead across the country. The world. Besides, left to his
own devices, Mason would overdose on those pills within weeks.
Maybe days.

"You're planning to kill me, then." Her voice trembled. What
could she do? Tomas was gone. She was a decrepit old woman with
a bad hip and an aching body. Maybe this was mercy.

"I do what I got to do." Mason's boots thudded across the living
room, and he paused as he faced the shelf again.

"Huh." He reached for a small statuette on the shelf. It was an
artifact of the 1970s, an ugly-as-sin big-headed little boy holding

up a Valentine. Tomas had bought it, back in the day. "My grand-mama used to have one of these."

"Everyone had them." Her voice shook.

"You got grandkids?"

She sucked in a small breath. He had recognized her as human. "Yes, five," Rosa said. Not by biological children, but the babies of the street children they'd supported over the years. Please, God, let them be alive. To survive those harsh years of neglect, then triumph with colleges and families and jobs, only for a bomb to go off and . . . She blinked back tears.

Mason cast her a sidelong glance. "Your old man's dead now, right?" His voice had lost its triumphant bluster, but his grip tightened on the gun.

Tomas's picture glared at her, one eyebrow arched. Ah, Tomas. He could still set her straight. Despair evaporated in her mind. No. She refused to give up on life. She couldn't.

"My Tomas died six months ago." She nodded to his framed photograph as she clutched the solidness of her cane. Maybe she could make this work. Maybe Tomas could still play her partner. "If you have to do this, then please, do it out at the edge of my back lawn. My Tomas is buried out there. Let me be near him."

Actually, Tomas was buried twenty miles away, just out of town, but the memorial along the edge of the woods could pass as a grave.

Mason remained quiet, his brow furrowed beneath his cap. "I can do that. Make less of a mess. I need this place. I don't got any more food, and I'm not going to share. I'm going to live."

"I understand." She did. It was one thing to point a gun, and another to use it. Mason was a bully, but no murderer. Not until today.

I am still La Rosa, she told herself, breathing through her fear.

She needed little prompting to go outside. He even helped her down the steps a little, one hand on her arm. She resisted the urge to strike him then, standing so close his tobacco breath seemed to stain the air. Rosa knew that with her back and hip as they were, she could never haul his body the fifty feet across the yard. The thought of that stinking corpse on her back steps—with her sweet kitties bringing morsels inside—made her gag. No, she needed to bide her time, just as in the old days. As Tomas would say, wait till moonlight reflects in their eyes.

The morning was brisk and blue-skied, complete with birds twittering in the trees. Rosa suspected the radiation wouldn't come their way for a while, or much of it. Not by the usual wind patterns. A white blur bounded through the leafless shrubs. Camille. Hopefully the rest of the cats had the sense to stay hidden.

"Where's this grave?" Mason asked. He used the barrel of his shotgun to adjust the angle of his ball cap.

"Just down the slope a little."

He grunted. His young, long legs passed her by. Rosa hobbled after him. Mason slowed as the grass ended. She quickened her pace, tears streaming down her cheeks as her hip clacked and fought against her.

Mason stopped, facing the woods. "Okay, old woman—"

The solid wood of her cane smacked across his face, twisting his body around. His cheek seemed to deflate, several teeth airborne. The next blow landed in his kidney, the knob of her cane so deep it threatened to impale him. Rosa's breath huffed and gasped, pain dizzying as she relied on the full pressure on her bum leg to keep her erect.

"My name is not 'old woman.' My name is Rosa Garcia." She smacked the opposite cheek. His jaw made an audible crack, like a breaking branch. "But you can call me La Rosa." The knob caught the scraggly cliff of his chin and jerked his head up and back. That pop was his spine. Mason's eyes rolled to white as he slumped to his knees and flopped over.

Rosa almost followed him down, gasping. The foot of her cane caught the ground just in time and she leaned heavily into the 40-degree angle. Killing. Today she became a killer, but not a murderer. Not like Mason. Back in the day, they had only killed three thugs, but Tomas had done all of the dirty work. Most of the criminals were left neatly hog-tied for the police. But this man, he needed killing. She smothered a sob against her trembling wrist.

"Oh, Tomas. Why did you have to leave me alone in a world like this?" she whispered. She had to kill Mason. She had to. Once he killed her, it wouldn't stop. Anyone on the road would become his victim.

Slowly, ever so slowly, she stooped to pick up the pump-action shotgun. With her short stature, she never favored long-barreled weaponry. She didn't fancy guns much at all, not after seeing what they did close-up. Rosa squinted. No release on the magazine. She held down the slide release until the chamber was empty, and then reloaded with a single shell. Mason hadn't been bluffing. That should have made her feel better. It didn't.

She set her cane against the nearest tree. With her toe, she dragged the bag of medicine from under Mason's arm and threw it behind her. The man still breathed, his neck crooked at an impossible angle.

"I could leave you here like this," Rosa said. "But I do believe in mercy." Out of habit, she motioned the four points of the cross and then raised the shotgun.

The blast sent birds fluttering from the trees. Rosa's ragged breath filled the vacancy of sound. She felt the urge to throw the weapon aside, but knew better. She might need it again.

She waddled back up the slope, shotgun, cane, and bag in her grasp. Pausing at the steps, she leaned against the railing. Round cat eyes stared from the rhododendrons. Her hip groaned, the fire burning deep in her pelvis. She needed food, then maybe she could stomach her pain medication. Then she could spend the afternoon burying the man.

Spritz had returned to his chair sometime during the drama outside. His head tilted against his stretched-out inky paws. Rosa shook her head in disgust. She set the shotgun in the nook by her chair, pausing to smooth the white doily on the back. The base of her cane lifted up the floor rug and revealed the hatch to the basement.

Her footsteps on the stairs were slow and pained as she took in her bunker of supplies. Hundreds of cans for cat or human alike, cases of cereal and granola, drums of water, everything they might need. This, Tomas had worked on, even hairless, his skin blanched like a grub. Because they saw the way of the world and how the gangs worsened, how world governments turned. They came here to retire, to get away. To be safe.

"I would have shared this with you, Mason." Her voice echoed against the ceiling. "I would have. I'm not going to live long enough to use all this." Her medications wouldn't last forever. But today, right now, she was alive. She fought back. She killed a man, and that act would not be in vain. The sun still rose each morning. Birds still tweeted. Her cats still shed tumbleweeds of fur around her feet. She was alive. She would keep fighting, even by herself.

Tears traced hot streaks down her cheeks. Rosa tucked a box of shredded wheat under her armpit and hobbled back up the steps to where milky morning light cast the floor in gray and black stripes.

CULINARY MAGIC

A RECIPE FOR RAIN
AND RAINBOWS

 THE WHOLE TOWN SHOWED UP for the big June
picnic. While Esther went off and played all those
little kid games, I helped Mama mind her table.
My Mama made the best pies in the whole valley, maybe the
whole world. She made every kind imaginable, all except pecan
'cause Esther was allergic. Mind you, her regular food was better
than most, too, but her pies were really something special. She won
the top prize at the county fair two years in a row until she stopped
entering. It wasn't fair to the other bakers, she said.

All of the pies sat in tidy white boxes with Mama's delicate
writing labeling the top. Next to us the other ladies sold lots of lemonade at a steep price. The entire proceeds from the picnic went to
the Doctorow Mine Widows' Association. Most everybody's husband or father worked up the mountain, and most all the women
were afraid to become members of the club. Mama always did her
part to help. Those ladies' casseroles kept us alive after Pa and Me-
Maw died.

Mrs. Patrick stepped up to the table, hesitating. "I think I'll get
buttermilk pie," she said.

Mama shook her head. "Amelia. You know you want apple cin-
namon."

Mrs. Patrick's eyes filled with tears. "That was Seth's favorite.
You know yesterday was . . ."

"I know." And she did, too. A box already had "Amelia Patrick"
written on it.

"You always know what's right," Mrs. Patrick whispered, pushing the dollars across the table. "The kids will like that. Maybe they can think of their big brother and not drive so careless on the highway."

I eyed Mama. They certainly would think of their brother, but not of his death. Even Mama's saddest-made pies weren't a mean sort of sadness. For me, they brought on the tightness of Pa's hugs and the way his shirt buttons had gaped on his big round belly and how his favorite chair stayed empty.

Mama smiled, watching Mrs. Patrick walk away. Mama was most always happy when she baked, and her pies made people feel that way, too. She called it empathy, sowing her feelings into the dough and fruit, making them taste the rain and the rainbows.

"Well, well," said a man's voice. I jerked up my head.

Mr. Reginald Yates was as old as Methuselah with a wild, wiry beard and skin as creased and dirty as an old wooden fencepost. Mama warned us to stay away from him ever since he got out of jail back at Christmastime. He lived down in the hollow on the far side of the valley. Mama's friend Miss Catherine said that was the closest a person could get to hell without moving to Yankee territory.

With sly fingers, Mama whisked the money box behind her back and to me. I hid it behind the stack of boxes.

"I want to buy a pecan pie," he said.

"I don't sell pecan pies." Mama met his steely gaze.

Sensing trouble, one of the lemonade ladies set off at a fast waddle towards where the sheriff's department had their dunk tank on the park's far side.

"Why can't I have my pie?" growled Mr. Yates.

"My Esther is allergic," said Mama.

"But I'm willing to buy," he said, then lowered his voice so only me and Mama were close enough to hear. "I've had my eye on you since your blue ribbon fair days. I know something's going on in those pies. I want a cut."

Mama recoiled. "Whatever do you mean?"

"It's marijuana, ain't it? I can keep it quiet, if, you know." He rubbed his fingers together.

"Mr. Yates." Mama's tone turned to ice. "I would never use any ingredient so vulgar. Leave this table at once."

"Or what?" He glanced at me, and then frowned and looked at the pie boxes. "If that's not the secret, what is?"

"It's not for you to know," she said. "I shudder to think about the kinds of thoughts that would make you happy."

I sucked in a breath. Never had I heard Mama so blatantly mention her special touch. Once, Esther said Mama's pies were magic, and Me-Maw told her to never say such a thing 'cause folks would talk, even if it was true. Me-Maw knew because she had the gift, too, and her mama before that. Mama said in a few years I could bake, and then I'd be a grown woman.

Mr. Yates's face turned a funny shade of red. "Why—"

"Reginald Yates." Three deputies stood behind him, two of them in long swim trunks with blotchy white sun block all over their bodies. The speaker, however, was fully dressed. "You causing a problem?"

"Ain't I always?" said Mr. Yates in a drawl. He gave Mama a pointed glare. "I still want my pie."

He turned and stalked off.

"Ma'am, I'm sorry about that," said the deputy. "We would have been here sooner, but . . ."

Mama waved her hand. "It's all right. He's gone now."

He frowned, fingering the bold buckle on his belt. "Well then, I may as well ask while I'm here. You got any strawberry left?"

Thank goodness the next morning I was the one who went out first to water the flowers. Pecans covered our whole porch. Mama made sure all the windows were shut and Esther's medication was handy. She called up the sheriff and the deputy that came said at most they could charge Mr. Yates with mischief.

We could hear them through the thin walls. "My girl is fiercely allergic," Mama said. I could almost see her puffing up like a hen.

"Tell you what. We'll clean it all up and wash the porch down for you, will that help?" he said.

"Mama's going to get all riled up," I whispered. "I hope she doesn't bake anything."

"She knows better," said Esther. She pressed her chin against her knees, her brown hair flopping down like a dog's long ears. "I just wanna go to school. The last week is all fun stuff and now I gotta miss out."

The next morning, Mama went out first to make sure it was okay. Me and Esther slurped up our cereal.

When Mama came in, her face was as white as if it'd been bleached.

"Mama!" I said, jumping out of my chair. "What's wrong?"

She held out her hand. From it dangled a shiny black stone on a hemp cord.

"Oh, no. Mama." I staggered to lean on the counter.

Esther looked between us. "What is it?" she asked.

Mama bit her lip and took a steadying breath. "It's the necklace we buried your Me-Maw in," she said.

"Then why's it here?" For a nine-year-old, she could surely be dense, but maybe that was good at a time like that.

"Why would he do something like this?" I asked. "It just doesn't make sense. All he wanted was a pie, why—"

"It's not just a pie to a man like that," said Mama. "It's control and anger and spite. He thinks he's being denied something, that he can push us around."

"I still don't get why Me-Maw's necklace—" Esther began.

"Ruth, get your sister ready for school," Mama said, then stopped. Her gaze focused on the aluminum pie plates stacked on the counter.

"Mama," I said softly. Anything she baked now would taste of sorrow and salty tears and Pa's funeral, but we'd still feel the compulsion to eat up every last crumb and relive every miserable thought.

She lifted her head and stared through me. "No. You girls are missing school again this morning. We're going to do a different sort of project. We need to teach Mr. Yates a lesson."

"But Mama, today is movie day and—"

"Esther." Mama wasn't in a mood for any whining. She fumbled through a drawer and found a notepad and a few pens. "You two girls are going downtown to ask everyone their thoughts and memories of Mr. Yates."

"Mama, you should really call the sheriff again," I said.

"This is beyond the sheriff." Something dark sparkled in her eyes. "I'm going to bake Mr. Yates a pecan pie."

A shiver traveled up my spine. For the first time in my life, I was scared of Mama.

When we were all done walking down Main Street, I left Esther at Miss Catherine's house in case Mama still had pecans out.

I expected the pie to be all done and ready, but Mama sat at the kitchen table, her head in her hands. The pie ingredients covered the counter.

"Here, Mama," I said and held out the paper pad.

Wet eyes peeked between her fingers. "I don't know about this, Ruth Annabelle," she mumbled. "I want to do this, I want him to feel . . ." She balled her fists, then got a funny look on her face. "Do you still forgive Derrick Johnston for running over Sprinkles?"

Well, that came out of the blue. "He didn't mean to hit Sprinkles, Mama, and we all know Sprinkles was the dumbest cat ever. Derrick was awful upset about it."

Mama studied me for a moment. "I can't stand to look at that boy, knowing how you cried over that cat." She sucked in a deep breath. "Maybe it's time for you to make your first pie."

My jaw dropped somewhere below the table. "You mean I mix it all myself?" I asked, almost squealing like Esther. "Not waiting at the table or in the living room?"

"Not this time." A soft smile warmed her face. "You're my sensible girl. It's time to see if you have the gift."

She stood behind me, her long arms overlapping mine. "Think on Reginald Yates, how he must have desecrated Me-Maw, how he wanted to sicken Esther."

The anger welled up in me like a tight red ball, a clenched fist.

I began assembling the pie crust ingredients. Shortening, butter, salt, cold water.

"Now think on everything you wrote down from your walk in town, Ruth. You mix with your fingers. I'll read." She set her reading glasses on. "Reginald Yates was a devil from the time he was a boy. It was his ma and pa's fault, treating him like a do-nothing, so that's what he grew up to be, a do-nothing."

The tightness inside me loosened, dripping like a bloodied nose. Every push and knead of my hands, I felt more droplets fall. Mama read on.

"I think he stole three lawnmowers from the front of my store. I reported it, but they never busted him. Then he had the nerve to come in two days later and buy extra gas cans. He smirked. I could have slugged him."

The dough was done, pressed into an aluminum pie plate. Without speaking, Mama motioned to the contents of the pie, all the syrup and pecans.

The old oven preheated, clicking and creaking.

"My daughter said he did stuff to her, but there wasn't no proof, and after that she went to live with her daddy down south and I wonder if that's why. I miss her so much. That Yates should never have been born."

Never been born.

A waste of humanity.

A drug addict, a molester, a sorry excuse for a man.

The pie slid into the oven and the door slammed shut, and all around me the world throbbed and wavered like I was in the oven, too.

He dug up Me-Maw to steal her necklace, all to spite Mama.

He tried to sicken Esther. Ran down puppies and laughed about it. Set the high school on fire.

Never should have been born.

Then, like a yellow flash of lightning, it was gone. The anger, the rage, the frustration at Mr. Yates causing so much grief for so many people.

Mama caught me against her shoulder.

"I want to hate him, Mama, but I can't, I can't," I said, sobbing. "He never had a chance. He's awful and he's mean, and I feel so sorry for him."

"Oh, Ruthie," she said, holding me there. Here I was supposed to be a woman at last, baking the magic in, and instead I soaked her shoulder through.

I didn't want my first pie tasting of sadness and anger and the hatred of twenty folks from downtown. I felt those final drops deep inside me, so deep it's like I had to hold my soul upside down to find them, and let them fall.

Peace crept over me like a rare snowy Christmas day, all cozy and perfect.

An hour later, the pie sat cooling on a rack. Mama was on the phone with Miss Catherine, asking her to watch Esther a few hours more. I figured my sister wouldn't be whining about missing movie day at school anymore, not after playing at Miss Catherine's house with her boys' load of video games and three puppies.

I heard the piece of crust hit the counter, but really, I felt it. It jarred me like a train coming down the tracks. Watching Mama out one corner of my eye, I reached over and grabbed the chunk the size of my thumbnail. Without giving it a thought, I stuck the piece in my mouth.

The crust could have tasted of bitterness, of a father yelling, and tangy bloody noses and playground dirt and rank prison laundry and everything Mr. Yates had lived through. Instead, the flakiness melted on my tongue and into something more. It wasn't the happy memories of Mama's pies. Instead, it tasted like the frozen lasagnas the mine ladies brought over after Me-Maw died, how the old hymns resonated through my chest during Sunday services, the harsh drumming of rain on the old roof right after the leaks were fixed.

It tasted like neighborliness, comfort, security. Hope.

The phone shut off. "We'll give the pie another two hours to cool and then we'll run it over to Mr. Yates's house," said Mama. Her voice lowered. "I'm proud of you, Ruth. If I had made that pie, he would have been dead and on the floor in his first bite. All I can think of is my mama ... Lord, I still need to report that to the sheriff, but I'm afraid to know the truth."

"He's still going to think we poisoned it, Mama," I said. My voice sounded strange and ancient to my own ears. "He never could trust a person, ever, and he had reasons. I don't know if he's ready for this sort of pie."

Mama nodded and laid her dishwater-wrinkled hand on my shoulder. "That's his choice then, Ruth."

I leaned against her hand. The warmth of her wedding band pressed against my ear.

"And we'll give him that choice and leave the rest to the sheriff," I said. "Your pies should always taste like rainbows."

"Can't have rainbows without the rain," she whispered, and I knew she was thinking of Pa and Me-Maw, 'cause I was thinking of them, too.

BREAD OF LIFE

IT WAS DANGEROUS—TRAITOROUS—for people to speak aloud of their memories of Earth. It meant they risked giving the Dendul exactly what they wanted. And yet, people often couldn't help but dismiss that peril when they entered Sonya's Earth Bread Shop.

Sonya looked up as a man entered her business. He was the typical sort. In his forties or fifties, his hair silver; not that different from her, gender aside. Both of them old enough to remember Earth in its glory. He paused at the door and breathed in. Grief flashed across his face.

"My god," he whispered.

"You must be Franklin with the order for rye. Your ship docked right on time."

Humanity had scattered across a dozen systems, yet Sonya didn't have to advertise her wares. Word managed to spread among any human crew members on the freighters and shuttles that passed through Kaji Station. Most ordered ahead to get what they wanted, but she always kept favorites on display. Bread rarely went to waste.

A thin visor wrapped around Franklin's eyes like a clear halo and did nothing to hide his dazed expression. "This place—how do you even get the ingredients?" He had a trim body like most deep spacers, as they relied on strict calorie packets when in transit.

"It's expensive. I don't make much profit." That was the truth. "I source my wheat and everything else through legitimate traders who specialize in human palatable foods. I beamed you that info when you ordered."

Sonya pulled out a bundle wrapped in white parchment. The paper was folded just so, as if she had swaddled a newborn baby.

"I read it. Maybe it seems too good to believe." He stared at the goods preserved beneath the counter's dome. "You have sourdough available in slices? And challah?" He leaned against the glass as if suddenly boneless.

Sonya stared at him, waiting.

"My grandmother. She used to make challah for holidays." He said it in the lowest discernible whisper. "This big braided round. She insisted it had to be done by hand, that it tasted best. The smell, when that loaf would come out of the oven." He inhaled, his breath rattling with checked emotion. "It even smells right here. I had forgotten. It's been so long since . . ."

The Dendul had obliterated Earth.

To them, humans radiated potent emotions in a way unlike any other species. Spoken memories, in particular, exuded deep flavors that the Dendul absorbed to ascend into a state of blissful intoxication. When they scorched Earth, their intent wasn't to slaughter the majority of humanity. No, they ripened memories for harvest.

"Most every culture on Earth had some kind of bread," said Sonya. "I make it all. I hear it all. I think almost everyone had a grandmother who baked. I even have people who come to me for those old commercial sliced breads."

He laughed, high and giddy. "The stuff in every kid's lunch box, with peanut butter and jelly, or that god-awful bologna. Even that sounds good these days. This challah in here? How much—" He blinked as she beamed the new total to his visor. The non-vocal response was habit for Sonya; the Kaji regarded the mention of money as crude. "I'll take the rest of that loaf. There's a woman on my crew . . . this will mean a lot to her."

Sonya wrapped it up. "Thanks for beaming your payment promptly."

He nodded as she passed the bagged bread to him. "Yeah. Yeah.

You do this . . . why? Doesn't it drive you crazy to remember what we lost, every day?"

"It would drive me crazier not to."

He backed away, his gaze distant, and said nothing as he departed.

Sonya looked up at the obscured sensors that recorded their conversation at much deeper levels than mere vocalization. A human with synesthesia might hear music and see colors; for the Dendul, Franklin's brief, emotional story would evoke catatonic ecstasy.

The Dendul had tried torturing humans to force out memories, but physical pain tainted the results. Made them bitter. Alcohol also changed the flavor in a distasteful way. The words had to be provoked in an unimpaired, natural way.

Many Earth foods proved to be good bait, but nothing was as powerful and universal as bread.

Sonya reached into the flash freezer for another loaf of challah for the dome, and to ready her next orders for the day. Portuguese sweet bread. Pita. Ciabatta. She breathed in the redolent, yeasty smell.

This memory trap was for her own selfish needs, too. To draw in the few humans who came to this far station, to hear them whisper history as a conspiracy. She drank it in. Savored it. As if she still ran the counter at her father's bakery in Denver. As if she wasn't on a revolving rod in deep space, a speck in a Diaspora of a million remaining human souls.

The door chimed and a white-haired woman entered. "There really is a bakery on this station! The smell here. It reminds me . . ." She drew silent, her expression pained.

Sonya said nothing. She waited. The stories would come.

STICHED WINGS

MADELINE FLED from her new governess and into the shadowy strangeness of the garden.

Strange, this garden, because she and Mother had scarcely been in that house for a week, and more so because Mother had expressly forbidden her from that part of the property. That made the garden the ideal hiding spot.

After their months in the desert hinterlands of Drell, the greenery of the stone-walled paradise delighted Madeline. Panting, she paused on the coarsely-laid brick path and breathed in the muskiness of lichen-laden branches. Something about such places always made her feel indescribably alive; Mother seemed to react similarly within her laboratory, surrounded by oil cans and metal detritus.

"Gertrude! Where are you, child?"

The voice carried over a great distance, but Madeline bolted forward. She needed to hide from Miss Shelly, and fast.

She crawled between grasping shrubberies, wiggling on her knees without care for skirts or lace. There, within a tiny cathedral of boxwood branches and desiccated leaves, she spied the fairy in the cage.

The fairy sat, twiggy legs akimbo. His tunic shirt and trousers seemed woven of moss, the intense green almost camouflaging him against the grass flattened by the cage. With one hand he wielded what appeared to be a whisker or quill, and with the other he held together a tidy stack of overlapped leaves.

"Hello!" A real fairy, in her garden! Madeline's filthy skirts rustled as she sat. "What are you doing?"

BETH CATO

"Makin' me wings for fall." He didn't look up. "Us lot, we make wings with what we 'ave."

"Who set the trap? Is it meant for fairies?"

"Haven't a clue who put the blimey thing here, but here it is, eh?" He lied. He knew. The awareness tasted like pickled onions— oh, how she hated pickled onions.

"I can let you out." She needed to let him out. Cages reminded her of Father, in his box.

The fairy met her eye then, gaze baleful. "I'm just idling for a while, minding me own business." More lies, with a hint of garlic.

He tested the hold of his spider-silk thread. The newly-sewn wing featured an array of small leaves in a dozen shades of orange and vermillion. His sort of sewing looked interesting—not at all like the drudgery Miss Shelly expected of Madeline, forcing her to sit with feet rooted to the rug as she stitched the hours away as a proper girl should.

Madeline had no intention of being proper. Mother had taught her that much, even as Mother expected domestication from her.

Madeline sat back, frowning. "What's your name?"

"Snuggleweed Rothchild the Third." He stitched another leaf into place.

"You're lying." The stench of his words made her stomach roil, though his untruths were nowhere near Mother's grand scale.

"That's the smartest thing you've said yet, it is. And what's your name, then, eh?" He met her eyes then, so briefly, and they pierced her in a way that made her shudder.

Names had power, Mother had said, which was why Madeline was not allowed to use her true name wherever they lived. With a name, they could be discovered by reeves, or soldiers, or worst of all, bank investigators.

"Gertrude," said Madeline, and tasted the foulness of her own lie on her tongue. Gertrude, her new name in this new place.

"Gertrude." The fairy chortled. "You lie like a fairy, you do. Mightily impressive for a human child of your age."

She pondered him for a moment. "Fairies lie a lot?"

"'Course not." He tied off the thread.

The sourness of his words lingered. She lifted the gate of the trap. "I don't want you to lie to me anymore."

He scowled at her most fiercely. "Well, now you dunnit. You done me a kindness and now I'm in your debt. If you'd left me alone to do me spot o' sewing, life woulda been much simpler."

"I couldn't just leave you like that. You could've starved to death." Madeline shuffled back to give him space.

He shuddered. "Even worse, a life debt. Damned and double damned." He ambled to freedom, and a peculiar smell grew stronger—that of fresh-cut grass, mouth-watering cheese, and dusty cat.

The fairy stood only two of her hands-spans tall, his body emaciated in the way of a deep winter twig. "I mighta lived. The queen coulda saved me. She could bust through that iron, maybe. Iron's tough on fairy magic, even hers, and she's the most powerful thing in this whole forest, she is."

Magic! Mother had recently muttered about magic as she studied her blueprints. Madeline clasped her hands. "Do you use magic to make your wings?"

"To attach 'em, sure. We gotta stitch wings each season, as magic fades after a time."

He held up his new wing. Bending his gangly arm in an impossible way, he angled the wing to rest at the top of his shoulder blade. That bizarre smell of him increased, as strong as the aether and butane in Mother's laboratory. A few twitches and the fairy stood straight. The wing had attached, even through his mossy shirt.

"Amazing!" she breathed. He did look a little smug at that. "And your queen can do much more?"

"Most assuredly. Glow like the sun, she can, though not much call for that sorta thing."

"Does she lie, too?"

"Best liar o' anyone." His truth was sweet as nectar.

"Ger-trude!" The two syllables belted out, off-key and far too close. Madeline and the fairy cringed.

"It's Miss Shelly!" Madeline looked around, keenly aware of the brightness of her red dress and the patchwork cover of the autumn foliage. "I'll have to talk to you more later."

"As you will," he said, though didn't seem entirely displeased. "Crawl straight on, huggin' the wall like them vines, 'n she won't see you. I best go deeper in the woods, avoid more temp-pa-ta-tion from these cages."

"Why? What's the bait?" she asked, angling her head around.

"Sugar cakes." He sighed his delight. "Bait like that, 'm bound to be caught 'gain."

Madeline could well understand that. "G'bye, Sir Fairy!" She choked back a yelp as the nearby garden gate creaked and footsteps crunched on dry leaves.

"Sir!" The fairy's voice was faint, but delighted. "You honor a nobody like me, little liar-who's-not-lying."

She wormed her way through the jasmine as she faintly heard him say, "And jess so you know, the name's Rowan."

Truth.

Rowan hadn't been lying when he said his queen was the best liar of all, but Madeline knew that was only because he hadn't met her mother.

Madeline sat at the big long dining table. Glass windows poured ruddy sunlight into the room, like pomegranate juice from a pitcher. An old servant shuffled to bring out food from the kitchen. Beside Madeline, Miss Shelly sat rigid as stone, napkin tucked over her lap just so.

Across from Madeline, Mother's place was set, food steaming in wait, as always.

At the head of the table sat the biggest lie of all: Father's seat. Food awaited him, as it had every night as long as Madeline could remember, even though he had eaten nothing in over five years.

When she was younger, she had believed the lie and thought Father would whirl through the door at any moment, smelling of horse and dusty roads, and his saber rattling at his side. She still recalled his fervent love when he looked her in the eye—she could taste it, sweet as sugar cakes—and the potent foulness when he walked towards the door so often and said to Mother, "I'll see you soon, my love."

Lie, and lie. The former was the realism that came with being a soldier, as he was most always away; the latter, because Madeline knew the love that made him return home from each campaign was for her and her alone.

But Mother's love for him was true and absolute. She was absolute in everything she did.

"Ah, dinner!" Mother entered the room, demure in a clean frock. Gloves covered the permanent stains of oil within the creases of her hands, and the two stubby fingers from an explosion last year. "Good evening, everyone."

Mother's chipper mood was a shock, nearly as much a shock as the elbow that jabbed into Madeline's ribs. She lurched to her feet at Miss Shelly's prompt. "Mother," she said, curtsying, and Miss Shelly stood and did likewise.

"Gertrude, my darling." Mother stepped close enough to plant a fleeting kiss on her cheek. By habit, Madeline did not cringe from the fog of falsehoods that clothed Mother. Indeed, her very clothing was false. Mother could play the part of a proper lady better than any actress on stage, but she was neither. She was a scientist and a thief, and Madeline was not sure where one ended and the other began.

She had, from a tender age, understood there were certain things not done by proper ladies.

Proper ladies did not give false names to everyone they met, and different names in different places. They did not enter strangers' houses and leave with new jewels, which were then exchanged for jingling bags of coins. Ladies did not choose which households to rent by the ability to adapt chambers into laboratories—in the case of their current abode, a ballroom—nor did they often set such households afire or create other disturbances that required fleeing in the night. And foremost, ladies did not keep their dead husbands hard-packed in salt like barreled cod, and continue to haul their pickled life-mate by dirigible from city to city for five years.

Madeline remembered the day the soldiers came with their giant metal box. She had spied on them through a cracked door; watched Mother nod, stoic as always. After the soldiers left, Mother rested one hand on the casket, so briefly, and went straight to her drafting table to begin the first of her many efforts to resurrect Father.

Even tasting the truth as she did, part of Madeline needed that lie, that sliver of hope, that Father would return. Love for him was the one thing she and Mother shared.

Mother's gloved hand caressed the back of Father's chair and she moved to sit opposite of Madeline. "Have you had a good day, my dear?"

"Yes, Mother." She tasted fermenting crabapples in the lie of Mother's love, and her own feigned obedience.

"She is doing well in her lessons?"

"Oh yes," gushed Miss Shelly. "She's such a bright child."

Madeline and the governess smiled at each other with the pleasantness of roving tomcats making an acquaintance.

"Good. My husband will be displeased if she's behind in her lessons." Mother began eating.

Everything Madeline did—her lessons, her etiquette training—all of it was a show for Father. She had realized this a few years before, around age seven, after an incident at a past residence. The staff abandoned them, and Madeline survived alone for a week and ate the pantry bare. Mother finally emerged from her locked laboratory and berated Madeline for not being clean— "What would your father say, if he saw you like this!"

Madeline stared at Father's chair as she chewed and wondered what he would say, about that and so many other things.

"I believe the master of the house will not be with us tonight, so you may go ahead and remove his plate," said Mother, motioning to the old man. "Perhaps tomorrow he'll return." Promise brought a rosy haze to her cheeks.

Something had happened in the laboratory today.

Madeline could not remember Mother being so happy since right before they had left the hinterlands—and then they had fled the city in the dark of night. Absolute dark, as the steam systems died, casting the streets into blackness that had rivaled Mother's ferocious mood. As their little airship rose, it was hard to discern the horizon between two spans of darkness.

"Madam?" The cook stood in the doorway, fidgeting. "I gots more made for you. Sweetened them up, I did."

"Very well. Bring them out," said Mother.

Madeline smelled the sugar cakes before she saw them. So sweet and citrusy, they brightened the very air. The tops of the little discs sparkled in the evening light.

Mother keenly inspected them, then took a precise, dainty nibble. "The sweetness could be tweaked," she said, one hand up to cover her mouth as she chewed. "Just a slight adjustment."

"Yes, Madam."

Why would a scientist like Mother want to capture fairies? She spoke of magic sometimes, true, but her talent was in machines.

"That reminds me." Mother pushed away her still-mounded plate and stood. "I do believe I'll walk in the garden." She practically skipped as she left.

A harsh doorbell resounded again and again from downstairs. Madeline placidly continued her stitchery, her posture perfect in the leather library chair. Finally Miss Shelly could take the obnoxious sound no more.

"Gertrude!" she snapped. "Continue your work. Where are those servants?"

Miss Shelly bustled off and closed the door behind her. Madeline lurched to her feet at the distinct click of the lock. The governess had locked her in! The nerve!

Through the floor, Madeline detected shudders and whirs. Mother was at work in her laboratory directly below, and had been all morning. Madeline could only hope to be so enterprising.

She tucked her needle into the canvas and looked to the rainbow-hued shelves around her. She could easily read away the hours, but she had no desire to read in captivity—she would be like Rowan, stitching his new wing within his cage. At the thought of the fairy, she dashed to the window.

The second story view showed several trees and the garden gate. She swung the pane outward. The peculiar magical smell of him tickled her nose, and she smiled.

"Rowan!" she hissed.

"What you goin' on about?"

It took her a moment to spy him, small and green-garbed as he was, perched atop a bush just below.

"Can you help me get out?"

"Mischief is a specialty of mine, 'tis true. Just jump down and I'll catch you, and bring that spot o' sewing in your hand so we can take a gander."

"You'll catch me?" The words confused Madeline, as they rang true. "How can you catch me? You're not even as tall as my arm!"

Rowan sighed. "You'll not come by harm, not from me. I'll keep you good 'n safe. This I vow, 'n folks like me don't take vows lightly, y'should know."

That truth shivered in its might.

Still, her heart twittered against her breastbone as she climbed onto the sill. She took two deep breaths, squinted her eyes shut, and jumped, barely swallowing a shriek as she fell.

Sticks cupped beneath her legs and grabbed her, sure and

strong. Madeline opened her eyes and gasped. Rowan was as tall as any grown man, his arms wrapped around her.

"How?!" she asked as he set her down on the grass. As soon as the warmth of his contact withdrew, he shrank down to normal size and scampered toward the bushes where they had met.

"Sizes 'n shapes can be lies same as anything, and like most lies, can't hold up for long. Come along now, girly-girl."

She brushed aside bared twigs as she crawled. "If you could get big, why didn't you break out of your cage that way?"

"Tut! That's iron. Binds magic within. Speaking of which, wasn't being exactly phil-ann-thropic when I brought you down." He pointed ahead to where the trap had again been laid, complete with a sugar cake. "See that? Stick me big-human-sized hand in there, and it'd box me magic right up. 'Fraid to know what'd happen ta the rest of me. There's a few more cages 'bout the garden now, 'n all. And a few missing fairy kin, dare say."

"Oh." She sucked in a breath. "I know where they are. Mother's setting the traps."

"Well, she can keep me cousin Dandelion. He's a twitter-twit, through and through. Here. Lemme see that stitchery you gots going while you fetch 'ere that cake."

She had almost forgotten about the sampler in her hand. She gave it to him, then disabled the trap and reached inside. The tiny cake was still soft, the dome crusted with turbinado sugar and candied bits of orange. Her mouth watered, but she offered it to Rowan.

"Split it as y' will." He unfurled the sampler on the grass between them. Madeline tore the cake in half, and Rowan nodded as he accepted his share.

The sampler was a twelve by twelve canvas, intended to be proof of her proper training as a young lady. Miss Shelly might be aggravating, but she did know how to sew, and her shrewd eye had honed Madeline's skill—well, prevented laziness, in any case. The sampler had been started only a few days before, but Madeline had accomplished an important bit: her name.

"My oh my, yes, I sensed the potency of this un from down here." Rowan traced a knobby finger along the "G" of Gertrude. "Lies are magnificent, knotty things, and this is a beaut. You must be havin' some fairy in yer blood, way back."

Madeline's tongue worked at a bit of candied fruit stuck between her teeth. "That doesn't make sense! People lie all the time, and they can't all carry fairy blood. My mother . . ."

"Oh, there's lies 'n then there's lies. It's how it's done, bein' aware of the words and still saying 'em. Some folks, they say a thing often enough 'n it become true to them, but not us fairies. Lies are Things."

"Do lies have a flavor to you?"

Rowan grinned, all gap-toothed. "Sweet as that cake."

"Oh. Lies taste bad to me, hearing or saying them."

"Sounds like some fickle human corruption of somethin' pleasant, it does. Fae blood's way back, but there, I'd bet me wings on it." Sure enough, he did have two full wings now, radiant in autumn glory.

"Ger-trude!" The syllables belted out from above, followed by a roar of rage.

"Does that mean I could stitch wings, too?" Madeline whispered.

Rowan tapped his chin. "I truly don't know that, girly-girl. It takes a lot of magic, doin' that kind of thing, even if you're fine with needle 'n thread. 'N what would you do with wings, eh? Big as you are?"

She averted her eyes, suddenly shy. "I don't know. Go away?" She grabbed a handful of dry leaves.

"Even when birds fly south, they know where 'bout they're goin'."

Madeline thought of the crazed moves with Mother, the rented houses, the midnight rides by wagon and dirigible, the names she had accumulated like dust after a hinterland windstorm. "Maybe I don't need to know where I'm going. Maybe I just want to go."

"Maybe." He squinted at her. "So why'd you let me outta that cage? And don't jess say you're bein' nice 'n all."

The suddenness of the question caught her off guard. "I—I had to. You didn't belong in a box. No one does." Not even Father, though she could never say that aloud. Mother's work had to come to some purpose, surely.

Rowan studied her for a long moment. "What'll it take to free you from yer cage then, eh?"

"I'm not in a cage! I'm here right now, aren't I?" The words, the thought, tasted as smooth as satined cream. She escaped Miss Shelly most whenever she pleased. How could Rowan even think otherwise?

The fairy's next words were so soft, the chilly breeze almost stole them away. "Told yourself that plenty, eh? Even caged birds 'ave space t' stretch their wings, little liar."

Madeline clenched her hand. Leaves crunched and crumbled in her grasp.

The next day, the estate emanated with heated sugar. Breakfast and lunch had been simple fare, as the cook was under orders to make sugar cakes all morning long—dozens of them. Hours later, the scent lingered even in the second floor library, where Miss Shelly drilled Madeline on numbers, letters, and how to walk with a dainty point to her toes. Below, ruckus radiated from the laboratory.

Madeline hadn't seen Mother since dinner two days before. If Mother had chosen to sleep or leave her laboratory, Madeline certainly would have seized the opportunity to sneak inside the repurposed ballroom. But Mother was in the full sway of her mania, and food and sleep meant nothing.

The busywork with Miss Shelly was good, in a way. It kept Madeline's dread to a tepid burble in her stomach.

Whenever Mother arrived at this point, everything always went wrong. Cities fell strangely dark. The house would burn. It meant long days bobbing on the wind, Father's coffin rattling within its tethers along with Mother's laboratory equipment.

The thought of leaving this place—and Rowan—brought tears to her eyes.

Something flashed by the window. Miss Shelly had opened the pane to let the sweet smell vent, and now Rowan perched on the sill.

Madeline forced her gaze to her verses on pistils and anthers. The peculiar odor of Rowan grew stronger as he flew closer.

"The queen is missing," he whispered, distress quivering in each word.

She sucked in a sharp breath. The fairy queen was the most powerful thing in the forest. Rowan had said so.

The floor rumbled underfoot as machinery clunked and groaned and whirred. Always, always, it was about Mother and her machines, about Father's dinner plate set and waiting each night.

"Please. 'Elp me."

The agony in his voice was what did it. Madeline closed her book and set it on the side table alongside her sampler and sewing kit.

"I need to talk to Mother," Madeline said to Miss Shelly. It felt strange and refreshing to speak such an outright truth. "She's doing something below, something very wrong."

"She is a busy woman and not to be disturbed. Now—" Miss Shelly's jaw fell slack. "Oh goodness. What is that . . . thing?" She froze, staring at Rowan.

Madeline cast him a quick look. "That's my best friend. Just wait here for me, please. I'll be back as soon as I can." Miss Shelly shrank back in her chair, and Madeline turned and walked from the room, empowered by honesty and rebellion together.

"Think the queen's below with all that thrumming and whatsits?" asked Rowan and he fluttered into the hall ahead of her. "Smells of metal, even from outside, it does."

"Yes. In Mother's laboratory." A place Madeline had not yet entered in this house. Fear quivered through her, just as vibrations quaked through the stairs.

"Queen needs a whole forest to let 'er magic breathe! Girly-girl, this is what's what. I'd gone mad, bound up with me magic in that iron cage for more'n a day, popped like a mosquito in a bonfire. Queen's got a thousand times more power 'an me."

She looked to him. "I'll get her out."

Rowan said nothing, but for a moment, the magic of his palpable faith squeezed her like a hug. She hadn't known such a feeling since Father died.

Madeline yanked on the double doors to the laboratory. Even with her full body weight pulling, they didn't budge. She looked to Rowan.

"Iron bolts inside, nasty stuff."

"The wall," she said. "It's wood and wallpaper, isn't it?"

"The metal's raised such a stink that I couldn't tell! Wood, I can work with, aye." He raised his hands. Starting at the baseboard, the wall tore like parchment and stopped at the same height as Madeline's tunnel through the brambles.

The noise worsened, the smell of oils and strangeness smarting at her nose. She dropped to her knees and crawled through, and saw Mother.

Here, the mist of deception evaporated from Mother's skin. She was utterly herself, surrounded by gaskets and gears, her black hair coiled so as not to snare, her brown dungarees happily layered in stains of various coloration. The vast room shuddered in cacophony, the racket made visible in the sifting of ceiling plaster and belches of steam.

Father's tomb rested nearest to the door. A habit, no doubt, from their quick exits from so many previous laboratories. He was fully encased, with pipes and tubes connecting him to the larger apparatus.

And now, Madeline could smell magic.

The potency was fiercer than Rowan's peculiar scent: a mixture of jasmine and garlic, horse sweat-soaked leather and the first rain of spring. Particulates gushed from vents in vivid hues of violet and green, shifting by the second like ornate stained glass rendered to powder against the light.

"She can't be contained!" Rowan's voice was scarcely a whisper against the din. He flew at a metal tank, but his leaf-and-web wings were buffeted backward by the awesome power that radiated from within.

"Madeline!"

Madeline flinched at the rare sound of her true name from Mother's lips. She took a step back, expecting Mother to fly at her, enraged at her presence. Instead, Mother glowed and spun in place like a girl gifted with a pony.

"This is it! I finally have a functional resurrection apparatus. Not even the steam generators in the capital created adequate power, but a fairy queen . . . ! It's the perfect meld of science and magic."

The vibrations intensified. Cracks lined the marble floor. A fog of powdered plaster burned Madeline's eyes. Gears clanked with the violence of a locomotive engine on the tracks.

Mother clasped her hands. Her voice was like a tinny whisper against the roar of machinery. "We'll have your father to dinner tonight, Madeline. Miss Shelly must curl your hair and press your best dress!"

"No!" Madeline shouted. "He's dead! He's dead! He's been dead five years!"

The joy on Mother's face didn't shift. She was oblivious, as always. Raw power stewed and swirled, and Madeline's lungs struggled against its weight and the heady scent of a hundred muddled things. The walls wiggled like an army of worms.

Yes, Mother had discovered a source of power. Too much. Mother couldn't sense it, not like Madeline, not like Rowan.

No fairy queen could be contained in an iron tank of that size, of any size.

Rowan flew at Madeline, his arms wide. Metal pinged and steam whistled. Bolts zinged free of a tank, the discordant symphony rising to a crescendo. Terrible tension quivered in the air as everything turned hot and cold at once.

Rowan grew to full human size, then more, his body seeming to expand like a sheet held to a gale. His bright colors dimmed as his essence poured out, thinning his body to translucent, and she tried to shout "Rowan, no! No!" but the cocoon of his power constrained any sound and suffocated her with its overbearing scent.

"Your vow to help me 'n the queen was good 'n true, and my vow to you stands jess as solid. I'm keeping you safe, Madeline-who-is-most-assuredly-not-a-Gertrude."

She didn't see his lips move, but she felt the words like needle pricks against her heart. Magic woven into the truths of a vow and a name.

Everything beyond turned red and black and pink, an explosion of color. A roar filled her ears and dissipated with a slight pop.

"Rowan?" Her whisper echoed in the vacuum. The house was gone.

Above spanned the cold gray autumn sky. No fire, no smoke. Rain filtered down, a rain of leaves in shades of brown with blackened specks. No, not leaves—books from the library. Shredded pages twirled and danced their way to earth. Not a foot away, her sampler sprawled out. The canvas looked splashed by yellow and blue dyes, but it was there, needle and thread still tucked to one side in wait of another dreaded session with Miss Shelly.

Of Mother's great machine, twisted pipes and mottled tanks remained, but Father's casket—the focus of that awesome power—was gone. Only two wheels and part of the brake system huddled there.

"Mother?" There was no answer, but that was so like her. A red blotch marked where Mother had stood.

Madeline knew she should cry—she had cried for Father late at night, so many times—but instead she blinked, dry-eyed, until she thought of Miss Shelly and the servants. Miss Shelly—Miss Shelly would have been standing in the library just above, waiting for her. Madeline had promised she'd be back, and she meant it. She glanced up at the gray sky as tears slipped down her cheeks.

"Rowan?" she called again, looking around. She spied a miniature mossy leg sticking from beneath a growing mound of paper.

She unburied him and touched his shoulder. His wings were gone—shredded to mere nubs. There was no need to check for a heartbeat or breath; she knew he was dead. He had given everything to keep her alive; his debt filled in full.

She blinked and breathed in the last wafts of magic as she sat on the crackled marble of the ballroom floor. Pages twirled downward like falling leaves.

Without his wings, Rowan looked incomplete. He needed to look true, and then she could take him within the forest—whatever remained of it—and lay him to rest.

Madeline reached for her needle and thread, fingers quaking, and cradled Rowan against one knee.

She plucked drifting vellum from the air. Just as Rowan had in his cage, she would use what she had. These wings would be stitched of abbreviated words and shredded rhymes. And when his wings were done, she would stitch her own.

Whether they worked by magic or not, it mattered little. One way or another, she would fly from this place.

That was truth.

MY BROTHER'S KEEPER

HALF THE COUNTY figured my big brother Samuel had bricks for brains. There was mighty good evidence in favor of that, like the time he decided to walk through downtown naked simply cause it was a hot day and clothes just plain didn't feel good. But I knew Samuel wasn't a dummy, just quiet, with his mind in a different place than the rest of us.

So when I heard him with two speakers of dark words, I knew to hunker down and listen. Here by the barn was the most private spot on our property—or would be, if I wasn't up in the rafters.

I smelled the bad guys before I heard them. Mama didn't get to teach me much, but she did teach me to heed my nose when it came to good and evil and all the gray in between, and those men stank like the septic tank being sucked out on an August afternoon. I gagged against my wrist to keep quiet, Mama's old chain bracelet warm at my lips.

"I want to kill Macaulay," said Samuel.

That name made me inhale with a hiss. Kill Macaulay?

"It's easy to kill someone you hate that much," said one of the men. "But if you want to join our circle, you can't simply kill for vengeance. It's too easy."

There was a long pause. "He's got a wife and kid," said Samuel. I recognized the scuff of his bell bottom jeans dragging against the dirt.

"Three," said a deeper voice, "There's power in that."

"Yes," agreed the other man. "You must kill the entire family, on the equinox, with this knife. Then you can join our circle."

"I want them books of yours." Samuel's drawl was slow, every word dragged out like his puffs from a cigarette.

"You'll have access to our knowledge in stages. It takes time."

"I can do it," Samuel said.

When Samuel took that knife blade in his hand, I felt the wrongness of it rattle down my spine. That knife was an ugly, cursed thing. The other men left, heading back down the trail towards the base of the hill. Samuel stood there, holding that thing, assessing it in his quiet way. I barely breathed. I kept a pencil frozen in my hand, same as it was when I first smelled them come my way.

After a while, Samuel thudded back down the hill. The stink of evil faded. Why was Samuel doing such a stupid thing? If Mama knew, she'd whip his hide. She'd been the only one to ever keep him in line, the only one who understood he was so smart underneath all that stupid. But Mama was dead and gone and beneath feet of red iron dirt, and now Samuel was set out to kill the whole Macaulay family tomorrow night, and for magic, too.

Anger got all tight in my chest. At least Samuel had some magic, had some words to go by.

I stared down at my half-done math homework. I hated math something awful. All those numbers danced around in my mind and the answers never came out right, but I'd rather do a full fifty pages of algebra than save those Macaulays.

Old man Macaulay was the one who killed Mama, blowing past the stop sign at Templeton Hill and crunching our car flat as a griddle. They said in town that Macaulay had enough whiskey in him to pickle him like a frog for science class, but he hadn't been the one who died.

I scampered up and left my math for the mice to nibble on.

Given my druthers, I'd rather help Samuel out than save those Macaulays, but Mama loved everyone. She used to be close to Grandma Macaulay, too.

Mama wouldn't want Samuel to meddle with darkness,

wouldn't want that blood on his hands. I just had to ignore whose blood it was.

Most all the other men around came back from Vietnam and fell into the bottle, but not my Papa. Nope, he fell straight into Jesus's arms.

Papa had the table covered with books for his seminary course and was all hunched over, muttering to himself. He didn't notice me going by, or flinch when I opened up a can of RC. But the second I headed towards my room, his pencil stopped scratching.

"Deborah?"

"Yes, Papa?" I turned around, the cola fizzling on my tongue.

"We're out of bread."

"I can go by the Pig later."

His head bowed over his work, and I moved on. I didn't have any kid brothers or sisters underfoot. Didn't need them. I had Papa and Samuel, and the fact that I was twelve didn't matter a doodle. I cleaned, I cooked. If it wasn't for the fact that I made Sunday dinner just like Mama, Samuel might have never visited the house at all.

I can't even say I held any fondness for Papa, not anymore. He was more like an extra piece of furniture around the house, something to take care of because it'd always been there. Just looking at him made that anger rise up again, all because of what he did the day after Mama's funeral.

He burned her books. The family books.

Mama never said that what she did was magic. It was as natural as breathing. The words were all for focus, she said. So she wrote down what she learned, just as her mama had, and her grandfather, and her great-grandmother. From the way Mama told the tale, her great-grandma was all sneaky about learning to read and write as a slave, and did it all so she could preserve the words and pass them along.

Papa burned every last shred of those books, a full century of songs about growing okra in a day, warding away mosquitoes, making babies form all perfect, and calling on rain. Papa sobbed as he did it, said that it was an awful thing that Mama was burning in hell right now, but he'd save us kids. I woke up because I felt the flames itching along Mama's old ink; it woke up Samuel, too. Mama had already started teaching Samuel. Me—she said I was too young.

Now I'd never know how to focus or sing the words, not unless Samuel taught me, and he didn't know much.

But I had been learning from Papa. Not that he knew those kinds of words, of course, but he had been writing down his experiences from Vietnam. Called it his "spiritual cleansing." Course, those weren't the kinds of things a girl my age should be reading, but it was an education in the ways a man could die and the way eating half-cooked chicken could make him pray for death as he spewed out his guts for days and days. I had the latest book tucked under my mattress, and just the other day I read something that would come in mighty useful.

Samuel was a big fellow at seventeen. I couldn't overpower him. I didn't even know where to find him now, though I guessed he was sleeping somewhere in the woods, somewhere within easy walk of our place.

Keeping Samuel away from the Macaulay's house would require some military strategy.

It would have been a brilliant plan if it hadn't involved math.

I spent the rest of that Saturday gathering supplies, so I headed out after dark to set everything up. I figured I had to establish a perimeter around the backside of the Macaulay shack, which would be the most direct way for Samuel to sneak up on them. Any car on the drive would be too loud. So, I snuck a full reel of fishing wire from Darrel Craigshead's garage, and a pop cap gun from Lewis

David's back shed, and I dragged myself through the woods to make a tripwire.

See, Samuel had this thing about particular loud noises—the pops of guns or firecrackers or car backfires. He'd cover his ears and hunker down and freeze. I figured that I could rig this tripwire and scare him away, and I could do it far enough from the Macaulay house that they might not notice. Turns out that farther away means a bigger perimeter, and big reels of fishing wire aren't so big as they look.

Also, it's cussed hard work in the dark, in September. My skin was sticky as a swamp.

I was so busy muttering that I didn't hear Ralph Macaulay till he was five feet away. He had a shotgun in his hands aimed straight at my head.

"Deborah Kinsey." His mouth gaped. The porch light from his house gleamed off his glasses. "What are you doing out here?"

Now I'd known Ralph my whole life but barely said more than a grunt. That's because from the very start of kindergarten, when I could barely count to ten, Ralph Macaulay knew his multiplication tables. Since 3rd grade, each afternoon he'd gone to the high school across the way to sit in on the advanced coursework. I hated him long before I hated the rest of his family.

"Ralph."

"You didn't answer my question."

I looked around. The pop cap gun was leaning against a tree way far away. I had no desire to confess to him that I was trying to save his no-good family from some sort of dark sacrifice.

His eyes narrowed behind that thick glass. "Is that an empty wire reel in your hand?" He stepped closer, his gaze on the ground. "You . . . what is this, some kind of trap?" The barrel raised towards me again.

"Oh, what, you gonna shoot me?" I was hot and sweaty and bone-tired. "I'm not setting a trap for you, stupid."

"Then who? Looks like you ran out of wire, anyway."

If I had possessed any understanding of how magic works, I just might have blown him up. "Yes, thank you so much, Mr. Einstein." How could he even tell that in the dark?

"If the wire's not for us . . . is it for Samuel?"

My jaw almost hit the dirt. "What? How?"

"Maybe you should come to the porch where there's light. We can talk there."

The thought of going near that house made my stomach clench like a fist. "Nuh-uh, I don't think so."

Ralph sighed, all deep and heavy. "Look. We know Samuel's up to something. I thought you were him, that's why I came out." He motioned with the gun barrel. "We know about the magic. Your mom used to come over and chat with Grandma about it all the time, about how it affected my dad, and me."

". . . You?"

"It takes different forms for different folks. For me, it's numbers."

"Oh." I couldn't help but ask. "Then what about your pa? He doesn't have any knack for math."

"No. No, he doesn't. He sees shades, and since he killed your mom, she's been clinging to him. She's the one who warned us about Samuel."

"Are you trying to tell me my mama's a ghost?" The thought didn't disturb me as much as it could have. I mean, better for her to be a ghost than to burn in hell like Papa said. I felt a bit of relief, really.

Ralph led the way through the brambles towards his house. "No. A shade is . . . a shade." Upon glancing back and seeing the dumb look on my face, he continued, "Ghosts haunt out of vengeance. Shades are like a shadow of a person, after the soul's gone on. If someone like my dad is responsible, the shade joins with theirs, like a reminder."

"So, Mama is clinging to your dad, and she can talk to him?"

I could talk to her? My heartbeat roared in my ears like a revved lawnmower.

"It's not that easy." Ralph stopped on the porch. "Dad dropped bombs when he was over there. That's why he drinks, to blur the shades all together. There are . . . a lot of them."

"I want to talk to him," I said, and went right up to the door.

"Deborah . . . !"

I didn't have Mama's insight, but soon as I stepped in that house, I felt that clog of spirits. Even with box fans bellowing at full blast, there was an extra stickiness to the air, something beyond humidity. Like cobwebs tearing against my face, prying at my hands. Raw frustration scratched at my throat. I wanted to see more. I wanted to see Mama. Hear her. Not just feel these . . . vapors.

Maybe if I had our family books, I'd know what to say so I could see, so I could understand, but I didn't have squat. I hated feeling so stupid and helpless.

But there was something familiar about the cobweb feeling. The air felt that way around Papa, too—not nearly this thick, but that weirdness was there.

"Deborah, listen. Dad says it's really noisy in his head. It took him weeks to figure out what your mama was saying. All he got out was that Samuel was going to come after us, and that you both needed to forgive and let go."

"Forgive?" I recoiled from Ralph. "Forgive your papa?" Mama would expect that of me. Mama always had high ideals like that.

"That's what he said, that's all I know."

"Is there a way to get the other voices quiet, so he can just hear Mama?"

"If he forgives himself and lets them slide away," he said, his voice low. "This point, they cling to him as much as he clings to them."

Ralph's papa lay stretched out on a couch. The blanket ended short, covering the nubs of his legs. At least he lost something when he killed Mama. His head didn't move but his eyes did, widening with something I could only call fear.

"No. Ralph, she can't be here." He pushed himself up on a flabby arm.

Good, he hated seeing me much as I hated seeing him. "My brother aims to kill you and Ralph and your wife tomorrow night. I'm aiming to stop him."

"Go away! You look just like her. God, you look just like her."

"What else has my mama told you? What can I do to stop Samuel?" What words should I speak? That's what I wanted to ask, what I wanted to hear. That maybe she had some legacy to pass along, just for me.

"God, get out of my sight! The shade is bad enough, I don't need you in color, standing there! Oh Jesus." He moaned and blubbered and he hid his face beneath a pillow.

I would have spit on the man but I saw the misery on Ralph's face, and for some reason I didn't hate him near so much now. Instead, I stalked outside and let that the old screen door shriek shut behind me.

Ralph and I stood there, staring at the dark outline of the pines for a time. "So," he said, a quiver in his voice, "How's he plan on doing it? Samuel, I mean."

"Some bad fellows gave him a knife. The thing is stinky evil. He's supposed to kill all you with it, then he's in their club."

"Oh." He took in a long shaky breath. "I can understand revenge against Dad, but . . . me and Mom, we liked your mom just fine." He hugged his arms close, like he was cold.

"Even I know there's power in threes. You're the math wizard and all."

Ralph shrugged. "I'll shoot Samuel if I have to, but I don't want to. How are you thinking to stop him? What magic can you do?"

I blinked back the tears and frustration, the musk of those burning books flaring in my nose like the fire was fresh-lit.

"You think I'd be laying tripwire at midnight if I could do something special?" My shoulders hunched up like they could hide my face.

"What? But . . ."

"I can't do a thing, you hear me? I can sense power, smell it, but I can't do anything. And Papa, he burned all Mama's books. I don't even . . . I don't even know how to learn. When you said her shade was in there, I thought . . ."

To his credit, Ralph didn't look at me, but at the woods instead. "I'm awful sorry, Deborah."

"Yeah." I didn't say anything for a minute, and just listened as the crickets hollered back and forth. "Why don't you all just pack up and leave the state for the day? Get away? He can't kill you if he can't find you."

"Dad's stuck on that couch, and Mom's working double shifts at the diner. She doesn't believe in this . . . stuff. She won't leave, and I won't leave either of them behind." His voice shook again, but he stood straight and tall.

I sighed all heavy. "I can't talk Samuel out of anything, either. Mama's the only one who kept him grounded. He only really comes home now to eat my cooking, cause I cook just like Mama. He probably hasn't said a word to Papa since . . ." I blinked. The cooking. I looked at Ralph. "Whenever I cook, Samuel always manages to show up, even though he's not staying at the house anymore."

"There could be something to that."

"Maybe." Mama always had said that recipes were a way of putting words together in that special way. But once I had Samuel there, I had to stop him somehow. Keep him from his awful ritual. Cooking wasn't the kind of power I wanted, but it was something carried down from Mama.

I thought back on Papa's diaries again, about his awful experiences with food poisoning, and I grinned.

At one o'clock prompt that Sunday afternoon, I set the last dish on the table. It was all Mama's best fixings, done in my hand: country-fried steak strips, fried okra, mustard greens, and cornbread. A lemon pie sat chilling in the fridge. Samuel slammed through the door at 1:05 with all the focus of a cat headed to a can of tuna. He grabbed a plate and started shoveling it in.

As for Papa, he was at the church, and would be all day. His books marked his place at the end of the table. Not for the first time, I wondered what he'd think if he came home to find them all burnt, but I knew it wouldn't mean a thing. He could just buy more.

I worked on dishes and eyed Samuel. He always ate his foods one by one and saved his meats for last. That steak strip coating's where I whipped in a hefty dose of ipecac. I threw together some barbeque sauce for dipping, with the hopes that'd cover up the super-sweetness of the syrup. I wasn't big on steak, so I could skip eating it and he wouldn't think a thing of it. I figured ipecac was made to make people throw up, so it'd do the job better than serving up half-raw meat. Samuel wasn't that stupid.

"Haven't seen you for a few days," I said.

Samuel grunted as he speared okra on his fork. The thick aroma of frying oil lacquered the air, but even so I could smell the stink of that knife. He had it clipped to his waist.

I wanted to watch him without looking like I was watching, so I sat down in an old recliner. Next thing I knew the light in the room looked something funny and Ralph was standing there, kicking at my foot.

"You were sleeping?!" His scowl turned his face red.

"I was up half the night! And what are you doing here, stupid? Do you want to get killed? Where's Samuel?"

"Out in the woods, sick as my old man after a night of drinking. Come on!"

I knew Samuel was up ahead on the trail, and not just because he was a veritable volcano of sickness. That knife stank like a manure truck.

"Ralph, you gotta stay back," I said, shoving him behind me. He had his shotgun, but by the quiver in his hands, he wasn't too steady about using it. Which was good. Samuel was already messing with his soul. If he died now . . . no, I couldn't let that happen. Not when Mama's soul was already in doubt.

Samuel was all hunched over and on his knees, his head in the bushes. The knife was on the ground right by him. I rushed forward, all sneaky-like, but not enough so. Samuel managed to sit up and clutch that evil thing close. He didn't say a thing, just looked at me, his face a funny shade of pale.

"Samuel, that thing is awful evil. You don't need that," I said.

"I do," he rasped. "If I want to get books that tell us how to bring back Mama."

Despite the sweet heat of the evening, all my blood went cold. "You . . . what?"

"I see the Macaulay boy." Samuel's thick fingers twitched on the knife's handle. "Got to do this."

"Mama . . . Mama wouldn't want to come back like that, Samuel, it's wrong."

"She's not going to burn!" Samuel's shout sent birds flapping from the trees.

Oh, no. That's what this was about, what Papa said. My own anger stirred up in my chest, fists balling. "Mama's a sweet and good person. She can't . . . she wouldn't go there." Would she? I didn't rightly know.

Samuel didn't need to say a thing. He worked to stand up, all slow. His pant hems dragged on the gravel of the trail. This was all about Mama, and not even revenge. He didn't care about his soul, what those dark words would do. He'd do it all to save her.

"Mama'd hate you for doing that," I said.

"Mama never hated a thing," said Samuel. He was right.

The first rock plunked Samuel straight on the forehead. He blinked, furrowing his brows. The second one whapped him straight between the eyes. He kinda tipped backwards and splatted on the trail. I stared a moment before looking at Ralph about fifteen feet back.

He held a palm-full of gravel, the gun at his feet. "Didn't want to kill him," he said. "It's all geometry and physics."

"Dang. If you could go all David and Goliath, why'd I bother poisoning him?" I started forward.

Ralph snorted. "You think he'd have stayed still like that if he felt well?"

The sheathed knife slid right out of Samuel's slack grip. He was breathing, his body still and limp as a sardine. The smell of that knife made me heave.

"What are you going to do with it?" asked Ralph.

I stared at that knife, focusing, trying to find words just like Mama. This was the important moment and all. This is when I needed that insight. Instead, the bugs just buzzed in the trees and my nose got used to the stink of the knife and I was left no wiser than before.

"Guess we'll throw it in the river," I finally said, hating how stupid and uninspired it was.

Ralph didn't say one thing or another. We headed through the trees and to the big river. This was the area where Mama said I could never ever swim because the current was so fast. I handed the knife off to Ralph, as he had math in his favor, and he prettily threw it some twenty feet till it splashed deep. Then he turned around and squeaked like a kitten.

Samuel stood at the edge of the woods. Well, hunkered there, leaning on a tree. His skin had an awful sheen, and a big old bump grew on his forehead.

"I don't get a second chance with them," he said, his words slurred.

It took me a moment to realize what he was talking about. "You shouldn't have even had a first chance with those speakers of dark words." I marched up to him. "Your soul's still clean. That's what Mama would want."

At least he wasn't doomed like her. I hated that thought, but it was still there, sticky to my brain like sweat on my skin.

"Will they come after you?" I asked.

Samuel jerked his head in a no, then leaned into the bushes. I waited till his guts emptied some more, then I grabbed him by the arm. Even with me half his size, I managed to prop him up and we staggered back towards the house. Ralph hung far behind, and I can't say I blamed him. The smell of my brother alone was enough to make a person gag, but at least it was the scent of sickness, not evil.

"How long will I be sick?" Samuel whispered.

That was pure Samuel. Didn't ask or care how I'd done it. "Till tomorrow, most likely."

We were halfway across the yard when I saw Papa's car parked there and heard the clink of silverware carry through the screen door.

I hadn't cleaned up the poisoned dinner. Papa was sitting down to leftovers.

Good, I thought. He deserved to get sick, sicker even than Samuel. This was all his fault, anyway.

Anger festered in my chest, all raw and awful, and that's when it hit me. Mama's shade hadn't been talking about forgiving old man Macaulay, though she'd want that of me, too. No, she was talking about Papa. Letting go of the anger about what he said. Letting go of the books and everything they meant. I blinked back hot tears.

"Ralph, can you wait in the barn?"

"Yeah. Sure," he said.

I wanted to speak the old words, not because I wanted power like Samuel, but because I wanted something of Mama. Cooking wasn't enough. I didn't know what would be enough, but I knew Mama wouldn't want me poisoning Papa. Even if he did deserve it.

Mama didn't deserve to burn in hell, either, but God and Jesus would know her best. Better than Papa, that's for sure.

I let Samuel lean on the railing and I bounded on up the steps.

Papa's shades whispered against me, that guilt and grief he tried to push away with Jesus. It was working, in a way. The shades didn't dwell on him like they did Macaulay. I was surprised at how that relieved me. I didn't want Papa to suffer, not really.

I just wanted Mama back, and that could never happen. Not even Samuel's dark words could make everything like it'd been.

Papa was still standing there in the kitchen, dishing up food on his plate.

"Papa, you can't eat that," I said, yanking him back. "The steak, I think it's gone bad. Samuel ate some and is sick as a dog." On cue, Samuel staggered in and past Papa.

"What?" Papa said, blinking at me. Unpleasant sounds shuddered from the bathroom.

I plucked the plate from his hands and in two steps dumped the whole thing in the trash. I didn't trust the whole surface, not after that meat had touched it. I threw away the few remaining pieces of steak, too, not that there was much after a hungry seventeen-year-old boy had had his way.

"Here. Have this instead." I pulled out the icebox pie.

"Is that lemon?" Papa asked. I swear I heard drool in his voice.

"Yeah. Yeah, it is. You listen in case Samuel needs help, okay?"

I walked out of the house. The rage wasn't in my chest now, just emptiness. I hadn't forgiven him, not yet. But without that heavy feeling on my lungs, it was easier to breathe, even in that sticky evening air.

The lights were on in the barn, but I didn't see Ralph. "Hey," I called.

"Up here!"

I climbed up the ladder and found him in my spot, those math sheets spread out. Figured he'd be drawn to the numbers.

"You got a few wrong," he said, voice mild as could be.

I snorted. "A few?"

"I could help you, if you wanted. Not going to cheat on tests for you or anything, but I could give you pointers, maybe."

I plopped down on some old straw, staring at this boy I hated for so long. "Maybe," I said. I stared out the slats at the fading light. "There's something your papa said. Do I ... do I really look like her? My mama?"

"Sure, you do," Ralph said. "Probably look more like her as you grow up, too."

I nodded to myself. Maybe the words would come in time. Maybe I'd learn the hard way, like my great-great-grandma did. But for now, I had some things from Mama, and that'd do.

"Come on," I said. "Let's have some pie."

DEEPER THAN PIE

grandma's the one who taught me
that spells were most potent
baked into pie

but now she has started to forget
first her keys, then her spells
memories thinned like her silver hair

doctors run tests
as grandma says she's not worth any fuss
I'm not fussing—I'm fighting

to preserve the bright spark in her eye
the joy in her laugh and the stories
that flavor our meals better than salt

I whisper Latin in a mantra
as I breathe in nutmeg, cardamom, and cloves
mixing apples and enchantment and hope

I sprinkle in unicorn eyelashes
almond petals kissed by a full moon's light
a pinch of Pacific Ocean white sand

I sift in my desperation with flour and spice
crumble a topping of butter and dragon's breath
set it to bake for 45 minutes at 350

ten minutes remain on the timer
when grandma heaves into the chair across the table
tugs the statistics book from my gaze

"You were heavy on the unicorn lashes,"
she says, though I smell nothing but apple
she smiles; I know she knows

we let the pie cool just enough
say nothing beyond the clatter of fork and plate
I taste fruit and so much more

each bite slow and savored
as grandma seeks to remember
and I desperately hope to never forget

ALL WHO WANDER

MAPS

CHRISTINA DREW HER FIRST MAP at age five, nubby red crayon in her fist. She thrust the sheet into her grandmother's lap, warring for attention against four squalling cousins.

"What's this?" asked her grandmother, her smooth, ripe lips pursing in a frown.

"That's where you'll die," said Christina.

The maps continued, etched only for herself or loved ones, though not all were dire:

"This is where I'll have my first kiss."

"This is where Jimmy'll fall from a tree and break both legs."

"This is where the jasmine will bloom, even though you don't plant it."

None bore a timeline, only saying where, not when. Her fingers preferred drawing in dirt most of all. No sticks, no rocks—nails and flesh furrowing through dust.

The social workers, the therapists, each noted it in her case file: "A manifestation of a turbulent youth, a desire to seize control over aspects of her chaotic life." Christina already showed strong anti-social tendencies, running away to the woods for hours at a time. A consulted magi theorized that maybe she contracted something there, but if so, it was impossible to tell; she was like a fly flitting through the undergrowth, still for mere seconds at a time.

Christina's grandmother died where depicted, despite her strong avoidance of that intersection. Cousin Jimmy broke his legs. Jasmine bloomed, fragrant as heaven.

Christina didn't want to draw her maps. She screamed and fought against the compulsion of her left fingers. Her hand, bound in bandages, would writhe its way free. In the night, her nails gouged pathways and words onto the headboard as she slept.

In a way, foster care was a blessing, distancing her from attachments and love, as that love seemed requisite for a map.

At age nine, on a rare visit to her mother, she battled against her fingers as they jabbed through the rock bed of the apartment landscaping to find dirt beneath.

"This is where you'll get AIDS," Christina said, hating the words, the way the knowledge trickled from her fingertips and up her arm, the sensation warm as pee. The map showed the apartment complex itself, an X on the residence of her mother's boyfriend, a man she had never met or known about.

Doctors, psychiatrists, and magi examined her, trying to deter- mine what magic graced her. When one told her she was blessed, Christina screamed and lunged for the shrink's eyes, her right fin- gers curved as claws.

She embraced her role as a rebellious teenager, discarding friends as a cat sheds fur, with no discretion, no attachment—or so she tried. Christina ached for companionship the way an early spring seedling ached for the sun, but at the first realization that she cared for someone, she made herself sever contact. She didn't want to know where the cancer would grow, where their brother would die in Afghanistan, where they would lose Jesus.

Withdrawing to her bedroom and online high school courses, her predictions focused on herself.

"This is where I'll fall in love."

"This is where I'll buy my first cigarette."

"This is where I'll be when I find out he cheated on me."

She broke her fingers after that—not for the first time—yet still they quivered out their diagrams, agony dappling her eyesight. She had tried to slice them off, only to lose a fight against her left hand.

Christina graduated from the foster system and acquired her case file, a disk drive loaded with encyclopedias of data. She skimmed for any clue of what caused her fingers to rebel, what made the words travel up her arm and escape her lips. There were no answers, only theories—a rare disease, a blessing, a curse, all of the above.

She shunned the city and escaped to the Sierras. Alone and isolated, the compulsion lessened, but when maps did come her independent fingers shivered in ecstasy.

At the fleshy distal points, her fingers began to turn as brown as the soil they loved.

The joints stiffened like twigs as the coloration spread. She perfected the use of her right hand for everyday tasks, her tapping on a cell phone or the flick of her lighter. Christina hiked through meadows and clambered across plutons, ignoring humanity and showers in her quest for an answer to her curse.

Her left fingers became useless husks, the bones within rattling like seeds in a gourd. Still, the messages came to her, written by nerveless flesh.

"This is where I'll catch a glimpse of God in the stars."

"This is where I'll see twin fawns graze."

"This is where my fingers will leave me."

She followed that map with urgency in her stride and stood at the edge of a swampy meadow, far, far from civilization. Christina stared at her fingers, feeling strangely devoid of emotion. The left hand didn't fight now. The pocket knife sliced through the base of her pointer finger as though cutting into crusty bread. No blood, no pain. The finger plopped into the water. A sprout emerged and bloomed a dazzling red flower, velvety petals begging to be touched.

She stepped back, suddenly understanding. Like poison ivy, this plant spread poison premonitions. If her right hand touched the bloom, the curse would spread again.

Christina sliced off her other fingers onto a nearby boulder, and with an expert flick of her lighter, she burned them. The seeds writhed as fire claimed them, but she didn't feel happy. She felt nothing at all.

She smacked down the bloom with a branch, herded the petals from the water and crushed them beneath her boots, pounded at the seedling until she could not breathe.

Her distorted reflection wavered in the dark water.

All her life she had run from love, run from the maps it evoked. Now she could visit her mother in the hospice, get a job, go to college—live. Now she had no excuse. Christina blinked at her maimed hand.

She was utterly lost.

OVERLAP

 TODAY WAS THE DAY Reyna Aguilar's Goodwill and junkyard jury-rigged teleporter was going to win her the New Avalon Scientifics Innovators Prize. No more setbacks, no more failures. This was it. The deadline was tomorrow.

The heavy industrial door clanged behind her as she hopped down two flights of concrete steps to her basement bungalow. Her lab/bedroom/home sweet home, complete with a borrowed portable toilet stuck in a far corner. Reyna liked to think that the smell granted the place some ambience.

The plastic grocery bag rattled against her thigh. In honor of the day, she had gone all out: a Marie Callender's Chocolate Satin Pie. That sucker wasn't even on sale, costing as much as ten of her usual ramen cups. Reyna stashed the pie in the freezer; the lower part of the fridge didn't work anymore. That's what happened when you mined electronics for spare parts that turned out to not be spare.

"Okay." She clapped her hands and looked around the basement.

Most of the space was devoted to her laboratory. Monitors cluttered several attached desks, while two teleporter pads sat about ten feet apart. They looked like showers because that's what they had been in their previous incarnation. She had ripped out the bases and replaced them with smooth steel and data receivers. Crammed in one corner, not far from her destination unit, was her mattress with its crumpled blankets.

Adrenaline thrumming, Reyna began her systems checklist and reviewed the contents on her screens. The list had been printed out for weeks, read to the point of memorization, but her gaze still traced every syllable. Long lines of numerals expanded on the monitors as she scrolled down.

She could not afford to screw this up, not if she wanted the NASIP and its million dollar prize, not if she wanted to attract the attention of hiring managers at CERN, not if she wanted to prove she wasn't a freaking failure.

Reyna had dropped out of college, five units shy of graduation, because of some stupid financial aid deadline. Then three weeks back, Taco Bell had fired her. Goddamned Taco Bell.

Three years working there, shift manager and all, and they fired her because some punk wrote a letter to the district manager. Because Reyna told the jerk not to grab hot sauce packets by the fistful as he walked out the door.

Her teleporter was going to work. It had to.

Her checklist and data looked good to go. Next she had to satisfy the requisites for the prize. She climbed a rickety ladder to where a mesh sling cradled her smart phone. That vantage point provided a perfect view of both teleporters. To reduce digital manipulation, contestants had to upload the raw feed of their experiments as they happened. It would go directly to New Avalon's databanks. Reyna could still edit the feed—and she would, for presentation's sake—but that raw version was required. She set the phone to start recording and placed it in its niche.

"My name is Reyna Aguilar," she said, voice raspy. She knew her face filled the lens. "And I'm about to make history."

This was a moment she'd been working towards since age five when she spied the cover of *A Brief History of Time*, wondered about the guy in the wheelchair, and started reading. Other kids in Fresno's south side read graffiti and emulated gang signs for fun; instead, in first grade she declared she was going to be a particle physicist when she grew up.

"I'm going to win, I'm going to win," she whispered beneath her breath.

She checked the teleporter pads. She had mapped their surface area and calibrated down to the micrometer so she could land within a precise zone. Reyna's basic data was greatly modified from laboratory work from the UK, where scientists had successfully beamed objects like pencils from room to room. What they had spent ten years researching, she had replicated in six months. She had tested a dozen inanimate objects, but she wasn't going to win the NASIP by zapping a talking Furby from point A to point B. To win, she had to go big. Animal testing should be the next step, but Reyna wasn't going to risk any living creature on something she wasn't willing to try herself.

So that's exactly what she planned to do.

It was dangerous. It was hella scary. One of the big theories was that teleporters didn't transfer exact material. Reyna could very well be killing herself, and then emerge on the other side as a copy. Or, by more crazy science fiction theories, she could rip holes in space time or invite in an alien race or something.

Well, that might win the NASIP, too. Or a Nobel.

Her computers hummed. The sound was comforting white noise as she removed her socks and shoes and tossed them beside her bed. She wanted to describe every sensation of transit, how it felt from the callused skin of her heels to the very taste of the air against her tongue.

Reyna took a deep breath. Glanced at the clock. 10:31. Years of work for something that would take less than ten seconds. She'd need to spend the rest of the day editing footage, perfecting her presentation. Eating that pie.

All systems were ready. She stared, absorbing that fact, then nodded. Okay then. She crossed herself as a precaution. Fingers shaking, Reyna clicked the mouse and began the countdown sequence. One minute.

God, oh God. The ten feet to the teleporter felt like a mile, or two steps. So far yet so close. She entered and closed the door behind her. Her thudding heart threatened to clog her throat, the world all a hum of electricity. She centered herself on the X and pressed her arms tightly against her sides, her chin up. Steel was cold and smooth beneath her bare feet. In the shadows, the green light of her phone's camera stared down. She raised an arm in a brief wave. A hello, not a good-bye.

The seconds ticked by as eternities. She stared up at the light, willing herself not to panic. It was going to happen, it was going to happen.

It happened.

The light was brilliant blue, dazzling like a Caribbean sea. Reyna felt her lips part in a gasp, but no sound registered in her ears. Sound ceased existing at all.

Then the light was gone. All light was gone. Then came the pain. Excruciating agony extended from both feet, its suddenness ripping a scream from her throat. Pain? Why was there pain? Where was she? The smell—the sharpness of ozone. The hum was gone—the computers were off? But the green light above, it was still there. She tried to move. Her right foot scuttled forward, slick with agony, but her left was anchored in place. She fell. Screaming, she dropped face-first into something soft. Her body bounced. White lightning bolts of agony zinged up both legs, and then blackness claimed her.

Searing agony woke her, and wetness, and cold.

Reyna's lips pressed against softness beneath her. Where was she? What happened? That pain—she gasped, reeling, fighting to stay conscious. Even in the darkness, white spots of agony dappled her sight. She forced herself onto her knees; one knee was higher, and the cushioning beneath adjusted to the movement, like a bed. A bed?

Her fingers explored, finding cloth. Sheets, blankets. Hers? She reached back along the length of her body, where wetness lingered, and grasped at her left foot, the one that didn't move.

It was inside the mattress.

Inside, literally. She felt strained cloth just above where her ankle should be, where it fused with her flesh. She hadn't landed on telepad B. She had landed in the mattress. Fused with it on an atomic level. Above the overlap, her calf swelled like a sausage casing. Shock and nausea rose in her throat, and she retched. Heaving only worsened the pain, driving her flat on her belly again in a pool of her own vomit and blood.

Something had gone very, very wrong.

Her mind raced over the algorithms. Something—something was off, some calculation. Damn it. She wanted to see her screens, figure out what happened. Even bleeding out, dying, this was a puzzle that needed solving. Dying. She could die.

That rational thought forced back the nausea and terror. Grinding her teeth, she reared onto her knees and probed with her hands again, this time reaching for her right foot. The leg wasn't locked in place, but something was still wrong. She grappled at her heel, pain causing her to dry heave for a moment. A flag of cloth covered most of her sole and was merged with her flesh. It was sopping with hot blood but the weave of the cloth was familiar. Her sock—she had landed partially on her discarded sock. Dizziness overtook her again and her face met the foul mattress.

It could have been worse. She could have landed in the wall, inside the floor. Died instantly. Melded with that port-a-potty across the room. Reyna tried to laugh and it emerged somewhere between a screech and a sob.

She refused to die here, alone. She pushed up onto her elbows. Okay. The power was out for some reason. The calculations—she should have landed on the second pad, just as the other test objects had. What had gone wrong? Reyna shivered. Cold—that was a sign of shock, right? Loss of body temperature because of the blood. She had to get out of the mattress, out of the basement. No time to analyze, not now.

Her fingers tested the fabric where her leg met the cloth. The strands were pulled tight, frazzled, soaked by blood. Thank God it was a ratty old Craigslist mattress, already weakened by wear. Gritting her teeth, she shredded the threads with her nails and dug deeper, digging her foot out from a mash of sponge and fluff. She couldn't feel many sensations from her foot now, but her calf was hot, bulging. No blood was circulating downward. Taking a deep breath, she yanked her foot upward. It jerked free and met the coolness of the concrete, something metallic clattering at one side of her foot. A spring. Nausea threatened her again, and she forced down bile.

If she didn't get out of here, she would go mad in the darkness with freaking feet joined with polyester and cotton and a goddamned spring. Everyone used to say she was crazy, anyway, making her own teleporter. Saying she was going to win.

The light of her phone remained steady as it recorded. Oh, God—the NASIP. No, she couldn't think of that now, that failure. She just had to get out of here.

Grinding her teeth to block out the pain, she eased her entire body onto the floor. She was cold. So cold. Thirsty. The fridge—it was so damn close, but the bottom compartment was empty. Her phone—seven feet up an already rickety ladder. She had to make the stairs, both flights. The door on the top—God, that thing was heavy on an average day.

The concrete floor was icy cold beneath her palms, causing her to shiver more. Move. Don't dawdle. Reyna dragged herself forward. The spring rattled and jostled from one foot, the merged sock heavy and dragging from the other. She found the plastic mats that covered the spider-webbing of wires across the floor. Her legs, her body, felt compressed by gravity. Sweat beaded her skin, dripped from her nose. The room should be thirty feet across. She knew the direction, roughly. It would be mostly open space.

The lights flicked on.

Blinded, surprised, Reyna cried out, dropping her head towards the floor. She panted, quivering. Lights. The teleporter must have knocked out power within a radius. She raised her head again. The stairs, ten feet away, stretched into the ceiling in stern gray.

She couldn't help it. She glanced back.

A snail's trail of blood lead back to the mattress. The computer monitors were all on start-up screens. Well, her server should have backed up everything to the moment of the outage. The camera would see her clearly now, too, if it was still streaming. Too bad it was all going straight to some NASIP storage server along with 1,300 other attempts at the prize. No one would see this as a live feed and call for help.

She turned back around, curling her body like a pill bug. God. What happened? How did she screw up this badly? The NASIP. This place, no job, no money—she would be homeless. The medical bills. End up back at her parents, cocooned by their pity, their murmured "there-there, you'll get all better, chica" condolences as they knowingly nodded amongst themselves. Because they knew she'd screw this up, just like everything else, and end up back home. No degree, not even a job at freaking Taco Bell.

Reyna screamed, but this time it wasn't from pain. It was from honest-to-God rage.

"I am not a failure!" she yelled, her voice bouncing back against the high ceiling. "I am not going to die, I am not going to fail!"

And she moved forward. Tears flowing, breaths heaving. Using her hands, she pushed herself up to the first step, and paused. Reality wobbled around her. Sitting upright—not a good idea. She lowered her torso against the concrete steps, then she began to climb.

She didn't count stairs, or flights. It was all about moving up, one at a time. Having committed some terrible mathematical error in her algorithms, this was all about basic math. One plus one plus one. To infinity, it seemed. Then she was staring at the dark gray of the door.

Placing her weight against her sock-merged foot sent white sparkles of agony dancing across her vision, but she propped herself against the door. Leaned on the push bar. Leaned harder. The door opened.

Reyna had rented the basement in an old commercial complex. Most of the places were vacant. The heavy door echoed as it shut behind her, the automatic lock clattering. Down the hallway she dragged herself. Almost out. There was daylight now, slits of summer sun through the high windows. Her elbows ached and bled, bone and blisters grinding on concrete. The next door was lighter, easier.

Reyna was on the sidewalk. It was hot, gritty. Stank of oil and asphalt and exhaust. There weren't any pedestrians, not here. There was only one way to get attention.

She dragged herself into the road.

The asphalt ripped at whatever flesh remained at her elbows. She was past sobbing, past pain. The world was brightness and heat and cold. The yellow lines in the road—those were her goal. She felt the truck coming, the mighty rumbles of a behemoth. She lacked the strength to move her head. The roaring grew louder, the stink of fumes increasing, then it stopped. Footsteps. Feet, in her vision.

"Hey, what happened? You all right?"

"No," she said, and rested her cheek on the pavement.

The best part of being knocked-out at the hospital wasn't the blissful absence of pain, though that was a major perk. No, it was that she slept through the deadline for the New Avalon Scientifics Innovators Prize.

Upon awakening, however, her consciousness didn't go straight to the beeping monitors, the draping intravenous lines, or the long creases of worry in her mother's face as she waited there at Reyna's bedside. It went straight to one thought:

I failed.

If she hadn't just fought so damn hard to stay alive, she might have been suicidal. Instead, she lay there, accepting Mama's fervent prayers, tears, and exclamations of joy; Papa's stoic hand-clasp; even her brother's tearful hug.

The doctors came next, then the police. She answered their questions as best she could and asked plenty of her own, making sure no one had messed with her laboratory.

Then the flowers started arriving.

"What the hell?" Reyna asked, as an attendant wheeled in an entire cart of vases and balloons.

"It's cause of that contest and your weird-ass injuries," said her brother, shrugging. "You been all over the news."

"Oh." Pity flowers. How nice. She looked to the attendant. "Can you take these to the pediatric or cancer wing or something?"

The flowers kept coming, then relayed requests from the media. A police officer was stationed at her door to keep out the nosey. Reyna slipped in and out of sleep. When she was awake, she lay there. She could see the algorithms in her mind. She traced over them, searching for the flaw, whispering beneath her breath.

Her ruminations were interrupted by a knock at the door. At her bedside, Papa jerked awake, eyes wide.

"Pardon me, ma'am." It was the police officer on duty. "There's a lawyer here, says she's from New Avalon."

Reyna's number stream froze in place. "New Avalon? Let her in." The officer nodded and motioned behind him.

"A lawyer?" repeated Papa, frowning.

The woman who entered was petite and precise in a white pantsuit. Tousled blonde hair framed her face and contrasted with thick black glasses. "I'm Lilah Caputo. You're Reyna Aguilar?"

"Yeah. Why are you here?"

"How are you recovering?" The woman's tone was even, as though Reyna hadn't asked a thing. She set a briefcase on a side table.

"I'm shorter. They had to cut off both feet, but they're already talking about prosthetics." Like Reyna could afford them. "But why's a lawyer from New Avalon here? I didn't complete my submission, but I signed off on the legal stuff. I'm not going to sue you." Not when this was her own stupid fault somehow.

"I'm not here regarding any lawsuit. I'm here because of your video."

Reyna sat up, wincing at pain from the motion. "The upload? New Avalon owns that video, I remember that much from the fine print. I'm not going to turn around and upload it to YouTube or anything. But my invention is still mine, as it is." Bitterness crept into her voice.

"As it is. You are the first teleported human being."

"Yeah. Minus my feet because I screwed up and missed my target."

"You teleported. You lived. You recorded everything. The dark portions were easily lightened for visibility. It's not simply what you've created, and what you have the potential to create. It's who you are. New Avalon needs people with that kind of tenacity, that resilience." Her voice softened, and she unlatched the suitcase. "I have paperwork, offering you a job with our company. The details are here. Actually, there are several jobs, depending on your interests."

Reyna only stared. ". . . Jobs?"

"Of course, there may be other forthcoming offers as well," Lilah continued. "Would you like to look at our paperwork?"

"Yeah. Sure." Reyna accepted the packet, blinking in disbelief. Her eyes scanned the sheets. Numbers stood out the most; numbers always did. For the first time in days, she had keen awareness of her heartbeat. "Oh."

"Ray-ray, you okay?" Papa leaned closer.

"Yeah. I'm . . . okay." She stared at the numbers again, comprehending. Job offers. CERN might even come knocking, but even if not, New Avalon . . . was New Avalon. That equipment, those extra resources, might be what she needed to get her teleporter working again—hers. She needed to make sure it still belonged to her, no matter who she worked for.

"I also had a favor to ask you. Don't feel any obligation, of course." Lilah's smile turned surprisingly shy. "I was wondering if someone in your family could show me to the basement where everything happened. I wouldn't touch anything, but I—and my peers—would love to have pictures of it all."

Reyna bet they would. She met Lilah's gaze. The lawyer might be poaching, but there was genuine joy and curiosity behind it.

"Papa?" she asked. He leaned closer, clasping her wrist. "I need a lawyer. The best damn lawyer you can get. I don't think money will be an object, not anymore. Call up some people and have them come here so I can interview them, okay?" She looked at Lilah, challenging her.

Lilah arched an eyebrow, but if anything her smile grew. "You have to look out for yourself. I can wait."

Papa stood and shuffled to the door, already pulling out his cell phone.

"No one in my family has wanted to go in . . . there," Reyna said. "But once I have this lawyer, I'll talk to them, see if they can walk you in. But we'll talk details later."

"Of course. No pressure."

Reyna may have screwed up, but this was her chance at redemption. She could make this right, make her teleporter right. New Avalon wanted to use her and her machine—all right. She could use them, too.

She looked at the papers resting against her chest. "There's one big favor you can do for me at my place, though."

Lilah tilted forward. "Oh?"

"There's a pie in my freezer that needs to be brought here to the hospital." Reyna grinned as algorithms danced in her head. "I think it'd taste really good about now."

MOON SKIN

BEULAH EMERGED FROM THE RIVER and into a brisk autumn night that made the waning moon shiver behind the clouds. Her vision, even with the color spectrum narrowed, was keen in the darkness, and she detected the movement of men amongst the few wooden buildings and tents near the shore. The vertical slits in her nose opened and she took in the ripeness of the swamp and the wretched stench of the *Dorchester*'s iron hulk.

With a tilt of her head, her seal skin peeled back to her shoulders. Smells altered, the marsh's rot more bothersome, the iron more annoying than appalling. She could see the *Dorchester* better now. The forty-foot submarine floated alongside a pier. Gray metal maintained a dull sheen beneath lit lamps. A few soldiers bobbed in a boat at the tip of the long spar where a torpedo would be affixed in place. If all went according to Papa's plan, tomorrow the submersible would engage the enemy.

"Miss Beulah's back!" a spotter called.

She sensed Papa's approach. His body glowed with innate magic, like a full moon that cast no shadows on the normal world. Annie's pelt, hooked to his waist, held a fainter glow tonight, like a lamp tucked beneath a quilt.

Oh, Annie. Her sister endured such agony right now. The dimmed pelt was proof of that.

Only her head above water, Beulah shimmied out of her pelt. She hunkered as she walked onto higher ground and obscured herself in the reeds. Her frail human skin pocked in goose bumps, she pulled on a thick robe she'd left hanging there and draped her long gray pelt over her arm. Her bare feet squished in mud as she walked onto land. Papa awaited her on the embankment. A glow behind him caught her eye. She stopped.

Amidst so many fellows in gray attire, the strange man didn't stand out at all but for his innate blue glow. He was a boy, really, close to her age. Skinny as a fence rail, his features plain. In water, she knew of everything around her by the current against her whiskers; the buzz of his magic was strong like that, the sense of it different than Papa or Annie. Like the difference between a wood fire and a gas lamp.

"Miss Beulah." Papa inclined his head, a dozen questions compounded into her name. He was never one to dither.

"Captain Kettleman, sir." She saluted. Even in private, she had not been permitted to call him "Papa" for years. "Two Union sloops still off-shore, three civilian crafts aside. One a fisherman, the others smuggling."

If anyone spied her, they'd likely think she was a porpoise. Seals were uncommon along the North Carolina coast; she had never met one in the wild.

"They must know we're hidden in the vicinity. Let the Yanks linger. All the better for tomorrow. Won't need to sail far to find our target." Papa fidgeted with Annie's pale pelt. He nodded at Beulah. "You're a good girl. You get adequate rest. Be ready for tomorrow." The words held a warning.

His care for her extended to her usefulness. As a child, she had been taught enough reading and arithmetic to manage as his secretary. Back then, she thought it was flattering, even if her literacy set her uncomfortably apart from the other house slaves. As if being the master's bastard daughter wasn't enough.

His treatment of Annie proved that anything of his blood was his property, to use as he will. Skin color had nothing to with it.

"Yes, sir." Beulah's teeth threatened to chatter.

She clutched her own pelt a little closer for both warmth and security as she walked past Papa. She caught the direct, wide gaze of the man behind him. It was pretty clear that he *saw* her, and not simply as a young woman in a robe. He appeared as skittish as a kitten in a dog kennel as he looked between her and Papa. He must have never seen magic in a person before. How peculiar.

"Miss Beulah?"

"Sir?" She stopped and faced her father.

"This man here, Chaplain . . . ?"

"Walsh, sir," said the stranger.

"Yes, Walsh. He will escort you once you're dressed."

"Not Lieutenant Groves, sir?" she asked.

"Lee believed a chaplain's presence would do the men well before we deploy, but we have no need of him yet." Papa's curled lip revealed he had no use for a chaplain, period, but Lee's word was akin to God's. "Lieutenant Groves has plenty else to do."

With that, Papa walked on, already bellowing an order to another soldier.

The man who glowed, a chaplain? Through thin lamplight, they stared each other down. His face was pale and pink, his nose blotched with freckles. Irish, then, like Papa's line. They'd carried a lot of old magic to American shores, though she'd noticed that glow in other folks, too. Most of them hadn't seen hers in turn, though.

"I be but a few minutes, sir," Beulah murmured, and scurried past him to her tent.

The tent had been her home for a brief while, until it became clear that she needed a quieter environment for sleep; shifting to seal and back left her drained, and if she was deprived she couldn't manage the change at all. Papa had begrudgingly arranged for her to stay with a loyal yet humble family nearby.

She emerged in proper clothes, hugging her coat close to her cotton dress. It was cold enough that she belted her pelt in place beneath her layers, girthing her like a saddle blanket.

Papa's soldiers nodded and sidestepped around her. She knew some made signs of the cross and muttered, but no one behaved cruelly with her secret known, and it wasn't simply because of Papa's command or that he was known as a selkie, too. She was respected in her own right—a peculiar thing, truly—for her service in the war. She'd scouted for the *Hunley* and more, and the *Hunley* had busted the Union blockade of Charleston. Until it recently docked for repairs, the submersible had prowled the South Carolina coast and sent Yanks fleeing northward.

A month after the *Hunley's* first success, Sherman had been obliterated on his march from Chattanooga to Atlanta. Peace and independence might be possible by the dawn of 1865, God willing.

Peace for white folk, anyway. But if Beulah had to be a slave, she'd be with Annie and Annie would treat her as well as she could.

Chaplain Walsh awaited her with a wagon; he seemed afraid to look at her. She sat on the bench seat and tugged blankets onto her lap. The chaplain clicked his tongue, and the horse pulled the wagon onto the bumpy road.

Beulah waited until the camp's noise was replaced by the chirps and trills of the marsh. "No need to worry, sir. Captain Kettleman can't see your glow."

He shot her a nervous glance. "But he's a selkie, like you, if I understand correctly? That is, er . . ."

"Yes, sir, he's my father, but men-selkies can't change form or use any magic they carry. You never met no one like us before?"

"You have?"

"A few times, yes, sir. Not that common, and not every person with magic can see or sense how it's carried in others. I got a sense that you're not of selkie blood, sir."

His grip on the reins tightened. "Can you sense what I am, Miss Beulah?"

What a strange conversation this was. She twined her hands beneath the blankets. The night was fiercely quiet. Back when the blockade was still in place and more Lincoln soldiers lurked close, Papa kept more guards around her. As if she'd run north and leave Annie behind, or even let soldiers steal her away.

She squinted at him. "I met some Indian spirits I don't know to name, and a dryad once. You glow like a pure drink of water, like nothing else I seen."

"Like a pure drink of water." He repeated it with a small smile in his voice. "The pelt the Captain carries. Who . . . ?"

"My sister. Annie." She noted the quick shift in subject.

"She's—"

"White, sir. His wife's child. She was a good woman, God rest her."

"I was 'bout to ask her age, the skin so small."

"Oh. She's seven, sir."

His brow furrowed. "It's hooked on his belt, too. Am I right to reckon . . . ?"

"She got a hole through her left hand. Size of a blueberry. Never heals. He keeps her pelt close here. For luck."

"God Almighty," he whispered. The horse snorted. An owl hooted from somewhere distant. "The other men say as much, that the skin's their lucky charm. That you're part of that, too, seein' as you made the *Hunley* succeed, and now you'll bless the *Dorchester* next."

Bless. She looked away to hide her revulsion. The *Dorchester* needed to succeed and then Papa would be promoted and then the bluebellies could blow it to kingdom come. Annie's pelt just needed to be away first, back near the rest of her flesh.

"I don't know what you expect me to say to that, Chaplain. I'm not particularly lucky, and my sister . . ."

"No one can know their own luck, I reckon. I'm just . . . still in awe that we see each other's magic in such a way."

The house was just ahead, a lamp on in the parlor window. Surrounding trees fringed the yard like dark lace. The woman of the house was likely peering through the curtains in wait. The wagon rolled down the drive and Beulah stood to disembark.

This man carried some kind of power and he was friendly to the point of foolishness. Maybe he could help her get Annie's pelt away from Papa. Beulah could run south, get her sister. How they'd make it north together, God only knew, but others had done it. *"Follow the north star,"* folks said.

"Everyone knows what I am," Beulah said slowly, "but no one knows 'bout you. You're the one with a secret."

His breath caught. "It's best they not know."

"What, you're not wanting to give everything for the cause? Sir?" She played a dangerous game, wielding power over a white man like this, but if it could save Annie, it was worth it.

"There's no givin' in this war. Just takin'." The door to the house opened.

"I tell you this. I won't tell no one, for now." Instead of feeling mighty with the words, the power, she felt all sour inside.

"Thank you, Miss Beulah," he said quietly. He didn't even sound mad. "I already been told I'm to fetch you 'bout midnight."

"Midnight," she murmured, and hopped from the wagon without looking back.

The missus greeted her with a scowl that'd scare away any soldier, blue or gray. A few minutes later, Beulah had cleaned off a whole plate of food, including the cold, cooked fish her human body craved so often now.

"Almost forgot," the woman said. "There's a letter on the desk. Reckon you can read?"

"Yes . . . yes, missus."

Beulah murmured her thanks as she retreated to her room. A rain-marbled envelope awaited her on the felt mat of the desk.

The handwriting was Annie's.

It was dated a mere week before; blessed fast, compared to how things were when Charleston was under siege. Annie's fat pencil loops quivered across the page. Beulah's eyes scanned back and forth as she read the seven-year-old's words, read beneath pleasantries about how Annie rode her horse with old Rickery's help, about how the leaves had started to shift color and whirl away.

Beulah pictured Annie sitting in her bed like a doll propped against down-filled pillows. Her little lap desk against her knees, her mousey brown hair kept up in curlers. A week ago, her pelt was brighter, too. Now she likely hadn't the strength to write.

That child's gap-toothed smile lit up Beulah's world with a glow greater than any magic. Papa and most everyone else had scolded Annie, told her to not treat Beulah like a sister. The girl wouldn't heed. She had a stubborn streak wider than the James River, bless her.

And Papa was killing her, slowly yet surely.

Beulah closed her eyes and rocked. The paper crinkled in her grip. Annie's pelt was so far away from her body. That was bad enough, but far worse, it was so often in the *Dorchester*. Iron gnawed on magic like hungry termites. Beulah's own pelt had been taken aboard the *Hunley*. She had been left bed-bound and wretched, and for the first time, the *Hunley*'s mission was a success. The submersible had blown apart the *U.S.S. Housatonic* and gone on to sink or scare off the rest of the Union blockade.

Now it was Annie whose pelt was to be their lucky charm. Annie, who Papa was sure had stronger and purer magic, being white and all. If the *Dorchester* did its duty along the North Carolina coast, Papa said he was sure to be promoted. He wouldn't need to go out to sea no more.

Annie had to stay stubborn and strong. She'd have her pelt back soon enough. Beulah would make sure of that, one way or another.

The night was strangely balmy for late October. Too hot for Beulah to belt her pelt beneath her clothes. She climbed into the wagon with her glowing skin draped over her shoulder and lap. She caught Chaplain Walsh's double-take upon sight of it. He clicked for the horse to move forward. The wheels found the ruts of the road.

"It's strange, seeing the same glow twice over," he said.

"I suppose so, sir."

"You needn't 'sir' me out here."

"It's best to stay in the habit. Sir." She frowned, discomfited by his friendliness even after her hint of blackmail the night before.

All was quiet but for the grind of wheels. "I don't hold with slavery," he whispered, as well he should. Dangerous words. "I'm from up in Virginia, the hills. Didn't think to join. They made me."

"The western side of the state, the Union part?" She heard a lot of slaves ran up through there, headed to Ohio.

"Yes. I was riding my circuit when . . ."

"You really are a preacher?"

At that, he smiled. "I am."

"Hardly seems smart to tell me this, sir, when I already know you hold some power inside."

"If anyone asks what I think, I tell them truth."

She snorted. Good grief. Here she hoped for the man's help, and he continued to prove himself a fool. "You won't have to worry 'bout Yanks shooting you then. Boys in gray will do it first."

"I'm not lookin' to die or be a martyr, but ain't about to lie, either. God sees all."

"How do you judge my soul, then, with what I do? Directing these fish boats so they kill hundreds of men in a night?"

He looked surprised. "Why, I don't judge your soul at all. Not my place. That's between you'n the Almighty."

She stroked her pelt, an anxious habit. In the water, Beulah could taste rendered metal, munitions, the tartness of blood and flesh. She knew she didn't have a choice in her duty, truly, but guilt weighed on her all the same. She worried for her own soul, but even more, she worried for Annie's.

"I wonder, d'you think—" she began.

A tailed critter—fox, coon, something—darted across the road. The horse reared in the shafts and the wagon lurched forward. The sky rotated as Beulah flung over the low back rest. The underside of her noggin cracked against wood. New stars lit her vision as terrible heat flared in her ears. She rolled, dazed, the world blurred. Wood and metal snapped—the back hatch of the wagon, busting open. Everything turned black. Dust filled her nostrils. She blinked. Her head felt hot and wrong and her right leg hurt in an awful way.

She had to be able to swim tonight. Had to. If she couldn't scout, if she couldn't keep Annie's pelt safe . . .

Beulah forced her body upright. The horizon spun around her and threatened to squeeze supper from her gut. She couldn't see the wagon, but even more, her seal skin wasn't right close by.

Gritting her teeth, she leaned on her knuckles and took several slow breaths to get her bearings. Her leg—oh Lord, her leg. Summoning all her gumption, she stood. Her other toes tapped for balance. Sheer agony almost melted her into the dirt.

Standing, she could see the wagon wasn't far ahead. A plume of dust still hovered in the air. The wagon was stuck in high grass along the road, and it rocked back and forth as the horse squealed and kicked. The beast sounded panicked more than anything. Where was Chaplain?

Beulah scanned for his glow and found it out in the swamp, some twenty feet away. Dark as the night was, their ability to see each other was handy. He swam straight toward her, her pelt in hand. He staggered up the embankment and flopped to earth, gasping. He was wet as a fish, and it was impossible to tell if he was hurt.

Dear God, he had her pelt.

He could blackmail her now, or damage it, or do any number of things. Even if she wrestled it away, she couldn't run, not with her crippled leg.

Chaplain Walsh still wore a gun at his hip. If she could get that . . . but then what? Papa still had Annie's skin. Beulah couldn't escape. Couldn't do anything.

"Miss Beulah? How do you fare?"

She took several long breaths to mask her pain and panic. "Alive, sir. And you—"

"Your pelt. It is indeed blessed. It just saved my life."

"What?"

"I flew off the wagon and landed out there in deep water. I swim as well as a rock. I was like to drown, but I reached out, found your skin. It pulled me to the surface. I could feel magic in it, warmth. And, and there was an alligator out there, I was not a foot away from the beast. It . . . it left. Ignored me. Praise Jesus."

Beulah's toes tapped the ground for balance. She cried out, and Chaplain Walsh pivoted to look up at her.

"What the . . . ? Miss Beulah?" He stood.

"It's my leg. It's not . . ."

"It surely is bad, so don't protest the contrary. Would it help you to change form?"

He held out the pelt to her. She stared at it. God forgive her. She'd thought to shoot him, and he handed her skin over with nary a mean thought. Beulah buried her face in the familiar gray and black fur. It smelled of dank water and saltiness and the comfort of her own self.

"No. I'd be a lame seal." Her voice was muffled against the skin. "I can't be lame, not tonight of all nights."

Chaplain Walsh looked toward the wagon. "I need to check on the horse. You—I wouldn't reckon you'd be so keen on the *Dorchester* succeeding."

"I hate that boat like nothing else." Agony loosened her tongue and her wits. "The iron's making Annie awful sick. The glow of her pelt, it's dimmer by the day. If Papa's promoted, he won't have to be on board, and Annie—"

Oh, blessed Annie, who'd hide handwritten copies of Elizabeth Barrett Browning poems in her Bible to read during her daily devotionals. The girl who had to be scolded to walk all ladylike, or she'd scamper like a crazed squirrel. Beulah knew just how Annie's little hand fit in her grip when they walked together in the far fields, their arms swinging.

Would Beulah know that touch again? She wavered on her feet. Chaplain Walsh grabbed hold of her arms while keeping himself at a gentlemanly distance. "Easy, easy," he crooned as he helped her to sit. Her hands found lush grass about wrist deep. Agony jolted down her hip. She buried her face in the pelt and sobbed.

"I'll be right back," he said.

The wagon wheels rattled and groaned as Chaplain shushed the horse, just as he soothed Beulah. A moment later, Chaplain returned.

"Had to make sure the horse didn't cause further mischief. He seems well enough for now, and the wagon's back on the road. Can I see your leg? I'm not—I don't have improper intentions."

"Most men say such things. You . . . you really do tell truth."

"I'm as much a sinner as any man."

She doubted that. She pulled up her skirt to tuck above her knees. By starlight, she could barely see the bulge of her thigh bone through her careworn, bloodied petticoats.

"Do you doctor, like some preachers do?" Her voice warbled.

His hands hovered over her leg, as if to warm them over a fire. "I do . . . something."

In a span of seconds, splinters of bone dragged through her muscle, the femur's shaft tugging into place with an audible pop. Red spots of pure pain dappled the ebony night. Next she knew, she was flat on her back, her skull tingling as if it held a hive of bees. Chaplain Walsh leaned over her, his pink face skewed in worry.

"What'd you do?" Her voice was hoarse. "How long . . . ?"

"You slept a minute. It . . . it was for the best. How d'you feel now?"

She raised a hand to her forehead first, then shifted both legs. "Sore, but not hurting like I was. This is what you do then, the magic in you?"

"Yes." He whispered. "It's at a cost. An awful cost."

She spanned her fingers into the grass. The lush, deep ground-cover had turned brittle. It crackled at her touch.

"I can't control how it takes from anything and anyone living close by. I try not to use it, but . . ."

"Why on me, then?" She clutched her pelt against her chest as she sat up. "Why give my skin back?"

Chaplain Walsh looked strangely old and tired. "You're the first person I met who uses magic—is magic, and who can see it in me. I . . . I want to be friends. You bein' a slave, it don't matter to me. I don't desire for you or your sister to suffer. I got little sisters, too. No magic in them, just mischief and giggles."

How like Annie he was, in his defiance. "You don't know your kin . . . ?"

"My mother was grabbed by fae folk back in Ireland. She . . . she fought to escape. She thought she'd been bound all of a night, but it'd been five years. She came to America, then I was born."

Beulah regarded him in silence for a time. "I won't tell no one about you, what you do. But you need to mind your own lips. You need to lie. It'll keep you alive."

"As you keep yourself alive, I reckon." It was simply stated. "You're a weapon for a cause in which you don't believe, you and your sister both."

She stood, pelt draped over her shoulders, and offered him a hand. He shakily stood and almost leaned against her.

"Pardon. Healing takes something outta me. You said . . . you said before that you want the Captain promoted and off the *Dorchester* to keep your Annie safe. How d'you reckon?"

"Why—Papa wants to work in Richmond, he's said as much—"

"That's not what I mean. What makes you think the *Dorchester* would do without a pelt? Men swear by its luck. The *Hunley*'s in port for repairs, and it's failed every sea worthiness test of late." He staggered forward a few steps.

"I—I hadn't heard such." Her mouth went dry. "Much as my scouting helps, they could use the surface to utilize the periscope instead. I . . ." The Confederates would rather have two submersibles run, most certainly. That meant she'd be bed-bound again, sick as a hound dog, her pelt going as pale as Annie's.

Dazed, she glanced behind them. A yellow scar of dead grass marked where she had sprawled, extending twenty feet wide. It encompassed both sides of the road and into the water. Reeds draped over, limp. The water looked almost lumpy, too. Maybe the fish were all dead. Maybe that gator, if it swam close. She shivered and turned.

Chaplain Walsh was falling, his eyes rolled back to whites. She dove forward and managed to catch his shoulders before his head struck the ground.

By the time Lieutenant Groves and his men found them, Beulah had managed to drag Chaplain Walsh up to the wagon. They tended him from there. He was conscious now and murmured to soldiers who sat in back with him. His voice slurred. An off-kilter wheel made the carriage to lurch with each rotation. Beulah clutched the bench seat as she bounced forward against her folded pelt.

"Are you well enough to swim?" Lieutenant Groves asked, an eye on her bloodied clothes.

No, she wanted to say, but what did her health truly mean to these men? They would steal her pelt, store it in toxic iron, leave her bed-bound and writhing in misery. She wanted Chaplain Walsh to be wrong, but her mind traced his logic like a dog chased its tail. He was right. She and Annie, they'd never be free. It wasn't up to Papa. Their role was bigger than him.

"I need to do my duty, sir," she murmured. "I can clean myself up. I can swim."

He studied her for a moment before nodding. "Our last reports placed the Union sloop *Woolton* at the river's mouth. Direct the *Dorchester*, as we practiced."

"Yes, sir. What about Chaplain Walsh, sir?"

The lieutenant glanced over his shoulder. "Head injuries are fickle things. Seen a man strip off his clothes and dance naked in a fire once, after a blow to the skull, and he didn't recall nary a thing after. Chaplain can do his prayer with the men aboard and we'll drive him to town in the morn. Don't fuss over him. You got plenty to do."

"Yes, sir."

The tension at the dock was at an intense simmer, the kind where everyone spoke at a murmur, lights dim, birds mute. Men scurried around the *Dorchester*. A boat bobbed on the far side, near the twenty-foot spar with its attached torpedo. The vessel would attack by tapping the mine against an enemy hull. A battery and copper wire would enable Papa to detonate the explosive once they were a safer distance away.

Papa was nowhere in sight at the moment, likely in the iron belly of the beast.

Chaplain Walsh stood in the wagon bed and leaned on a soldier for balance. Beulah's eyes met his for an instant and she turned away. He'd set the sailors' souls right with a prayer, then maybe he could rest to recover from her healing.

What of Beulah's soul? Because of her, the *Hunley* had killed or captured over a thousand men. Now here she was, leading the *Dorchester* to its prey, all for the sake of Annie's pelt. No more. After tonight, she'd find a way to save her sister's skin. It was time for them to them to go north.

A few minutes later, Beulah waded into the river.

The warmth of her pelt settled on her shoulders, then settled deeper. Heat nestled in her marrows and viciously tingled down and back up the lengths of her arms and legs as they receded. Colors shifted. She wiggled her new tail, water embracing her like cool silk, then she dived.

Fifty feet away, the *Dorchester* wallowed, to her attuned senses more putrid than any cesspool. Its ballast tanks sloshed and echoed as they filled with water, and the submarine lowered into the depths. Reverberations carried from each rotation of the hand crank that propelled it forward.

She surfaced in the middle of the river. Her seal eyes showed her a world hued in blues and greens. Bubbles marked the submersible's wake.

At the end of the dock, a blue glow caught her eye. The figure waved at her.

". . . pelt won't work!" she barely made out. "No glow!" Other soldiers surrounded Chaplain Walsh, gripping his arms, trying to calm him.

Beulah swam closer, her mind blank, her heart racing.

"No glow!" he shouted again. "She got no glow!"

No glow? Annie's pelt had no glow? No. Beulah sank into absolute darkness. Chaplain Walsh had to be lying. He just wanted to stop her, stop the *Dorchester*. He was a Yankee at heart, and a man of God. He had every reason to want this to fail.

Ripples slapped her whiskers as the *Dorchester* thrummed by. Beulah twisted in the water and swam alongside. She rested a flipper against the icy hull. The metal gnashed her limb as if with spiny teeth. In her mind, she heard her human self scream in agony as she struggled to stay conscious. Her senses fought through the accursed iron to find Papa within.

She knew his magic the way she knew the murmur of indistinct voices a room away. He stood five feet distant at command position. Metal groaned as the crew powered the crankshaft, but she could not discern the individual men with her magic. Nor could she find any other glow. The skin may as well have not been there, but she knew it was; the men wouldn't have sailed without it. Chaplain was right.

The submarine pushed past in a torrent of bubbles. She drifted, limp. She was scarcely aware of how her flipper ached and throbbed and how lingering convulsions rippled across her skin.

Annie's pelt was empty. She was dead.

Papa killed her.

You're a weapon for a cause in which you don't believe, you and your sister both. Chaplain's words pierced through the numbness. Papa's cause had killed Annie, and would kill Beulah, too. Her and so many more. The Union ship was out there, with hundreds more burdens on her soul.

Papa's good luck charm was dead. Without Annie's magic, the *Dorchester* would eventually fail, as the *Hunley* had. Maybe take its crew of ten with it.

Beulah couldn't wait. If she was going to be a weapon, this'd be the last time, on her terms.

God have mercy on her soul.

She swam, her body a sleek torpedo. She surpassed the submarine, powered by pedaling men, and passed the wooden spar with its explosive. She knew the river's sinuous curves as it broadened into the Atlantic. By her whiskers and the flow of the water, she knew the channel's depth, the anxious and erratic paths of fish. She stopped to let the submarine catch up.

Beulah's flipper banged on the hull, fast enough that it didn't scald her. Tap-tap. Tap-tap-tap. Tap. An obstacle ahead, bear right. *You're a good girl,* Papa always said. He trusted her to be obedient, to do as she ought.

After a long pause, it began to turn, oh so slowly. It was a perfect maneuver, one they had practiced time and again. The new angle aimed the torpedo-laden spar directly at rocks thirty feet ahead. The submersible was at full speed.

Beulah swam hard, but not far enough. Not fast enough. Metal crunched and whined and not a second later the explosion shoved her through the water. She sensed shrapnel shoot past, and she dove deeper. Her tail, her every muscle pushed her forward. To what? A shore, swarming with Confederates who would want to know what happened? To a world without the brightness of Annie awaiting her back home? She swam by blind instinct until she could take it no more. She shot to the surface.

Her head craned from the water and she screamed. The hoarse bray echoed. The sound of the explosion had faded, though something still crackled in the distance. She didn't turn around to look. The dock was not far away, still adorned with the blue glow of

Chaplain Walsh. Men scrambled and yelled from the shore and pier. Oars slapped the water.

"I see Miss Beulah!" called one of the men. "She's out there!"

"Miss Beulah?" echoed Lieutenant Groves, panting. He sat in the lead boat, not ten feet away. "What happened?"

She sensed Chaplain Walsh's gaze on her. He knew she had done this. Would he condemn her, as part of his honesty?

Still in deep water, she pulled back her skin to the shoulders. "Lieutenant!" she cried, hoarse from her scream. "Something went awful wrong. I tried to catch up, but I moved too slow. They plowed straight into them rocks down at the fork."

"God Almighty. All our hopes . . ." Lieutenant Groves looked so weary and old as he gazed in the direction of her voice. "That Union sloop may send men in to investigate. Might be a battle here soon enough, but we can't let them get salvage. Get ashore, girl. The men'll get you inland."

"And Chaplain Walsh, sir?" she asked. "Is he well? I thought he yelled somethin'."

"He's to stay still. Ain't right in the head." Lieutenant Groves motioned a soldier to continue paddling. Boats hurried past. The other men on the pier had dashed away, readying for battle.

Chaplain Walsh looked directly at her. "Your sister . . . I'm so very sorry, Miss Beulah."

"So am I, Chaplain Walsh, for so many things." Tears streamed down her cheeks. "I'm going. Before they use me as a weapon again. Before . . . before I end up like Annie."

"Yes. Yes." He stared away and she wondered if he was about to faint again. "I'd swim away with you, if I could." The words were so soft, she barely heard them.

"No. You don't believe in their cause, but they made you vow to serve. Knowin' you, you'd still hold yourself to such a thing."

He snorted. "You know me so well, so quickly."

"Yes, and you . . . you're gonna to end up dead yourself. Battle or sickness or because of your own mouth. I wish you could lie. I wish you'd try. I wish you'd stay alive."

"Thank you for that." He paused. "I'll do what I need to do."

Beulah stared at him in dismay, emotion choking her throat. The fool. The wonderful, stupidly stubborn fool.

In the moonless blackness, his magic made his pale skin glow all the more. "I'll pray for you."

"Yes. I'd like that. Pray for me. Please. I need your prayers, Chaplain Walsh."

Beulah pulled herself deeper into her own skin, deeper than she had ever gone before. Water thrummed against her whiskers, her vision of dark colors, the human color spectrum a mere memory. She tucked her flippers flush against her sides and swam. The river flowed against her, but she'd fight it every inch of the way.

THE CARTOGRAPHY OF SHATTERED TREES

SINCE THAT TERRIBLE NIGHT six months ago, Vivian had tolerated her body as a foreign, broken thing. She took care to never look at herself naked, yet as she stepped from the shower that morning, she glimpsed something strange in the mirror and paused. Instead of mere scars, a map adorned her skin. A highway of red traced the curve of her breast and flowed down to her belly button. The flecks and scars of wooden shrapnel had shifted to create the outline of hills and the undulation of a river. Her city rested above the knoll of her heart, thatched by cross-streets and byways.

Her fingers glanced her skin. The scars felt like divots, the fern-like spread of her burns in soft ripples. According to doctors, the Lichtenberg figures should have faded months before. Now those fractal burns had metamorphosed into something more.

Repulsed and fascinated, she followed the red route south to her navel. Did the map go where . . . it happened? Shuddering, she clenched her fist.

"I need to get ready for work," she said aloud.

Yet she still stared at herself, mesmerized. Despite the burns, despite the horribleness, there was something beautiful about the map.

She reached into the darkness of her closet and pulled out her old portfolio. Disturbed feathers of dust were set adrift in the air. She propped a large pad of paper against the bathroom counter and, with glances at the mirror, began to sketch. Her head pounded as it had so often since the lightning strike, and she furrowed her brow as she struggled for focus.

The line veered, gouging at the paper. She flung the pencil away with a wordless scream.

Vivian used to draw, paint, exist for the muse that overflowed from her fingertips. She used to live.

Her therapist had told her that if she wanted to create art again, she would find a way, even with the lingering nerve damage. Such trite, arrogant advice from a man with an illegible signature.

She didn't just want art again, she wanted her old life back. She wanted her innocence, for her body to be a clean slate, free of burns, free of the lingering memories of Andrew's heavy hand dragging her down.

Vivian ached to feel whole again, to fill the emptiness that constantly echoed beneath her breast.

She scrambled into her work clothes, smothering the memories beneath cotton and polyester. Her feet knew the path to work. She needed no map.

The throbbing drumbeat of pain worsened as the day continued.

The pain itself was nothing new; it had been a constant companion all these months. Doctors had bluntly informed her that she could experience dementia, chronic headaches, motor impairment, personality changes, or even amnesia—oh, how she prayed for the latter.

On the contrary, Vivian remembered every detail of that night. The throbbing pain made it easier to fall into the past, when the agony had been fresh and intense. If she could still paint, she would have portrayed it with a foreground of bobbing blades of grass and a high, stark wall of trees beyond. It had been the first day of May, everything green and lovely beneath the moon.

And then Andrew's fingers jerked her down like manacles and the tree trunk scraped her elbows and she screamed, "Help me! Someone help me! Get off, Andrew, get off me—" and a bird's silhouette swooped against gray swirls of clouds and thunder rumbled and . . .

Vivian shivered out of the memory. Chatter continued in the surrounding cubicles, everyone content in their carpet-walled boxes. She was content here too, usually. The mindlessness soothed her. No need to think. Just read, type, code.

Heat flared just above her heart and, like a dragging finger, seared its way to her navel. She curled against her keyboard, gasping through the agony. As suddenly as it had appeared, the pain was gone.

Headaches, she knew. This—this was something more.

Vivian shoved away her desk. She kept her gaze down, avoiding eye contact that might have raised questions or concerns, and staggered down the hall to a singular bathroom. Another hot wave arced down her chest as she turned the lock. Moaning, she crumpled to the floor. When the spasm passed, she clutched the lip of the counter to pull herself upright. She tugged off her shirt.

The hard line of the roadmap glowed in ugly red. All around it, the divots of her scars radiated blue like stars against a pale sky.

On that night six months ago, lightning had channeled through a tree and blasted into her and Andrew. A brilliant flash and crackle quivered through her marrow as part of the tree exploded, piercing her with shrapnel beyond count. The doctors never removed all of the splinters. Her body would work them out in time, they said.

Now those splinters—or where they once lay—shone like a thousand distant constellations, tiny pinpricks aglow. Vivian splayed a hand against the lights. Her skin felt normal in temperature, the texture as mottled as it had been that morning.

The heat returned, and like a laser beam, the pain traveled from her heart to her belly. The map burned within her flesh.

"I don't want to go there," she whispered to herself, to the strangeness of her own body.

The pain lashed her again. Again. Again. She braced against the counter and rocked with the waves. It was strange, really, to feel something so intensely after such emptiness, but the agony brought no relief, no catharsis. Sweat slicked her fingers and coursed the taut lines of her neck.

"And what happens if I go there?" she asked herself. Vivian had long avoided the sight of her own skin, but somehow she knew the map hadn't been there before today. It had waited until now, until Halloween.

The blue lights sparkled with such intensity that they radiated through the thick cups of her bra.

Vivian had loved Andrew. In hindsight, she understood it was a naïve, stupid love, that she had been desperate for anyone to love her or show the slightest interest. He was a brooding artistic genius in the university fine arts track, the person she admired from afar since their freshman year. At the end of their first date, she dismissed the roughness of his kisses as mere eagerness.

On their second date, May Day, he drove her south. "To find a good make-out spot," he said, as the road curved through the hills.

Suspicion quivered in her belly but she wore a smile. In her senior year high school yearbook, she had been described with one word: 'Nice.' Nice to a fault. Nice in the most gullible way.

Andrew said he liked nice girls.

Now, six months later, she drove south by herself.

At the fringe of the city, she passed children in costume, their treat bags in hand. One little girl wore a purple witch's hat that shimmered in the glow of passing headlights. It almost made Vivian smile. During her teenage goth phase, she had tried to summon spirits on this night with its thin veil between the real and the spiritual. After hours of chanting and giggling, the only thing she and her friends successfully summoned was the pizza delivery man.

As she drove onward, the physical pain withdrew but memories gouged her. She knew these landmarks, not only from the map on her torso, but from that distant night. She recognized the particular bow of an old oak tree, and the gas station with its neon sign screaming CERVEZA. She knew the long curve of the road as it followed then crossed the river, just as the line flowed over the ridge of her ribs as it worked southward.

Vivian's arms, rigid as rebar, gripped the steering wheel. She wanted to stop, but feared if she did the pain would return and paint her world in red dapples. She felt used. Herded. Just as Andrew forced her on this route, now something inexplicable was forcing her again.

The realization caused her to lurch to the side of the road. The car braked with a violent crunch of gravel.

What if Andrew was doing this again?

This was Halloween, the night of ghosts and spirits. What if he awaited her? What could she say to him, what could she do?

She opened her car door and retched.

Andrew never acknowledged that he had done wrong, never had that chance. "I drove you all the way out here. Isn't this a romantic spot?" he said, pointing to the beautiful oak that towered overhead.

"No," she said. "No. I want to go home, I don't want to—"

She had always admired his hands in class. One usually thinks of painters with long, delicate fingers, but Andrew had the wide mitts of a football player. He gripped her slender wrists so tightly his fingers touched.

He had died with his pants wadded around his ankles.

"No," she said, punching her ribs and the map. "I'm not going. You can't make me."

Vivian backed up the car, the tires grinding as she angled them north. Pain crashed into her again. She had enough presence of mind to lay all her weight into the brake. The scars, hidden beneath her shirt, flashed so brilliantly they illuminated the blackness.

"No. No. No." She panted as she leaned on the steering wheel. She had repeated those words to Andrew, and they were just as effective now as then. Maybe she was the ghost.

A light reflected against the silver hood of her car. She looked up. A full moon gleamed through skeletal branches, as though it were snared in the spindly grasp of twigs. Watercolor clouds in hues of black, purple, and navy softened the sky.

"I could paint that," she whispered. Fury uncoiled in her gut. She used to be able to paint scenes like that.

Vivian wanted to paint again. She wanted steadiness to return to her fingers. Instead of that constant emptiness within, she yearned for the overflow of her soul onto canvas or paper. Hot rage compounded her headache.

Six months ago, she was broken. Tonight she could confront Andrew. She was alive, not him. He had no power over her, not now. She refused to be herded to the scene of her attack. No, she'd go there willingly and face the bastard down.

She turned south again, her rear wheels peeling on gravel as she roared back onto the road.

Vivian took a side street darkened by tall trees. At a right turn, the map sizzled on her chest, and she knew to turn left instead. She wound her way deeper into the hills until she reached a broken wooden fence all too familiar to her nightmares. In the field beyond stood the tree.

She wanted to hate it, but instead, she stared in awe.

The gnarled branches of the oak scraped the sky. The nearest trees cowered as saplings in comparison. Vivian absorbed the eloquence of the tree's composition. Like a bonsai tree on massive scale, it looked utterly natural yet unreal in its asymmetrically balanced perfection—Wabi-sabi, as her college Arts Aesthetics professor would have said.

She hadn't been able to take in all of that before. She had been talking to Andrew, her shoulders braced, her hands shoved in her pockets. By the time they were within the tree's shadow, he had grabbed her arm, and the images of the tree became a mixture of utter clarity and terrified blurs.

Vivian stepped over the broken fence and approached the tree along an intermittent muddy path. She remembered the mud. She had crawled back to the car, to her purse and phone, even as her skin zinged in continued electric agony.

Andrew had landed some twenty feet from the big oak. She looked for him there now, her arms clutched close, her throat dry with fear. Acorns and dry leaves crunched beneath her feet and she shivered within the deep shade of the tree's canopy. No stereotypical ghost stood in wait. She frowned. Things glittered in the grass, as though a bottle had been broken and scattered.

"Don't you recognize yourself?" asked a woman's voice, creaking with age.

Vivian whirled on her heel, gasping as the scars across her torso flickered with cold. Not pain, just—strangeness.

The trunk of the large tree stood five feet wide, and from it leaned the body of woman. The branches of her arms flexed and bowed in greeting. Vine hair trailed over her shoulders to the adolescent curves of her chest and down to where her waist melded with the tree itself.

Vivian stared. "What . . . what are you?"

"What are you?" The woman cocked her head to one side.

"I'm . . . I'm Vivian. A woman. Human."

"You are more and you are less," the tree said, her ebony eyes narrowing. "I expected more growth. You're little more than a stump."

"What? A stump?" Vivian licked her dry lips and looked around. "I thought . . . I expected a ghost here."

"A ghost?" The tree sounded incredulous. "You wear part of me within your flesh, its magic lighting your path here on this night of power, and you expect a ghost?" The bark-skinned woman shook her head in clear disgust.

Vivian pressed her hand against her shirt, her mind rapidly trying to take in everything. This being in the tree was something straight out of a fairy tale or Greek myth.

"You're a dryad," Vivian whispered. "Why—why do I see you? I didn't when I was here . . . before."

"You see me because of what you carry. I have stood here for three hundred circuits of the sun. I have hosted picnics upon my roots, blanketed lovers with my leaves, and shared in such joy. And then," the dryad said, her eyes blazing like coals, "one fool human sought to use my trunk, my roots, to shatter you. I will not be used in such a way."

"Andrew," Vivian whispered.

"I thought to spare you, but the damage was done. You beings are so brief and fragile. Part of your soul fragmented like an autumn leaf." The dryad nodded towards the sparkles in the grass. "The pieces are over there, visible on this night and Beltane."

Vivian closed her eyes. She remembered her hands clawing into the roots. Andrew's heavy weight, heavy breaths, heavy presence crushing her. "Someone help me! Help!" she had cried.

Then the lightning came.

"It was you," Vivian said. "You brought the lightning."

The dryad nodded, her leafy hair swaying in the breeze. "It is an easy thing, at my height, to stretch towards the sky."

Heat uncoiled in Vivian's chest, but not the heat of the burns or the map. "Do you realize what it did to me?" she screamed. "Do you know how much it hurt, how it still hurts? And my hands." She thrust them out towards the tree. "I can't . . . do anything." Draw, paint, live.

The dryad blinked, unfazed. "I have been struck by lightning dozens of times. I hold no fear of it."

"Well, you're a tree!"

"And you are a human."

Vivian's shoulders shook as she breathed rapidly. "I haven't been the same since that night."

"You expect to stay the same? This day, my roots have sunken deeper into the ground. I've shed a hundred leaves."

Vivian turned away from the tree and swallowed another

scream. Her throat burned with the effort. She didn't want to stare at this pompous being, this thing that caused so much pain even as it meant to save her.

She stooped to pick up a piece of her soul. It was the size of a fingernail, iridescent, weighing nothing against her palm. Looking around, she spied a dozen more shards.

She needed to be whole again. She pressed the piece to her lips and swallowed.

Vivian walked back and forth to find and swallow every shard. Heat curdled in her chest again, and she breathed through the pain. She faced the dryad. The heat instantly subsided.

The woman in the tree studied her with an impatient frown.

"Enough of that! Come closer. The night grows older, and your ilk isn't meant to carry my magic. Let's do this and be done."

Vivian stopped, staring down at her body. Once upon a time, she would have been delighted to carry such magic. A blue glow lit her shirt.

"Don't hesitate or I will do this until you come close." The woman in the tree flicked her spindly fingers. Pain shivered down Vivian's torso. "I'm content with my roots planted here. I have no desire to graft with a human."

The pain was all the motivation Vivian needed. She took a few steps forward and the dryad grasped her with a wooden hand.

Pinpricks of cold intensified across Vivian's breasts and ribs. The world glowed vermillion and black as agony rippled across her body, as though the lightning struck again. Vivian blinked and saw tree branches directly above, though she had no memory of falling or closing her eyes. Her hand clutched her shirt and found holes—dozens, hundreds. The map had been ripped from her skin. She held a hand up to the moonlight and didn't see any blood.

Vivian pressed a fist to her stomach, which had abruptly turned queasy. "That's not—that's not all, the bigger splinters were pulled out at the hospital—"

"I lose branches to the wind and it is no loss, but my essence isn't meant to be melded with yours." The voice was fainter. Even its appearance had withdrawn, more fused with the tree.

Vivian sat upright. She didn't feel different, or did she? She lifted her shirt. In the scarce light she could barely see the Lichtenberg figures. Maybe they would heal now. Maybe . . .

Her stomach burbled, and she had just enough time to face the ground before she became ill. Shards of her soul sparkled across the dirt. They were as bright as ever, unaffected by the absence of the dryad's magic.

Above her, the dryad laughed like a wind whistling far away. Her branches clattered. "As if ingesting your soul will restore it. It's a soul, not rainwater." The words were scarcely audible.

Vivian picked up a single fleck of her soul. She turned it between her fingertips. The shard glowed in her hand, its edges jagged yet not sharp. None of the pieces were alike. It was an impossible puzzle.

They could never go back inside. They were never meant to.

An odd sense of peace fell over her.

Vivian sat, gazing up at the tree. She could barely see the dryad at all now, those dark eyes as whorls. The burn scar on the trunk began at Vivian's eye level and extended to the roots. That was where the lightning channeled through, struck her, then passed on through Andrew. Her fingers hovered over the scorched wood.

The tree had taken the blast and survived, even thrived. It stood, magnificent and old, braving the wind and winters and whatever else came this way. The burns and lost branches did not take away from the dryad's perfect imperfection. Wabi-sabi.

Vivian scooped up the fragments of her soul and stood.

Her body was ugly. Scarred. But she was alive.

In a violent motion, she flung the shards back into the grass. The fragments sparkled like a hundred prisms as they arced through the air and bounced into the carpet of green. They resembled strange glass flowers of rainbow petals, glowing and iridescent.

She would paint them someday.

If her fingers could never hold a brush, she would use finger-paints. Somehow, someway, she would capture this scene again. The tree would loom in the background, holding up the moon and a dome of stars with its ancient strength. Vivian was just as strong, just as resilient.

"I'll come back someday," she said to the tree. The lower branches bowed in acknowledgment.

Vivian did not need a map to find her way.

Roots, Shallow and Deep

Folks say first impressions mean everything. Well, Hanford tasted like dirt. I stepped off the train to a face-full of the stuff, plus a waft from some restless cattle nearby. I coughed to one side and headed toward the depot. The passenger train had been about half full, most folks likely headed on to points west like San Francisco. The town of Hanford was young—it smelled young, by the fresh pine of nearby construction—and businesses bustled along the north side of the tracks.

Peculiar, considering how I'd been rushed here to investigate a matter of plague.

I'd expected a scene of eerie quiet, maybe bodies in the street. Certainly not cheery howdy-heys of farmers and barefoot boys scampering after a leather ball.

"Pardon! Mr. Harrington! Are you Mr. Evan Harrington?"

I turned to confront a man as he nearly pushed aside a few fellows in his way. I caught the dark looks they gave him.

"I'm Mr. Harrington," I said, and extended my hand.

"I'm Mr. Johns, from the Southern Pacific Railroad. I was sent to meet you and acquaint you with our predicament."

He assessed me in a glance and self-consciously smoothed his slicked blonde hair. His brown suit didn't sit square on his shoulders, like a child playing dress-up in his big brother's clothes. I notice these sorts of things. Clothing makes the man, as folks say. Or in my case, makes the black woman a white man.

I wore a suit I'd tailored for myself, modeled on the latest fashion from New York City. The sack coat featured a narrow lapel and buttoned high to reveal a blue silk vest and the drapery of a gold pocket watch chain. A starched collar pressed against my neck and looked bold behind a black cravat. A derby hat rested at a jaunty angle. It was an outfit that spoke of smartness, success, and of some maturity. Exactly the persona I needed my glamour to exude. While so attired, only I could see my true coloration with my eyes or in mirrors. Photography inexplicably smeared my image.

I walked alongside Mr. Johns. Twenty years of experience had trained me to force my strides long and confident. "The city is not what I expected."

He shot me a nervous glance. "Yes, well, that's not something to discuss out here."

A crowd of farmers huddled around a hitching post. They grimaced at Mr. Johns and eyed me with wariness.

We entered a board-constructed building within sight of the railroad tracks. The furniture was sparse and mismatched. Two desks mounded with paperwork were pressed to the far wall. Mr. Johns sat behind the central desk like a king settling onto a throne. He pulled out two glasses and a decanter of amber liquid.

"Damned sand-lappers out there. They usually spit when I walk by. They're on good behavior for you." He began to pour.

"Pardon me, sand-lappers?" I took out my notepad and pencil.

"A local term for these . . . obstinate settlers." He slid a glass toward me. I did not reach for it. The impairment brought by drink was not something I could risk. "You are aware of the melodrama here, them versus the Southern Pacific?"

"There hasn't been much published about it in Portland. I really need to know more about this plague and why business appears so normal here, Mr. Johns."

"This legal fight and the plague are tied together, or I'll be damned." He scowled into his drink. "See, I sell and rent Southern Pacific railroad land and collect our grain rents. The railroad owns a stretch of land out west of here in Mussel Slough. A number of settlers are squatting on our parcels, refusing to move even when we sell the land out from under them. I've been threatened and burned in effigy. The Circuit Court ruled in our favor about a month ago. A week later, my two partners here in Hanford were killed by this strange sickness." He hesitated.

"Speak freely, Mr. Johns. I'm proprietor of Extraordinary Investigations. I deal with ... the unusual. Sprites that invade like locusts. Lycanthropes. Foul sorcery—"

"Is it like in the dime novels?" He leaned forward. "Girls, travel, stalking monsters through the night?"

Oh, how he'd react if he knew he spoke with a Negro woman born a slave. "No. The worst monsters work days and wear suits." That took him aback. "I'm not here to palaver about personal matters. I need to know more about this illness. What leads you to think it's magical in nature, not poison?"

"Mr. Bunyan and Mr. Heisen came down sick one at a time. They each turned gray, like statues. Like the life drained from them. They both lasted three days exactly. After they were both dead, someone else came down sick. Random, it seems. Always one at a time. Doctors can't do nothing to stop it."

"How many others have died?"

"Don't know. My associates passed on three weeks ago. I been begging for someone like you to come here and find out what's-what. The local marshal certainly doesn't want to meddle with something that reeks of dark magic. Damned railroad nabobs in San Francisco finally listened to me to hire you."

Victims going gray and lifeless one at a time. Medical intervention useless. More and more, this reminded me of a case about a decade back in Santa Fe. Beautiful woman afraid of getting old summoned up a miasma that sucked other people dry and granted their vitality to her. By the time I hunted her down on a mesa near the Pecos, she'd aged herself to look fifteen years old.

I glanced past Mr. Johns to an 1880 calendar still pinned a month behind, on March. "If this plague keeps going, word will get out. The railroad's property values will fall for sure. No wonder your higher-ups decided to care." His grudging nod affirmed that. "The sick folk. Are they all in Hanford?"

"Close vicinity. Hanford to Grangeville to Armona. No further out than that."

"These settlers. Any known magi in their ranks? Or gossip of anyone who is suddenly healthier than before?"

"Some folks do magic, sure, but good enough to be called a magus? Don't know. I don't hear much in the way of gossip."

No. If he was grabbing land from established settlers, people would likely rather pet a spider than palaver with Mr. Johns. "How've you stayed alive these three weeks?"

His grin was tight and ugly. "Come five o'clock tonight, I'm on a train to Fresno to stay at a boarding house. I'll be back in the morning. It's damned inconvenient, but I see the pattern. I'm no fool."

As an assassination technique against railroad men, this sickness struck me as damned inefficient. There were other 'accidental' ways to kill a person. Too many other people were dying.

I tapped my pencil. Life-eaters like this were common across many world cultures. The good news for me—and most everyone else local—was that across all pantheons, the simplest solution here was to find and kill the magus.

"Thanks for the welcome, Mr. Johns." I stood and picked up my luggage. "I have a great deal of work to do by nightfall."

"Do you want me to show you around? Major Lederer's head of the Settler's Land League. He's out near the slough in Grangeville." He looked downright eager.

"No, thank you. I can see myself around."

"Oh. Well, meet me at the station by five and you can be assured I'll get you a train ticket to Fresno for the night. And remember, this needs to be kept quiet. We can't have people panicking."

"No. Of course not." I turned away. Out of the corner of my eye, I watched him throw back my full glass of liquor.

Some stalwart fellow this was. Keep things quiet, indeed. He was fine with other folks dying so long as his own skin was safe. I'd call him a donkey by another name, but I hate to insult any kin of a horse.

I acquired a hotel room and took the time to tidy myself. My suit needed to be dusted off, my shoes shined. Cologne applied to the pressure points. I checked the vital accoutrements of my job. My silver knife, sheathed at the utility belt at my hips. A vial of holy water. Pouch of salt. Pouch of iron nails. A loaded pistol, for troubles of the human variety. I checked my appearance. The utility belt added a debonair, gunslinger flare to an otherwise trim, neat suit.

Mr. Johns and everyone else saw me as the kind of man you'd expect in such attire. White-skinned. Well-off. Handsome, even. I couldn't see what they saw, and from what I understood, no one viewed me in exactly the same way.

The real me had skin like a moonless night. A broad nose. Round, brown eyes. Hair cropped close. I kept my breasts bound— not that I had much to hide. I tailored everything to hide the curve of my hips. Wasn't often I wore a proper dress.

I liked being a woman, truly. *Evaline.* My given name, the one no one said anymore. But I liked the independence of being a man of privilege. *Evan Harrington.* It was awful lonely, being some-where between Evaline and Evan. Being someone different with clothes on and off. The attention of women grieved me something fierce.

Not that I had time to spare on such thoughts now, not with a malevolent spirit on the prowl. Maybe that's why I kept at constant work.

Another train had pulled into the depot across the way. This one delivered cattle, machinery, and lumber. I hadn't often been through this part of California in recent years, but I understood the region's forced reliance on the Southern Pacific. There was no competition. Every passenger or parcel or food grown here *had* to take the Southern Pacific to travel in an expedient manner. Hanford itself was founded by the railway and named after one of its employees, according to literature I'd read on my trip down.

Considering these facts—and the demeanor of Mr. Johns—I could well understand why the "sand-lappers" were riled. Not that this excused the sorcery set loose here.

At the livery stable nearby, I acquired a chestnut mare. I rode west through a verdant spring countryside crisscrossed by irrigation ditches filled with Sierra snowpack runoff. I could have ridden on forever with a smile on my face. More I saw of the country, the more I liked it. I had a home these days, but not a home-home. Hadn't had such a thing since I was a fool child, bound to the plantation. These folks made the desert bloom through sheer work and gumption. I envied that.

The Lederer homestead was a single-story structure surrounded by massive rose bushes in an array of colors. I couldn't help but take in a deep, blissful breath. My old missus used to grow roses. I think that was her one redeeming quality.

A Chinese manservant didn't meet my eye as he welcomed me inside and to a formal parlor. The sweetness of roses was replaced by something faint and foul. To other folks, magic smelled pleasant. To me, it stank. The darker the magic, the nastier the odor. Mind you, I can't cast spells; my glamour doesn't tax my energy the way spell-work drains a magus. I put on clothes, and the glamour is simply . . . there.

I don't know what sort of fae my father was, but he certainly passed along some curious skills.

A few minutes later, Major Lederer introduced himself. He looked as I'd expected: silver hair, coiffed beard, his frock coat well-worn but of high quality. His eyes were rheumy and vacant, as if he'd been ill.

I passed him my calling card, describing myself as simply an investigator of recent illnesses in the area. "I was admiring the roses out front."

A wave of grief passed over his face. "They were my wife's joy. The roots came from England. They've grown here some fifteen years. She . . . she went to the Almighty a few weeks ago."

Another death. "Was it this sickness . . . ?"

"No. I'm not sure of the illness of which you speak. My Sally struck her head and didn't awaken after."

"My deepest condolences. I didn't mean to intrude."

"No. I should . . . make an effort to get out. Our friends have tried, but it's been difficult for me." His smile quivered. "We were together forty years. We met when I was a young man sent abroad. She was British-born, but passionate for California. Our home here means—meant—everything to her."

I glanced at his hands. Magic required bare skin on herbs and ingredients, and the resulting stains were a point of pride among practitioners. Major Lederer's cuticles and nails were trimmed and unremarkable. That left the house staff and the late Mrs. Lederer as suspected magi.

Occultism was all the rage in Britain, and had recently become a hobby across America. Many wives' clubs gathered to exchange cantrips and socialize. Other club members would know about Mrs. Lederer or other locals with the knack. Investigating the house staff would require a different tack.

"I heard you were head of the Settler's Land League and led the fight against the railroad," I said.

His laugh was bitter. "Officially, I still am the head, but I'm as good as resigned. You need hope in order to fight the octopus that is the Southern Pacific, and I haven't any hope left. This ranch—what does it mean, without any family? No wife, no boy . . . Our son died in the war, you see."

Three portraits on the nearby table featured a pale boy, the Major in his full Confederate regalia, and the late Mrs. Lederer, her pale hair in ringlets.

"I understand what it means to lose your kin and to lose your home." I stopped myself. I didn't need to say more about my own shallow roots. "But if you're the leader, there're other families looking to you. Don't forget them."

The Major seemed to look at me for the first time, as if he just woke up. He pulled my card from his pocket again. "Extraordinary Investigations. I've seen your sort before. This illness you're asking about must not be normal."

"No. I suspect it's sorcery to benefit the magus. Was told there's an afflicted child near death in Hanford now."

"A child? Do you know the name?"

"I don't, sir."

Grief drenched his features. "I'll inquire. But if anyone is engaged in dark chicanery, it's those Southern Pacific men. Heisen, Johns, Bunyan. They want to sell us our own land and charge us for the improvements we made. Since we won't pay, they're keen to run us off."

"It'd be hard to ask Mr. Heisen and Mr. Bunyan as they succumbed first to this plague," I said.

Major Lederer's jaw gaped. "They did? Then you . . . that's who is paying you to investigate, isn't it? The railroad?" He was no fool. I wondered if he'd throw me out, but instead he looked thoughtful. "And here you were talking me into continued work for the Settler's Land League."

"I'm not here about the legal fight over the land." God knew, the legal system and I disagreed on many things. I stood. "I'm here because dark magic is killing railroader and settler alike. If you need to contact me, I have a room at the Livermore in Hanford. Good day, Major."

I stepped outside and paused to breathe in the roses again, to clear that awful residual magic from my lungs. This was a shaded spot of pure peace.

My pause was longer than I realized, as Major Lederer soon joined me with clippers in hand. I eyed him with wariness, but his manner was not threatening.

"She would hate how overgrown the roses are now. She always tended to them herself. I . . . I should take care of them. Would you like a white bloom for your lapel, Mr. Harrington?"

"I don't usually wear one in such fashion, but it might freshen my hotel room."

"Or maybe you can gift it to a lady in town. Sally liked when her roses made people smile. Here." He cut the thornless stem a few inches long and wrapped it in his own silk handkerchief.

"I'm much obliged," I said, ignoring the yearning evoked by his statement. The wrapped bloom just fit inside an interior jacket pocket I most often used to carry an extra pistol and silver bullets.

"We never thought we'd find a place we loved more than Tennessee," he said softly, and not to me. "This California valley was our promised land. Home in the truest sense."

Home. I liked Oregon well enough, but he made me think of South Carolina and the life I left behind. The guilt hit me in the gut sometimes. That I escaped. That I wasn't true to my own self, my kin. I sent money to my cousins there every so often, as if that could absolve me of my insecurities. I doubted anything could. My fae blood was half of me, but I didn't understand that half. I knew the names and faces of my mama's folks, and the misery I escaped.

For the first time in many a year, I felt a yearning to sink in my roots, make a real home, damned fool notion though it was. I couldn't live in utter isolation, and if I lived near folks, I wouldn't be accepted as an equal due to my skin and gender. At this point, I would settle for no less.

So I wouldn't settle. I'd take job after job, stay restless as ever. I had plenty to do. Too many folks suffered from the misuse of magic and ancient machinations born anew. Then there was my own quest for answers about my fae nature.

I rode east toward town, sober with memories. The sun was high overhead. Clicking my teeth, I encouraged my horse to trot.

Every minute ticked closer to that three day point when the life-eater would shift to a new victim.

There's a common misperception about where to find the best know-it-alls in a small town. Bartenders know a lot about men's business, true, but the best gossip is where the liquor or juice is sipped once a week.

The afternoon crawled on as I visited every local building with a spire. The priests and preachers were downright courteous, though I finally found what I needed when a reverend was out on rounds. His wife, the kindly Mrs. Shute, invited me in for tea. There was an unmistakable whiff of magic about the place.

"I'm delighted you were able to speak with Major Lederer. The poor man." Mrs. Shute reminded me of an unbaked bread roll with her doughy complexion and rounded body. The cap of black frizzy hair, barely contained by a snood, seemed to be an afterthought. "Since his wife passed, he's shut out the world. The circumstances there . . . terrible."

"I was told she had a head wound."

Mrs. Shute leaned forward. "I heard that as well, Mr. Harrington, but also that she was a suicide." She motioned two fingers against her wrist. I couldn't help but notice the telltale ingredient stains on her fingertips. She was likely the sort who wore fingerless gloves in public for that very reason. "Which, really, makes no sense to me. She was a vivacious woman in a loving marriage."

"Did you know her well?"

"In our club, yes. We'd get together to quilt, collect food for families in need, maybe fiddle with a spell or two."

She said it to impress me; the occult was popular, after all, and here I was, the sophisticated out-of-towner. I arched an eyebrow. "Does the reverend . . . ?"

"Oh, Mr. Harrington. It's all in fun. Dabbling, that's all." She giggled like a schoolgirl.

"Was Mrs. Lederer particularly talented?"

"Better than most of us, I'd say. If you want to find the darker arts, well, you go to China Alley." She leaned forward, tapping her chin. "My husband is trying to get the heathens removed. The smells down there are awful, then there's the gambling, the opium. It's terrible. Sugar?" She held out a cup of sugar cubes.

"No, thank you, ma'am." Directing this conversation was like herding a cat. "I mentioned at the start I'm investigating these local illnesses. Has your husband tended some of the others struck down?"

"Oh my, yes. The graying, they call it. Young Cliff is almost gone. The poor dear."

Sunset neared. That child would die for certain unless I found the magus. Mrs. Shute wasn't the source. The scent of magic here was mild, the sort of minor household enchantments that kept linens crisp and flies out. In my wandering about town, I hadn't come across anything as pungent as in the Major's house. That left the servants as suspect, or . . .

I'd dealt with undead magi before. That transformation required incredible magical aptitude and a deep-rooted selfish need for power that seemed strongly at odds with everything I'd heard of Mrs. Lederer. Even so, I'd been at this too long to fully dismiss her as the culprit.

"Is there anyone else in the area with an aptitude for magic? Or anyone who is looking exceptionally healthy?"

She arched an eyebrow. That tidbit of gossip would be spread about for sure. "No one especially gifted, no. This town barely has its roots in the dirt, Mr. Harrington. We have to go to Fresno for proper spell-work."

A thump came from the back of the house, followed by footsteps. A young Chinese woman stepped within the doorway, saw the two of us, and hastily bowed.

"I bring," she said.

"Wonderful. Thank you, Mimi. Her father has quite a garden.

Good Christian folk. You should see their strawberries!"

I stood and bowed as I tucked my notes away. The girl took a step back and offered another hesitant bow in turn.

House servants knew everything that happened within their walls. A local grocer, with such trusted access to homes, might know a thing or two as well.

"Ma'am? Might I speak with you?" I asked her.

Her eyes widened. Her nod was quick, fearful. Good God, how must my glamour make me look to her? I knew from experience that when well-dressed white men came to visit and asked after the younger slaves, there was nothing good about. Chinese women were rare to see in California, and ignorant folks assumed all of them were ladies of the night. Likely the presence of the reverend's wife was all that kept Mimi from bolting from the house completely.

Nauseous at my own ineptitude, I knew I needed to cut this short. "Have you heard of the sickness going around, ma'am? That makes folks turn gray?" At her increased alarm, I knew I had erred again. "No, I am not saying your people are the cause. Have any of yours been sick?"

She looked between me and Mrs. Shute.

If I asked if she'd heard of any bad magic about, I wouldn't get an answer. The question was too incriminating. California boiled with anti-Chinese sentiment, and folks looked for any excuse to lynch, shame, or attack her people. And here I was, in my glamoured guise.

Finally, she nodded.

"Thank you, ma'am, that's all I need to know. Have a pleasant day."

She remained still like a rabbit caught in the open, as if she could render herself invisible, then burst into motion. Her feet pattered down the hall, screen door clattering behind her.

"She's a good girl. Terribly shy around men. We encourage her family to come to church, with the hopes she'll spread the Good Word."

I had lived in my own glamour for so long, God help me, I forgot. I forgot the fear.

I clutched my trembling fists at my hips. My suit felt wrong on my body. Soiled. "Mrs. Shute, thank you very much for enduring my questions. The tea was quite fine."

With that, I skedaddled with just slightly more control than the Chinese woman. God help me. I needed to get back to my place back in Portland, lock myself inside, and stay naked for days. I needed to remember my own skin.

The walk toward downtown calmed my nerves. Windows along Sixth Street were aglow with electric light. A train whistle pierced the evening; I wondered if it was Mr. Johns' train, or if he had already fled. I encountered the town druggist as he closed up shop. He provided directions to the home of the child gone gray.

The sky turned fully dark on the short walk there. The front door was open and the wailing of family was discernible from the street. The inevitable had occurred.

I lingered near the front gate, guilt like iron in my gut. If I'd gotten to Hanford faster. If I'd found answers sooner. If I wasn't such a damned fool. My encounter at Mrs. Shute's house had left me rattled, made me think of things I didn't want to think of.

From the side of the house, I heard hoof beats that increased in intensity as the rider bolted into the street at a reckless canter. I hugged the white fence. The rider sped by not five feet away. Dust kicked against my trousers.

"My God! Are you all right?" The man's accented voice came from the other side of the fence.

"Yes. Startled more than anything."

"The Major shouldn't be riding that fast in the dark."

"Major? Major Lederer? Why was he here?"

"He heard of Cliff's illness. He was quite shaken. Let me find the latch—I should have brought a lamp, but my walk home is short." A gate creaked open. "I'm Doctor Resinov."

"I spoke to the Major earlier. It seemed he had become something of a recluse since his wife passed on."

"Yes. Her death was a tragedy. One of those simple falls in the bedroom that turns out to not be simple. The Major hasn't been himself, and I think his senses are still addled. He pulled me aside tonight, in front of everyone, to ask if I was sure his wife was dead." His laugh was loud and awkward. "Really, what kind of a question is that?"

One very relevant to my investigation. "Thank you for your help, doctor," I said, and began to walk. After crossing the street, I ran.

This all came back to the railroad and Major Lederer and Sally Lederer. I gripped my utility belt as I ran, verifying my knife and everything else was where it ought to be.

I retrieved my horse from the livery stable and set off for Mussel Slough again, following a road cast pale gray by moonlight.

No one answered my hail in the yard, though illumination shone through the homestead windows. The roses were as fragrant as before. I entered the house with a hand on the pistol beneath my jacket.

Wary, I let the stink of magic draw me deeper into the house. Floorboards creaked beneath my soft treads. I found myself in a unkempt bedroom wallpapered in paisley.

The place reeked of magic. Blood magic, recently cast. Rot and decay with a whiff of iron. I avoided the center of the floor as if it contained an open pit. The stain there was invisible yet as dark as a senator's soul.

What had happened here? How had Mrs. Lederer truly died? Suicide, or a head injury? Or was she not truly dead at all, as the Major now suspected?

Daguerreotypes on the dresser caught my eye. Another image of the Major in his regalia, and a separate one of a young soldier. I did a double take when I realized the soldier was their son. He wore Union attire.

"Father versus son. One survived and the other did not," I murmured. Such was the nature of that war.

The house and barn were empty of people. I heard an approaching wagon on the road and rode to intercept it.

"Yes, I saw the Major a while back," the farmer replied to my inquiry. "He was riding up Lake Avenue with a shovel and lantern. I found that a mite strange."

I sucked in a breath. "Is the cemetery that way?"

"Straight up the road, sure. Why, whatever—"

I pressed my horse to a gallop. Wheat fields and orchards of spindly saplings flanked the road in moonlit blurs. Miles passed. I would have dismissed the cemetery as just another field but for the taller trees throughout the lot. These grounds had likely been settled before most of the surrounding towns. I slowed my horse to a walk to grant him time to cool, then dismounted to encourage a quiet approach.

A lantern glimmered out yonder. I secured my horse's reins to a tall headstone and advanced, doing my utmost to not break my own neck on low headstones or brush. I gripped my pistol in my right hand and the silver dagger with my left.

The soft snick and slide of a shovel against dirt was clear to my ears. The stink of magic filled my nostrils. The shovel struck something solid. I sidled behind a monument some ten feet away.

"Jesus, have mercy. Jesus, help me," I heard. The shovel was tossed aside with a thud. There came a wrenching of wood and an agonized wail that made the hair on my neck stand on end. "Oh God! Sally! Are you alive? Are you? What have you done?"

I rounded the headstone, weapons at ready. "Major Lederer, please back away from the grave."

He was on all fours beside the open earth, sobbing. "I had to see. When you came earlier, I got to thinking, and then I saw that boy die . . . it wasn't natural, that sickness, and I knew my Sally, she didn't intend that. She'd never take away anyone else's child, Mr. Harrington."

I edged around the dirt pile to see what the lantern illuminated. The potency of magic quivered in the air like a heat mirage. Inside the casket, Sally Lederer looked all of twenty—not nearer to sixty, as she should be—and this was no glamour. Her age had been undone, just as in my previous case in Santa Fe. She looked almost perfect.

The exception being the top of her head. Through the perfect torrent of blonde hair, her head grotesquely bulged. There was no blood, which made it worse, in a way.

"What did Mrs. Lederer intend?" I asked.

"We lost the Circuit Court case a month ago. Her sister just sent over some old grimoires from England. Sally said, maybe there's something in there that can help us. She wanted to make the railroad men sick. That's all I knew. I went up to Fresno for business. When I came back . . ." He heaved with sobs. "There was so much blood, and her head . . ."

"This kind of sorcery requires blood," I said. "She cut her wrist, didn't she? But she cut too deep and with the blood loss, she must have gone faint and struck her head."

My mind raced through the bits that the Major wouldn't know, didn't need to know. Ignorant as Sally was about magic of this caliber, she'd successfully shackled the spirit to her. It'd done its duty and sickened two of the three men it was sent for, and now she was incapable of stopping the spell.

"She lived a few days after and then . . . we thought she was dead. Doc Resinov said so. Her heart stopped. She wasn't breathing."

"She's still as good as dead. Maybe she did die, back then. This magic she worked is stealing the essence of other folks around town. It's making her younger, but it can't actually heal her. Look."

I set down my dagger long enough to use the shovel's handle to turn over her arm. It still showed a bright, unhealed cut from wrist to elbow. The poor, foolish woman. She hadn't a clue what she was doing. To anyone else, a cut like that was suicide. No wonder the rumor had spread.

Or maybe this wasn't fully of her own volition. The summoned spirit could have manipulated her during the casting, insisted on more blood. These creatures weren't stupid, and this one had earned an extended stay with three-day smorgasbords one after another.

"But she looks ... she looks beautiful," Major Lederer whispered.

"Her brain is beyond repair, Major. You served in the war. You've seen others with wounds like this."

"Sally's magic will let her get better—"

"Sally had some small skill with magic, yes, but not for this sorcery. The only way to stop this is to truly kill her—"

"No!" He lurched upright, reaching to his waist. "I can't let you. By God's mercy, she'll heal—"

"How many more children do you want to die? It ..."

I smelled the miasma's approach before I saw it. I switched my silver blade to my right hand; my pistol would be useless as a feather now. "Major! Get away from the grave!"

He gasped as the creature entered the halo of light. It was like a bag of black vapor stretched into a long, serpentine form. No head, no eyes. It oozed over the side of the pit and onto Mrs. Lederer.

"No!" The Major yelled and started to fling himself into the grave.

"Fool!" I lunged to grip him by the collar in time. It said something of the potency of the life-eater that the Major could see it at all.

"It's—that thing—it's going to—"

"It's the only reason her body's still alive at all." We watched in mute horror as the shadow coiled and writhed. The body beneath did not move or react in any way, even as the stench increased. It was emitting the life force of that boy. The shadow shivered and glided up the other side of the grave.

Right toward us.

I hauled back the Major with a firm hand on his shoulder. The spirit hesitated as if to consider its options.

I considered my own choices. I needed to attend the ugly business of severing the dark link Mrs. Lederer had formed.

That meant I needed Major Lederer incapacitated.

I shoved.

The shadow swarmed over him. One instant the Major was there on his knees, trying to rise. The next, he was sprawled flat on his belly. Limp. The miasma was fully inside him.

I shakily lowered myself to the dirt. "God forgive me," I whispered. I looked into my own quaking hands, my pale palms, my dark fingers and knuckles. Major Lederer's eyes were still open wide. They tracked me as I stood.

"Once she's dead, the spirit will go back whence it came," I said. "You'll be able to get well. Just stay put for now. I'll be back for you."

He whimpered.

With that, I assessed her body and the tools at hand. I needed to burn her heart and brain to cinders to break the perverse bond, and return what remained to the grave. Then the Major needed tending, and there'd be other business, too. I adjusted my derby hat.

This'd be a long night.

Relentless sunlight beamed down on the Southern Pacific depot in Hanford the next morn. Folks clustered around in wait for the next train. I leaned against a wooden post. My back and arms ached, but even so, if I closed my eyes for more than two blinks I could have fallen asleep. The labor was hard for a solitary person, and my figure wasn't quite so imposing as it appeared to others.

Major Lederer's body had been laid waste after mere hours of affliction. Fortunately, I'd found a ranch nearby with good folks who came to our aid. At sun-up, the talk with the local marshal hadn't been pleasant—meetings with such folks rarely are—but my position as a contract worker for the Southern Pacific granted me some authority. It earned me plenty of derisive looks, too.

The train pulled up to the station with a magnificent gush of dust. The place stewed with people.

"Mr. Harrington?" Mr. Johns approached, waving. "You survived the night!" He looked so bright-eyed, I could have slugged him.

"I did. You won't need to flee every third night now. Check with the local marshal. He has his report, and mine will be ready to mail to your people by the time I'm back in Portland."

"Damn fine work. Dare I ask—who was behind the sorcery?"

Weary as I was, that's when my brain pieced together the repercussions of the night. Mrs. Lederer had done wrong, but that didn't make the railroad right. That's not how it'd look to the press and so many other people, though. The odds had always been against the settlers, but now their cause was damned for sure.

I wondered how many more bodies would be added to Grangeville Cemetery by the time this fight with the railroad was done. I wondered if when the railroad sold the Lederer homestead, if the new owner would uproot those magnificent roses.

I couldn't bear to see Mr. Johns' pleasure at the Lederers being at fault. "You'll need to read the report. I'm not one to gossip."

"Oh. Well. Thanks, anyway." He looked disappointed as we shook hands.

I boarded the train. The status of my ticket allowed me a full row to myself, which I planned to occupy lengthwise soon enough.

I pressed my face to the window for a last glance of the young town. My gut felt hollow, and not for lack of food. I'd envied what these people had. God help me, I knew I'd done the right thing here. Sally Lederer's botched spell-work had to be undone. I wasn't at fault for the homesteaders' impending losses. And yet . . . and yet . . .

I wasn't even forty, and I felt so damned tired and old. I wanted to get home. Home. Whatever that meant.

Most everyone had left the rail station, but I did spy the Chinese girl from the day before. She walked along the street, a yoke laden with produce across her shoulders. She didn't even glance toward the train as it rolled forward with a lurch.

I pulled back from the glass enough to see my true reflection stare me in the eye. Through my visage, fields and orchards blinked by. My suit was filmed with dust and that's all I could smell. Better than the stench of magic, anyway.

I shifted in my seat and detected a lump within my jacket. I pulled out a handkerchief, and inside found Mrs. Lederer's white rose. The petals had begun to wilt after being crunched close to my body for most of the day. I brought it to my nose and breathed in, as if I could fill the hollow ache.

A steward approached. I beckoned him over. I needed a glass of water to hold the stem. Maybe, just maybe, I could eke a few more days of life out of the bloom as I traveled north.

CARTOGRAPHER'S INK

NOT EVEN THE SOOTHING HEAT of a full cup of tea could ease the agony in Sir Oren's hands. Each finger joint throbbed as if it contained a burning coal. He cursed, trying to cradle the cup between his palms, but the brew sloshed and speckled his velvet housecoat. Oren exhaled in frustration and set the cup aside.

If he couldn't drink tea, how in the ten hells was he supposed to manage pen and ink? The secret of his pained hands had been kept this long because the king had no immediate need of him, and his other commissions had far-off deadlines. Oren claimed headaches, avoided the map room entirely, and tried every available concoction to heal his hands. Nothing worked.

If King Atsu didn't see an update on his linked palace map soon, there'd be another messenger. His Majesty would already be marshalling his soldiers to march on Jal and reinforce the Gray Watchtower, so recently cut off by the meandering river. He must draw the new map lines to assert their claim against those Jalian ingrates.

Oren heaved upright and hobbled towards the atelier. He dare not take the pen in his unsteady hand, and yet he must. King Atsu flogged his horse for being skittish on a windy day. Old men were far more expendable than a blooded stallion.

Pride was Oren's downfall. He should have retired years ago, ignoring the pressure to celebrate forty years in his prestigious position. Or, had he possessed any brain, he would have never become Royal Cartographer at all. Never to dabble with red inks that took ten years for priests to steep and bless, never to cope with courtiers whose moods shifted like a summer midafternoon sky. Just maps—his beloved sheets with lines of black and purple, the chance to study the curves and stones of the land, the joy of testing the enchanted spikes in the thousand places they stabbed the soil of Qen. A life of near poverty, perhaps, but wealth of a different sort. Maybe his wife would not have died five half-years past, leaving sweet Tavi motherless far too soon.

His fingers quaked, reminding him of the dire circumstances of the day. Fool. Dreaming old fool. Reality remained harsh and hopeless, with not even an apprentice to aid him. That damned fool boy died in a drunken horserace two months ago, just as Oren's hands began to ail. With a half-year of mourning to complete, Oren couldn't take a new heir to his craft. One curse atop another. If he were religious, he might surmise this was penance for his sins.

He stopped in the hallway. The door to the map room was cracked open. His steps slowed as he leaned to peer inside.

Tavi stood at the master map, pen in hand. Her lips moved in breathy hisses as arcane words dripped into the paper along with the red ink of Qen. Oren clutched at the door frame, barely breathing. For Tavi to even touch the priceless inks was treason, but to say the incantations? If the truth were known, punishment would be neither swift nor kind.

He dared not startle her, lest she freckle the countryside like a pox. Oren mouthed the words, and as though unfurling a scroll, the kingdom of Qen revealed itself in his mind.

The enchanted spikes hummed and sparkled like stars in midnight heavens, each bolt of metal aligned to an intersection on the grid-lined paper map. Over mountains and dipping through valleys, all across the living continent, black ink separated farm from town, sheep lots from cattle. Tavi's casting carried Oren's inner sight across the countryside to stop at the burbling and swollen River Nev.

Red and blue inks floated atop the water like a thick sheen of oil. They oozed with the river's flow. The fresh blue ink stood bold and dominant, but Tavi's addition was fresher yet. Oren traced the red as his daughter's pen met the spirited map and appeared in physical form.

A distant roar met Oren's ears. The soldiers in the Gray Watchtower saw the crimson line. The truest show of a Royal Cartographer's power—ink blessed by God, reassuring them of the rightness of their cause.

How many soldiers would die against Jal in the coming days? These were mere boys, barely growing beards. He shoved the thought aside. They chose the sword.

Oren opened his eyes. Tavi remained ignorant of his presence. She picked up the pen for white next, dipping the nib just so, and in smooth strokes blotted out the old border. The presence of enchantment carried through the air like hot cardamom.

Brilliant, stupid girl. Even if Oren had thought to ask for her help, he would not have; he had done his utmost to discourage her from taking on a cartographer's cowl. Now she had made her choice, foolhardy as it was. If the king had the generosity to end the mourning period early, Oren could formally apprentice her. He held back a snort. King Atsu was only generous in cruelty.

Oren waited until the red and white pens returned to their berths.

"Tavi," he said.

Her head jerked back, loose brown hair rippling over her shoulders. God, she looked so much like her mother. "Papa." Her golden skin blanched.

"That map is priceless beyond compare. Thousands of lives balance on the actions of a pen. It's not a task for a fourteen-year-old girl of unbound hair. You cannot—"

"And what of your life, Papa?" she cut in, her gaze shrewd. He flinched. Yes, what of his life? "You think you can hide it from me, the trembling, the pain?" Her voice softened. "If you can make it till Cleric's Day, you can resign your commission with honor, but that's more than a half-year away. I remember what happened last year when Hensa lost the king's favorite cloak. He died of pneumonia in the gaol. Papa, he and the king had the same wet nurse as babes. How would Atsu treat you?" Tears flooded her eyes as she bit her lip.

Oren took in a rattling breath. "Better to let me accept my fate alone. I can't imagine the punishment both king and guild would extend to you for drawing on the spirited map, Tavi. You have not yet practiced your art on the property maps."

"Haven't I?" She turned with a rustle of skirts, flinging her arms towards the tables that lined the periphery of the room. "When were you last in this room, Papa?"

Weeks. Mayhap a month. Dread soured his stomach as he walked the walls. Many of his non-royal commissions appeared ready to send. Neat black lines illuminated the redrawn road maps for the district south of the palace that had so recently burned. A map for a property dispute in the North Country contained careful forgeries of his own script in paperbound purple ink. Ten others sat in a neat stack. Touching his hands to the papers, he could sense the rightness in the magic and how it aligned with the earth itself.

These smaller projects had always been his joy; his connection with the land more intimate, his clients less fickle. That, and no one ever died by the actions of a black pen.

"I didn't know," he muttered. "The deadlines were so distant." He rubbed his aching knuckles and palms together, feeling the burden of each gray hair and wrinkle.

"Papa," Tavi asked, "How did I do?" She pinched her lower lip between her teeth.

"Beautifully." He pressed a kiss against her ear, even as tears of worry burned in his eyes. "But it's a dreadful burden you've undertaken."

"When I was little, you told me that red ink was worth a stable of the king's finest horses, and if I ever so much as walked within

five feet of an open jar you'd tie me over a nest of scald-bite ants."
Though her tone was light, she focused her gaze on the massive
map.

He gave her arm a light pat. "So I did. Lucky for you, it's not
scald-bite ant season." Oren took his customary seat and studied
the spirited map with his eyes. The red ink shivered on the page,
and he grunted. "Finish the invocation, girl. It's waiting for you."

"Oh." Tavi flushed. Magic danced from her tongue as the final
words flowed. The red ink gelled on the map.

Oren nodded his approval. Jal's own cartographer would see it
now, on paper and topography, and she would offer a quick rebuttal.

"Always remember, Tavi, that this is no mere map. As my old
master liked to say, "Royal Cartographers peddle in ink, earth, and
war.'"

Oren paused. When he was a boy, he'd entertained the notion
of training to be a soldier as his cousins had. Now as an old man,
he had come to accept that he had slain more men by his pen than
he ever could have by sword. He thought again of the boys in the
watchtower. His fingers ached.

Tingles swirled in his head, driving his attention to the paper
map. The blue ink of Jal grew bolder, retracing their claimed border
around the tower.

"Papa, look." Tavi didn't point to the contentious border along
the River Nev. Instead, she motioned to the drawn high peak just
beyond their own city. A round letter took shape in flowing script
and its companions followed until the words were emblazoned for
all to read. GOD'S WILL.

The stool's legs scraped across the floor as he rose to his feet.
"Come," he said. His old limbs gained new strength as he propelled
himself up the stairs, down the hall, and burst open the door to the
storage room. Tavi assisted him in wedging the bolt loose, and they
threw wide the double doors to the balcony.

Sure enough, there it was. Beyond the red high-peaked roofs
and the elegant spires of the palace, the impudent letters glinted

like sapphires against the pale green hillside. Below on the streets, almost everyone pointed and gawked. Up the hill, he could see the rider in Qen-crimson livery galloping their way. He could well imagine what the king would say to him now. Oren shut the two doors, his arms trembling.

"Jal can't do that," said Tavi. "They can't. One must never, ever, use blessed ink to write words upon the spirited map. That's what plain purple is for. Why—"

"If their intention is war, what have they to lose? What is the censure of a cartography guild compared to that of a king and his legions?" Oren secured the door in the hallway. The king wouldn't be content with a redrawn border now. This called for a brilliant, showy response, and all Oren had to show was clumsiness.

"Papa." Her lips parted as if to speak, but remained silent.

He rubbed his bristled chin and sighed. There would be no time to shave. "Can you call Ando into my quarters? I need to change into my silks, and I cannot manage the ties on my own."

"Papa, you're so certain that the king will want an audience?"

Already, he heard the rapid knocking at the front door. Oren laid a heavy hand on his daughter's shoulder, his fingers quivering like plucked harp strings.

"Yes. I'm sure."

This would not go well. The surety rested in his gut like a supper of crusty bread and stew.

Still, Oren would make a good show of it. His red silks hung loose off of his gangly frame and matched his fine white-plumed hat. Tavi helped him belt a dagger at his hip, and Oren adjusted it to rest at a jaunty angle. He admired himself in the mirror. Yes, he could still cut a fine figure when he chose.

Tavi helped him roll the great map and secure it in a tube as long as a claymore. The travel-sized ink jars were checked for freshness and judged well.

"I love you, Papa," she said from the doorway, her words soft and warbling.

He took a single step then turned around. "Tavi, tell me. Do you wish to be Royal Cartographer someday?"

She shook her head, frowning. "No. I want . . ." Her voice trailed off.

"Yes?"

"I want to draw property maps for the North Country. When I use black ink there, I can hear the birds sing." She tried to hide her blush behind her billowed sleeve.

Oren nodded, a slow smile stretching across his face. "Yes, yes you can," he said, and walked away.

Tarrying would not help his situation, regardless of what await-ed him. The palace guards welcomed him with stiff bows and es-corted him within the gated courtyard. Abnormal hustle and bustle punctuated the arcade. Preparations for war were well underway, just as he had suspected.

"Sir Oren." King Atsu paced the long ornate rug in the map room. "God, I thought you would never get here, my man. Did you see what they did, that affront? You must dispose of it, and then I'll dispose of them."

Oren only nodded as he set his parcels down. Several of the royal attendants stepped forward, and with their gloved hands they spread the spirited map on the table and lined the edge with stones to prevent curling. The mate to Oren's map adorned the full wall at the end of the room.

"Well, are you going to eliminate those words?" The king's nos-trils flared.

Oren continued laying out his gear, setting the red vial in its wooden cradle. "Your Majesty must be patient. By guild guidelines, any violation or error must remain set in paper for a full day to re-mind the cartographer of his or her own humility."

"This was no error. This was provocation. I order you to apply white ink immediately."

"I am sorry, I cannot do that, Your Majesty. Once their ink has melded, it needs time to complete its drying on both paper and earth. If white is applied too quickly, the inks may wash. Would you prefer the entire hill be dyed in Jal blue? Or the city itself?"

"No." The king's enthusiasm dampened. "Well, if you can't eliminate their words, we must answer in kind."

Oren scuffed his knuckles against his chin. He expected as much. The guild would not chastise him for issuing a response, but still. One didn't use red ink for words.

"Your Majesty, if I may suggest, avoid words," he said. "Your troops will march on Jal soon enough. Let your swords be their answer."

One of the attendants stepped closer, frowning and toying with the ermine trim of his cloak. "And yet, Your Majesty, the cliffs over their capital would provide a fine canvas for your retort of choice. Swords would only reinforce your wisdom."

"Hmm. Yes. Yes indeed they would," said the king, stroking his smooth chin. "Sir Oren, a response at this time is a necessity. Jal must know that Qen will not tolerate such an abuse of land and pen. Now I must think of the appropriate words." He resumed pacing along the rug.

Damn the meddling sycophant, and damn the king for being so readily swayed. Oren checked his pens, then uncorked the blessed red ink. Acrid tang filled the air. He grappled the pen, trying to ignore the aching tremors that coursed the length of his arm.

King Atsu muttered as he walked. "'God is of Qen?' No. 'The River is but a River?' No, no, that's too dreadfully long. Perhaps I should call a committee, but half my men are in the field, readying to march. God, why must the Jal be so difficult?"

"It's in their nature, Your Majesty," one of the other attendants soothed.

Oren's tongue sat heavy in his mouth. The truth would be known. Forty years of reputation and career gone. And Tavi, sweet Tavi. He dare not even think on her, or the trembling in his hands would overtake his entire body.

"What about staying simple?" the king asked, spinning on his heel. "Perhaps just write 'No', or 'The Gray Tower is Qen.' Or go for the direct threat and pronounce that 'Jal Will Fall.' How is that?"

"Succinct and all too true, Your Majesty."

"Very well. Sir Oren? Sir Oren?"

His fingers twitched and searched for a steady hold on the pen. "Yes, Your Majesty?"

"God, man, we're having a vital discussion here. Pay attention. Write 'Jal Will Fall' above their city. Ah, it even sounds poetic."

"'Jal Will Fall.'" As will I, Oren thought. He licked his dry lips and gripped the pen tighter. He dipped the nib into the vial.

The ancient words slid from his tongue and the trembling claimed his fingers again, but Oren could not stop the words, not now, not at this critical juncture. The glass vial thudded against the table. Dread and horror almost strangled his throat, but the words flowed onward. Warm ink drenched the heel of his hand. He clenched his eyes shut in denial even as the attendants and King Atsu gasped.

After a dozen galloping heartbeats he opened his eyes to witness the devastation. The vial had tipped in its rest, spreading a tide as bright as a severed artery. The capital of Jal drowned in red.

In the thrall of ink and magic, Oren knew the panic in the distant city. Screams, crying children, frantic goats. The sparkling waves washing over mud, over cobbles. With the ink so thick and unset, it tracked and sloshed underfoot. If someone stood on a normal line as it was drawn, the ink may darken their soles for a half dozen footsteps, but this? Thousands upon thousands of footsteps reverberated through the fresh ink. He could feel the impressions the citizens' bodies made as they fell into the muck. The ink was not thick enough to drown them, but—Oren gasped.

Foundations faltered along one particularly steep hillside, and with an audible snap the old property lines broke as the buildings slid downhill. In a cascade, the tenements in the crevice below ceased to be, the old lines drowning in rubble and Qen red.

Cacophony. Chaos. Red, blood red.

He forced himself to full consciousness. He dropped the pen to one side and lifted the wooden cradle upright and away from the map. The glowing ink continued to spread. Damn it all. That small vial had been open for twenty years, and could have lasted a dozen more. The cost—no, he dare not think of the expense. It would hardly matter now compared to the loss of so many lives. Jalian lives, to be sure, but lives nevertheless. These were citizens, not soldiers. He tugged a rag from his case and mopped the red ink from his hand. His creased skin remained spider-webbed in crimson.

Oren's eyes burned with held back tears. A whole hillside, obliterated. The city . . . It was enough that his ink bolstered the soldiers, encouraging war time and again. A baby's wail echoed in his mind.

The king's lips held an unusual pallor. "God, what have you done?"

Oren bowed his head. "I apologize, Your Majesty. Regardless of the consequences, I should have addressed this first, but when it comes to men and their pride—"

"Well, you should have told me what you had in mind. God, it's brilliant! Better than mere words. The people of Jal must be running and screaming through the streets. Ink as a weapon. It's perfect." A rare smile lit the king's face. "Blood red ink at that. Their streets will run with the real thing soon enough. I'm glad you didn't tell me what you had planned, Sir Oren. Better to surprise me, surprise us all." The king clapped his hands, and an attendant bowed. "Have the captain ready my horse. We ride for the River Nev immediately."

Oren stayed very still as he absorbed Atsu's reaction. The fool didn't know—didn't realize. More of the old black boundary lines wavered, and Oren whispered the final words of setting to freeze the ink. Belated mercy to those already drenched in red.

"Leave your handiwork in place until I order otherwise," said King Atsu. "That will be well beyond the single day required by your guild, I assure you. I can't get over this magnificent stain. It's ingenious. We must notify our own countrymen in case Jal should make a like counterattack. Thank God, our hills are not as steep as theirs."

With a wave of his hand, one of the attendants dashed away, undoubtedly to warn the mayor and the rest of the city. The king moved behind Oren and placed both hands on his shoulders. "Anything else I can do? Anything else you need?" Giddiness warmed his voice.

Sir Oren sat up straighter underneath the king's touch. This was the moment. "Yes, Your Majesty." The words were hoarse. "If you sign a writ permitting an early end to the mourning period of my belated apprentice, it would be much appreciated."

The guild would fume over the exception—as would the boy's family—but such things could be soothed by time. At the very least, he could survive past half-year with his commission intact. He grimaced, staring at the spillage. Others would recognize this folly for what it was.

"An unusual request, but considering your devotion to my father and now me, I shall grant it." The king snapped his fingers, and an attendant brought him pen and paper. He went to the other end of the table.

Oren blotted more ink from his wrist and forearm as he studied the map and saw beyond to the screams, the chaos, the readied swords. His parched throat ached as he swallowed.

Within a minute the waiver was done, and King Atsu whirled from the map room with lackeys in his wake. The stone walls shuddered from trumpet blasts as the royal entourage galloped from the courtyard. After several attempts Oren recorked the empty vial.

"'Ink, earth, and war,'" he whispered, staring at his soiled hands against the map. This would be his legacy: a puddle of crimson. A legacy earned. Perhaps he should have been a soldier after all.

Beyond the window, a bird warbled in song. Oren lifted his head, listening. No, this stain was not his entire legacy. Tavi would be a fine cartographer, one wise enough to never wear red ink on her hands. He thought again of what she said, and smiled.

Many years ago, Oren had known where the birds of the North Country sang their sweetest. Perhaps they awaited him still.

The Quest You Have Chosen Defies Your Fate

 You are reading a book, and within that book you now walk through the iron gates of the junior high school of your youth.

You don't understand how you are reading of a real place within this old fantasy book of adventures you found in the closet of your childhood bedroom. These particular pages didn't exist before, here in this volume that you read until its white spine was bowed, sway-backed, broken.

Today you have fallen between the plotlines, the inked illustrations, the bookmarks you once placed at the major decisions you were asked to make—yes, your cheating is known. The bookmarks are gone. You can no longer flip back to choose between releasing the unicorn on page 32, or continuing into the forest on page 210, or the various other forks in your literary path.

Instead, you are at your old school. Again.

Fog shrouds the buildings and open corridors of the campus. A backpack weighs down your left shoulder. Your AD&D books must be in there. They were your lunchtime salvation. The one time each day you could cast magic spells.

You were supposed to be a wizard, after all. To awaken one day with extraordinary powers. But you lived on contemporary Earth, and reality shriveled the brilliant dreams that empowered you through the night.

A boy emerges from the fog. Your first bully, from fourth grade. "Hey, stupid!" he calls. "Oink, oink! Fat, ugly, stupid!" Weeks and months of daily abuse are compacted into a torrent.

Other figures emerge from the mist. That horrible boy from seventh grade math. The girls from eighth grade P.E. Your brother, frozen as he was at an angry twelve. Their jibes flow together and compete for precedence.

You back away, then stop. Hopelessness clenches your throat like a zombie's hands. What's the point of resisting? It'll only continue tomorrow. You are doomed.

That's why you sometimes read this book and purposefully made the wrong choices, the ones that led to literary suicide. You were a loser in reality. May as well be a loser in an adventure book, too, right? The quarry was the quickest death, page 70. Or the dragon's lair, page 111—that had a nice illustration. Or being enchanted into an eternal stupor in the witch's cave, page 53. These pages knew your bitter laugh when you reached an intentional THE END.

Why are you still reading this book right now? These words revive the fatness and futility you knew at thirteen. Why did you even keep a book that evokes such terrible memories?

Because your fantasy wasn't constantly mired in despair. This book also brought hope that you could leave behind your Podunk village. That your magic would manifest itself. That you could save the world—that you mattered.

So many emotions are crammed between the pages. So many almost-forgotten crumbs and stains.

The bully mob swarms. Their words are like knives that pierce deeper than the open scissor blades you often held against your wrists. If you tore your eyes away from this page and pulled up your sleeve right now, you'd find the scars. Those old tally marks, so stacked and close they are impossible to count.

As a teenager, you thought your reality offered you no choices.

Well, you have a choice now.

You can hunch your shoulders, ignore them. You don't want to be a tattletale. Not like the teachers would care, anyway. Do you stand here and endure, as you once did?

If so, turn to page 10.

Do you start to run?

If so, turn the page.

You run.

The backpack pounds your spine with each stride, but you won't drop it, not even to move faster. You won't let them take the one magic you possess. So you run. Your lungs and throat sear with need for oxygen. Your body jiggles and quakes—oh yes, their jeers on that ring out loud and clear—but you keep going through the fog, past the statue, past the band room.

In reality, it wasn't until college that you really discovered running. It was mortifying at first—the rhythmic slap of butt cheeks and thighs—but for some reason, you kept waking up at five o'clock. The world looked different at that hour. Full of potential—magic, of a sort. You run, and you are a galloping unicorn, Hermes, the wind itself. Your feet devour the earth.

You run across the basketball courts and through the field. The movement is easy now. You have found your groove. You're not running out of cowardice; you run because it sets you free.

In a blink, a wall emerges from within the fog: the chain link fence with its diamonds draped with dew. You slam into the wires; they chime and bounce you backward. Water droplets fling from the fence and shock you with cold.

The fence falls away with a violent, metallic shudder. There is no path ahead; there is complete openness.

Everything goes to black.

Turn the page.

Congratulations. You are still alive.

You're in your bedroom, leaning against musty cardboard boxes. You have returned from the spaces between the pages.

Your hands are large as you grip the cover. You wear a ring. The high-pitched voices of your children carry from the backyard.

Beyond them, you still hear the decades-old specters in the fog. Times like this, their catcalls are so loud that they penetrate reality, but you keep moving, even when you are still. You are swift and strong.

Your choice is clear.

Close the book.

AFTERWORD

THE SOULS OF HORSES

This is my favorite story, and probably one with the longest gestation period. Back in 5th grade, I advanced from my long-held obsession with reading horse books to reading novels and nonfiction about the Civil War. I even won my school district's Friends of the Library essay contest for my grade level, saying I wanted to write novels about the Civil War, perhaps from the horse's point of view.

Around 2010, I had the idea to write about someone placing the souls of horses into carousel horses. Over the next year or so, I made several attempts to write the piece and gave up. The elements didn't come together. The "aha!" moment finally came several years later as I read a nonfiction book, *Horses and Mules in the Civil War* by Gene G. Armistead. My story idea developed into a novelette. I polished it, submitted it, received feedback, rewrote it again, submitted it, and so on. I had a revision request from a pro market that asked me to cut it down by about 3000 words. I did, making it a tight short story; it was rejected, again. Mind you, I've become so accustomed to rejections over the years that they don't tend to bother me, but that one made me bawl. I loved this story and I desperately wanted it to have a good home.

By this time, I was running out of pro markets, but I kept sending it out when new places opened. That's how "The Souls of Horses" ended up in *Clockwork Phoenix 5*. That acceptance made me cry, too, but this time from sheer joy. After all the rejections and rewrites, it was especially validating to see my story called out in a starred *Publishers Weekly* review and get a recommendation from Ellen Datlow on Twitter.

WHAT WE CARRY

As you might surmise by this book's section of horse stories, my writing often harkens back to my childhood passion for horses. The cartoon *Rainbow Brite* started when I was about 4, and her horse Starlite became my first great love. I think Starlite is imprinted on my subconscious, as my own version of him often revisits me in works like this poem.

BEAT SOFTLY, MY WINGS OF STEEL

The title of this piece was a story prompt up for the offering during a contest on Codex Writers. I snared the title, then had to churn out a story within like a two week deadline. I thought of "The Souls of Horses," still in its endless cycle of submission-rejection, and figured I'd write a different take on war horses with errant souls—and maybe this one would actually sell.

HUNTER

This poem was specifically written for the *Metastasis* anthology around the theme of cancer, and I cannot read it without sobbing. It's inspired by my cat Palom, who in 2012 developed sarcoma on his chest and succumbed within two months. Palom was the most vivacious, mischievous, obnoxious cat I have ever known, and I miss him every day. He adored people. He welcomed them in the door, tried to steal their purses and shoes, and yowled happily all the while. He could jump six feet to rip tacks out of walls, open any cabinet, and thought Christmas trees and presents were his grand opportunity to play Godzilla. Palom and his sister Porom were my solace throughout our years as a Navy family, through multiple cross-country moves and deployments and upheaval. I was far from my human family, but never alone.

Writing "Hunter" gave me a chance to pay tribute to a cat I will forever love and miss.

HEADSPACE

I wrote this story for an anthology called *Cats in Space*. I tried to think of a way to literally get a cat in space, in a space suit, and came up with the tale of a kitten named Trouble. I was pleasantly surprised when this story was a finalist for the WSFA Small Press Award.

THE DEATH OF THE HORSE

I love the idea of an imaginary friend not being imaginary at all. That's how this poem emerged: an alien horse only the girl can see who has trained her to become a future ambassador for humanity. The idea of the horse fading away goes back to my own childhood terror of growing up and losing my imagination. This was a potential catastrophe I became consciously aware of when I was about ten, and I made a vocal vow to myself that I would not forget to look for magic everywhere.

RED DUST AND DANCING HORSES

Another one of my all-time favorite stories. I visited the Phoenix Zoo once a few years ago, and it turned out they were holding a Day of the Horse celebration. They had a riding arena open with brief rides available. I couldn't resist the opportunity even though I hadn't been on a horse in almost twenty years. As I did my quick circuit around the ring, I could see the vivid red rocks of the mountains within the zoo grounds. I thought, "It's like I'm riding a horse on Mars. But horses can't exist on Mars. Can they?"

WHAT HAPPENED AMONG THE STARS

This is something of a sequel to "What We Carry." I wanted to explore their mission from the perspective of the magical horse who loves his girl, and is well aware of the tragedy she will endure. This poem was published in *Niteblade Magazine*; Marge Simon used my poem for her cover illustration; I bought the original watercolor and have it framed and hanging in my house.

BIDING TIME

This flash story was my first pro-paying publication, and it remains one of my favorites. The story arose from hearing a discussion on the news about a man being sentenced to life in prison because of a horrific crime; I was left thinking, what if he outlived his sentence? What would that mean to the family of his victims?

HAT TRICK

I wrote—and fully rewrote twice over—a future-set urban fantasy novel about people with superpowers. I signed with my agent because of that book, but it wasn't able to sell because there was already a glut of fabulous urban fantasies on the market. Giving up on that book broke my heart, and I almost gave up on writing novels.

When I saw the call for a story anthology about people who only kinda-sorta have superpowers, I knew I wanted to return to my book's world. There are really only a few words that connect my novel and this story, but it still delighted me to finally have a piece of my book's world see publication.

BLUE TAG SALE

I live far away from my hometown and my family. My grandma went through a bad patch a few years ago. I couldn't be there to help, so I wrote a number of stories on the theme of granddaughter-grandmother relationships to cope.

When I was in my early teens, my grandma volunteered at my hometown City of Hope Thrift Store, and I happily volunteered right along with her when I had days off from school. I still love shopping at thrift stores. There's nothing like the bond that comes from being with friends/family when you make a good thrift store find! To me, that's a shared joy worth celebrating, and that's what I wanted to write about here.

NISEI

I grew up listening to my grandpa's stories of his time in World War II. He was of proud Okie and Arkie stock, raised in California, and he wasn't ashamed that the sight of a rippling American flag brought tears to his eyes. His hometown of Armona was also home to many Japanese residents who were sent off to internment camps during the war. I wanted to look at the experience of Nisei ("second generation") Japanese and their patriotism, but through the eyes of a grandchild like myself. Kappa mythology seemed to fit right in.

TOILET GNOMES AT WAR

This story emerged from a spontaneous comment that a problematic toilet's issues were surely the fault of toilet gnomes. I then paused and said, "Huh. That'd make a good story." And so it did. I continue to make toilet gnome jokes with friends and family.

MINOR HOCKEY GODS OF BARSTOW STATION

I was invited to submit a story to a Baen anthology inspired by the Olympics, but on a galactic scale. I asked to write about hockey, and then spent a number of months gathering up the nerve to actually write the thing. This story challenged me on a number of levels. It's a harder type of science fiction than most of my works, and I struggled to not info-dump in the world-building. I also had to write about hockey with technical details. Mind you, I've watched a lot of hockey—my family holds season tickets for the Arizona Coyotes—but writing about it for sports fans is something else entirely. My husband patiently went through the story with me and even drew out rink schematics so we could position my characters properly.

AN ECHO IN THE SHELL

This is one of my darkest published stories. Again, I drew on my relationship with my grandma. We spent many, many hours watching game shows together, though we didn't watch *Match Game*.

Whenever I reread the whole story, I feel this weird sense of "Wow, I wrote something this deep, but wow, it's *horrible*." The ending feels right within the story, but it will never cease to horrify me.

213 MYRTLE STREET

I live near Phoenix, Arizona. The housing downturn hit the area hard. For a few years, there were sale and foreclosure signs everywhere. As I drove home from a grocery shopping trip one day, I started thinking, "How does a house feel when that happens?" The sentient household at 213 Myrtle began to take shape in my mind.

This story also likely has my largest—and most unwilling—readership. It's used for high school graduation testing in both Canada and Texas. Someday, I'd love to know what questions are asked about my story on those exams!

THE HUMAN IS LATE TO FEED THE CAT

My cat Porom acts like it's the end of the world if she doesn't get her twice-daily canned cat food. I decided to explore that as if it really was the end of the world, and how a cat would perceive it. The tale was written as a poem first, and I was sucker-punched by the emotion in it. I decided it needed more space to develop, and so I wrote it as a flash fic.

THE SWEETNESS OF BITTER

I fondly recall this as the story that almost gave me a mental breakdown. No exaggeration. I wrote an initial draft and sent it to a few pro markets, but it was rejected. I then submitted the story to be critiqued at the Cascade Writers Workshop. This was my first time traveling to a writing convention of any kind. My story was shredded in critiques—not in a mean way, but the experience left me dazed and overwhelmed. I returned home, determined to fix the story. Somehow.

Within days of returning from Cascade Writers, I found a tumor growing on my cat Palom's chest. His health quickly deteriorated.

At the same time, there was another writing issue that cast a large shadow: my agent was about to send my novel *The Clockwork Dagger* out on submission. Since my previous novel hadn't sold, I was sick with dread of a repeat experience and that I would be a total failure as a novelist.

The one thing I could control was this story. I was going to fix it. I was going to make it work. I kept only the bare bones of the plot and I rewrote from scratch. The sorrow and grief in this story is real, as I was an emotional wreck throughout the intense writing process.

POST-APOCALYPTIC CONVERSATIONS WITH A SIDEWALK

Sometimes, weird offhand comments can inspire a story. One of my favorite authors tweeted that she fell but a sidewalk caught her. I started thinking that it would be neat if a sidewalk actually tried to catch people to keep them safe, and that's how this story came about.

A DANCE TO END OUR FINAL DAY

This flash story is probably one of my most personal works. I write a lot of post-apocalyptic stories. My son is autistic. One day I wondered how I could possibly explain to him that a cataclysm was about to befall the planet, and I realized I couldn't, but that was okay because he'd be his happy self up to the end. I wrote the story as a way to explore those emotions.

A LONESOME SPECK OF HOME

Since the Power Rangers became a big thing back in the early '90s, I have joked about how awful it'd be to live in their city. The real estate values! The giant foot prints in the yard!

I hit on the idea to write a more "realistic" story about the Power Rangers, and the only protagonist I could picture was a cranky old man like in the animated movie *Up*. The sort to yell, "Get off my lawn!" even if the guilty party happened to be a giant robot from outer space.

This story has one of my favorite first lines, too: "The goddamn robots were at it again."

LA ROSA STILL IN BLOOM

My mom sometimes gripes that too many stories are about young heroes. So, I wrote a story for her about a retired superheroine who might be in poor health, but she hasn't lost her fighting spirit.

A RECIPE FOR RAIN AND RAINBOWS

Pies are magical. This is common knowledge, yes? When I saw an anthology call for stories set in Appalachia, it seemed only right to turn to the subject of pie. Mixing in faith, family, and magic served to complete the recipe. This story was among my first pro-paying sales, and it's still an old, dear favorite of mine.

BREAD OF LIFE

A Codex Writers flash fiction contest included a prompt in the form of a Markov chain, a computerized jumble of text. As I skimmed through the strings of nonsense, one word stood out several times: 'bread.'

That I felt drawn to this word won't come as a surprise to most folks who know me. I maintain a food blog called Bready or Not. I'm known for my evil cookies and delicious bread recipes.

When I latched onto the prompt of 'bread,' I decided to tackle it from a science fiction perspective. What would bread represent for humanity if we no longer had a home world?

STITCHED WINGS

My imagination created an image that I couldn't let go of: that of a young girl sitting in the gutted remains of a library where a violent explosion just occurred, the shredded books still falling around her like leaves. I needed to figure out how this happened. The image ended up being the very last scene of the book. I think this is my only story I've created backwards in this way.

MY BROTHER'S KEEPER

I like writing about girls who are about ten to twelve years old. I see it as a time of incredible power and innocence and potential, when magic can still be very real. In this story, I wanted to break the trope of the child saving the parent, and have the central relationship be that of a brother and sister. I also wanted to show that redemption isn't a tidy concept.

DEEPER THAN PIE

This poem gets to me. Again, it's in my grandmother theme, and channels some of my own raw emotions. I'm still not sure how the poem came together as tidily as it did. It needed to be written, I think.

MAPS

Sometimes, writing a story feels like trying to pluck out leg hairs one by one. Sometimes, the words flow, and by some miracle, a cohesive story forms. "Maps" is the latter. I started writing and I journeyed right along with Christina.

OVERLAP

An anthology call required that submissions use three words as their story prompt: madness, darkness, and mattress. My mind somehow went to clipping as a problem in video games. 'Clipping' is when the graphics glitch and your perspective merges with a wall or some other thing that your character shouldn't stand in. Like a mattress. I decided to use that clipping concept in a plot where teleportation goes wrong.

MOON SKIN

Whenever I read a nonfiction book on the Civil War, I seem to be inspired to write a story. I started pondering how the war might have gone differently if the Confederate submarine *Hunley* hadn't gone down in its first successful foray off the coast of South Carolina. What might have helped their success? "Magic" seemed like an obvious source to me.

I decided to twist selkie mythology and grant fae seal pelts with some extra powers. I love selkies—they are one of my very favorite mythological creatures—but a lot of selkie stories follow the same basic plot. It's hard to find that right balance of an original but recognizable take on such an overused subject. I'm glad it worked out here, and I sure want to write more selkie stories if I can figure out some fresh ways to go about it.

CARTOGRAPHY OF SHATTERED TREES

This story emerged from another Codex Writers contest. For this one, two other participating writers provided me with prompts: a luopan, which is a Chinese magnetic compass used in Feng Shui, and lichtenberg figures, the scarring that results from a lightning strike. The luopan put me in mind of maps, and from there I thought—what if there was a map in fractal burns on someone? What would cause that?

ROOTS, SHALLOW AND DEEP

I was born and raised in Hanford, California. The city's claims to fame are being the hometown of original Journey lead singer Steve Perry and being the location of one of the most infamous old west shoot-outs. I first heard about the Mussel Slough Tragedy when I was in 3rd grade, and rushed home from school to point an accusing finger at my mom. "Why didn't you tell me something like this happened here?!" followed by "Take me where it happened, please!" The location has a large stone historical marker and otherwise looks like any farm field around town. Still, my imagination was hooked.

One of my early publications was an alt history piece about the Tragedy and its gun battle between angry settlers and railroad agents. Looking back, I see that story as clumsily written and in need of tremendous revision. Therefore, I wanted to write a completely new take on the event. I bought several history books on the Tragedy, thoroughly did my research, and this time I'm very happy with the resulting story. I think my 3rd grade self would be pleased.

CARTOGRAPHER'S INK

I wrote this story at a point when I was starting to get bold, innovative story ideas that I couldn't quite figure out how to write. This is now a pretty common problem with my longer stories as I experiment in different ways, but back then, I really didn't have a support network around me to help me fix what was wrong in the story. I floundered. I sent it on submission, had it rejected, poked at it more, tried a few more submissions, became frustrated, and gave up. I couldn't leave it in the trunk, though. The story concept was just too intriguing. I worked on it more, asked for help, and sent it out again. The story sold at last! The whole process taught me a lot about revision and tenacity.

THE QUEST YOU HAVE CHOSEN DEFIES YOUR FATE

"The Quest" emerged from another Codex contest. The title was up for offering, and I claimed it as my own. It immediately resonated with me as a Choose Your Own Adventure kind of story, so I went with that. It was very experimental for me—this is my only story written in second person! However, it needed that point of view because it's semi-autobiographical. I describe my junior high school. I describe my own emotions, the bullying, the despair, the escape into fantasy. I never succumbed to cutting (tried it, didn't like it) nor do I run (thanks to childhood foot injuries), but I do use daily exercise and other tools to help keep my mental health in balance.

Achieving that balance is a daily struggle. It always will be.

I hope that this story helps other people who still hear their childhood bullies loud and clear, and I really hope it reaches teenagers who are in the midst of that hell right now.

I wanted to end my collection with "The Quest" because of how the story itself ends: with hope, empowerment, and the closing of a book.

Thank you for reading.

About the Author

Beth Cato hails from Hanford, California, but currently writes and bakes cookies in a lair west of Phoenix, Arizona. She shares the household with a hockey-loving husband, a numbers-obsessed son, and a cat the size of a canned ham. She's the author of *The Clockwork Dagger* (a 2015 Locus Award finalist for First Novel) and *The Clockwork Crown* (an RT Reviewers' Choice Finalist) from Harper Voyager. Her novella *Wings of Sorrow and Bone* was a 2016 Nebula nominee. Her new alt-history steampunk trilogy begins with *Breath of Earth*, and continues with *Call of Fire* and *Roar of Sky*. Follow her at BethCato.com and on Twitter at @BethCato

PUBLICATION NOTES

"The Souls of Horses" originally appeared in *Clockwork Phoenix 5*, April 2016 | "What We Carry" originally appeared in *inkscrawl #6*, August 2013 | "Beat Softly, My Wings of Steel" originally appeared in *PodCastle #405: Artemis Rising 2*, 29 February 2016 | "Hunter" originally appeared in *Metastasis: An Anthology to Support Cancer Research*, October 2013 | "Headspace" originally appeared in *Cats in Space*, May 2015 | "The Death of the Horse" originally appeared in *Remixt Magazine*, September 2016 | "Red Dust and Dancing Horses" originally appeared in *Stupefying Stories #1.5*, March 2012 | "What Happened Among the Stars" originally appeared in *Niteblade Magazine*, June 2015 | "Biding Time" originally appeared in *The Pedestal Magazine #55*, December 2009-February 2010 | "Hat Trick" originally appeared in *Oomph: A Little Super Goes a Long Way*, October 2013 | "Blue Tag Sale" originally appeared in *Buzzy Mag*, September 2012 | "Nisei" originally appeared in *Mythic Delirium #4*, June 2014 | "Toilet Gnomes at War" originally appeared in *Stupefying Stories #2.1*, November 2012 | "Minor Hockey Gods of Barstow Station" originally appeared in *Galactic Games*, Baen Books, June 2016 | "An Echo in the Shell" originally appeared in *Waylines #1*, January 2013 | "213 Myrtle Street" originally appeared in *Flash Fiction Online*, April 2012 | "The Human is Late to Feed the Cat" originally appeared in *Nature*, issue 7595, March 2016 | "The Sweetness of Bitter" originally appeared in *Orson Scott Card's InterGalactic Medicine Show #35*, September 2013 | "Post-Apocalyptic Conversations with a Sidewalk" originally appeared in *Nature*, issue 7519, September 2014 | "A Dance to End Our Final Day" originally appeared in *Every Day Fiction*, May 2011 | "A Lonesome Speck of Home" originally appeared in *Blue Shift Magazine*, August 2013 | "La Rosa Still in Bloom" originally appeared in *Crossed Genres #32: Sidekicks and Minions*, 2011 | "A Recipe for Rain and Rainbows" originally appeared in *Mountain Magic: Spellbinding Tales of Appalachia*, October 2010 | "Bread of Life" originally appeared in *Nature*, issue 7546, April 2015 | "Stitched Wings" originally appeared in *Beneath Ceaseless Skies #137*, December 2013 | "My Brother's Keeper" originally appeared in *Fantasy Scroll Magazine #6*, April 2015 | "Deeper Than Pie" originally appeared in *Uncanny Magazine #10*, May 2016 | "Maps" originally appeared in *Daily Science Fiction*, February 2013 | "Overlap" originally appeared in *Cucurbital 3*, November 2012 | "Moon Skin" originally appeared in *Swords & Steam Short Stories*, Flame Tree Publishing, September 2016 | "Cartography of Shattered Trees" originally appeared in *Fae*, May 2014 | "Roots, Shallow and Deep" originally appeared in *Urban Fantasy Magazine*, May 2015 | "Cartographer's Ink" originally appeared in *Daily Science Fiction*, August 2012 | "The Quest You Have Chosen Defies Your Fate" originally appeared in *Daily Science Fiction*, August 2015

OTHER TITLES FROM FAIRWOOD PRESS

Other Arms Reach Out to Me
by Michael Bishop
trade paper $17.99
ISBN: 978-1-933846-65-1

Cat Pictures Please
by Naomi Kritzer
trade paper: $17.99
ISBN: 978-1-933846-67-5

The Experience Arcade
by James Van Pelt
trade paper: $17.99
ISBN: 978-1-933846-69-9

Transfigurations
by Michael Bishop
trade paper $17.99
ISBN: 978-1-933846-70-5

Seven Wonders of a Once and Future World
by Caroline M. Yoachim
trade paper: $17.99
ISBN: 978-1-933846-55-2

Amaryllis
by Carrie Vaughn
trade paper: $17.99
ISBN: 978-1-933846-62-0

On the Eyeball Floor
by Tina Connolly
trade paper: $17.99
ISBN: 978-1-933846-56-9

Traveler of Worlds:
Conversations with Robert Silverberg
by Alvaro Zinos-Amaro
trade paper: $16.99
ISBN: 978-1-933846-63-7

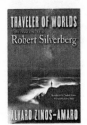

www.fairwoodpress.com
21528 104th Street Court East;
Bonney Lake, WA   98391

CPSIA information can be obtained
at www.ICGtesting.com
Printed in the USA
LVOW11s1735071217
558993LV00007B/886/P